5/17

ᴛᴏᴜ

Books should be returned or renewed by the last
date above. Renew by phone **03000 41 31 31** or
online *www.kent.gov.uk/libs*

tv

Libraries Registration & Archives

emotion. No one can paint each page with equal parts
triumph and tragedy the way Molly McAdams can'
Jay Crownover, *New York Times* bestselling author

'Consuming. Enthralling. Sexy. MIND-BLOWING . . .
A must-read that will have you questioning all
your er

C   D0269220

Blackbird
MOLLY McADAMS

HEADLINE
ETERNAL

First published in Great Britain in 2017
by HEADLINE ETERNAL
An imprint of HEADLINE PUBLISHING GROUP

1

Cataloguing in Publication Data is available from the British Library

ISBN 978 1 4722 4751 3

Typeset in 10.75/14 pt Garamond MT Std by Jouve (UK), Milton Keynes

Printed and bound in Great Britain by CPI Group (UK) Ltd, Croydon, CR0 4YY

Headline's policy is to use papers that are natural, renewable and recyclable
products and made from wood grown in well-managed forests and other
controlled sources. The logging and manufacturing processes are expected to
conform to the environmental regulations of the country of origin.

HEADLINE PUBLISHING GROUP
An Hachette UK Company
Carmelite House
50 Victoria Embankment
London EC4Y 0DZ

www.headlineeternal.com
www.headline.co.uk
www.hachette.co.uk

For Rachel.
Because I absolutely adore you.

ACKNOWLEDGMENTS

Cory – None of this would be possible without you. I love you for everything you are and for how you take care of us. Thank you for being wonderful, incredible you.

Mom – Thank you for being such a champion for this book from the very first day. I love you so much.

Rachel Elliott – Really, I don't think this book would've ever happened if it weren't for you. He will always be for you. I love you, seestor.

A. L. Jackson – I don't know what I would do if I didn't have you to come to. Having you there for me means the world. Thank you for being the best writing partner, rambler, and inspiration.

Amanda Stepp – I feel like I've already said everything so many times before. I love you . . . I'd be lost without my soul friend. Besides, we both know I can't write a blurb to save my life!

Kevan Lyon – Thank you for letting me have this. Your support means the world to me. I couldn't have asked for a better agent to be on this journey with.

Molly Lee – I'm so thankful to have found the other half of my Molly Squared. Thank you for everything—the calls and endless messages mean the world to me.

Letitia, Marion, Karen, and Julie – Thank you, thank you, thank you! A million times thank you for helping me through this transition period. You've all made it such a wonderful experience.

My Readers – I absolutely adore all of you, and I hope you've enjoyed finally getting *this* story . . . I know it has been such a long time coming. There has not been a single day in almost three years where someone hasn't asked for this story, and I love that I could finally give it to you.

Blackbird

Prologue

Briar

"Trust me." His voice was low, his tone barely hinting at his plea as he placed the material over my eyes, wrapping it around my head and tying it in a knot. Making it so the darkness and his voice and the terrifying memories were all I was aware of.

His mouth passed across my cheek then my lips . . . lingering there as he spoke. The ache in his whispered words nearly bringing me to my knees. "I'm sorry I have to force you to relive those days, but I'll do whatever it takes to keep you safe."

I wanted to reach out for him when I felt him move away from me; I wanted to cling to him and his voice and his words . . . but memories began to grip and suffocate me. I could no longer move. No longer breathe.

A shuddering breath finally burst from my chest and my body began trembling. My lips automatically began moving out of fear as a song begged to be freed.

My entire being thrashed and rebelled against the memories that flashed through my mind as I stood in the enforced darkness. Memories that felt so real as if they were happening now instead of all those months ago.

My body shook harder, and I nearly screamed, *"How can this be happening to me?"*

But it wasn't real. Not anymore.

I'd lived a life made up of rules and appearances. I was told what to wear, how to act, and when to speak—or sing.

Even when I'd found the man I thought I wanted to spend my future with, nothing felt like it was my own. But I'd been happy with our life and excited for the days to come.

Until they didn't.

Until I was forced into a world I'd been blind to and came face to face with the devil.

A man cloaked in darkness—a man who would set me free.

A man hidden in a world I vowed to destroy with him by my side.

"Briar."

I whipped my head to the left when his voice sounded from across the room, barely loud enough to hear. My shaking grew stronger, and when I felt his dark, dark presence slip behind me, the song I'd been trying so desperately to hold back bled out as a whisper.

"I know him. I know *the man behind me,"* my mind screamed. But those screams couldn't be heard while I was consumed with memories *he* wanted me to surrender to.

His breath stirred the loose hair on my neck, and just before his arms wrapped around me, he spoke in a low, sinister tone that sent chills up my spine. "Fight me."

Chapter 1

THE DARK ROOM

Briar

I didn't know day from night, or how many hours or days had passed while I was unconscious. I only knew the nausea and headache when I awoke, and then the awful stench soon after.

It smelled like human waste and bile, and soon I added to it as my stomach forced up any trace of food it held. Hard sobs wracked my body as I tried to free my hands from where they were zip-tied behind me, but it didn't give.

Oh God. Where am I? I need to get out of here.

"Help," I croaked then gagged again. "Help." I repeated it louder and louder until I was screaming it.

"Stop."

I froze at the hushed word and strained to hear anything in the dark.

"Hello?" I asked hesitantly.

"Stop," the feminine voice pled again.

"Who are—?"

"Hush."

I heard the rustling of a body—bod*ies*. I couldn't tell how many, but it sounded like a lot.

"If you don't stop, they'll come in here."

I wanted that. I needed to get out of wherever I was. "Someone help," I screamed. "Help me!"

More women were hushing me, some in languages I didn't know, but I didn't stop.

A metal door slid open and slammed shut, and I paused as unease crawled through the room and made its way to me, fear sliding over me like oil. I didn't know what had just entered the room, but I bit my lip to keep from making another sound.

The room was dark enough that I couldn't see the floor, and I hoped the darkness would hide me from whoever was here with us . . .

The sound of heavy boots grew closer and closer, every now and then hitting what sounded like a puddle or squishing something. My stomach rolled.

Just when I thought the boots would pass by me, a hand pressed my head roughly against the floor.

"No, no, n—" I thrashed against the strong hold, screaming when something pinched my neck.

My loud sobs tore through the room, echoing back to me as the heavy boots moved back in the direction they'd come. When the metal door screeched open, I pled for someone to help me. But my words were soft and slurred.

No one hushed me again, and no one came to save me as darkness engulfed me.

"Beautiful," a familiar voice whispered into my ear. A pair of warm arms curled around my waist, pulling me back against his chest.

I bit down on my bottom lip, abruptly cutting off the song that had been flowing from my mouth. Despite my sudden unease, I couldn't stop my smile as my fiancé's lips ghosted along my neck.

"Don't stop," he pled just as gently.

My smile slipped even as a hum of appreciation slid up my throat from the feel of Kyle's teasing lips on me, but I didn't continue singing. He knew I wouldn't.

When seconds ticked by with nothing, he laughed against my shoulder. "You're so confusing, Briar Rose."

My body stilled, already knowing what he would say next.

"Never heard a voice like yours, but you won't let anyone hear it."

"That's not true." I turned in his arms when another breath of a laugh left him and worried my bottom lip as he studied me with a challenging expression. "I just . . ." I lifted one shoulder when I couldn't find the words to explain it.

"Won't let anyone hear you," he provided, echoing his previous statement.

"You've heard me . . ." I blinked quickly as I tried to think back, then sputtered out, "countless times."

"And you stop singing every time you realize I'm listening. Is there anyone you don't stop for when you realize they're close enough to hear you?"

Not anymore I thought as stabs of pain and betrayal sliced through my anxiousness.

My nanny's face flashed through my mind, and I heard her words as clearly as if she were whispering them to me. "Every fear and every worry fades to nothing when you sing, Briar Rose. Your voice is your comfort and your security . . . don't let anyone take it from you."

My parents had attempted to do exactly that years later. It was the first time I could remember them paying attention to me, pretending to be the loving parents they always should've been.

It took a few years too long to realize their love was conditional.

Ever since, I'd been leery of anyone who pushed me to further my future with my voice, and eventually anyone who wanted me to sing for them.

I tried to ignore conversations with Kyle when he asked instead of pushed, and kept telling myself one day he would understand. But that day had still yet to come.

"What could you be afraid of with a voice like yours?" he asked when I didn't respond. "People would crawl over each other to be able to listen to you. Others would fight to represent you if that's what you wanted."

My lips curved at the corners in the faintest of smiles, and I reached up to wrap my arms around his neck. "I'm not scared," I said, soft enough so he wouldn't detect the tremble in my voice. "I grew up in a world where nothing was my own.

I want my voice to remain mine. Not something on display . . . not something my parents try to control."

"This? Where we are? It's no one's world but ours, Briar." Kyle's head dipped low so his mouth could brush across mine. "Confuse me. Just don't stop singing around me."

After four years, he still couldn't understand, and I was beginning to doubt he ever would.

I forced a smile when I pulled away from the kiss and tried to change the direction of his thoughts and the conversation. "Technically this house is only yours for two more weeks."

"My ring is on your finger, your clothes are in the closet, and I came out to find you making coffee, wearing nothing but my shirt. Ours."

"And what would the governor say if she found out about that?" I asked with a wry smile and raised brow. He lifted me onto the granite island countertop—his hands slipping under the shirt I was wearing.

"I'd like to see her try to say anything."

I inhaled sharply when Kyle's fingers moved over my breasts as he pushed the shirt up, up, up—

And exhaled just as fast when his phone began ringing.

His light eyes flashed with annoyance, but he and I both knew who was calling at this time on a Sunday, just as we knew he had to answer her call.

"Speak of the devil," *he muttered under his breath as he released the shirt and grabbed the phone from his jeans pocket. Irritation leaked through his tone when he answered.* "We've never forgotten a brunch before, Mom, we're not going to forget today— Because you aren't calling at the best time." *Kyle's grin was slow and mischievous.* "Yeah, she's here— Yes— I'm sure you're extremely surprised." *His free hand traced up one of my thighs and forced them apart when I tried to squeeze them shut.*

"You are on the phone with your mother," I hissed, low enough that my voice wouldn't carry through the phone.

"Mom, I need to go. We'll see you at brunch."

I bit back a whimper when he ran his fingers over where I was bare and ready for him, and slapped at his chest when I noticed the hungry, yet amused, look on his face.

"You can tell me this at brunch. I really need to go— Mom— Mo— Never mind. Bye." *He hung up and tossed his phone on the island countertop next to me, and grinned wolfishly when I smacked his chest again.*

"That was not—" *He cut off my reprimand with his mouth on mine, and swallowed my moan when he pressed two fingers inside me.*

"She knows now," he said through the kiss. "And you know she won't be able to say anything at brunch because we'll be in public."

My eyes fluttered shut, and I leaned away from him, keeping my hands secured to the back of his neck for support as his fingers brought me closer and closer to the edge. "You're terrible," I said halfheartedly, my focus mostly on what Kyle was doing to me.

"What was that?"

I sucked in a quick breath when his thumb pressed against my clit and murmured something unintelligible.

"That's what I thought," he said quietly, his tone laced with humor.

I woke up in the dark place sometime later, gasping and screaming in a pool of my own vomit. Almost immediately, I was forced back into unconsciousness the same way as before.

"Who's that?" Kyle asked an hour and a half later when we were stepping out of the house to meet his parents for brunch.

I glanced up, my chest tightening when I saw her.

Jenna, a girl I worked with, was standing next to an idling car at the end of the driveway.

Even from where I was, I could see that her arms were wrapped around her waist tightly, and she was shaking.

"Jenna," I whispered, and gave Kyle a knowing look before hurrying over to her. "Hey, wh—oh my God, Jenna. What happened?"

Her mess of blonde hair fell like a protective curtain around her face, but it didn't stop me from seeing it. Her bottom lip was split open and her right eye was red and purple, and so swollen I doubted she could see through it.

In the year she'd been working with me at Glow, I'd noticed a couple suspicious bruises along her arms, but she'd always had an excuse for them. That is . . . when she'd spoken to me.

No one knew anything about her or her home life since she was incredibly shy and never said much to anyone. And she hadn't said a word to me for nearly a month after I'd brought the bruises up.

I'd always mentioned my worries to Kyle, but it was obvious Jenna hadn't wanted our help back then. Now . . .

"I have to go, Briar," she said through her trembling. "I have—I have to get out of here."

I stared at her in shock for a few seconds with my head shaking before I nodded quickly. "Of course, what do you need us to do? We can take you where—"

"No," she said quickly, harshly. "I have a car, but m-m-my dad . . . he thinks I'm on my way to work right now, and he has my phone. If I don't show up, they'll call."

I wasn't understanding what she needed. All I could focus on were the bruises and the cuts on her face. The violent shaking of her body and the raw fear in her voice.

"Your dad?" I asked lamely, and wondered for a second how old she was. She had to be at least twenty-one to work in the restaurant. "What do you need, Jenna? Tell me what I can do. Do you need money?"

"N-no. No, can you cover for me at work? P-please, I n-need time to get away, Briar. I need time, and if he realizes I'm not there, he'll come looking for me right away."

"Of course," I said without hesitation. "Of course I will. What time is your shift?"

"It starts in ten minutes."

I nodded again, and tried to get my mind straight. "Okay. Okay, I'll call and tell them I'm running late. That I forgot we switched. Are you sure we can't help you in any other way? My fiancé can—"

"No, just—I just need to leave."

"Jenna, my fiancé's mom is the governor, so she can do something about your dad if he's the one who's been doing this—"

"No! Please don't get anyone else involved. If you do he'll come after me, I know he will. Just let me leave," she begged, and the desperation in her voice tore through me until I was shaking too.

How could a father do this to his own child?

I could feel her fear start to consume me until a song was just a breath from leaving my lips—but I forced the impulse back, knowing distantly that the fear wasn't my own. I needed to hold it together for Jenna now.

"Okay, go," I whispered, as if her dad might be near. Before she could turn to leave, I pulled her into my arms, and tried to keep my hug light in the chance there were more bruises I couldn't see. "Be safe, Jenna. Get far, far away. You deserve so much better than this."

A sob tore from her throat when she pulled away. I watched her turn and run toward her car. My shock mixed with confusion, rooting me to the ground.

The next time I woke, it was from the harsh spray of a hose. The other females in the room were screaming, and I wondered if this was the end. If this had been some unknown torture, only to drown us.

I was so focused on keeping my mouth shut so things I didn't want to think of wouldn't fly into my mouth, that I hadn't noticed that the screams of the girls had started dying out. I hadn't noticed that the spray of the water was focused more on my part of the room, or that I was surrounded by people who hadn't been there just before. It wasn't until that familiar pinch was at my neck that all of that came back to me. I welcomed the darkness like an old friend, hoping recent memories of Kyle would be there.

"Briar . . ."

I looked up when I heard Kyle's voice, my face tensed with worry and fear as I hurried to tell him what had just happened.

Though he seemed worried for a girl he didn't know, and just as furious and disgusted as I was with the kind of man who would hurt his own daughter, I could see his frustration when he realized what this meant.

I wasn't just backing out on brunch, I was doing it last minute after he'd more or less let his mom know that we'd been living together. Something she'd specifically *told us was forbidden in case the media caught wind of it. Anything that could make her family look anything less than perfect wasn't allowed . . . ever.*

A lifestyle I knew all too well being raised under my parents' roof. Not that Kyle or I had cared about either of our parents or the consequences when he'd given me a key to his place and asked me not to leave.

As soon as I was done explaining what I knew about Jenna, I called the res-taurant, hurrying through the house as I did to change into the satiny uniform dress and stilettos, and then Kyle was rushing me to work.

Working had been a constant argument with both my parents and Kyle's. They didn't like that I was a waitress, even if it was at a place that only catered to those with pockets as deep as the Atlantic Ocean. Kyle's mom thought it was an embar-rassment to her family, and my parents thought I was embarrassing them by embarrassing the governor. Kyle hoped I would stop once we got married, but he knew I had plans to return after our honeymoon.

He didn't understand, but it wasn't for lack of trying on my part.

I'd grown up being handed everything and had watched as my parents threw money away as if it were nothing. I'd thought it normal. After all, that was how my friends' families were as well.

It wasn't until my parents had tried to use me as a pawn for their own personal gain that I'd realized how disgusting their money was—how disgusting the world I'd grown up in was.

From that moment on, I'd wanted to earn everything I had.

And, with the exception of Kyle and his need to spoil me, that was exactly what I'd done.

"I'm sorry," I said to Kyle for the fifth time as we pulled up to Glow. "Please ask your mom to forgive me, and let her know I won't miss next Sunday."

Before I could hop out of his truck, he grabbed my hand in his and pulled me close. "Stop apologizing, Briar. My mom can get mad if she wants to; it won't be long before she'll find something or someone else to be mad at. Do you know if it had been my mom or one of my sisters, they would have sent Jenna away without helping her?" He brushed my hair away from my face with his free hand, and said in a soft voice, "I'm thankful for the woman you are, and I'm proud of you and proud to call you mine. I can't wait until I can call you my wife."

My lips stretched into the widest smile as he spoke. By the time the last word left his mouth, I was pressing my lips to his.

In a move made effortless from years of kissing each other, Kyle pulled me closer. One arm was wrapped around my waist, hugging my body against his, while his other hand was cupped around the back of my neck to deepen the kiss.

The second his tongue met mine, heat flooded low in my belly. The feeling was intoxicating, and I knew I could easily get lost in that feeling and that kiss for hours. But even through the haze of Kyle's kisses, we were in the parking lot outside work, and I was already running late for the shift. A shift I needed to work for Jenna's sake.

"So I guess you kinda love me, or something, huh?" I whispered against his lips, and pulled against his hold.

A gorgeous smile tugged at Kyle's mouth as he let me back away. Grabbing my hand in his, he ran his thumb over my engagement ring, and vowed, "Until we're old and gray, and then long after."

My eyes slowly cracked open to pitch black again, but this seemed different. The movement of my eyelids seemed sluggish when I blinked. It took me a few seconds to realize there was a blindfold around my eyes, and I immediately tried to remove it, but my hands were still tightly bound. I rubbed my face against the cold floor, trying to get the blindfold to move, but had no luck.

Something wasn't right—something had changed. I lay still, listening for long moments until I realized I was *hearing* something. A loud whirring I couldn't place. It sounded like obscenely loud white noise, but it was familiar. And there was no smell. For the first time since waking up in the dark room, there was no smell of vomit or other waste.

I took a deeper breath, but wished I hadn't when my stomach rolled. Whatever was in that syringe made my stomach uneasy.

I wondered if the other women were with me. Fear slowly crawled through me when I realized I couldn't hear them above the loud whirring.

If they're gone, what happened to them? What's going to happen to me? Where am I?

Tears burned my eyes and my throat tightened.

How long has it been since I was taken? Hours . . . days? Does Kyle know? What is he thinking? What is he doing to find—I choked back a sob and curled in on myself against the cool floor.

That movement also felt odd and caught me off guard. I straightened then curled into a ball again once . . . twice before I realized why it felt wrong.

I wasn't wearing any clothes.

No dress. No underwear. Nothing but the blindfold and zip ties.

My jaw trembled violently and a jumbled prayer flew from my lips.

I repeated that prayer over and over, and eventually began mouthing the words to songs until I was singing to myself.

Relief flooded me when the first "Hush!" came.

"You're still here?" I asked quickly.

"Hush!"

But again, I didn't. I couldn't. I was terrified. The loud whirring was probably drowning me out for the most part anyway. It didn't matter that there were others around me or that they could hear me. I sang when I was afraid, always had, and it was nearly impossible to stop.

"Stop. They're going to come again."

I didn't stop, and the men with the needles never came.

"I'm waiting on one last check, then I'm taking my lunch," I called out to the manager halfway through the shift.

I eyed the two full bags of trash sitting near the kitchen door that led outside and hurried over to them. It wasn't part of my job, but I had nothing else to do while I waited, and Jenna usually threw them out on her smoke breaks.

In the hours I'd been at work, I'd worried Jenna's dad would show—not that I would know who he was even if he had—but no one had come in asking for her. No one had given a vibe that he'd been beating his daughter for who knew how long, and had chased her out of town. But I hadn't been able to shake the feeling that at any second, I would turn around and Jenna's dad would be standing there, demanding to know where she had gone. I'd felt anxious and uncomfortable in my skin throughout the shift, and was actually contemplating calling Kyle to see if he would come sit in my section for the next handful of hours.

I had finished throwing the bags into the dumpster and was walking back toward the building when I noticed the odd, almost ominous quiet around me. I was telling my feet to move faster, but fear was slowing them down.

No birds were singing, no bugs could be heard, and the air around me felt suffocating.

A song kissed my lips as my body began trembling, my soft voice sounding too loud in the quiet outdoors, and I focused on nothing but the words flowing from me and the door to the kitchen just twelve feet away.

Eleven.

Ten.

A cloth-covered hand clamped over my mouth and an arm wrapped around my waist. I screamed against it, panic and raw terror flooding me. The large person behind me lifted me off the ground and hurried backward.

I kicked at the air and clawed at the arm near my face, but my movements were already subdued, my screams dying out.

The person holding me fell back, landed with a thud, then began yelling in a deep voice, "Go, go, go!"

The light of day disappeared with the sound of a door sliding shut. I kicked uselessly at it when the vehicle took off, tried to breathe as little as possible, and thrashed my head back and forth to get away from the cloth. I attempted one more scream and felt a sharp pinch in my neck. Seconds passed before I realized my legs were no longer moving and I was no longer scratching the man holding me. The ceiling of the van blurred and the edges of my vision darkened as multiple men spoke quickly over each other, their words jumbled together and slowly faded to nothing.

Time dragged on as I sang, and eventually the other girls stopped telling me to be quiet. Occasionally some of them joined in. Others sang and murmured in different languages, the sounds all mixing together. My voice became hoarse, but I continued on when muffled cries could be heard throughout the room—knowing at least some of them needed this as much as I did—until our room suddenly dipped.

Gasps filled the room as we tried to figure out what was happening. Frantic screams and demands filled the space.

The jolt when we landed seemed to send an unspoken message through the room as we all fell silent and waited.

Oh God, oh God . . .

Where have they taken us?

The whirring eventually died down, but none of us moved or spoke as seconds turned into minutes. And minutes turned into hours.

Chapter 2

ROOM OF MIRRORS

Briar

Hours passed before a charge suddenly filled the room—or airplane—and fear flooded me. Unable to stop myself, a near-silent song left my lips.

"No, don't," someone hissed.

I wished I was smart enough to know how to listen to her. Fear suffocated me, pulling each breath and each word from my lungs, and I was helpless to stop it.

I was suddenly yanked off the ground by my elbows and hauled away.

A scream tore from my lungs, and I thrashed uselessly against whoever was holding me. "Help! Help—someone, help!"

"Quiet, bitch," the man holding me commanded; the words were muffled, as if something was covering his mouth.

I was dragged for a little while longer before I heard a door slide shut behind us, then I was forced to stand.

"Please, let me go. My fiancé has to be looking for me. His parents—*please*."

Someone in front of me scoffed, and the person gripping my elbows released me when another person grasped my shoulders roughly. I felt a cool, thin material slide over my body from behind, and recoiled from it until I remembered I was naked.

"Fiancé," the man in front of me said with a sneer, and the man behind me laughed.

"Help me," I screamed, and stumbled back into the man when a hand slammed down over my mouth.

"Listen, bitch. You don't get chosen now, you come again with us, we take you to a house to please many men."

My shocked cry was muffled by the hand against my mouth. Whoever had been keeping me in place was now holding me up as my knees gave out. Though I couldn't see, it felt like everything was tilting to the side. I was going to be sick.

I screamed again and tried with every ounce of strength inside of me to break free from the zip ties.

"If you don't shut your mouth, no one will want you. One man or many. Your choice."

I couldn't figure out which man was talking. They sounded different, but the same, and it seemed like they were coming from the same place now instead of in front of and behind me. My head spun as their words replayed over and over, and I wondered how this had happened to me.

This can't be happening. This is a nightmare. Please, God, let this be a nightmare.

"Up. Up," one of them commanded, and eventually I was lifted to my feet. "Walk. I said walk, bitch."

"Please. Please, don't do this," I begged hoarsely. "Let me go home. Kyle—" I choked out a sob and stumbled, but the men didn't let me fall.

They spoke in a rush, in voices too low for me to hear, and I wondered if these were the same men who had taken me from work. I stumbled awkwardly down a ramp and across a flat surface. It never got brighter behind the blindfold, but I had a feeling we were outside from the sudden warmth.

I sucked in a deep breath, but a hand smashed down onto my mouth before I could scream again.

My empty stomach churned at the taste of his sweaty, dirt-covered hand. I jerked, trying to get away, but his hold didn't loosen.

"No one can see you. No one knows you are here," the man in front informed me. "Keep walking."

Within another minute I was hit with a blast of air conditioning, and I planted my bare feet onto what felt like a hardwood floor. "N-no. No! Let me go." I needed to get back outside. I needed to run.

"Walk," the one behind me barked then mumbled a curse.

The man in front made a confirming grunt. "To the whore house for you then if you don't shut up."

My knees shook violently and hard sobs burst from my chest.

"Ah," the one in front continued, "yes. Do that instead. Some might like it."

Both men laughed, the sounds grating and taunting.

We slowed to a stop, and my head bowed as grief ate at me.

"Look at me. Look at me," one of them demanded, and a hand grasped at my cheeks, forcing my face up. "One last time. You listen, bitch, okay? Cry if you want. Some like that, they will pay for that," he said quickly, his voice still muffled. "You talk, you beg for help, they won't want you. They don't want a talking bitch. Got it?"

When my head shook, his free hand roughly cupped my sex, and I cried out, "Don't touch me."

"You talk . . . this will be used day and night, day and night, by anyone. You will be forced into a room to wait for the next man who pays for you. Got it? *Got it*?" he barked when I didn't respond.

"Y-yes," I said, trembling. A man who wasn't Kyle was touching me, and it was crushing something inside me.

"Let's go." He released me quickly only to take my arm in his grasp.

I heard a door open, and I bit back a cry as we stepped through it. Wherever we were now made the hair on the back of my neck stand up. The silence here was heavy, wrong.

"Three steps right . . . *now*," the man at my arm said softly, but it still crashed through the weighted silence of the room and made me jump and trip over the first step.

No one laughed as the man brought me to an abrupt stop, and I wondered briefly where the second man was. Then I thought about the other girls still on the plane, and realized I didn't want to know.

My heart raced and stomach swirled with disgust, fear, and horror as I wondered again how I had ended up here. But as I waited for something—*anything*—I stood completely still with my jaw clenched tight, determined not to let my emotions show.

The man holding me squeezed my arm and hissed a low reminder to stay quiet, but just as quickly his grasp loosened and he breathed, "Yes. Yes."

I didn't want to know what had made him excited. His words were making me lose my hold on my fragile composure.

His hold disappeared altogether, and suddenly his voice came from in front of me. "You do not move; you do not speak."

I can barely breathe.

"Do not react," he commanded urgently, but soft enough that I barely heard him.

My jaw shook and my breath came out in a hard rush at his words. I didn't want to know what I wasn't supposed to react to—his threat alone was more than enough to make me want to.

The thin material covering me was pushed from my body, and I fought against my zip ties to cover myself.

"Don't," he hissed. "They like you; do not mess it up now, bitch."

"Ple—"

"Don't!" He waited for a few beats before his fingers went to the back of my head, and I wanted to beg him to leave the blindfold alone.

I didn't want to know.

I didn't want to see.

The material fell away, and I blinked against the dim light in the room. It felt as harsh as the sun after being in pure darkness for so long. Once my eyes adjusted, I saw what my captor had been seeing, and a cry fell from my lips.

I was surrounded by dozens of one-way mirrors—each one taller than me, and just as wide. Every handful of seconds, a small, round light would turn on above one of them, only to turn off when another lit up. Then another. Then another. Faster and faster, like the lights were at war with each other.

Without realizing what I was doing until the grip on my arm tightened, I began quietly singing. All the lights stopped blinking, and another hiss came from the man beside me.

"Bitch," he said on a breath, "stop."

Just before I dropped my head and squeezed my eyes shut, a light to my left came on and didn't turn off.

Chapter 3

DAY 1 THE AUCTION

Lucas

Adrenaline coursed through my veins as I waited for the auction to begin, but despite the fact that I couldn't see any of the other bidders and they couldn't see me, I kept a calm front of indifference.

I glanced around the box of a room I would stay in throughout the process and took note of everything. It was small, but clearly no expense had been spared. The chair was more comfortable than some beds I'd slept on, and I considered sleeping through the first few girls as I rubbed at my eyes.

No, I couldn't. I knew if I fell asleep now I probably wouldn't wake up until this entire thing was over, and then I wouldn't have anything to show for a second round. My mentor told me it would be unacceptable if I came home empty-handed again, and frustrating him wasn't something I could afford.

I changed the music channel in my room until I found one to settle on, then continued looking around the room. There was a mini-coffee station, a fridge filled with water and energy drinks, and a phone with a menu next to it, but I didn't feel like I could eat now. On the other side of the room, closest to the window, were a basket of lotions and a jeweled box of Kleenex.

I rolled my eyes and drummed my fingers against the desk.

My phone chimed, and I glanced at a text from my mentor reminding me not to choose the first girl.

I nodded to myself and dropped my phone on the desk before resuming my anxious drumming. My fingers paused briefly when the door to the viewing room opened but continued as I reminded myself to be patient.

"The first girls are never worth it," my mentor always told me. *"They're the ones the sellers know will bring in the most money, so they put them up first."*

I would wait.

I dropped my head into my other hand and rubbed at a headache forming from lack of sleep. I was starting to think about that coffee maker again when the lights on my built-in desk screen went wild.

I straightened in the chair and watched in surprise for a few seconds as the bids poured in. Not once had they come in that fast during my visit six months before.

My head jerked up when the bid for her rose faster than expected, and my mouth slowly fell open.

Despite her small build, she stood tall and fearless, although I had no doubt she was anything but. I moved around my desk toward the window and let my eyes roam over her.

Her blonde hair was long, falling to her waist. Her legs were slender, and now that I was staring at them, I could see they were shaking. My gaze snapped up, and I noticed her jaw was too.

The man holding on to the girl released her to step in front of her, and although I had been turning to go back to my chair, I couldn't move. I needed to see this girl.

The man pushed the robe from her body, and immediately the girl thrashed against whatever was binding her hands. Gone was the bravado; in its place was trembling and fear.

She looked to be in her mid-twenties—just a few years younger than me, as most of the girls here today would be—and so completely pure I had no doubts that every man here was drooling at the thought of having her.

I glanced away from her long enough to see rooms light up with bids. When I looked back, I wished I hadn't. The blindfold was gone from her eyes, and now all I could do was stare at her face.

Her body bent and it looked like she cried out—and for some irrational reason, I wanted to go to her. I wanted to protect her from what she was seeing. And that was something I couldn't allow to happen. Not there, not ever.

I forced myself to turn away from her and clenched my hands into fists over and over again as I went back to my chair.

I had seen dozens of faces from a room like the one I was in. Not one of them had pulled any kind of reaction from me. They weren't supposed to.

"And she didn't either," I mumbled as I loosened my tie, trying to play it off as some side effect from my lack of sleep.

My eyes stayed focused on the screen as bids continued to come in, so I saw the second they halted. I stared at the screen, confused. There hadn't been two or three bidders going back and forth over her, and it hadn't slowed to a stop. There had been at least ten or more men bidding . . . and then nothing.

Although I tried to keep myself from it, I glanced at the girl, then leaned over the desk to look more closely at her. Her full lips were moving slowly, methodically, and I felt my own tug up in response.

It took a few seconds before I understood, and then a low laugh built in my chest. "Are you singing during a bidding war?" I whispered to myself. "You *are* brave."

As if being compelled by some force I refused to acknowledge, my fingers flew over the desk screen, and my blood pounded through my veins when I pressed the submit button. No one attempted to outbid me; I hadn't thought they would. I'd offered double the last bid to shut the other bidders down before they could decide to start up again.

Looking at the brave girl in the viewing room, my face slid back into that practiced mask of indifference as I thought of how she would soon be broken.

Chapter 4

DAY 1 WITH GIRL

Lucas

I pulled on the cufflink at my left wrist as my mentor droned on over the phone ten minutes later. "Because there wasn't a point in staying, like I told you before." I let out a slow breath through my nose to calm myself when he scoffed, as if I was a kid who didn't know any better. Before he could inform me of all the reasons to stay, I reminded him, "After everything I had to fix for you last night, I'm exhausted and ready to go home. I got what I came for; I'm leaving with a girl. There isn't a reason to buy another."

"You will grow bored with one."

My jaw tensed in frustration. I doubted that. "There will be another group in six months. If you're right, and that's the case, then I'll buy my second at that auction."

Another scoff. "I wonder about you, Lucas, I do. I wonder about your ability to do what you're supposed to. I think I put too much faith in you . . . I'm not sure you can do this."

I narrowed my eyes at the fogged privacy glass in front of me. "Only an idiot would question the man he's trained to pass as his shadow. Only a man with a death wish would question *me*."

There were a few beats of silence before he said, "I will need to come inspect her."

"Like hell you will," I said with a surprised laugh. "That is not how any of us do this, don't even attempt to deny that."

"How dare you tell me what I will and will not—"

"Did your mentor ever once come to *inspect* any of your women?" I asked quietly. Dangerously. There was warning in my tone of what would happen if he went against the rules.

"This is different, things are expected of you. You are *my* protégé," he yelled, and I laughed bitterly.

"Don't deceive your old mind into believing that you're someone greater than you are, with more power and holding than you have," I sneered. "No. This is no different, and you are no different than the rest. You are a mentor—nothing more—and mentors do not visit or *inspect*. *I* will visit *you* with her when *she* is ready."

"Lucas—"

"Trust that you trained me well, William, and remember that it *was* you who trained me. Mentor or not, do not cross me. You already know the consequences, since they came from your own mind." I ended the call before he could say anything else and dropped my phone onto the seat next to me.

I'd just rested my head on the back of the seat when there was a light tap on the back window of the car.

My eyes shot open, and I raised my arm to glance at my watch before leaning over to roll down the window. It hadn't been fifteen minutes since I'd finished buying the girl; she shouldn't have been ready yet.

"Sir?"

"What?" I growled, and narrowed my eyes at the seller trying to get a glimpse into the car.

His eyes darted back to me, and he scrambled to grab something out of his pocket. "You purchased 48-1, yes?"

I only continued to glare at him. Considering we had talked just minutes after the purchase had been finalized, he and I both knew I had.

"Yes. Here. As requested." He shoved an old, crumpled piece of paper into the car and jerked his arm away as soon as it was in my grasp.

I didn't offer my thanks. I looked away in dismissal and waited until the window was back up before I allowed myself to read the scrawled notes about the girl.

Atlanta, Georgia.
Loner.
Only goes between work (restaurant – *Glow*) and home.
Dad only. *Abusive*.
Dad deals out of home.
Girl does not use.
Perfect!

There wasn't anything to help me know more about the girl I'd just bought, but I had figured it was too much to hope for. The sellers' jobs were to study girls, finding ones who fit a certain profile and would be easily forgotten from their old lives. Nothing more.

Once I'd read the few descriptions they'd given me on her enough times to memorize them, I balled the crinkled paper into my hand and let it fall to the floor of the car.

My mouth twitched into a grimace when I thought about the girl again, trembling and crying out. The initial reaction she'd forced from me—the one to go to her and protect her—rushed to the surface and was quickly met with old memories.

Not the same, I told myself harshly as I rested my head on the back of the seat again. *Not the same.*

"Mr. Holt?"

I slowly cracked open my eyes and immediately noticed that the privacy window was down.

"Mr. Holt?"

I tensed when I realized the voice was coming from next to me and the back door was open. When I tilted my head enough to notice the driver standing there, I relaxed. I straightened in the seat as I cleared my throat and fixed my tie, though it was fine. "What?"

"They're coming with her—I thought I should warn you. You aren't going to be happy."

I stopped trying to fix my tie. "Why?"

My driver looked nervous to deliver the news, as if he was worried about my reaction. But I was already getting frustrated with the way he hesitated and scrambled for words. "They said she was scream-ing . . ." He looked at me uneasily when I stilled.

"You have exactly three seconds to tell me what happened if you want to keep your life and your job." My voice was deceptively even, but it still had the desired effect.

I wasn't to be ignored. Ever.

I watched the man turn into a scared kid. He swallowed thickly and his face paled.

"Yes, Mr. Holt. They uh, they said she was fighting them and she was uncontrollable."

"What happened?" I demanded harshly, each word clipped.

"They knocked her out; s-she's still unconscious. I'm sorry, Mr. Holt, I—"

"Move," I ordered, and barely waited until he was out of my way before I got out of the car. "How did you find out?"

"One of the men came to tell us."

I nodded, accepting his answer. I shrugged out of my jacket and threw it into the car, then shoved my hands into my pants pockets as I stared at the building ahead. My body vibrated as I resisted the urge to pace. "Knocked her out how?"

"Some drug, he didn't say what."

A growl built in my chest and cut off abruptly when a few men exited the building, one of them carrying the girl. She looked lifeless.

Barely concealed rage pounded through me by the time they reached us, and I gently took the girl from the man's arms. I studied her chest until I saw it rise and fall a few times, then I let out a slow, relieved breath.

"You bought a wild one," the man who handed her over said.

"She was uncontrollable, huh?" I tried to make my tone light but knew I didn't succeed.

"She's been trouble since we took her," another man responded. "All the others stayed silent, this bitch wouldn't shut up."

All three men laughed. My driver and I joined in, but my driver shot me a nervous look when I turned to put the girl in the backseat of the car.

He was worried. He was smart to be.

I paused from straightening out of the car and glanced over my shoulder when one of the men behind me said, "I had to drug this bitch constantly just to keep her quiet. Surprised anyone wanted her."

"Surprised she's still alive," another said with a laugh.

"Surprised you are," I added coolly. I wrapped my hand around the handle of one of the guns I had hidden below the seat and took aim when I turned around.

The three men began yelling and backing up, but I just spoke calmly over them. "We don't ask in this business, right?" I didn't wait for them to answer. "You don't ask what I do; I won't ask what you do. You don't judge me; I won't judge you. But you just harmed something that now belongs to me. I did not pay all that money for you to bring me an unconscious girl or for you to decide what happens to her when she acts out. Do we understand each other?"

The men were still slowly backing up, hands now raised, and murmuring their agreements and apologies.

"Next time I won't be so forgiving," I warned, dropping the arm holding the gun.

The men exhaled roughly, and one even laughed nervously.

The same man who had bragged about drugging the girl joked weakly, "My life just flashed before my eyes."

"Why would I kill you?" I mused darkly. "She's still breathing."

And there are rules . . .

Before he could react, I lifted my arm and fired once, hitting him in the knee.

Chapter 5

BLACKBIRD

Briar

I rolled over in bed, lifting my hands above my head to stretch, but paused when my body ached in protest.

Why do I hurt?

I tested out my muscles slowly, starting with my arms and working down to my legs. The entire time I tried to remember what I had done to be aching so much and when our bed had ever felt this incredible.

I absentmindedly ran my fingers over the cool sheets as I went through what had happened yesterday, but I couldn't seem to get a grasp on it. Everything was foggy and just out of my reach. I would get glimpses before they drifted off. Something about Kyle and phone calls in the kitchen. Work and worrying about someone ... someone ...

No, I couldn't have worked yesterday; I never work on Sundays. Brunch with Kyle's parents ... where did we go again?

I pressed my hands to my head, trying to force away the pounding and hoping in vain to clear my mind so I could sort through the confusing memories. *Why can't I remember? Why am I in so much pain? And why can't I open my eyes?*

My wrists ached. I rolled my right one a few times before grasping it with my left hand . . . and stilled. All the oxygen seemed to be sucked from the room when I felt shallow cuts that circled my wrist. Switching over to my left wrist only to feel the same, I sorted through a dizzying assault of memories as my heart raced.

"Jenna," I gasped loudly and flew into a sitting position on the strange bed.

I forced my eyes open and had to blink a few times to get them to stay open, then looked wildly around a darkened bedroom I had never seen before. My body swayed as the room spun, and I grasped my head with the hand that wasn't holding me up on the bed.

Everything came flooding back at once, and hard sobs tore from my chest as reality slammed into me. Being kidnapped, the darkness, being sold, being prepped for my buyer . . . "No, no, no, no. Help me. Someone help," I screamed, and scrambled to get off the bed.

I staggered to the side and then back toward the bed before finally finding my balance. I ran to the first door I saw and fell into the next room when the door opened easily. I looked into the small bathroom for less than a second before crawling out of it and struggling to my feet again.

The next door didn't give, and I slammed my hands against the thick wood. "Somebody. Anybody. Help me!" I cried out. "*Please.*"

My knees weakened, and I slid down to the floor, my palms slapping listlessly against the door. I bowed my head as I continued to plea with anyone who might be listening, and soon my pleas turned into songs.

Soon after, I heard a key in the lock and hurried to stand.

My body shook violently through the seconds that felt like agonizing minutes, and I hoped for strength and safety as the door swung toward me, and I ran for the opening.

I didn't even get through the doorframe before strong arms caught me and walked me backward, never seeming to care as I kicked, scratched, and screamed for help.

My screams turned frantic when I realized he was taking to me to the bed, and my efforts to get away from him doubled. "No, no! Let me go."

The man never released me, and instead of laying me down, as I had feared he would, he sat on the edge of the bed with me cradled in his arms like a small child. He kept his head bowed to his chest to protect it from my futile attack, and his arms wrapped tightly and possessively around me as seconds turned to countless minutes.

The screams and cries for help had long died out, and the struggles to get away from him had ended in a mess of shaky limbs not long after.

"Are you ready to eat, girl?"

My body tensed at his question. It was the first time I'd heard him speak. Was this the man who had *bought* me, or another one of the captors?

His voice was deep and hypnotic. And although I couldn't tell his age from his voice, the way he said *girl*, as if I was so much younger than him, made my stomach roll. How old was he? What was he going to do with me? What did he expect me to do for him?

My jaw trembled when that thought crossed my mind. *I can't do this. I can't do this.*

"When was the last time you ate?" he asked minutes later.

Even if I knew what day it was, I wouldn't have responded to him. Even if I were hungry, I wouldn't have told him.

I knew I needed food—my stomach had long stopped growling—but I didn't want to think of food right now. The nausea I had become so familiar with during my time in the pitch-black room was still present, and he wasn't helping by keeping me in his arms.

"It's early Wednesday morning; now tell me when you last ate."

My mouth opened with a soundless cry. I didn't know what was most shocking and upsetting: that I had lost two and a half days, that Kyle and both of our parents would know I was missing, or that my entire world had been ripped away from me in such a short time.

I knew they would be looking for me. I knew that, despite the frustrations Kyle's mom had, knowing we were living together and with me continuing to work at Glow, the governor would be using her status to do everything to help find me.

But I didn't even know where I was. And it left such an odd and uncomfortable feeling in my stomach. *How is someone supposed to find me when I don't even know where I am?*

"No?" he murmured, and his chest vibrated with his hum. One hand released me, but then he was pulling the silk robe I was wearing off my shoulder.

I flinched at the first contact of his fingers on my skin, though the touch was so soft it felt as though he had trailed a feather over me. My heart beat wildly in my chest as I waited for what would come next. My mind raced with the sickening possibilities, and my body became still as stone when his hand trailed down, down, down.

"Did the men touch you during the transporting?" he asked in a dangerous tone.

Someone help me, someone help me, please save me.

I cracked.

I trembled uncontrollably when his strong hand fell to my ankle then traveled back up my leg. I jerked when he reached the top of my thigh, pushing the bottom of the robe up as he went, and a quiet sob rushed from my lungs in the same breath that near-silent words started pouring from me.

His touch stilled for a second, and that vibration in his chest happened again, and I knew he was enjoying this.

Enjoying my terror.

"There you are," he said, and curled me closer against his chest. His nose pressed against my hair, but he didn't seem to be breathing. It was as if he was only listening to me.

I wanted to stop—*needed* to—but didn't know how.

"Fitting," he said after a moment; his husky tone almost sounded amused. "Over time, you'll see how perfectly that song fits you, my blackbird." He stood then, and turned to deposit me on the bed. "I'll be back with food soon."

I didn't look up at him as he walked away. I didn't want to see his face. I didn't want to know what he looked like. I didn't want to know *him*. I just rolled to face the wall as my body continued to shake. My throat tightened, strangling the words as I continued singing.

"Blackbird fly, blackbird fly. Into the light of the dark black night."

Chapter 6

DAY 2 WITH GIRL

Lucas

I bit back a frustrated groan and clenched my hands into fists when I saw the name on the screen of my cell phone. As much as I didn't want to take my mentor's call right then, I knew I had to. *This*, at least, was part of the rules. However, I was afraid of what he would say because I knew if I answered that call I would tell him what was happening.

The girl was driving me insane.

"William," I answered through gritted teeth.

"How did the day go?" His tone said what I knew he wouldn't. He was expecting the worst.

"She won't eat," I finally admitted and hissed a curse when he laughed. "Yes, laugh at me. That's what I need instead of a way to figure out how to keep her alive. She hasn't eaten for two days that I'm aware of, and however much longer from when she was taken and transported."

I sat roughly on the couch in my home office and ran my free hand over my face. I'd only had her in my care for a day and a half. Even though I had taken her three meals today, she hadn't once looked at me or touched a bite of food.

I'd tried to force her, I'd tried to coax her, I'd tried to be patient— but my patience had worn out quickly each time her body trembled and quiet songs fell from her lips. At least I had learned one thing today: she sang when scared. It seemed involuntary, but damn it, it was . . . it was endearing.

"It's only been two days, Lucas. She'll eat when she gets hungry enough."

I bit back my automatic response and blew out a calming breath. "*Again*, that I know. I don't know how long her transport was."

I refused to tell him that she'd been unconscious when I received her, and I had been worried she wouldn't wake at all when she slept through the day *and* night. Or, when I'd checked her body once she woke, she'd been covered in bruises.

Covered.

Because I knew it wouldn't matter to William. Knew what he would say.

"What difference do some bruises make? You're bound to give her more. It cannot matter to you what condition the girl is in. Unless she is dying, let her stay that way."

"If I recall, it was my fourth who did the very same thing."

My brows lifted at his unexpected comment. "And what happened?"

"Ah, I almost lost her. I had to call in a doctor who hooked her up to an IV to rehydrate her. I didn't leave her side for days even after she recovered . . ." His joking tone had disappeared, replaced by a voice I so rarely heard from him that I sat in shock for moments after.

It was full of affection and love, everything we could not feel when it came to the women—and everything he clearly showed for only one of his.

One no one knew, because he wouldn't allow anyone to know his weakness—*her.* He never showed favor toward whoever she was, but it was there in his voice. You knew when he talked about her, and you knew he was in love with her, but the mystery remained because he'd never mentioned her name. Knowing she was his fourth didn't help solve the mystery, since only the first women in a house could ever go by their number.

"You have two options, Lucas," he continued sharply, and I knew the subject of that woman was over. "You either let her starve herself until you need to get her medical help or you force her."

"I've tried forcing her."

"No," he argued, "you have not."

I lifted my hand then let it fall back to my leg. "Since you haven't been here to witness it, let me assure you—"

"You can say what you will, I will maintain that you have not. She is your property. She is to do exactly as you say when you say; eventually she will need to learn that. Some of the girls need to be taught immediately who is in control—yours might be one of them."

I breathed in sharply through my nose when I finally understood what it was he *wasn't* saying. "She isn't ready," I said gruffly.

"She isn't, or you aren't?"

My jaw clenched painfully at his blatant challenge.

"I was wrong thinking you could be brought into this life, Lucas. I thought I saw something—I was wrong."

I gripped the phone tightly in my hand and threw it across the room when he hung up. Launching myself away from the couch, I paced like a caged animal in my office as adrenaline surged through me and my anger grew.

Anger at the little blackbird in the level above this one for driving me insane and making my mentor question my abilities. Anger at myself for wanting to go easy on her when I knew that was the worst thing I could do for the both of us.

The girl had to be taught. I knew that.

Despite how much the thought made me want to offer up my own name on a bullet, I *had* to break her. I knew I couldn't let her turn into what William's fourth was for him: a weakness.

I stalked toward the doors leading to the rest of the main level of my house, and at the last second, grabbed my tie from the day before that was draped over a chair.

Chapter 7

THE DEVIL

Briar

I woke slowly when my door was thrown open. The sound of it slamming into the adjacent wall reverberated throughout the room, but I didn't attempt to move from my curled-up position.

I didn't have the strength to.

Other than the times the man had forced me to move that day in a vain attempt to eat, I had stayed right there, facing the wall.

I had wondered how long it would take my body to shut down from lack of nutrition, and I tried to figure out if it already was.

I hadn't had anything Sunday morning before Kyle and I had been on our way out the door and had been abducted before I could take my lunch at work. I remembered being given one small cup of water while they'd prepped me for my buyer, but other than that, I hadn't put anything in my stomach since Saturday night. I'd vaguely noticed that during all of my crying today, there hadn't been any tears, and I couldn't remember when I'd last used the restroom. I was just so tired.

Just as my eyes slid closed again, the man roughly forced me onto my back. It was easy to keep my eyes closed now—I wondered briefly if I could sleep through this attempt at giving me food.

A scratchy whimper of protest sounded in the back of my throat when he grabbed my sore wrists and yanked them high over my head. "Please let me go," I whispered hoarsely as something smooth slid over one wrist . . . and then the other.

For a second, the material felt so nice that I wondered if he was doing something to heal my cuts, but then it tightened painfully and my hands were pulled higher until my shoulders were screaming in pain.

The tension eased momentarily, but when I tried to move my arms down again, I couldn't.

I sluggishly leaned my head back on the bed and peeled my eyes open, but it took me a second to understand what I was seeing. My hands were tied to a wide section of the wooden headboard. I pulled harder with no give from the wood, and looked down, panic flooding me when the man opened my robe, exposing my body.

I pressed my legs together and tried to pull them up, to curl into as much of a ball as my position would allow, but the man gripped the tops of my thighs and slammed them back onto the bed, spreading them wide.

"No, no. No!" I screamed, and tried to thrash with what little energy I had left. "Please, no."

"You are mine, do you understand that?" he seethed, and the muscles in his arms flexed as he held me down.

He was shirtless, and the jeans he'd been wearing throughout the day were unbuttoned and barely staying up. He was tall, with a broad chest and shoulders that tapered down to narrow hips. Every inch of him was tanned and muscled, but the scars and tattoos that littered his body didn't seem to fit a man who bought kidnapped women.

They didn't seem to belong to a man who spoke to me the way he did. They didn't boast of his money or power.

They screamed he was dangerous. They screamed to run.

My head shook subtly as a sob burst from my chest. "No," I whimpered.

His head snapped up then, and I froze as I got my first glimpse of this man.

He was younger than I'd thought. Maybe a few years older than me. His dark hair was cut short on the sides and longer on top, and looked as if he had been running his hand through it all day. His nose and jaw were strong, and the dark stubble that covered his face somehow highlighted his full lips that were in a sneer now. But his eyes—those dark eyes were as murderous as they were mesmerizing . . .

He was darkness.

He was my own personal demon sent from hell.

"No?" he asked. His voice held no emotion anymore. He released my legs and straightened his body as his strong hands moved to the zipper on his jeans. I shut my eyes and my jaw trembled when I felt the bed dip. "You can try to kill yourself, Blackbird; I will keep you alive. When I tell you to eat, you eat. Do you understand?"

"Please stop, please stop, please stop," I begged as his hands grasped my thighs again so his denim-covered hips could settle between them, my voice growing louder with each word. "No, no. Stop!" I screamed when one of his hands trailed up to my hip, his grip tightening. "Stop!"

I squeezed my eyes harder, not wanting to see any part of this. *This can't be happening to me.*

His other hand slowly moved to the inside of my thigh, my entire body now shaking with fear and hatred and disgust.

"I understand," I yelled. "Just please *stop*. Don't do this."

His hand stilled, and seconds that felt like lifetimes of torture passed by before he released me and slowly covered my trembling body with his own. I flinched when his lips met my ear, but otherwise I didn't move.

"I own you, Blackbird," he said in a deceptively soothing voice.

I let my head fall away from him, and opened my eyes to stare at the same wall I'd looked at all day as I responded, "Never."

His fingers gripped my face and forced me to look at him, and like before, he looked murderous. Beautiful and destructive.

Chapter 8

DAY 2 WITH BLACKBIRD

Lucas

I paced the length of the living area on the upper level for nearly an hour after I left Blackbird and still couldn't seem to find the strength to stop.

That had been her first *lesson*. I had shown her who was in control, as I knew I had to. I had taken the first step in breaking her.

William was under the impression I'd done more than I had, and he was satisfied.

I wanted to die.

I wanted to tear my heart out if it would get her screams out of my head, if it would get that look of hatred and brokenness out of her green eyes.

She had called me the devil, and I felt like it after tonight. But she would never hate me more than I hated myself.

I dropped down to a low squat and ran my hands roughly through my hair and over my face as I tried to do so many things: force myself to go downstairs, talk myself out of what I was so close to doing, and get her damn screams out of my head.

A roar of frustration filled the room, and I was storming away within seconds. Only this time it wasn't to continue pacing—I needed to try to get her to eat one more time even though it was nearly midnight. She had looked so fragile and pale. Her lips had been so chapped and dry. I couldn't get the image out of my head, and I was fucking terrified to think how much worse she might be if I left her until morning like I was supposed to.

"They must stay isolated for at least eight hours after a lesson," William always said. *"It's a lesson for them, and you will look weak if you go to them before they would come crawling to you."*

As soon as I had some water, fruit, and a sandwich made, I went back to her room and unlocked the door. Unlike last time, I opened the door and stepped in slowly to give her time to prepare for me.

The lamps were still on even though she looked like she was asleep. She was curled up on the bed with her back facing me, as she had been most of the times I'd come in today, and again she didn't turn around.

I set the plate and water on the nightstand, and reached for her shoulder, but withdrew my hand before I could touch her. "Blackbird," I said gently. My hands fisted when I noticed her rapid breathing, but I knew we had a long road ahead of us before she wasn't afraid of me.

Her fear . . . it was something I had been prepared for. Something I'd been trained for. I just hadn't been prepared for how much it would bother me.

"Blackbird," I called again, and finally touched her shoulder to turn her toward me when she didn't respond in any way.

Her eyes were shut and jaw trembling, but for once, I had a feeling she wasn't avoiding looking at me.

"Blackbird," I said sharply and shook her shoulder. "Girl!" I rolled her fully onto her back and pressed my fingers to her neck.

Her pulse was weak, but felt like it was going as fast as a hummingbird's wings.

"No, no, no, no, shit," I roared, and brushed my hand over her face then paused. Placing my hand on her cheek again, I moved it up to her forehead and swore.

I grabbed at my pockets, biting out another curse when I remembered throwing my cell phone against a wall, and took off out of the room to grab one of the landlines.

William answered on the second ring. "Lucas, wha—"

"Get a doctor here now!"

There was a pause, then, "Did you already go back to check on her? How long has it be—"

"Did you hear me?" I yelled as I ran back to the girl's room. She hadn't moved. "Get a doctor here. Have him bring the IV drip and anything else he can think of." I hung up and dropped the phone on the bed and ran my hands over the girl's face again. Her skin was on fire. "Shit," I whispered, and moved one hand to her throat and the other to her wrist.

I hurried into the small bathroom attached to the room and ran two washcloths under cold water, then wrung them out and folded them as I rushed back to her. I placed one on her forehead and held the other to the back of her neck as my free hand gripped her wrist until I found her rapid pulse again.

I felt helpless waiting for a doctor to show up, but I knew I had no other option. Taking her to a hospital right now wasn't possible. Not when she had just been taken from her home days before. Not when she would scream for help as soon as she regained consciousness. No . . . I couldn't risk everything for this girl, but in the ten minutes it took for the doctor to arrive, I considered it more and more.

"Leave the room, Lucas," William called out as he entered the girl's room behind the doctor.

I looked up in surprise, and growled as my eyes went back to the girl. "No. You shouldn't be here."

"Lucas—"

My head whipped back up, my eyes already narrowed. "Don't tell me to leave." My tone was a mix of warning and plea, and it shocked my mentor.

His eyes traveled over to my blackbird. There was hesitation in the way he looked at her, as if he were suddenly afraid to. His gaze lingered on where I was now gripping her hand, and one eyebrow rose in disapproval. "I see."

The doctor didn't ask questions. He just checked her vitals, hurried to find a vein in Blackbird's dehydrated body and started pumping her with fluids, then checked her vitals for a second time. The entire time murmuring things to himself that he needed to remember before he finally stopped to write it all down.

"When did she last eat or drink?" he asked suddenly.

"I have no idea. I've been trying to get her to do both for two days."

He nodded to himself as he wrote. "Has she been sick?"

I ground my jaw. "No."

The doctor continued nodding, then pointed to her with his pen. "New one?"

"Yes," William responded for me.

"Then we wait," the doctor said as he turned to check the speed of the IV. "Her body is in shock. A few more hours, she would have slipped into a coma."

I rubbed my hand over my face, then rested my elbow on my knee and my mouth on my fist. My eyes shut and my stomach churned when I thought about how close I had been to leaving her for the night.

"Lucas."

I opened my eyes and slowly slid my gaze over to William.

He shook his head subtly. I didn't need his words to know what he meant.

I shouldn't be reacting this way. Even though only William was present—doctors like this one were the best around, and were paid to keep quiet . . . be invisible—I shouldn't show this kind of emotion over a girl. It showed weakness.

The women could become attached, but the men never did. The men never showed that they cared at all, not outside private times in the bedroom at least.

William was one to talk.

"Leave," I demanded quietly.

He didn't, and I went back to ignoring him as the doctor set up a machine to track Blackbird's vitals.

The doctor stayed until the girl had shown enough improvement for him to feel optimistic. I let William walk him out since he'd brought him in, and I still wasn't ready to leave Blackbird's side even with the improvements.

She had woken briefly before falling back asleep, but her heart rate was slower and stronger, her blood pressure was higher, and she was on her third bag of fluids—this one dripping much slower than the first two had—so at least my worry had eased. Slightly.

"We must talk."

"I don't see a reason to," I said when William came back into the room. "You can leave. I needed the doctor, not you. Now I have his number for future reference."

William sat with a huff in the chair he had dragged into the room earlier. "You came back to her before you should have. Eight hours, Lucas, and you didn't even last two."

I gave him a dark look as I reminded him, "And she would have been in a coma if I'd listened to you."

He waved off my words. "That's beside the point. Clearly she's going to be fine." He slapped his hand onto his leg when I huffed. "You were not ready for this."

A muscle in my jaw popped from the force I was putting on it, but this time I wondered if he was right. Instead of threats or dark warnings, I admitted, "She was the first."

"What?" he asked, having not heard my soft words.

"She was the first," I said louder, then clarified, "at the auction."

He scoffed. "Child. You are a child, and you think this is a game. This is my life. This is *their* lives," he said, gesturing to the wall, as if dozens of men would suddenly be standing there. "This is how we—"

"This is my life, too," I argued. "The moment I saw her face I knew I *needed* her." William's expression fell, but I continued talking. "I turned my back on her, I ignored her. But then she—" I broke off quickly, not wanting to tell him about her singing. I shrugged helplessly. "I hated the thought of someone touching what was mine. I owned her before I ever bought her, and there was no way I wasn't buying her—first or not."

"Lucas, who owns who?" I'd never seen my mentor as disappointed as I did then.

"I do," I growled. "As I proved tonight."

William shook his head. "You have to let her go."

Shock and anger tore through me, freezing me in place.

"This isn't acceptable this early in. You are going against everything I have taught you. Buying a first, showing that you care, not being able to follow through with the entire lesson . . ." He searched for something to say, and finally settled on, "You can't keep her."

"Take her from me," I challenged darkly, knowing full well he wouldn't if he valued his life. "You wanted me to finally begin, and I have. I have my first girl. Yes, I didn't leave her alone after a lesson, but there was reason for that. I was already worried about her lack of eating and drinking, and then I put her through a *lesson*. She fought me—"

"As you should expect them to in the beginning."

My right hand fisted, and I forced myself not to punch the smirk off my mentor's face. "She used energy she didn't have to fight me. She exerted herself. All of this might not be happening if I wouldn't have tried to teach her a lesson tonight, do you understand that? Can you understand why I feel guilty and don't want to leave her side?"

"Whether you feel that or not—which you should not—you do not let it show as you have tonight. If she saw you, she would know she had you in the palm of her hand."

Although I felt drawn to, I refused to look down at my blackbird. I kept my gaze on William's, and asked, "Did *she*?" When confusion covered his face, I said, "Your *fourth* . . ." I let the word hang in the air. "Did she ever see you show the emotion that you fail to hide in front of the rest of us?"

Rage quickly replaced the confusion on William's face, and I knew I had him. But just as fast as the rage had come, it was gone and his expression was calm and indifferent. "If *this* is how you repay me for finally allowing you to play this game, I clearly trusted you with too much and let you move through your training far too quickly."

"Allowed me?" I asked darkly, and hurried to turn it around on him. I hadn't done all I had in the last few years for him to doubt me now. "You chose me. You trained me. You urged me to buy into your company and then you pushed me to buy my way into this life. And when I came home six months ago without a girl, you nearly lost your mind. But now I have an equal claim in our company, and I'm finally in the world you so desperately wanted *me* to be in. I think the real issue here isn't how I'm handling the girl I now have, it's that you're panicking because you've realized your mistake."

The calm on William's face slipped just a fraction, but it was all I needed.

"The man *you* trained is smarter in this world and in our business than you've ever been . . . and will one day replace you," I growled, the threat in my words clear. I nodded toward the door. "Leave, and don't come back. We'll come to you when she's ready—and she *will* be ready."

Chapter 9

UNANSWERED QUESTIONS

Briar

The door to my room opened and shut, but I didn't move to look at him from where I sat cross-legged on my bed. I continued to run my hands through my wet hair, staring at the wall as though there were a window there.

I wondered what it looked like outside here . . . wherever *here* was.

"Blackbird."

I froze for a second then started finger-combing my hair again. In the four days since I'd woken up to a doctor taking an IV out of my hand, the devil hadn't attempted to speak to me. He had brought me meals regularly—the first day staying to make sure I ate—but had otherwise left me alone.

When he spoke again, frustration laced his name for me. "Blackbird."

"I have a name," I said numbly and looked over my shoulder in time to see him fight back a smile. "I have a name, and I have a fiancé and parents and people who are looking for me."

His smile abruptly fell, his face now void of all emotion. "You don't have anyone looking for you."

My fingers stopped running through my hair. Ice-cold dread filled me. "W-what? What did you do— What did you do to them?"

I yelled, and turned to fully face him. "They didn't do anything—*I* didn't do anything to deserve this. I don't understand why I am here," I yelled as a mixture of sad and angry tears fell to my cheeks.

"Stop," he commanded gently, coldly.

I gripped at my chest as different scenarios flashed through my mind. "*Please* tell me what happened to them."

"You want me to play this game with you? Fine. What happened to who, Blackbird?" he snapped. "There is no one looking for you, because you *had* no one. Why do you think you were taken?"

It took immeasurable seconds to understand what he was saying.

"*. . . you* had *no one. Why do you think you were taken?*" Whoever they'd meant to take . . . it wasn't me.

Which meant Kyle and his parents—*my* parents—were safe.

Relief filled me so fast and so profound that it made me dizzy.

"Then it was a mistake," I choked out. "I had them, I had Kyl—" A sob forced its way from my chest. "You took everything from me," I whispered. My right thumb and forefinger automatically went to where my ring had been on my left hand before I'd been taken, and my chest ached as I thought about Kyle.

"There's no point in lying, you can't leave," the man said.

"Ly—" I cleared my throat and shook my head. "I'm not *lying*! I was taken by mistake. I'm supposed to be getting married in a week."

The devil's dark eyes narrowed in frustration, and he turned to leave as I continued shouting.

"My name is Briar Chapman," I called out as he reached the door. "My fiancé's name is Kyle Armstrong. His mother is the governor of Georgia. I was taken by mistake." Then to myself, "This is a mistake."

Hours dragged by before the door opened again. Not that it was uncommon for so long to pass between each time he visited, but I had been hoping for something different after I had given him my name and something to think about.

Then again, I doubted he cared.

"Are you ready to talk calmly now?" he asked with one dark eyebrow raised when I turned to face him.

I didn't respond.

He walked closer until he was standing at the corner of my bed, and my hatred for him grew when I realized some distant part of my mind appreciated the way he looked.

The tie he had been wearing earlier was gone, and his shirtsleeves were now rolled up. His hands were crossed over his chest, revealing corded muscles and the scars and dark tattoos that contradicted the man he was.

Then again, it fit for a devil.

He is darkness, I reminded myself.

I flicked my gaze up to where he was staring down at me, waiting for my reply, and instead asked, "Do you have my ring?"

"What ring?"

I lifted my left hand for a second before dropping it back into my lap. "My enga—"

"Enough," he hissed, and slowly relaxed his arms to slip his hands into his suit pants pockets. "You do not have a family, and you do not have a fiancé—I was told about your life when I bought you. Your lying will only frustrate me and force me to teach you another lesson."

It took far too long to understand what the first lesson had been, and my lunch soured in my stomach. "T-the . . . the other night was a lesson?"

His nostrils flared, but he didn't respond otherwise.

"You—I thought you were going to rape me," I cried out, "and that was a *lesson*?"

"Keep pushing me and see if I don't," he threatened in a dark tone.

A shuddering breath tumbled from my lips before the room fell into a heavy silence. "I mean nothing to you," I whispered, mostly to myself, then slowly looked up at him. My voice shook as I spoke.

"Why do you want to . . . to keep someone locked in a room whose life and body mean nothing to you?" I pressed a hand to my chest.

"Because they mean something to me." When he didn't respond, I begged, "Tell me why I'm here."

"Because I own you."

I shook my head quickly. *No. Never.* "What does that mean for me?"

"It means you're mine." He didn't seem to care that he wasn't giving me the answers I needed—and was afraid to have—he just continued to stand there with a look of eternal patience on his face.

My body trembled when I thought about that night—about the *lesson*—and my question came out weak and breathy. "Am I here for sex?"

He huffed through his nose. "Not exactly."

"Not exactly?" I mouthed, my body shaking harder at his response. "Then what exactly?"

"Next question."

I was so horrified about the thought of having been taken and sold into some sex trafficking ring that it took almost an entire minute to ask, "Can I please have clothes other than the robes?"

His sinful eyes roamed over my body, making me feel as though I wasn't covered. "Not yet."

"Yet? When can I?" I asked, but he didn't respond, and my shoulders fell as I searched for another question. "Will I always be in this room?"

"Do you want to be?"

"No," I said immediately. The room wasn't small, but it felt like a dungeon. "There aren't any windows, I haven't seen outside in . . . in . . . in nearly a week," I realized bleakly. "I don't even know where I am."

"Are you done asking questions?" he asked after a short pause. Again, he looked like he had all the patience in the world, and it was infuriating.

"You've barely been answering the ones I've asked."

"Answer that one," he demanded.

I stared at him as my frustration and fear swirled through me. By the time I spoke, the fear had won out and my voice was nothing more than a breath leaving my lips. "Yes."

He moved to cross his arms back over his chest, and thought for a second. "This is a starter room, Blackbird. When I think you're ready, you'll be allowed to move out and have free rein of the entire upstairs of my home. There is a kitchen up here, other bedrooms that you can choose from since no one else is here, and plenty of windows. Once I completely trust you, you will be allowed anywhere in this house, and out of it as long as I've approved where you're going."

"Out?" I whispered. "You would let me out?"

A wicked smirk pulled at his full lips. "Like I said, that will only be once I trust you. By that point, I won't be worried about you trying to run."

There would never come a time where I would want to stay.

"If we don't ever get to that point, you won't leave this level of the house," he added quickly, diminishing my hopes of running from him. "Once you're out of this room and have picked a new one, you'll have a closet that we will fill. Until then, you're only allowed the robes because you need to understand that you *are* mine and that means your body is mine. I want you comfortable in nothing around me."

My head shook as he spoke. Again, something that would never happen.

"Your body is mine, but that doesn't mean you're here for sex, Blackbird. If you'd been bought by someone else, you might have ended up as a sex slave. Most of us don't see the women we buy that way. You'll help cook and clean, take care of the house . . ." He lifted a shoulder in an easy shrug. "You'll take care of me and I'll take care you."

I blinked slowly, trying to process what he had told me. "I-I-I," I stuttered, then stopped trying to speak, because I didn't even understand how to phrase the question in my head. Instead, I said, "You said no one else was here."

He nodded. "Yet."

My eyebrows rose. "Yet? Who will be coming here?"

"You are only one of many women who will end up in this house."

"How long do we each stay?" I asked, and embarrassed heat filled my cheeks when he barked out a laugh.

"Forever, Blackbird. My mentor has thirteen women in his home."

Thirteen?

It felt like I had been punched. "Thirteen? I don't—why? Why do you—why can't I just go then? Who wants or can handle that many wives?"

"Wives?" he asked condescendingly. "No. Women. Life partners. I will never marry any of you. I will never enter into a relationship with any of you. As I said, I *own* you, just as I will own them. There is nothing more to it."

Tears burned at my eyes, and my fingers automatically went to play with my ring before I remembered it wasn't there. As I had so many times over the last week, I wondered how I had ended up here.

I was supposed to be getting married soon.

We wanted to have kids and move to a large plot of land where we could have horses, cows, and goats. And instead of a farm and the man of my dreams, I got the devil and twelve other women.

"You aren't meant to have multiple life partners. There's supposed to be one and that's it," I whispered, and clutched at my chest, trying in vain to pull the invisible weight from it. "A life partner is someone you love and want to spend the rest of your life with. Not someone you claim to *own*. You can't force someone into that—or multiple people for that matter."

One dark brow arched in response. In challenge.

I gripped at my chest harder, still searching for the weight pressing down, and tried to force my tears back.

And then it struck me. The man said if I ever gained his trust, I could leave.

I knew what I had to do. I had to do whatever it took to get out of here. To get out of this nightmare and back to my life with Kyle.

The man suddenly snatched my left hand from my chest and brought it closer to him, as if inspecting it.

I slowly looked up at him, but never asked what he was doing.

"What is your name?" he asked gruffly.

Was he testing me? I thought of the furious look on his face before, and said, "B-blackbird?" making it sound like a question.

An amused smile played at his lips for a second before it was gone. "No, what is your name?" he demanded.

"Briar Chapman."

His eyes drifted to the side, away from me, and after a moment he dropped my hand. "Not anymore. Your last name is Holt, do you understand?" He didn't wait for me to respond before he turned and left.

Once the door slammed shut and locked, I glanced at my hand.

What had he been looking at?

Chapter 10

DAY 7 WITH BLACKBIRD

Lucas

I stared at the screen of my computer as minutes came and went, unable to make myself do what I wanted—and knew I shouldn't.

She's just getting into your head. They probably all will. They'll all lie.

I thought about the paper with the notes on it about *Atlanta*, and tried to tell myself that that was the truth. That everything *Briar* had said about parents and a fiancé had been a lie.

But I had seen the grief when she'd said his name. I had seen the faint tan line on her finger from a ring. And now I was about to break the rules and destroy myself to find out the truth about her when it was the last thing I should ever know.

I pulled up a news page and went to the list of breaking news links. My eyes darted down to the second one, and my hand tightened on the cursor.

Missing Georgia woman, "Briar Chapman", details.

Just below that, another.

Georgia Governor, Judy Armstrong, speaks out about missing future daughter-in-law.

Forcing myself to breathe, I clicked on the top link and dropped my head to stare at the desk.

I was fucking shaking.

I tried to talk myself out of looking at the news story, but before I could click out of the web browser, I caught sight of the picture of a smiling blonde and felt the same pull I had every time I had looked at her this week.

Dread deepened as I read every word of the article. Certain parts stood out: *hard worker, loved by all, weeks away from wedding, graduated summa cum laude from University of Georgia.*

"Christ," I hissed as I continued on, and found where they had interviewed Georgia Governor's son, Kyle Armstrong . . . her fiancé.

Everyone was sure she wasn't a runaway. Her fiancé explained that they'd been headed out to brunch with his parents when a friend had come asking for help, and Briar had gone into work at the last minute for said friend.

. . . never worked a Sunday . . . Armstrong thinks friend might be in danger, too . . . friend's father brought in for questioning.

Friend's father.

Her father.

Shit.

I shoved away from my desk and gripped at my hair. My breaths came out in hard rushes and sounded like I was in pain. I wanted to be. I wanted to be in the worst kind of pain, only to find something that hurt more.

They had grabbed the wrong girl.

Briar hadn't been lying. She'd been taken by mistake.

Her words and her life triggered something I'd locked deep inside me, and I was quick to force it back before it could overwhelm me, like I knew it so easily would . . .

Not the same, I told myself.

"Why do you want to . . . to keep someone locked in a room whose life and body mean nothing to you? Because they mean something to me."

Her broken voice floated through my mind, making me want to tear at my heart all over again.

A dozen responses to her question had crossed my mind then, and were flooding it now. If I voiced any of them, it would be dangerous on too many levels.

I went back to the desk and scrolled up until her smiling face was on my screen, and let out a heavy sigh as I stared at the girl I would never deserve.

Coward.

I was a goddamn coward.

I hadn't even looked in Briar's direction when I'd put her plate of food inside the doorway for lunch or dinner the day before. And though I doubted she noticed since she was usually facing away from me when I entered, I still knew.

I knew everything I wished I didn't.

If I would've seen her face—the broken way she looked at me—I would have said things that couldn't be voiced. Would've apologized for things I couldn't be sorry for.

And despite my need for more time away from that face and those shattered eyes . . . I couldn't take it.

I stepped in that next morning with her breakfast in one hand and a chair dragging from the other and immediately her singing halted. Her body visibly tensed as she took slow, calculated breaths before looking over her shoulder at me.

The hatred that poured from her hit me hard enough that a weaker man would've stumbled. Instead, I let that calm wash through me until I felt nothing. I needed to feel nothing if I was going to get her through this.

If she was surprised that I was coming toward her, she didn't show it.

If she wanted to hide her fear, she needed to work harder.

"Blackbird," I murmured gruffly, set the plate on the edge of the bed, then stepped back and positioned the chair so I would be within reaching distance of her. Once I was settled in it, I dipped my head toward the food, and said, "You might as well eat, because I'm obviously not leaving yet."

She held my stare with narrowed, hate-filled eyes for a few seconds as her shoulders lightly shook before finally turning around and taking a bite of her food.

"We need to work on your progress," I said once she'd taken a few bites.

Her hand halted on the way back to her mouth, and her eyes widened. "My progress. What progress?"

I relaxed into the chair and folded my arms across my chest. My eyes dipped over her robe-covered body in silent answer before I said, "We need to get you out of this room."

It was immediate, the hunger that replaced the confusion, and then the fear and revulsion that replaced that hunger. She wanted out of the room just as badly as I needed her out of it, but she wasn't *ready*. I knew she wasn't, but I needed to push her or she never would be, and *never* wasn't an option. There was an expected timeline she had to follow, and I couldn't afford for time to run out with her still in this room.

The hand that wasn't holding a piece of fruit slowly moved up to grasp at where the robe covered her chest, as if to make sure nothing could be seen. The shaking of her shoulders gradually grew stronger and stronger until her entire body was trembling.

"I can have a conversation with you and not scream for help or try to run," she said on a breath. "Can't that be enough?"

My head tilted, and my voice hinted at the driest amusement when I asked, "Do I really need to tell you that that isn't how this works?"

But she didn't respond, and she didn't move. She sat there shivering with her hand still clasping the robe together and that piece of melon still suspended in air.

"Why are you shaking, Blackbird?"

A harsh, mocking laugh burst from her chest. But again . . . nothing.

"Briar," I said in a low murmur, and waited until her frightened eyes snapped up to meet mine. "It's just a question. I'm sitting in a chair and you *could* be eating breakfast. So why exactly are you shaking right now?"

The melon slipped from her fingers and fell to the plate as a stunned breath filled the space between us, and her small frame jerked with a full-body shiver. "Because of w-who you are and what you've done."

"What have I done?"

She looked at me incredulously, and tried to voice the words again and again before they finally came out. "The other night I thought you were going to rape me, and you said you woul—"

"I'm not going to hurt you," I said, and my voice swam with honesty.

"Right now? Or today? Or does that include tomorrow too?" she asked as her voice cracked and tears filled those broken eyes.

I bit back my initial response and instead echoed, "I'm not going to hurt you. But we need to get you out of this room." I shifted forward, and watched every movement of her body as I rested my arms on my knees and clasped my hands together.

Her chest hitched and her body jerked, but she didn't move away from me.

"Now, tell me why you're still shaking."

"Because I can't do this," she said immediately, her voice weak. "I can't do what you want me to." I opened my mouth to speak, but she asked, "Is this a lesson?"

Her question slammed into me and made me lose my hold on that calm as everything I *shouldn't* feel assaulted me again and again . . . The way those broken eyes made me want to beg her to forgive me. The way her screams made me want to tear out my heart.

Within seconds my calm was back and filling me, and I let my lips slowly curve into a wicked grin. "You'll know when I'm teaching you a lesson." Once her hatred from my statement had dulled, I nodded toward the plate again. "Eat."

Only seconds had passed before she picked at the fruit she'd been eating, and after she'd taken a few bites, I slowly reached forward.

She stilled as my hand neared the robe just above her breasts, and her chest's movements became exaggerated when I slipped my hand inside to slowly drag the material off one of her shoulders.

When I looked up, fear-filled eyes were watching my every move before darting up to my face when I withdrew my hand. As soon as my hands were clasped again, I mumbled, "Eat."

A full minute came and went before she shakily resumed, and as before, I slowly reached forward after she'd finished taking a few bites.

Her breath rushed out when I grasped the other side of her robe. "Please, d-d—" she said breathlessly but didn't continue.

My eyes darted up to hers once her other shoulder was bared, and I forced myself to ignore the way they pled with me and the way they glistened with unshed tears. "You need to be comfortable around me, Blackbird. Eat."

After another minute, she grabbed for the piece of toast. But even then, she just held on to it as she continued to violently tremble.

I stood from the chair and walked to the edge of the bed. Pressing my knuckles to her chin, I waited until she was looking at me, then slowly dropped my hands to where she was grasping the satin material against her breasts.

"You want to leave this room, and I can't let you leave it until we've passed this point," I said in a low, soothing tone as I removed the tight grip she had on the robe and bent to whisper in her ear, "Close your eyes and clear your mind. You *can* do this."

But I wasn't sure that *I* could.

Because my calm was crumbling, and I couldn't hold on to that *nothing* that I so desperately needed to cling to in order to get through this.

This girl and those eyes were crippling me in a way I'd never known—and couldn't afford now.

I knew what I needed to do, and yet . . . I wanted to protect her from this, even though I was the one pushing her. I wanted to pull her closer so I could feel her body pressed to mine. I wanted to brush my lips across hers—

Nothing. Feel nothing, I maintained as I fought between covering her up, and continuing with what I knew we had to do.

I forced that calm and that *nothingness*, and the tips of my thumbs brushed against her breasts as I bunched the material in my hands. Just as I was about to release the robe and let the material pool around her hips, a song fell from her lips, hushed and broken, and the sound made me pause.

I looked at her face to see it tight with fear, and again, I lost my weak hold on my calm. Only that time, I didn't try to snap it back in place. I let everything I felt consume me as I pulled her robe back over her shoulders and stepped away.

"Another day, Blackbird," I mumbled and let her voice follow me out of the room.

Chapter 11

PUSH

Briar

Days dragged on, yet blurred together. I wasn't sure how long I had been here and wished I had a way of knowing. I had started counting the breakfasts, but eventually I couldn't remember which day had been the day before. I'd spent days crying before my body stopped producing tears and a numbness settled over my heart and mind. As the numbness receded a few days later, the boredom settled in.

I spent whole days singing, others staring at the wall just *wishing* for a window so I could see the outdoors, and still others waiting in fear, wondering what the day would hold.

There hadn't been another *lesson*, but there had been two more failed attempts of trying to push me into being comfortable with a man I hated with every fiber of my being.

He seemed frustrated by my lack of progress, but I didn't know what more he could have expected. He was evil incarnate; he had *paid* for me after I'd been stolen from my life and the man I loved. He'd tried to teach me a lesson by making me think he was going to use my body . . . all because I'd refused to eat when I'd first arrived.

I knew I needed to gain his trust, and part of that was doing what needed to be done to get out of this room, but it wasn't as easy as he thought it should be.

This wasn't letting a man undress me as anticipation pounded through my veins and made me ache for him. This wasn't letting the man I loved look at me, bare and vulnerable and ready for him. This was dancing with the devil and attempting to come out of it unscathed.

The door opened, but I didn't look toward it as my throat closed up, effectively ending the song.

It took a few seconds, but I noticed there was a charge in the room that hadn't been there yesterday or the day before, and it sent a chill through my spine.

He was staying . . .

I blew a steadying breath out before I found the courage to turn my head to look at him from where I was lying on the bed.

His power, darkness, and masculine beauty stunned me, as it had every time I looked at him, but I didn't react to it. I watched him as he watched me, and I looked up at the ceiling when his eyes fell from my face to my body.

Sin. He was pure sin. I hated him.

"Blackbird," he whispered in that voice of his. That invigorating, throaty mixture of warmth and softness that hinted at regret was just another part of his attraction . . . another part of his deceit . . . another part of him I hated.

"Devil."

His face came into view then, his lips twitching into a brief, amused grin before falling, and then he was saying the words I didn't want to hear . . .

"Show me that—"

"Is it the weekend?" I asked quickly, cutting him off.

His dark brows pulled low over his eyes as he studied me, and instead of repeating what I knew he'd been about to say, he asked, "Why?"

"Your shirt," I responded automatically and hated that embarrassed heat filled my cheeks. "Um, you're just normally in a button-down."

He glanced at himself. "Do you prefer those?"

I looked at the black shirt that stretched over his tanned, muscled body and shook my head as I pushed myself up so I was sitting on the bed. "I don't have a preference. I've just been trying to figure out how long it's been since I was taken from home."

He looked away, but not before I saw the way his face fell. He swallowed thickly and seemed to think about what to say for a while before he spoke. "Don't think of it that way." His voice was laced with some emotion I couldn't place, but it shocked me all the same.

I had only ever seen him angry, annoyed, or menacing. To see any other kind of emotion that suggested this devil might have some humanity made him intriguing—no. He wasn't. *This is all a trick, all part of his darkness*, I reminded myself, and forced the sound of his voice from my mind.

"How am I supposed to think of it?" I asked softly. My throat tightened and my eyes burned, but no tears came. I wasn't sure I had any tears left in me. "I missed my *wedding*. I missed marrying the man I—"

"Enough," he bit out, cutting me off. Dark, dark eyes met mine as his chest rose and fell with each rough breath that left him. After an eternity had passed in our agonizing silence, he spoke. Every word was automatic, detached. "You're finally free here with me. You don't need to count days."

"*Free*? I was *kidnapped*. You *bought* me. I've been locked in this room for *weeks*. In what world could any of those things ever be considered *free*?" What had started out as whispers had turned into tortured yells, but he didn't react to them.

He just watched me until I was finished, then calmly said, "In my world, Blackbird."

"*Your*—" I began, somewhat taken aback. I hadn't thought he would respond to those questions, and I certainly hadn't expected *that* response. "What world *is* this? Where did they take me? Where are—what country are we in?" I demanded, my voice rising with each question.

The devil looked at me with forced amusement. "Where do you think you are?"

I didn't even know where to begin with my thoughts on where they could have taken me. I'd been unconscious for the better part of two days while they'd brought me here. And I'd been so naïve to think that sex trafficking would never touch my world, that I didn't know much about it. I thought it only happened in foreign countries, and I still had a feeling I was in one. "Not the United States," I finally whispered.

He glanced down at himself for a split second, and when he looked up again, his eyes were cold. "I'm American, Blackbird. What would give you the impression that we aren't in the U.S.?"

"Are we?"

"Why would I want you close to where they took you from?" he responded vaguely, trying to confuse me even more.

I shook my head slowly and pleaded, "Just tell me where we are."

"In a room you should've been out of a while ago," he said in a dark voice. "Show me you can handle this."

"I can't do this," I whispered back immediately, and some distant part of me noted that I didn't begin trembling as I had the other times.

"You can," he argued gently, and he placed a hand to my chest to gently push me back so I was lying down again.

He put one knee and hand on the bed, and leaned over me as the hand on my chest ran up along the edge of the robe I was wearing. Our positions, his touch, and the way his eyes burned and betrayed his emotionless mask . . . it made this feel too real, too intimate. Made my mind confuse this for something it wasn't.

Because he wasn't a lover and his touch shouldn't steal my breath. But it did.

He was darkness, and I couldn't allow myself to forget. No matter how he'd tried to backtrack with me ever since that first night. No matter how he'd stopped and covered me every time it had gotten to be too much and I'd started singing out of fear . . .

He was still pushing me for something that wasn't natural. He was still keeping me here against my will and claiming to own me when all I wanted was to get back to Kyle.

Kyle . . .

A sob caught in my throat as Kyle's face entered my mind while the devil above me pushed the satiny material off one shoulder in the beginnings of our slow, seductive dance—I began trembling as grief ate at me and fear consumed me.

His head shook subtly as he leaned down, and his lips brushed against my ear as he whispered in a tone that was at once pleading and soothing and longing. "Show me, Blackbird."

But for the first time, my fear had nothing to do with what the man above me could do to me. And instead, was solely based on the devastating realization that I would never get out of here, would never go back home. Because I knew . . . I knew I couldn't do what the devil was asking of me.

And like it was as natural as breathing, my mouth opened and the first words of a song tumbled from it.

The devil stilled above me just as he finished pushing the robe off my other shoulder, and I desperately tried to choke back the song and tame my shaking. Knowing if I could just get through this, I would be one step closer to seeing the man my heart was aching for.

When I felt the devil push away from me and start sliding my robe back into place, I panicked. "N-no, I ca—" But my words died when I looked at him to find his face twisted, as if *he* was being tortured . . .

But just as quickly it was gone, and that look of irritation and disappointment I'd come to know so well was all that lingered in his expression, and I knew I had to have imagined his pain, imagined that a devil could feel what I was enduring.

"Do you want to leave this room?" he asked as he sat back, his voice weighed down.

"Yes. Yes, you know I do."

His head shook with a slowness that made me feel his disappointment in the pit of my stomach, made me want to apologize for not being able to do this, and I hated him for that too. "You know what you need to do to leave, and you aren't trying."

There was no point in arguing how wrong he was. A man like him would never understand. "I thought when I left this room I would get clothes," I said quietly instead.

"You will."

"Then why do I need to be comfortable naked? Will I have to be that way often?"

A grin pulled at the corner of his mouth that didn't match the somber mood of the room or the coldness of his eyes. "Only if you want to be."

"Then I don't . . . I don't understand why it matters if I—"

"What are you doing right now?" he asked in a rough voice as he reached out to touch the edge of the robe again, but he didn't try to move it away. "You're hiding from me by covering yourself. Why would I trust you to leave this room when you're so afraid of me that you still feel like you need to hide?"

My mouth slowly opened as I wondered how he still didn't get it. "I don't understand how you can expect anything different from me."

"I expect you to try for yourself so I won't have to push you." Even though his tone remained calm and even, it was dripping with venom and promised so many nights like that first one that my blood ran cold. "This room and the robes—this whole process—it isn't for the sake of having sex or being naked. It's about getting to the point where you trust me and feel comfortable being near me. When you get to that point, I'll know you're ready to leave the room. Completely covering yourself, flinching before I can even touch you, and trembling when I do, shows me that you aren't."

I nodded absentmindedly then shook my head. "But I won't." When there was no response, I risked looking at him again. His brow was furrowed, and he was staring at me intently. My voice shook through my next admission. "I don't—I mean, I'm not that girl. I didn't think any other man would ever see me without my clothes on. I'll never leave this room because I'll never be okay with some man looking at me or touching me."

"Some man," he said, and his dark eyes flashed with frustration. "I own you."

"No, you don't," I reminded him.

His lip curled, but without saying a word, he got off the bed and began walking away from it.

"*Another day, Blackbird*?" I asked as I sat up on the bed, mocking his normal parting words, and immediately knew it was the wrong thing to do.

Even if it hadn't been for the deadly calm that washed over him when he turned to face me, I would have known from the way his hands slid into the pockets of his jeans as he did.

For a man that exuded such evil—and could easily destroy my heart and my soul during a few minutes with my body—he had been patient with me during these *progress days* . . . all things considered.

As much as I hated him and hated what he was trying to make me do, I knew it could be so, *so* much worse . . . as he'd just reminded me.

I needed to be glad it wasn't.

I needed to not provoke him.

"Watch yourself," he growled in warning. He glanced at his expensive-looking watch, then said in a low tone, "There are people who should be here any minute for you."

I froze as a dozen different thoughts, horrors and dreams alike, flew through my mind. "F-for me? Why? What's happening?"

"They're coming to change your hair color."

I glanced down at where my hair was falling to my waist in waves. "It's only ever been blonde."

His eyebrows rose, as if I was missing something crucial. "And that needs to change."

He looked away when the doorbell could be heard throughout the house and glanced to his watch again. "They'll come in here. Don't bother asking them to help you leave. You aren't the first girl they've visited."

I hated him.

The women who had come to dye my hair hadn't said a word to me the entire time they were there. They had tilted my head down and up as needed and had disrobed me and shoved me into the shower to wash the dye out, but they hadn't spoken. When I had exited the shower, they'd handed me a plush robe to dry off in and forced me into a chair as they began the process of drying my hair, but again, no words.

When they were done, they once again stripped me from their robe, dragged me in front of the mirror, and waited.

"It looks beautiful," I said honestly.

Gone was the blonde and in its place was a warm brown. It transformed my face even ... but the sight made my chest ache. The naked brunette in the mirror was not me. Briar Chapman was disappearing.

Both women had kissed my forehead before leaving, and I had turned around to grab one of my robes from the small closet in the bathroom.

Only the third robe was gone, as were all of my towels.

My brow furrowed as I walked out of the bathroom to my room, wondering if I had left the robes in there, and I stopped abruptly when my feet hit the carpet.

I hadn't had to look around the room to see if the robes were there or not. The stripped-bare bed told me all I needed to know.

I hated the man in that house.

After searching every corner of the room and bathroom for anything I could have used to cover myself and coming up empty, I had curled into a ball between the bed and wall, and hadn't moved since.

My legs had cramped up, but I knew the second I moved would be when the bedroom door opened, so I continued to sit through the pain as I waited.

And waited.

Dinner must have come and gone, judging from the way my stomach painfully growled before eventually stopping, and after nearly falling over too many times from drifting off to sleep, I finally stretched my legs out on the floor and rested my head against the wall. But he never came, and my eyes grew heavier and heavier until I couldn't keep them open any longer.

I woke later to the feel of him lifting me off the floor.

I gasped and instinctively pushed against his chest, trying to get away from him when he began lowering me to the bed.

It didn't matter that he'd done the same thing just *that* afternoon. That afternoon I'd been covered. That afternoon I could at least still hope for the kinder side of the devil as he tried to push me to progress. But he'd sent a blaring message by taking everything from me: Our "gentle" *progress days* were done.

"No, no!" I said desperately just before my back unexpectedly hit cool sheets.

"Stop," he commanded gently. Grasping my wrists in his hands, he forced my hands to the bed with little effort, and captured my gaze with his.

"P-please, no." My body trembled, and though I tried to close my legs, his still-clothed body kept them open.

"Stop moving, or the bedding is going to be taken away again, and your days in here will continue."

I immediately stopped fighting him, but the trembling continued. I clenched my teeth together in a useless attempt to stop my shaking jaw, but it only made my body shake harder.

"Show me you can handle this." It was a plea and a demand, every word coated with desire.

Despite everything—my hate, my revulsion, my fear—the sound

sent a shiver down my spine. A rush of air blew past my lips at the pleasant feeling, and I looked up to find his dark, sinful eyes locked on mine.

"Show me, Blackbird."

I hated him for taking away my choice. I hated his voice and those eyes. I hated that somehow, these days with him had caused me to not only want to succeed in this for me—but for him too.

I owed him nothing, and still . . .

No! He is darkness. He is the devil, I reminded myself as my breasts brushed against his broad chest. *I want nothing from him, and I owe him nothing. I hate him . . .*

"I can't do—"

"Briar," he whispered, his voice strained—the sound reminded me of his tortured expression earlier that afternoon. But other than letting his eyes shut then, his face remained blank. "I *need* you to do this. *You* need to do this. Don't make me force you," he pled so quietly that if he hadn't been pressed to me, I wouldn't have heard him. Then he dipped his head so close that he was my air, and I was his, and his dark eyes met mine again as he begged, "*Show me.*"

My breath caught in my throat at the haunted look that filled his eyes before he was able to force it away, and my fingers automatically curled around his hands.

I swallowed past the tightness in my throat, and after the briefest hesitation, I moved my head . . .

At first, shaking it subtly as some part of me tried to maintain that I couldn't—*wouldn't*—do this, before I quickly nodded.

I can do this.

"Briar."

I owe him nothing.

"*Don't make me force you.*"

To gain his trust and get out of here, I can do this.

"*Show me.*"

He held my stare for a few more seconds before releasing my hands and sitting back, and then his eyes dipped over my body in a way that felt violating and thrilling all at once. As his gaze moved leisurely back up, my breaths became rougher, harsher, but for once, it wasn't out of fear or disgust . . .

And from the shift in the devil's expression when he studied my eyes and took in my parted lips, he knew it too.

One of his large hands moved toward my face but paused in the air for a few seconds, as if he was debating whether or not he should do what he was about to. His dark brows drew together, and just when I thought he was going to drop his hand, he reached forward to curve it around my cheek, cradling my face gently.

My chest heaved with a trembling breath at the tenderness of his touch mixed with that same haunted look from earlier. And as I had before, I automatically reached down to grip his hand in one of mine.

Keeping my fingers locked in his, he slowly moved my hand back to where my other still rested on the bed above my head, and dipped his head until his lips were at my jaw.

My shiver was instant and not unwelcomed.

Heat moved through me, slow and intoxicating as his mouth moved down my throat in a series of sensual kisses.

Stop this. Stop him, I screamed at myself, but was only able to bite down on my bottom lip to stop a whimper from escaping me.

After releasing my hand, he placed one last kiss at the base of my neck before sitting back up, his dark eyes a mixture of need and indecision—and the need was winning . . .

In both of us.

He traced my cheek lightly, grabbed the length of my hair, and twisted until his hand was fisted at the base of my neck. A surprised huff blew past my lips when he pulled, forcing my head back on the bed, exposing more of my neck to him.

His free hand trailed down my throat lightly, the tips of his fingers leaving a tingling trail in their wake, and an erratically pounding heart in my chest. Wherever his fingers touched was no longer a cool burn, but an open flame.

Each breath and each second brought him closer and closer to my chest, where my bare breasts were on display for him despite my need to cover them. But then his fingers brushed over one of my nipples, and instead of trying to disappear into the bed, I arched against his touch.

The touches continued—light and demanding—until it felt like I would lose my mind. I needed them to stop and I needed them to continue. I twisted and bowed off the bed, trying to get away and get closer all at once, and inhaled sharply when I brushed where he was straining against his jeans.

Stop this, Briar, why aren't you stopping him?

My hands flew to his chest to push him away, but one gripped at the material of his shirt in an attempt to keep him close—both hands at war with each other, just as the rest of my body was.

A whimper sounded low in my throat when his fingers trailed over my breast again on their way down, down, down . . . and he responded by wrenching my head back.

I cried out in pain, but the cry ended with a soft moan when his fingers trailed over a part of me I thought only one man would ever see again.

"No," I said breathlessly, but my whimpers and moans and the way I pulled him closer begged for so many things that I hadn't voiced, and not one of them was for him to stop.

Because there had been pain, and I had wanted to get away from him. But heat was pooling low in my belly, and some traitorous part of me wanted this feeling to continue more than I wanted my next breath.

I couldn't make sense of what I was feeling.

"More."

It took too long to realize *that* word had left *my* lips. I shook my head, trying to force that small piece from my mind, and I tried to twist away from him as his fingers began teasing me, but his body between my legs didn't allow me to get far. "Please . . . please stop. St—" Another moan tumbled from my mouth and was followed by the slightest, most invigorating tug on my hair.

Shame filled me and my head shook as much as his tight hold would allow. My mind and my body were completely at war with each other. In my mind I was screaming at him to stop touching me, but the throaty sounds coming from me matched the way I was trying to get closer to his hand . . . not my thoughts.

My core tightened and another plea for more caught in my throat.

How can I want this so much?

Guilt tore through my chest.

Why am I not pushing him away?

I clutched his shirt tighter in my hand when he slid a finger inside me.

God, yes . . .

Then Kyle's face slipped through everything going on inside my mind. Guilt and shame overwhelmed me, threatening to choke me.

Kyle. Oh my God, what am I doing?

I was letting another man touch me. A man who I wanted to continue touching me just as badly as I wanted him to rot in hell.

It felt like I was going insane.

I wrenched my eyes open to find the devil's face just above mine. In movements too fast for him to stop, I shoved him back with one hand and slapped his face as hard as I could with the other while I screamed, "I said *stop!*"

He grabbed both hands before I could make another move and slammed them onto the bed as I continued to yell, "You have no right to touch me."

"I own you, Briar!"

I gathered what little saliva was in my mouth and spit in his face, regretting it instantly when his dark eyes turned murderous. But he didn't move, and he didn't speak again.

"You don't, and you won't," I gritted out when nearly a minute had passed.

Each ragged breath that we took forced our chests to brush against the other's and reminded me that my body was still betraying me—that I still wanted his touch.

But with each brush of his chest, and with each craving for more that rushed through me, I told myself over and over again it was all a lie. That it was nothing more than what should have been an anticipated phase from being stuck in that house with the man who bought me after I'd been kidnapped.

"This is all a process to get me comfortable around you," I mumbled, throwing his words back at him, and I hated how weak and defeated I sounded while doing it. "It isn't about sex. And yet . . ."

His face went void of all emotion, even his dark eyes looked bored. After a minute of studying me and steadying his breaths, he said, "And yet, I still own you."

A sharp pang hit my chest at his callousness after the chaos he'd just created inside me. "I hate you." The words slid out easily, and I refused to regret them.

But seconds ticked by without a response from the devil, and eventually he released me and got off the bed. A moment later he laid the comforter over my body then walked from the room.

Chapter 12

DAY 19 WITH BLACKBIRD

Lucas

"I hate you."

That weak, broken voice sounded in my mind again and again. The adrenaline coursing through my body grew, mixing with my own hate and the need to have the girl in that room until it became too much. A growl ripped from my throat, and I lashed out, punching the wall closest to me. I stumbled back to the opposite wall in the hallway and gripped at my hair with both hands as I forced myself not to move.

Because I wanted to go back upstairs, but not for the reasons I needed to. Not to teach my blackbird the lesson I knew I *should* be giving her. But because all I'd wanted in that instant after she'd said those three words was to fall to my knees and beg her to forgive me—for so many things. Because I wanted to tell her things that couldn't be said.

Stupid bastard.

William had said I wasn't ready.

He'd been right.

Chapter 13

WILLIAM

Briar

I hadn't spoken to the devil in the last day and a half, and I hadn't faced him when he'd brought my food. Then again, he hadn't tried to talk to me or get me to look at him since that night . . . and that made this all so much worse.

His silence made me wonder and worry about what I would be met with the next time he decided to speak to me, because I was terrified it would be a lesson. But a part of me—that stupid, traitorous part that had craved his touch—worried that if I looked at him, I would see that unnerving composure that revealed nothing.

I just wanted to know that he'd been living with some of the uncertainty and confusion that I was. Wanted to know that that night had affected him as much as it had me.

Flashes of those haunted eyes and his tortured look, and then his calm, indifferent expression, plagued me more than I wanted to admit even to myself.

I owe him nothing. I hate him, I told myself again. But even in my mind the words didn't hold much weight.

I didn't know what time of the day it was—as usual—but I usually sang for hours between each meal. And it hadn't felt nearly long enough when I heard a key in the lock.

The song abruptly died in my throat, and dread filled me as I scrambled to cover myself with the comforter since I still didn't have any robes.

My breaths were rough as I worried and wondered why he would be coming back so soon, but they stopped altogether when the door clicked shut, and an unfamiliar voice called out, "Hello, *First*."

I turned, my hesitation apparent in every slow, calculated move of my body.

An older man I had never seen before walked toward me nearly as slowly as I had turned. Something about him seemed familiar, but I couldn't place it until he was sitting on the edge of my bed. Although his were a pale blue, his eyes had that same cold and terrifying look as the devil's. His expression suggested he had all the time in the world.

I scooted away from him and pulled the comforter tighter to my body. My skin crawled when he smiled wickedly at my actions.

After long moments of staring at each other, he finally dipped his head to the side. "Truly, you don't need to fear me. I am only here to see how you are—to check on your progression." His proper British accent surprised me, and somehow, made him more terrifying. When I still didn't respond to him, he said, "I can only assume from your expression that Lucas has warned you about me."

I couldn't hide my shock or confusion.

Who was Lucas? Was he the devil? And who was the man in front of me that someone as terrible as the devil would warn me about *him*?

The man gave me a once-over that chilled me to my bones even though I was mostly hidden from his sight. "Your new hair color becomes you, even more so than the original. Lucas made a great choice."

I was now certain that Lucas was the man who'd bought me, and I rolled his name around in my mind a few times as I thought of him. *Devil* suited him so much better.

"How do you know?"

"Ah, you do speak." The man laughed. Something about the sound pushed ice through my veins. "How do I know what?"

"That it looks better than the original."

"I was here when you had your spell with dehydration."

I didn't know if I believed him. Everything about him made me not want to trust him, made me not want to be in the room alone with him—but that might have been because he was perfectly comfortable sitting there when it was obvious I was naked under the comforter. "Are you a doctor?" I finally asked.

"No, darling. I'm Lucas's mentor. My name is William, in case I forgot to mention that before."

I nodded because I didn't know what to say and looked around the bedroom until my restless gaze landed on the closed door. I waited, silently pleading for the devil to walk through there.

It surprised me, and I hated that I wanted him there at all, but I would rather the devil than the man sitting on the edge of my bed. And despite the evil that radiated from Lucas and the fear that had so often filled me in his presence, I somehow knew he would keep me safe from William.

"Where is Lucas?"

William's lips pulled into a sinister grin when he answered. "Work."

Chapter 14

DAY 21 WITH BRIAR

Lucas

I straightened my already straight tie, and messed with the cufflinks on my shirt as I watched the city pass by me. The scowl on my face deepened with every mile traveled.

I had a home office for a reason. All the men in this world did. For the first two months, none of us were expected to leave our new girls. I could do everything I do at the office at my house—including this meeting I was supposedly needed for.

My eyes rolled when my phone rang, showing one of the partners' names on the screen. I lifted it to my ear, and didn't bother with a greeting. "I should be there in fifteen."

"Where?"

"The office for the board meeting."

There was a pause before he said hesitantly, "There are no meetings today. Aren't you working from home anyway? I was just calling to get your opinion on—"

"No meeting?"

"No . . ."

I thought for only a second before I hissed a curse as my stomach dropped. "Is William in?"

Another pause. "No, he left for—"

I didn't wait for him to explain. I hung up and yelled for the driver to turn around and go home. I searched for William's cell number and had the phone back to my ear within seconds. My thumb and forefinger squeezed the bridge of my nose as I silently begged for him to pick up his phone.

"Hello?" a feminine voice answered.

"Who is this?" I demanded.

The woman chuckled. "Do not use that tone with me, Lucas. You do not scare me. I will find a wooden spoon, and we will see who is scared then."

I blew out a ragged breath and smiled. It was William's first. "Karina, is he there?"

"No, he's at work. The old fool forgot his phone," she said affectionately.

My body went rigid, but I bit back a curse. "Thank you, Karina, I'll try him there." As soon as I hung up, I barked, "Drive faster!"

I needed to get back to my blackbird—needed to get to her before he did. Because if he got there first . . .

I didn't want to think about what might happen.

William alone with Briar would be some of my worst fears coming to life for so many reasons.

My mind raced as I thought about the girl in that room, and my chest tightened with dread as we drove far too slowly.

I shouldn't have left her alone.

Should've never given William this opportunity.

Should've never let him trick me this way.

He'd been hounding me every day about how behind Briar was. As if I wasn't already aware. I'd been worried that he would visit us in a couple weeks if she hadn't made it out of that starter room.

I hadn't expected this.

And after what had happened between us the other night, her hate for me was only going to grow . . . and I wouldn't have anyone to blame but myself.

I never should have touched her that night . . .

As much as the thought of breaking her destroyed me, I knew it was something that had to be done. Just as there was a list of things I had to do when it came to Briar.

Pleasuring her wasn't on that list.

But I should have known from those first minutes during the auction that it would've been inevitable.

My days of trying to ease her into getting comfortable weren't working. And after the way she'd spoken to me before the women showed up to dye her hair, I knew I needed to teach her a lesson—one I still hadn't been able to do.

So I'd taken her robes and anything else she could have covered herself with in a last-ditch effort, because I couldn't continue to give her time.

Time that had run out long before.

The girls were expected to progress faster. She should have been out of that starter room by the end of her second week at the very latest.

But in trying to push her, I had become so enraptured in her perfect body and the longing in her eyes I hadn't been able to stop myself from kissing the smooth skin of her throat. I hadn't been able to stop from fisting my hand in her long hair, and then she'd moaned . . .

Those moans and whimpers had fueled my need for a girl I couldn't have in the way she was making me want her.

The women weren't allowed any type of pleasure from us for the first year. It made them want more, expect more, and then it made it harder for them to remember that what was between us was only a bond through ownership and not a relationship.

I had known that, but I hadn't been able to stop. Hadn't been able to stop from wanting to give her everything . . . only to be reminded how I'd already destroyed it all.

And now a man who made me look like a goddamn saint was with the girl who was terrified of me.

My fingers were twitching by the time we drove into the garage, and I was stepping out of the car before it finished rolling to a stop.

I ran through the garage into the house—and my heart stopped and blood ran cold when I heard loud sobs followed by her screams.

"Briar!"

Chapter 15

FALLEN ANGEL

Briar

"This can be scary at the beginning, I know, but it isn't the beginning anymore," William criticized. "You are behind where you should be. Do you want to stay in this room? Do you want to show Lucas that you can't move on with him? Now stop crying."

I couldn't, I hadn't been able to for some time now.

My head bowed as sobs tormented my body. My arms and shoulders ached, and my right calf was cramping, but I knew he had no plans to release me unless I did what he was asking.

Sometime before—what had seemed like hours, but I knew wasn't—William had grabbed my arm and forced me across the room to an alcove that I had always thought was a small, unfinished closet. Now I was rethinking the purpose of the space. A metal bar ran the length of the alcove high above me, and after tearing my comforter away, William had stripped off his belt and used it to tie my hands to the bar as I'd screamed and kicked at him.

He had looked at me as if my kicks were nothing more than a kitten pawing at him.

I had been on the balls of my feet ever since to take away the feeling that my arms were about to be ripped from their sockets, but my calves and thighs were shaking and I didn't know how much longer I could stand like that.

"Stop crying," William demanded again. "You have to be comfortable naked. You have to be comfortable with him watching you. You can't cry while he does that. Do you understand?"

I nodded, but my tears fell harder. I could hear the devil's words in William's, and I knew William had not lied to me.

William had to be Lucas's mentor.

The same words, the same demands, the same heartless tone. I found soon that my heart was big enough to hate more than one person.

"You have to look up," he gritted out, and suddenly he was in front of me, yanking my head up. "You have to make eye contact; you have to be proud; you cannot be scared. Stop crying!" He released my head, only for the back of his hand to come across my right cheek.

The force of his hit stunned me and made me lose the balance I'd been struggling to maintain on my toes. A sharp cry tore from my chest when it felt like my arms would tear from the sockets—my shoulders bearing all my weight until I could get back on my toes. Blood coated my tongue from where I'd bitten down on my cheek, and I had to fight to catch my breath when my sobs came faster than before.

"I have never had a girl struggle this much, or for this long, with this part of the process," he said in a bored tone when my cries became steady again.

"I can't do this," I sobbed.

"You have to. Stop crying. People stare at themselves in the mirror all the time. Studying their bodies, finding imperfections," he lectured harshly. "Think of Lucas as that mirror."

Hard sobs continued to force their way from my chest, and I shook my head quickly. "I—"

William gripped my cheeks roughly in his hand, forcing me to look at him, ignoring the way I tried to jerk away from him when my cheek smarted from the action. "*This* no longer belongs to you. It belongs to Lucas, and he does what he wants with it. You no longer hide it. Do you understand?"

I couldn't respond but tried to nod against his firm hold.

He released my face so forcefully it was as if he shoved my head back. But just as fast, his hands were on my breasts, painfully squeezing as he tested their weight and squeezed my nipples.

"No," I yelled, my voice hoarse as I tried in vain to twist away from his hold. "No, no, *stop*!"

"*These* no longer belong to you. They belong to him, and he does what he wants with them. You no longer hide them. Do you understand?"

"Stop touch—"

"I asked you a question, and you will answer me, *girl*," he seethed. "When Lucas asks you a question, you answer. You do not make demands." He paused for only a second before repeating, "Do you understand?"

I nodded numbly as the room filled with my cries. I choked over my tears and thrashed in the alcove when he suddenly cupped my sex, one of his fingers sliding into my folds just as roughly as he'd touched the rest of me.

"Stop!"

"*This* no long—"

Long ago memories flashed, and I screamed, "Don't touch me!"

"*Briar!*"

My head snapped up at the loud boom I would have sworn shook the house, and my heart raced. More tears pricked at my eyes—these different, these from the intense relief that pounded through me.

"Briar!" Lucas yelled again, closer.

William stepped back leisurely to stand silently a few feet away from me, looking at the closed doorway to my room expectantly. He almost seemed bored as he waited.

The devil, however, was anything but bored. His dark eyes were murderous when he charged into the room, but the look fell when he saw me being forced to stand in the alcove.

"Briar," he whispered, and quickly closed the distance between us. His hands went to my face first then my neck as his eyes searched my face wildly. "Are you okay? It's going to be okay," he assured me before I could answer.

"She needed to learn," William said from behind Lucas, and like a switch had been flipped, the murderous look was back in his eyes.

Lucas wrapped an arm around my waist to lift me off the ground as he untied the belt, and a muscle in his jaw popped while his nostrils flared. "This is too far; this is outside the rules. She's not yours to fucking touch," he hissed. His eyes never left my face, but it was clear his words weren't meant for me.

As soon as my hands were free, I let my arms fall like dead weights around Lucas's neck, curled my legs around his body, and sobbed against his white button-down shirt.

"It's okay." He ran his hand over my hair soothingly while he walked me back across the room. "It's okay." William began talking, but Lucas gritted out, "Enough!"

William continued on smugly. "It worked. You are welcome. She's progressed greatly today if she's also clinging to you rather than trying to get away."

When Lucas set me on the bed, his face was frozen in a terrifying mask of rage, and it didn't fit how gently he cupped my cheek. "Cover yourself."

I scrambled to pull the sheet over my body and flinched when Lucas turned and punched William in the jaw. Just as William started to stumble away from the force of Lucas's fist, Lucas grabbed him by the collar and forced him closer until they were face to face.

Other than working his jaw a couple times, William showed no signs of having been hit. His breathing remained calm and face impassive.

Lucas looked as if he was trying to talk himself out of doing it again, or more.

"You do not have the right to touch or teach what is mine," Lucas snapped.

"Ah ah, I didn't teach," William said, attempting a smug grin. "There *are* rules after all, Lucas. I merely . . . *bent* her so she would be more willing to comply to you."

Lucas's face became unreadable. The dark tension in the room became suffocating as he silently raged.

"If you were anyone less, you know exactly how this would end," he seethed in a calm, terrifying tone. "Now leave my home and don't come back unless you're invited. And if you ever touch Briar, or any of my girls, again, know that I *will* end this, and it will be with a heart-beat on your door."

I wasn't on the receiving end of those threats, but I was shaking from them. Most of the words meant nothing to me—didn't make sense—but it was his voice and the look in his eyes. Detached, dark, lethal.

He is darkness; he is the devil.

William maintained his aloof expression as he shoved away from Lucas. "I will expect your thanks soon," he called out as he walked from the room.

My mind was racing, trying to decipher the cryptic threat. "What do you mean, *a heartbeat on his door*?" I whispered softly when William left.

Lucas paused on his way back to me, continued, and shook his head. "Not today, Briar."

From some of the horrific images that came to mind, I wasn't even sure I wanted to know, so I didn't push for him to explain. I just clung to his forearms when he held my face in his hands.

"What did he do to you?"

I shook my head absentmindedly, my gaze drifted to the alcove when I wasn't able to speak.

He breathed out roughly through his nose, and if I hadn't been holding on to him so tightly, I might have missed the way his body began vibrating. "How long was he here?"

"I don't know," I choked out.

"Blackbird," he whispered soothingly, "I need to know if he hurt you. I need to know what he did to you."

My tears came harder as I tried to tell Lucas everything that had happened. Once I'd finished, I choked out, "Why does it matter? He's your *mentor*. I could hear you in his words. Your words in his voice."

Lucas's body stilled. His dark eyes bored into mine and his head tilted as if he was going to deny it, but he paused for a second and then sighed. "Yes, he's my mentor, but that doesn't allow him to be in this house without me, and it will never give him permission to be alone with you. It doesn't give him permission to touch you. And it matters because what happened today shouldn't have. Do you understand? I will do everything to make sure no one ever touches what's mine again."

I understood. I just wasn't sure if I responded in any way because I was suddenly at war with myself, questioning my sanity.

My unexpected thought that his touch felt nice and wanted during his explanation left my mind reeling. I told myself to let go of his arms and push away from him.

My fingers betrayed me by gripping tighter.

I looked from his eyes to my hands then back again. The entire time I was internally screaming, reminding myself I was clinging to the devil and needed to get far away—but another part of me shouted that *he* was also my safety.

No! No, he will never be safe.

But he came for me. He protected me.

I thought of the way his voice twisted with torment when he yelled my name, of the way he looked when he ran into the room: like an avenging angel.

Fallen angel, I automatically corrected myself. *Because he is darkness, and he has done worse to me than William. Stop thinking that any good can come from him.*

But some disturbed part of me still wanted to fall into his arms, to let him comfort me. My body was aching with the effort it took to keep myself from him, and a harsh breath rushed from my lungs as I continued to fight.

Fight with what I knew of the devil and the angel I was making myself believe I had caught a glimpse of.

Back and forth, back and forth.

He was still cradling my face in his large hands, and I had yet to let go of him. Every now and then he would brush his thumb across my un-bruised cheekbone, and I hated how much I craved those little brushes. But I did.

It didn't make sense. None of it made sense. I felt safer in that moment with Lucas than I had since I'd been stolen from Atlanta. The idea of feeling safety within his arms should terrify me, but the only terror that day had been in William's presence.

Dark eyes searched mine as he said my name like a question.

The sound of my name from his lips made me tremble with unspoken words that were bursting from that traitorous part of me. *Safe, safe, safe.*

No!

He is darkness. He is the devil.

My eyes fell to his mouth, and mine opened when my breaths grew heavy.

And I want him.

What is wrong with me?

I looked up when I felt his arms tense and found him staring at my body. Before I could follow his line of sight, his eyes met mine behind those thick, dark lashes, desire and sin swirling there.

Gently enough not to hurt me, but forcefully enough that I couldn't stop him, he released my face and removed my hands from his arms.

"Where are you going?" I asked without hesitation when he took two steps away from me.

He rubbed at his jaw then shoved his hands into his pockets. Just like that, Lucas was gone and the devil was back. "Leaving. When your time with William wears off, your hatred of me will return. The only reason you aren't afraid of me right now is because I'm the lesser of two evils today. You're safe and will be all right. I won't take advantage of this time where you *think* you want me around."

I pressed my lips firmly together before my lust-hazed mind could spout off something I'd regret.

His eyes dipped to my body. "After lunch you can pick a room."

I finally glanced down to see that the sheet had pooled around my hips and hurried to cover myself—but he was already gone.

What is happening to me?

Chapter 16

DAY 21 WITH BRIAR

Lucas

I stormed through the house agitatedly, and by the time I made it to my room on the main floor, I was cursing myself.

I had been about to kiss that mouth of hers that consumed my mind . . . not allowed. Ever.

I had wanted to claim her body but had walked away so she wouldn't hate me more than she already did. I would undoubtedly destroy another part of her spirit in the coming days, and I had *walked away*. Stupid bastard.

I turned back toward my bedroom door, knowing I needed to go up to her room again to regain the control that had slipped away. Needed to show William I still had it before he showed up here again to check on us. The fact that he had at all—when it wasn't allowed—was disastrous. But each time I turned around I saw the crushed hope in her eyes, and I knew I wouldn't survive seeing them up close.

Yanking at my tie until it was loose, I pulled it over my head and tossed it on the bed, then made quick work of taking off the rest of my clothes when the need for her grew to be too much.

I stepped into the bathroom and turned the water on in the shower, stepping in immediately to let the cold water clear my mind. But nothing could clear my mind of those full lips parting, of the rise and fall of her chest as her breaths grew ragged, of the indecision and want in her eyes, of the perfect way she had looked clinging to me with her breasts exposed.

I changed the temperature of the water until it was too hot, and fisted my erection in my hand, welcoming the assault of all that was Briar. I moved my hand slowly at first as I thought about every part of her body I wanted to explore, then faster when I thought about that mouth. That *mouth* that could easily bring me to my knees. The need to feel those lips in place of my hand was nearly painful.

I rested my free hand against the shower wall, using it to hold me up as I pumped my hand faster, squeezed harder. A moan built in my chest and her name crawled from my throat. A flash of images flooded my mind, and my hand moved faster still. Briar on her knees with her face pressed to the bed. My hand fisted in her long, dark hair as I drove into her. Her face in a mixture of pain and pleasure.

Over and over again, claiming her, that beautiful face in ecstasy, and doing more for her than I was supposed to—and things I wasn't allowed to. But God, I needed to. I needed to taste her. I needed to feel her body tremble beneath mine for a reason other than fear. I needed to hear her moans when she came. I needed it all.

I came with a low curse and dropped my head back to face the ceiling. My rough breaths curled the steam from the shower away from my face, and I tried to focus on that, focus on something mundane . . . but my blackbird was there in my mind.

I wanted to know what she was doing to me.

Yes, she was my first girl, but part of training with William had included "dating." If it could be called that. I had never had a problem with remaining detached from those girls. I'd never wanted to hold or kiss them. I'd never wanted to please them. I'd never wanted to give them anything—I'd never wanted anything from them at all.

One look at Briar's false bravado, and I'd needed her. A few seconds of watching her sing during an auction, and I'd been gone to her. It had been a mistake to buy her, but I would never be able to give her back.

As the hot water beat down on me, and with that thought in my mind, feelings of déjà vu washed over me. I stilled, struggling to force back memories I couldn't allow to surface.

Not the same, I told myself. *Not the same.*

I called my driver and told him to pick up the personal shopper and lunch, then I dressed casually and went into my office. As I had every day since first reading the news article on my blackbird, I pulled up Facebook.

Briar's profile was public but there wasn't a reason for me to stay on it for long. I had already gone through it a dozen times before, and it only frustrated me to no end. Her profile picture showed her laughing and looking up at Kyle as she stood in his arms, an engagement ring on display on her left hand.

Throughout her profile, there were pictures showing exactly how loved and loving she had been. Over the weeks those had been hidden by the mass of comments from people praying for her safe return or begging her to come home.

Today, like recent days, I only stayed on her profile long enough to glance at the new comments, then clicked on the link to Kyle's profile, since he posted every news update I could ever need to read on Briar.

I loathed the guy, but I was thankful he made it easy.

As soon as his profile flashed onto my screen, I noticed it. The large banner photo across his page had changed since yesterday, and the sight stilled me.

He was holding a long, rectangular sheet of construction paper. Painted on it were the words: *Until we're old and gray, and then long after.*

I clicked on the picture and realized I was shaking while reading his caption. *Come back to me, Briar Rose. I'll wait for you.*

"Goddamn it," I hissed, shoving away from my desk.

It was probably better that I didn't look at her updates. There was a reason I wasn't supposed to look up the girls I bought, and I had learned that reason extremely well upon reading that first news article.

But it was impossible to stop.

If anyone found out I was keeping close tabs on her disappearance, I'd told myself they would understand if they knew she'd been taken by mistake.

The argument had been weak at best, even then.

No one could know I knew about her old life. No one in this world could know I hated myself for doing this to her. If you broke the rules, you were a threat to the way we lived.

We took care of threats.

I had only calmed down marginally by the time my driver arrived with the shopper and food.

I led them upstairs and had the driver leave the food on the kitchen counter and wait for us there as the shopper and I walked into Blackbird's room.

She was sitting up in bed, covered in the sheet with an expectant look on her face.

"Briar, this woman will be your personal shopper for some time to come," I explained, and gestured to the woman.

We didn't learn the names of the people who helped us. They preferred it that way. It kept it impersonal and helped them feel better about taking our money and keeping their mouths shut about what they knew went on in these houses.

"I'm going to need you to stand up so she can take some measurements."

Briar hesitated, but finally stood. Her eyes anxiously darted to the open door behind me before settling on the woman.

"Drop," the woman said sternly, and she gestured to the sheet.

That conflicted gaze flitted to me briefly. With a slow, shaky breath out, Briar closed her eyes and dropped the sheet.

"Gorgeous," the woman said in the same tone. "This will be easy," she murmured to herself as she went about measuring. "Bodies like this look good in anything."

"She likes to be covered," I said gruffly.

The woman stopped writing down a measurement to send me an annoyed glare, and Briar's eyes flew open.

I gestured to my blackbird and said, "Don't make her uncomfortable in what you choose for her." The threat in my words was clear.

The shopper tapped her pencil quickly against her pad of paper once the fear receded from her face. "I can do beautiful and modest. She will be gorgeous . . . alluring."

"She already is."

Briar's sharp inhale let me know my words had been spoken out loud.

I swallowed a curse and held her surprised stare, daring her to respond to my comment instead of pretending the words had never been vocalized. Because now Briar was looking at me with a mix of surprise and that same indecision from earlier, which only complicated things for us more than my need for her did.

As soon as the shopper took a few steps away from Briar, I broke our eye contact to look pointedly at the sheet on the floor, then held up a hand in a silent command for her to stay as I walked out of the room—leaving the door open.

"I'll be back tonight with all she needs," the woman snapped as we walked toward where my driver stood.

"She has nothing. No shoes, under—"

"I know how this works," she informed me quickly. A knowing smile flashed across her face. "Nothing will be forgotten. Formalwear will take longer, but I'll put in the requests today."

I nodded my appreciation. "Until tonight then." I left them to go back to Briar and forced my expression into a mask of calm when I felt anything but.

She was standing exactly where I had left her with the sheet covering nearly every inch of her.

I stopped just inside the room and crossed my arms over my chest as I studied her thoughtful expression.

"You're testing me," she finally murmured.

My false calm was immediately overridden with confusion until I saw her glance at the door again. "No, I told you that you would be picking a room today, which means you will be allowed anywhere on this level on the house."

"But you just told me to stay."

And you did, I thought with a surge of relief. I closed the distance between us slowly and uncurled one arm from my body to caress her cheek that was bruised from William's hand. "I want you comfortable with me, but not other men. My driver was waiting out there."

Blood rushed to her cheeks and her head dipped in an unsuccessful attempt at hiding her embarrassment.

"Come on, lunch is in the kitchen."

My jaw ached from the pressure I was exerting as I walked out of the room with her right behind me. Today could push us forward or send us spiraling backward. With Briar, I was worried it would be the latter, but I knew I couldn't keep her from this any longer.

I waited for it—for any sign of her shock when she realized she wasn't as far from home as she'd originally thought. A gasp, singing, something . . . but it didn't come.

We were halfway through the main room of the upper level before I turned to look at her, and found her staring intently at her feet instead of the wall of windows as she followed.

I slowed until she caught up with me and placed a hand gently on her back to lead her to the far corner. She would be able to see everything from there. A lake stretched out to our left, the city to our right. A multimillion-dollar view to most, but it would probably be nothing more than a view from a cage for the girl next to me.

Folding my arms over my chest, I steeled myself and failed at forcing my calm façade into place. "Briar," I began, my voice was soft but with an edge from my nervousness as she lifted her head, "open your eyes."

At first, there was nothing. Then her eyes slowly widened and her face filled with something close to hope as she started taking it all in. Recognizing it, even if she'd never seen it. One sheet-covered hand came up to cover her trembling mouth, but there was no response otherwise. After an eternity made up of seconds passed, her other hand pressed against the window, followed soon by her forehead as she stared out at the familiar.

"We're in the United States, aren't we?" she asked, her voice cracking on the last words.

I dipped my head in confirmation even though she wasn't looking at me. "Yes."

Houston, Texas.

Only eight hundred miles from her home when she'd thought oceans stood between her and the life she wanted back.

I didn't ask to hear her thoughts even though I was aching to know what was going through that mind of hers. I just watched and waited, slowly going mad.

When a lone tear fell down her cheek, I broke.

My shoulders dropped and I automatically reached out for her, but stopped myself before I could touch her. I recoiled from her instead and clenched the hand that had been so close to her as I fought to move away. My chest was moving roughly and my arms were shaking from exertion by the time I was able to turn my back on her.

I don't care. She doesn't affect me. I can't care. Briar . . .

I hadn't even made it halfway to where my driver had left the lunch before I turned and stalked back to where she was still standing. This time there was no hesitation. I pulled her from the window and into my arms, and like it was the most natural thing in the world, she fell against me, her body fitting against mine perfectly.

She buried her head on my chest when her shoulders started

shaking with muted cries. Her hands showed the same indecision that had been playing in her eyes recently. Still covered in the sheet, one hand pressed against my chest and began pushing while the other gripped at my shirt and pulled me closer.

Oh, Blackbird.

I pressed my mouth to the top of her head in a moment of stupidity and weakness that was emphasized by her cracked plea. "Let me go . . . *please*. I just want to go home."

The hand that had been rubbing her back soothingly abruptly stopped moving, and for long seconds I stood like a statue holding my mistake.

I let my training fill my mind as that mask of indifference settled over my face again and internally berated myself for letting this girl have any type of control over me.

Caring she was hurt and comforting her wasn't allowed, and I worried about what would happen if William found out. If anyone found out . . .

"You are home." Gripping the girl's hands, I pushed her a step away from me and nodded toward the kitchen when she looked up at me with her tear-streaked face. "Eat lunch, then choose a room. Do whatever you want, just don't leave this floor. The shopper will be back tonight with your clothes."

"Wait, where are you going?" Briar asked anxiously when I turned to leave.

I paused mid-step and looked over my shoulder. Narrowing my eyes at her, I cocked my head to the side and asked in a deceptively soft tone, "What makes you think you can question what I do? Eat."

Chapter 17

FIGHT ME

Briar

"Everything has been laundered, you can wear it immediately."

I nodded slowly, unable to close my mouth as I stared at the newly filled walk-in closet, which was about the size of my starter room. "Why do I need so many clothes?"

The shopper laughed mockingly. "What a stupid thing to ask from a stupid girl. More clothes have been ordered for you. I will deliver them when they're ready later this week. Are you the first?"

I tore my eyes from one side of the closet to look at her questioningly. She had a stern voice and words, but every now and then I caught her sending me kind looks. I didn't understand her, but I wasn't sure if I was supposed to since she refused to give me her name. Still . . . those looks had the crumpled paper in my hand burning hotter and hotter. "The first?"

"In this house."

"Oh." Heat filled my cheeks and I looked away. "Yes," I whispered, as if admitting to a sin.

"Then this won't be all that you get. Consider yourself lucky. In all the houses I shop for, the firsts are always treated the best. They don't have to share rooms with the other women, and they receive the most gifts, clothes, everything . . ." she trailed off, then pointed at me and gave me a stern look. "You are *lucky*, little girl, don't you forget it."

My mouth opened, but no sound left for a few seconds. The other day the devil had said I was free in this life, and now this odd woman was telling me I was lucky? "How can you say that? I was two weeks away from my wedding when I was taken."

She *tsked*. "Stupid girl. No, you were not." She lifted her hands as if to gesture to more than just this closet as she spoke. "There is no *before* anymore. There is only *this*. Only *him* for you."

"No, that's not—that's not true." The paper in my hand felt like it could burn this house down and take the devil with it, and I knew I had to try.

I'd found a blank journal in my new room earlier, and knowing the shopper would be coming back tonight, had taken what I'd worried would be my only chance.

I stepped toward her and held my hand out between the edges of the sheet clutched tightly in front of my body. "Please, this is my fiancé's name and number. Just, if nothing else, call him and tell him that I'm alive. *Please*," I said through the tightening of my throat.

The shopper stared at me as if I'd just attempted to take her life, and for a moment I wondered if maybe I had. I wondered what would happen to someone like her, or the women who had dyed my hair that weekend, if they were caught helping any of the stolen women.

"Please," I echoed, my voice nothing more than a breath. "Please tell him."

She dipped her head in the slightest of nods. "I'll tell him, girl." After a moment's hesitation, she snatched the paper from my hand then began walking out of the closet.

"Thank you for my clothes," I murmured to her back.

Her response was a scoff followed by a quick, warm smile thrown over her shoulder.

Such a strange woman. But even as she walked away, something inside me ached at losing the only person who had spoken to me since I'd been taken that didn't radiate evil.

My head dropped, and I rubbed at my chest as I began turning to look in the closet, but her voice stopped me.

"Girl," she said in a hushed tone, and I looked up in surprise at seeing her in the doorway of the closet again. "It gets easier. You *will* get through this sad time, and you will be happy. I have never met a girl in all my years of doing this who wasn't happy."

I didn't believe her, but she didn't give me a chance to say anything else.

Once she was gone, I looked back at the closet and blew out a deep breath. A whispered plea left my lips that my message would make it to Kyle, and that plea effortlessly turned into a song in a subconscious attempt at relaxing my mind and my heart and my body.

I wanted to go through every piece of clothing for the sake of being able to touch fabric that I could cover myself with, but I refused to do it. I didn't want Lucas to think he could make me happy with an absurd amount of clothes when all I had wanted was something other than the robes.

It felt like my parents all over again—trying to buy my love when they'd really only wanted my voice. The devil's money and unwanted gifts would never change anything . . . would never make me forget who I was or where I'd come from.

I went to the large dresser that sat in the middle of the closet and searched through drawer after drawer until I realized I had already passed what I was looking for, and my voice suddenly disappeared.

If this was what the shopper thought would make me feel comfortable, I worried what she would have picked otherwise.

My entire underwear drawer was lace.

But after weeks of nothing, I was thankful for it, and hurried to put on the first pair my hands touched.

Shock filled me when I found three entire drawers of sexy teddies, see-through nighties, and nighties that were only slightly less revealing, and I wondered if the women in these situations ever actually wore these for the men who bought them, because I had no intentions of ever touching mine.

I looked through one entire side of the dresser for a pair of shorts or stretchy pants to put on without luck, and was on a second drawer full of different colored camisoles—this drawer cotton, the previous satin—on the opposite side when I heard heavy footsteps on the tile of my new bathroom.

I shoved the sheet I had been wrapped up in all day away from me and hurried to shrug into one of the shirts. I barely had it pulled over my chest before Lucas appeared between the double doors of my closet.

He stood strong and still with his hands in his pockets, and my heart pounded as the first trickle of fear spread through me. I was beginning to notice he only stood that way when he was the devil—when he was about to remind me of every reason why I hated him.

My gaze darted back and forth from his sinful eyes to his hidden hands as I waited for what he wanted, and though I tried to stop it, my mouth opened as a breath of a song left me, too low for him to hear.

"Do you like your clothes?" he finally asked with a tilt of his head.

My shoulders lifted in the slightest of shrugs. "They're just clothes."

One dark brow ticked up at the indifference in my tone. "*Just* clothes, or not, you'll still thank me."

"Thank you," I said quickly. "Thank you for all of them."

I *was* thankful. Any clothing after only having tiny robes and then nothing was nearly as satisfying as finally seeing the sun this afternoon after all that time away from it.

When nearly a minute had passed in silence, I bent to pick up the sheet off the floor, but stilled when he spoke again.

His voice was deep and rhythmic, but it was impossible to miss the underlying bite in his tone. "Four seven zero, five . . ."

My knees were weak as I straightened my back, and I had to grab the top of the dresser to keep myself standing while he read the rest of Kyle's phone number and name out loud from the piece of paper he held in front of him. "No," I breathed.

His dark eyes burned with rage as he slowly tore my paper in two, and then tore those pieces in half again. "Out." His lip curled when I didn't make an attempt to move. "Don't make me drag you out of there, Briar."

"Please," I said weakly. My stomach churned, and I swallowed back bile. "Lucas, plea—" I broke off quickly when I saw the shock covering his face at the sound of his own name.

But just as fast as the shock had appeared, it was gone, and his anger was back and worse than before. "*Out.*"

I was screaming at myself to move, to walk out of the closet, but my legs weren't working. It was as though they were no longer a part of my body, and I continued to stand frozen in fear. My body trembled, but no tears came this time.

His first step into the closet finally forced my own—only it was the wrong way. I stumbled backward with each of his long, quick steps in my direction.

"No, no, no!" I screamed when he reached me.

He grabbed my wrist and yanked me away from where I was trying to disappear into a wall of clothes, then pulled me roughly behind him.

"Let go of me," I continued to scream, and fought against his tight hold. "I *hate* you. Let me go." My feet got caught in the bunched-up sheet on the floor and I started falling, but before I could hit the floor, the devil grabbed me and threw me over his shoulder.

He continued his trek through the closet and equally large bathroom to the bed without seeming to care as I punched his back as hard as I could, over and over. "You should have walked out on your own when you had a chance."

"I hate you!"

"So you've told me."

The next punch aimed at his back ended up clipping his shoulder when he shoved me onto the bed. I was swinging for his face before I finished settling onto the bed, but he caught my hands in his own and used my fists as leverage to pull me up toward him.

Once our faces were no more than a breath apart, his lip curled and his dark eyes pierced mine. "You want to fight me, Blackbird? Then fight me," he goaded. "Fight *this*. I want you to."

In moves too fast for me to try to stop, he slammed me back down onto the bed and flipped me onto my stomach, all while keeping a tight grip on my fists. My hands were now pinned between our bodies, and my already sore shoulders screamed in protest when he pulled my wrists closer together, stretching them far down my body.

"No!" I said with a gasp when I felt the satiny material slide over and wrap around my wrists. "N-no, stop. Please stop."

"I've gone easy on you since you arrived. No more." His last words were a growl, and then his weight was gone before he roughly forced me onto my knees. "You'll learn your place here, Briar. You will learn that you're mine."

"Never. I will *never* be yours," I spat against the comforter. My next words died in my throat when I saw him standing at the side of the bed in nothing but his jeans . . . and they were falling to the floor.

He was there suddenly, his hands flat on the edge of the bed, straining as they held his weight up, and his face so close to mine I knew I should've recoiled, but I didn't move—*couldn't* move. His breath was mixing with mine, and that traitorous part of me was craving more from him, and I hated myself for it.

His dark eyes pierced mine, mocking me as a wicked smirk pulled at the corner of his mouth. "Never?" he asked, and a low laugh sounded in his chest when a shiver tore through me.

But then the humor and the taunting and the *seduction* . . . all of it was gone and was replaced by the cold indifference, and I found myself a breath away from pure darkness.

He leaned closer—his voice rumbled deep in his chest and his lips brushed along my ear when he growled, "Your denial stopped meaning anything the moment you begged me for more."

"Don't do this," I pleaded one last time as he pushed away and stepped toward the foot of the bed in nothing but boxer briefs, but all the power had been sucked from my voice.

His voice was detached, lifeless when he repeated, "Fight me, Briar."

Disgust rolled through me, and I forced my eyes closed and clenched my jaw so neither a song or plea for him to stop would leave my lips as he crawled between my legs. I didn't move, and I stopped trying to free myself from the too-tight binds behind my back. If he wanted a fight, I refused to give him one.

But there was nothing.

No touch. No sound except for my breaths that slowly got heavier and shakier as I waited for what would come next. Because I had a sickening feeling I would prefer the previous *lessons* over what I had coming for me.

Still, I knew he was there. Even if it wasn't for the weight of him at the end of the bed, I would have known. I could feel his presence in the room.

Heavy and dark. Sadistic and taunting.

As the seconds turned into minutes, my original fear of this lesson felt like nothing compared to what was paralyzing me now. It felt like something had taken my heart in its grasp and was slowly crushing it. It felt like I was gasping for air. My entire body was trembling, and there was no way to control it.

I wondered if he was enjoying my suffering.

I cried out when his hands suddenly gripped my hips and pulled me back, so I was pressed against him. Once I was settled there, he released me, but just as quickly his fingers trailed down my waist and over my hips. The tips of his fingers barely curled around the top of my underwear, moving them down a fraction of an inch.

Do not move.

Do not react.
He is darkness.
He is the devil.
I hate him.

The touch was soft and soothing, yet somehow strong and possessive, and soon he reversed his path. And I hated him for everything he was and for that touch . . . and for making me crave it more than I had anything in my life, when just seconds before, I'd waited in fear for when it would come.

My shirt was pushed up, each inch taking a lifetime, each inch sending my heart rate into chaos. He left the bunched material just below my breasts then began the agonizing process all over again. A small tremor began in my stomach when his fingers curled around the edge of my underwear again, but I fought to keep it contained and was disgusted with myself that it had been more out of anticipation than hate.

Do not move. Do not react. He is darkness. He is the devil, I chanted again.

Nothing. He would get nothing from me.

I hate—

My mouth opened with a nearly inaudible moan, and my pulse sped up when his large hands cupped my breasts as he exposed them.

Do not move. Do not—

"Don't ever forget who this is for," he said darkly as his hands slowly tightened. "Don't ever forget that no matter how much you deny it, you *are* mine."

My next breath was soft and broken, and felt like it shook the whole room. I'd known . . . I'd known it was coming, and I'd been stupid to forget. I'd been stupid to let him make me want his touch when he was just waiting to remind me who he really was and why we were here. What I'd been taken from.

I felt dizzy when those thoughts came flooding to my mind, and

I realized I'd been right. This *lesson* was worse than anything I'd endured with the devil so far. Because now I no longer simply hated him . . .

Tears pricked the backs of my eyes, but I held back the choked sob when he forced my underwear down my legs.

"Are you going to say it?" he asked as he gripped my thighs and forced them farther apart. "Are you going to tell me that you hate me?"

My breathing was hoarse. My heart numb. I shook my head against the bed, and whispered, "I hate myself."

I felt the shock that rippled through his body as if it were my own. "Briar . . ."

A few seconds passed in silence before my underwear was quickly pulled back up, and then his fingers went to the tie at my wrists, all the while I wondered if this was a trick.

"What are you . . ." he began softly. "What are you doing to—goddamn it, Briar!"

I jerked from the sudden roar of his voice and whimpered when my hands were released. Pain pounded up my arms, but I was unable to move them as they lay like dead weights at my sides when he helped me to my back again.

Lucas murmured something incoherent as he pulled my shirt back over my chest, then climbed off the bed to put on his jeans. Not bothering to button them, he took two steps away from the bed but paused and ran a hand through his hair, gripping it tightly. Seconds passed as he faced away from me, indecision rolling off his body. He then let out what sounded like a growl and stormed out of the room.

And I ached, but I wasn't completely sure from what.

Chapter 18

DAY 21 WITH BLACKBIRD

Lucas

What is this girl doing to me?

She was going to be my ruin. And I couldn't let that happen—couldn't let her destroy everything even though destroying *her* was something I knew I *had* to do.

Had to . . . and couldn't.

William had boldly and stupidly shown up at the house not long after the shopper had disappeared into the upstairs of the house with Briar, gloating about what he'd done to my blackbird earlier that morning and asking how the rest of the day had gone.

Not noticing how I'd been seconds away from tearing into him.

Ignoring that he'd broken the rules by teaching and touching what was mine.

Baiting me to see if I'd lash out again . . . but I'd already retaliated when I'd hit him. I'd already done all I was allowed to.

Between the men of this world? Lives were threatened to show power, but like for like was how the game was played.

All threats were taken seriously because the man joking with you today could be the man who decided you were a risk tomorrow . . . and then all bets were off.

Between William and me? Like for like would always be how it was played. Two of the most dominant and untrusting men were unlikely as partners. But *keep your enemies closer* was the only way of life we knew.

Despite the anger simmering in my veins and the need to turn my earlier threats into actions, I'd forced that calm to cover it the entire time he was there, and I answered his questions in the same bland tone he delivered them. Because I knew why he'd been so reckless to show up again, and I knew it was necessary.

He was testing me.

He wanted to see how I would react to him after most of the day had passed, and I needed to tread carefully.

I knew he was checking to see if there were signs I wasn't doing what I should be—that I wasn't teaching Briar the way I needed to. I knew he was watching every movement I made and any shift of my eyes to see if I was becoming attached to her in a way that wasn't allowed.

For a second, I'd even started to believe my detached words . . .

And then it had all gone to hell when the shopper came downstairs and handed me that crumpled piece of paper, announcing in front of William whose number it contained.

Kyle. Her fiancé.

William's eyes had snapped to mine. "What is the meaning of this?" he'd demanded.

I'd tried to control my panic and my anger, but I knew it had leaked out as I'd jerked my head once in denial. "She's been lying about having a fiancé ever since I got her."

William had stood then and taken a calculating step toward me. "Get control of that girl, Lucas, or I will do it for you." His eyes had drifted to the ceiling, then back to me. "I'll expect an update on what follows me leaving this house."

Another test. Another warning that made me want to hit him over and over again. Another reason for me to remember why I had to teach the girl on the floor above me a lesson for what she'd done—why I had to break her.

And I'd failed again.

I'd spent a lifetime doing things I despised. I'd had to in order to survive. I knew how to shut off what I was thinking and feeling in order to do what needed to be done. But this girl . . . this damn girl shook my very existence and made it impossible to block it all out.

"I hate myself."

Her broken voice played through my mind on repeat, haunting me with images of the shattered expression in her eyes and what I would have done to her . . .

I sagged against my bedroom door when a distinctive ringtone started playing, and reached into my pocket to pull out my phone. One glance at the screen had rage burning so deep inside me I nearly smashed the phone into the nearest wall in the few seconds it took for me to answer.

"What?" I growled.

Silence.

"If you're going to call me, then speak."

"What's happened?" It was a demand, not a question.

"Nothing."

There was only a beat of silence before: "I can't help you if I—"

"I said *nothing*," I hissed.

But the curse that filled the other end of the phone let me know he didn't believe my bullshit. "I *can't* afford to have you losing your mind now. Not after everything we've gone through to get you to this point."

A loud, mocking laugh tore from my chest and then died into nothing. "Don't take so much credit for *my* life. And there's nothing to worry about. He was here about fifteen minutes ago; it's done."

"We need to go over—"

"I said it's done." I hung up without allowing the man to respond then let my phone fall to the floor as I stumbled to my bed and sank onto the mattress.

Memories I'd kept locked away for years struck like a tidal wave, breaking me open and tormenting me. Every mistake I'd ever made—each day with Briar—was laid out before me, pulling me further and further down until all I knew was suffocating darkness. Drowning me.

I knew I deserved it—this destructive darkness. It was all I'd ever been and all I could ever be. And if I could've then, I would've laughed for even imagining I could have something as good as Briar Rose.

Not in this world or any other.

Chapter 19

STUPID GIRL

Briar

I hadn't seen Lucas for three full days.

In all the time I'd been here, whether we'd spoken or I'd avoided looking at him, he'd still been there at least three times a day. And now he wasn't.

It was unsettling, and more often than not I'd retreated back to my room as panic had consumed me and a song had poured from me—terrified that this would be the new normal. That I would go days or weeks without seeing him.

That whatever had happened the other night had pushed him to avoid me altogether.

I didn't know what it was, what had forced him to suddenly stop and leave. I was thankful for it, but I was confused and alone and terrified. I wanted answers, I wanted the sweet side of Lucas I'd caught a glimpse of, and I just wanted to go home . . .

I flew to a sitting position on the bed when someone knocked on the wall outside my room, but my racing heart abruptly sank when the man I'd been waiting days for wasn't the person to step through my open doorway.

The shopper.

"Hello, stupid girl," she said in that dry tone of hers and snapped her fingers behind her.

Two young women followed her, weighed down by clothes covered in zippered bags.

The shopper's cold gaze darted over the two girls before she snapped, "I don't think I need to tell you where those go. Get to it, then go get the rest of the shoes." Once the girls had disappeared through the bathroom and into the closet, she set her confusing stare on me. "I told you I would tell him."

And there it was. Blunt, unapologetic.

Despite the fear of the lesson that had turned into a confusing mass of emotions that night, I didn't hate this woman for her betrayal, and I wasn't sure I blamed her.

My voice was steady even though my chest ached with the need to see Kyle. "You and I both know that when I begged you to tell him, the man who owns this house and hired you and bought those clothes was not the *him* I was referring to."

She shrugged, once again unapologetically. "I did what was best for you because you were too stupid to know what that was, and I did not lie to you."

"Best for me?" I asked with a laugh. "You don't know me; how can you determine what's best for me?"

The shopper pursed her lips as the young women hurried through my room to get what I assumed would be the shoes and waited a few more seconds before saying, "I saved your life, that is how I know it was best for you."

"My—saved *my* life?" I asked incredulously, and shook my head quickly. "I knew in asking you to help that it could have meant horrible things for you, and I'm sorry that I put you in that position, but I *had* to try. But saving my life? No. If it was anyone's life you were worried about saving, it was your own."

She *tsked* in that way she liked to and murmured, "Stupid girl. One day you will realize that I saved your life by not doing what you asked."

I stared at her blankly for long moments when I realized she truly believed what she was saying. "I don't know what kind of women in my position you've encountered, or what lives they had before they were taken, but I'm not like those women. I was taken by mistake."

"Were you?" she asked with a challenging grin, but she didn't say anything else when her helpers came scurrying back in.

And I was getting too frustrated with this strange woman to try to respond.

Once they were finished in my closet and leaving my room, the shopper walked up to me and cradled my face in her hands. "Hundreds. I have encountered *hundreds* of women in your position, just as I have had the displeasure of working with dozens of men in *his* position. When you have seen all that I've seen, you cannot tell me that you were taken by mistake."

"But—"

"Stupid girl," she said softly then placed a motherly kiss on my forehead. "You, above all, I will look forward to seeing again." Without another word, she turned to go.

And though I didn't know her, and though I didn't understand her or her confusing nature or why she always called me stupid, I wanted to cry as I watched her walk away.

Once she was out of the room, I took a hesitant step in the direction she'd gone, and then another and another, intent on begging her not to leave, but came to an abrupt halt when I rounded the doorway into the hall and found Lucas standing in the living room with his arms folded across his chest, a solemn look on his devastatingly handsome face as he watched the women leave.

My heart faltered before taking off in a too-fast sprint I wasn't sure I could survive. And I hated him—I hated him for being there after being gone for so many days. I hated him for the way my body betrayed me and ached to go to him. I hated the intense relief I felt just knowing he hadn't abandoned me. *Hadn't left me.* And I hated that, after craving his presence, he only entered this level of the house because of the shopper's presence.

His head slowly lifted, and those dark eyes burned and begged and screamed a thousand silent things.

And despite the way my body rebelled against it, I let my anger and hatred for him show and forced myself into my bedroom, shutting the door behind me.

I'd barely gotten settled on the bed when the door opened and his dark presence filled my room.

"I didn't give her a number or ask her for any kind of help," I said through gritted teeth, keeping my focus on the comforter beneath me.

"I know," he said, and I listened to his slow footfalls that brought him deeper into my room.

Once he was standing at the foot of my bed, I glanced up at him and silently cursed myself for the way my voice shook when I asked, "Is this how it's going to be now?" When he lifted a brow, I clarified, "You've been gone."

"No." He blew out a slow, resigned breath before continuing, "I thought time away from you would help remind me who I need to be."

I took in his expression and hesitantly assumed, "And it didn't?"

"I remembered," he said in a chilling tone. "But that doesn't mean I can be that person with you."

"I don't—I don't understand."

A huff of a laugh left him, soft and mocking. "You don't?"

I didn't know why everyone in *this world*, as Lucas had called it, expected me to understand their confusing personalities and vague words—most of all, the man before me.

From his reaction when he found me with William, to his sudden coldness before lunch, to the lesson that had ended as abruptly as it had begun, to days of pure silence afterward, to the number of things I felt . . .

Having the ability to have me terrified to needing his touch, to hating his darkness, to wanting that avenging angel side of him all within the span of a few minutes was dizzying and something I hadn't anticipated—and just another piece of him I despised.

I didn't like that he could affect every one of my emotions so deeply, so thoroughly.

Especially when I didn't want him to be able to affect me at all.

When I didn't respond, his head shook absentmindedly. "I can't . . . none of this is allowed. I can't let this . . ." he trailed off, seeming to search for the right words. "It goes against our way of living, Briar," he explained. "But not only that, it's dangerous for us. For *you*. William obviously knows, if any of the other men—or our enemies— were to find out . . . Christ."

"*What* goes against your way of living, and *what* would be danger-ous?" My voice rose with frustration as I continued. "Do you have any idea how difficult it is to keep up with *anything* that is happening when I can't even keep up with your moods or your confusing, cryp-tic words? Do you have any idea how difficult it is to try to *progress*"—I sneered the word—"when in the matter of hours, you went from sav-ing me and caring about me, to *again* making me think you were going to rape me?" I scoffed, but the sound and my voice when I spoke again didn't hold any of my frustration, only lingering pain and humiliation from that night. "And you wondered why I was still afraid of you, and why it was taking me *so long* to get comfortable around you."

Lucas's face fell and his eyes shut with a slow exhale.

I tensed as I waited to see how he would look when those eyes opened again, but he only looked defeated.

"That's the problem. I don't—" He stopped, then corrected him-self, "I *can't* care about you, Briar. None of the men in this world *care* about any of their women past the bond of owning them."

My heart ached at his words.

I blinked quickly and hated that my eyes burned with unshed tears.

"But that morning. You looked—when William was here . . ." I couldn't figure out how to explain the look on Lucas's face that morning without embarrassing myself, because now I was sure I had imagined it. And, again, I didn't want this devil or anything he did to affect me. "You . . . when you came in, you—"

"I *can't* care, Briar. That's my problem. That is *our* problem. I was never supposed to care about you, and you've had me breaking rule after rule because you've gotten so far under my skin. William saw it the night I had the doctor here for you, and saw more than enough the morning he tried to *teach* you." Lucas ran his hands over his face, covering the agony for only a second.

I still didn't understand why he would look this tortured. "What is so wrong with caring about someone?" I asked quietly.

"Because they can get to me through you," he answered darkly. "If anyone ever wanted to hurt me—to send me a message—they would do it by going through you." His eyes met mine. "Don't tell me I'm wrong, because I can promise you I would do the same. But then there's our way of life. We have rules we have to live by. If one of us starts breaking the rules, it risks everything. We can't let risks live, Briar, you have to understand that."

My mouth popped open when his words clicked. "So because a man *cares* about someone, that's reason to . . . to . . . to kill him?"

"No, there would need to be more rules broken. But, trust me, with how many rules I have thrown out the window in these weeks with you, they have grounds to get rid of me. William won't say anything about how he thinks I'm starting to care about you because he broke one by coming here the other morning and an even bigger one by touching you. But if he knew about any of the other rules I've broken . . ."

"He's your mentor!"

Lucas laughed. "And?"

That brought me up short, and I remembered Lucas's threat to William on the morning everything had changed . . . "Doesn't your relationship mean enough that he would try to stop them from killing you?"

"No, Blackbird. He would just kill me himself."

My shock was apparent in my sharp intake of breath, because I knew from the look in his eyes that he was telling the truth. What kind of life was Lucas talking about where men would do this to each other? "That's heartbreaking."

"It's really not," he said honestly, and rounded the edge of the bed to sit on it. Leaning forward, he cupped my face in his hands. "What's heartbreaking is watching *your* spirit shatter—and knowing it's my fault—while years of training tells me that it's what I have to do, that it's what's right." His full lips pressed to my forehead and stayed there when he spoke again. "I'm *sorry*, Briar. I am so sorry. You can hate me all you want. I'll always hate myself more."

"Then don't be this way," I begged, gripping at his arms. "Don't do these things."

When he pulled away, I could see that that wasn't even an option. "I *have* to be like this. I *have* to teach you."

"But you aren't that man, you said you couldn't be that man. And I've seen that you don't want to be, I can see it *now*. Maybe you thought that you needed to do these things and live a certain way, but that was before you bought me . . . before you had your first girl, so—"

"No. I can assure you that *this* wouldn't be happening if I'd bought another girl that day," he said firmly. "I needed you from the moment I saw you, but I knew that need for you would get in the way of what I had to do to you, so I almost didn't bid on you."

"Why did you?"

"Bid?" he asked, and the second real smile I had ever seen lit up his face, making him so achingly beautiful. "Because, Blackbird, you started singing."

His admission had old suspicions rising in my chest. "The seller was mad when I started singing . . ."

"I'm sure he was. Every man there stopped bidding as soon as you started. I remember thinking you were brave for singing in the middle of an auction. Obviously I know now that it was because you were scared, but it doesn't matter. I couldn't let anyone take you after that."

My eyes snapped up to his. Even through my suspicion, I couldn't stop feeling surprised. In the four years I'd been with Kyle, he'd never once noticed or understood that singing went hand in hand with fear. And this man had figured me out within weeks, maybe less.

"What other rules are you breaking with me?"

He watched me for so long that I thought he wasn't going to answer. "Some things are better left unknown—at least for tonight, Blackbird."

I nodded, accepting that. He still evaded answering every time I asked how long I had been gone. For all I knew, the women weren't allowed to know the rules, and he would continue to say that same thing.

"There have been a few times I was supposed to teach you a lesson for something you did or said, and I couldn't bring myself to even try," he confessed, surprising me. His next words seemed detached, and he wouldn't look at me. "The times I *have* tried . . . William thinks that I've actually raped you. I was supposed to. I know how to teach girls lessons by showing them that I am in control at all times—never them—and not care, but I couldn't force myself to do that to you. Then after each lesson, I'm supposed to leave you for a certain amount of time, but I hated myself after that first night with you and just needed to check on you. Thank God I did," he said with a huff. "But the other times, I just kept thinking about that broken look in your eyes, and I couldn't bring myself to give you a lesson. I forced myself to leave instead of going through with it. The other night . . . William had come back and was with me when the shopper came to me with the number."

My surprise that William had come back, and that Lucas had let him inside, didn't go unnoticed, but he simply gave me a look that let me know it wasn't a subject he would discuss.

"Even if William hadn't been there, I would've known I needed to take back control with you. But your screams before I even touched you made me want to die. I don't know how long I sat there as years of training flashed through my mind while I tried to tell myself to leave before I could hurt you."

My eyes widened, and something in me clenched, knowing I'd had it all wrong. The fear that had built during that silent time hadn't been something he'd planned or been enjoying, but had been minutes of his own torture.

His large hand slid around the side of my neck, and his thumb brushed along the hollow of my throat when he said in a low, rough voice, "Girls are not supposed to receive any pleasure for the first year. It makes them think they have power when they shouldn't." The corner of his mouth twitched, hinting at a smile. "I think last week already proves I can't control myself with you."

At that time, his touches had felt like a lesson in itself—it surprised me that they hadn't been allowed at all.

My cheeks burned as I remembered every touch from him, my breaths deepened at their memory. Or maybe my response was from his touch and his voice now . . .

I could feel something changing, a shift in the air between us, and though I knew I should try to stop it, I was powerless to do so. "Oh." I pulled my bottom lip between my teeth, and some distant part of my mind wondered when we had gotten so close, and who had moved toward the other. "Is that all? For tonight anyway?"

Lucas's eyes danced over my face again and again, indecision and worry twisting through them. "And this," he said roughly just before his lips fell onto mine.

Chapter 20

BLISSFUL DEATH

Briar

A whimper of surprise sounded in the back of my throat and I became lost in our kiss. My first reaction was to stop it, because the man with his lips pressed firmly to my own was not my fiancé, and I knew . . . I *knew* from the bottom of my heart that I needed to continue hating the man holding me. But even if I could stop that man and get away with it, there was no stopping *that* kiss.

The emotions that rushed through me when his mouth moved against mine were a force all on their own. I was lost to them and him.

My hands wove through his dark hair in a weak attempt to keep him there—to keep *Lucas*. I was terrified of the moment he would wrench himself away from me, the moment his eyes would turn cold and murderous, but my movement seemed to incite something inside him.

A deep rumble vibrated in his chest, and he released my face to wrap his arms around me. One hand fisted in my hair while the other arm wrapped tightly around my back, holding me closer to him.

There was something possessive in the way he was holding me. And for once, I didn't mind it. Right there in his arms . . . that felt *right*.

It shouldn't, I screamed at myself, and tried to conjure images of Kyle, but all that I saw behind my eyelids was a handsome man with a wicked grin wrapped in darkness.

A devil.

Lucas tugged on my bottom lip with his teeth, eliciting a moan from me from the warm, welcome rush that followed the pain when he bit down.

His mouth moved to my jaw and then down my throat, and I tilted my head back, exposing my neck for him in a silent plea for more.

"Let me take care of you," he begged when his lips found that sensitive spot behind my ear, his voice dripped with seduction. But there was a hesitation that hadn't ever been there before.

My mouth parted, but I couldn't make my throat work. I needed to tell him no but didn't know how. All I knew was his lips and my racing heart and the heat that was spreading from my belly through my body and the *need*.

I tightened my grip in his hair and forced his mouth back to mine, and shivered beneath him when he growled in response.

The tips of his fingers traced faint, teasing patterns against my body as he moved slowly down my stomach. The barely there touches and eternal patience he seemed to have as he took his time were driving me crazy. The anticipation was dizzying and made it hard to breathe.

Dark, dark eyes captured mine when he broke away from me. His long, strong fingers pulled one side of my shorts down, and then the other, then repeated the process with my underwear. I lifted my hips off the bed to help him and released a shaky breath when the clothing passed my feet and Lucas tossed them on the floor. Like the touches down my body, his movements were painfully slow as he opened my legs and traced lazy designs on the inside of my thighs.

He was giving me time to stop him.

That time was gone for me. Holding his stare, I nodded subtly and exhaled with a rush when his fingers finally touched where I was now aching. Aching from the need. Aching in anticipation. Aching for him . . .

My head dropped back onto the bed and my eyes fluttered shut as that white-hot knot inside of me tightened. I pressed closer to his hand, trying to get more. But a small part of me shied away, afraid of what *more* would be like with this man.

"You're beautiful, Briar."

I looked up at his hoarse confession to find him watching me with awe.

He captured my mouth with his, but I had to break away when breathing became too difficult. He gripped my chin and brought our lips together again. Taking and taking, a silent reminder of who was really in control. A silent reminder that I would always get the devil with Lucas.

As if I could forget.

My chest ached with the need to breathe, but I continued to give more of myself to that kiss and welcomed the way he took.

With the last of my air, I whispered, "More," against his lips.

That wicked grin I had seen so many times pulled at his mouth, but no fear entered my body. The sight of it, combined with the look he was giving me, had me vibrating expectantly, because I knew he was about to give me what I'd asked for.

He sat back until I released my hold on his hair, but his fingers never stopped their pleasant torture. My hands fell to his shoulders then slid to his chest where he gently grabbed both of my wrists in his free hand. After brushing his mouth across my joined wrists, he looked up at me from under those thick lashes, and that grin came back.

He bent, his mouth finding my nipple through the thin cotton of my shirt, as he slammed my arms down on the bed above my head and bit down at the same moment he pinched my sex.

I cried out in shock and pain but then moaned at the body-wracking shiver that moved down my spine immediately after.

He sucked on my nipple through the shirt as his fingers brought me to a high I couldn't explain.

And just when it got to be too much, there was the same pain followed by even greater pleasure, and I wondered if a person could die from this kind of ecstasy.

It felt like our bodies were a battle of the brightest day and the darkest night—and I wanted to lie in the wake of their war.

But somehow, even in that moment, I knew our war was far from over.

My body tightened and my breaths came out broken, ragged. "I . . . I," I forced out. "Lucas, I—"

I felt him grin against my breast, and again that flash of pain shot through my body.

I was floating, and all time seemed to stop. No sound, no racing of my heart, no nothing.

This was death, and it was beautiful with my devil hovering over me.

The world came flooding back and my body shattered. "Lucas!" I trembled violently between him and the bed as heat rushed through me, my mouth opened with a silent moan.

He released my wrists only to press his forearm against my elbows, still effectively keeping my arms pinned to the bed for reasons I didn't understand until the rush of pleasure became too much . . .

I bucked against him and whimpered in protest when his fingers continued their assault.

"No more," I said weakly.

His eyes danced with that wicked grin. "You asked for more, Blackbird."

My head shook sluggishly as I tried to close my legs over his hand. "No. Too much. Too much," I complained, but every now and then another moan would slip from between my lips.

As some of the strength came back into my body, I bucked harder against him and tried with no avail to pull my arms out from under his.

I groaned in frustration, and he laughed darkly as his lips brushed against mine. Close enough for mine to tingle from the contact and make me crave more, but far enough away that the *more* was out of reach.

My next aggravated cry tore from my throat, and he laughed louder. "There you are, Blackbird." His lips met my ear, and he whispered, "Fight it, Briar." This time it wasn't a taunt. This time it was pure seduction wrapped up in that deep, hypnotic voice.

And I did.

Because it was still too much and not enough.

I needed to feel his lips that were now hovering just an inch over my own again.

I needed to run my hands through his hair and over his muscled body . . . and I couldn't.

But the sensations that continued to pulse through my body from where he was touching me were far too much.

I arched off the bed as my body shattered again suddenly, and I experienced this feeling like it was new. Because it was. This was wholly different than the first time. The first had felt like a blissful death, and this was all-consuming.

Lucas freed my arms and crushed his mouth down onto mine, swallowing my moans. Rising to his knees, he pulled me into his arms and sat against the headboard with me tightly curled against his chest to try to calm my uncontrollable shaking.

I clung to his neck as the minutes wore on and the shaking subsided, leaving me exhausted and satisfied. Lucas didn't let me go, he only moved me so he could look into my face for a few seconds, as if he was checking on me.

"Beautiful."

Blood rushed to my cheeks, but I was too tired to respond or try to hide it.

"So fucking beautiful." His eyes searched mine, and then his lips were on mine again, soft as a feather. "Sleep, Blackbird. We'll talk in the morning."

I only had a few seconds of peace when I woke the next morning before I was flooded with guilt, shame, and heartache.

I had willingly betrayed my relationship with Kyle. I had wanted that pleasure, had eagerly given in to the temptation of all that was Lucas. I was waking up in a bed that wasn't Kyle's, with a man I wanted to hate, but couldn't after all he had told me the night before.

He's just as trapped as I am . . .

But that didn't excuse what we had done.

One of my legs was pinned between Lucas's and my head was tucked into the crook of his arm. His other arm was draped heavily over my body, pinning me to him possessively even in sleep. I noted absently that he wasn't wearing a shirt, and the material against my legs didn't feel like the denim he'd been wearing the night before, but I didn't care that he had left at some point in the night.

This was my room and my bed, not his, and even though I'd been anxious over his withdrawal from me the night before, I now wished he would leave again so I could deal with my grief alone.

My thoughts went back to Kyle and my chest tightened. If I ever got away and found my way back to him, what would he think of me? My eyes burned with unshed tears because I knew . . . I knew he would never forgive me, just as I didn't know how to forgive myself.

How could I expect him to still want to marry me after what I'd done? How would I be able to hide that a demented part of my soul wanted the man currently holding me? How could I ever expect him to understand that I had craved the touch of a man who'd wanted me to think he was going to force himself on me on numerous occasions?

"Blackbird," Lucas mumbled, his voice thick from sleep.

I lifted my head to look at him, but his eyes were still closed.

"You're tensing." Two words, but his unspoken question lingered in the air.

"Thinking about things," I admitted and hoped he didn't make me clarify.

A noise sounded deep in his chest, like he was acknowledging my words, and his arm tightened around me. "Like?"

My chest deflated. I swallowed thickly as I tried to think of what to say. "Last night . . ."

The corners of his mouth twitched up.

"Kyle."

His eyes flew open, and his expression fell. "Don't," he said in a low warning. "Don't say his name when I'm holding you in bed, Briar."

Before? I would have argued and screamed at him about ripping me away from my life.

Now? I didn't know what to say when I had never been so confused in my entire life.

I both wanted last night to never have happened, and I wanted to repeat it. I wanted to fall into Kyle's arms, sobbing as I begged him to forgive me, and I wanted to beg Lucas to *stay* Lucas, and stay far from the devil I knew he could so easily become. I wanted to cry for the life I had been taken from and missed, and I wanted to beg to feel just one more kiss from the man next to me.

"I'm sorry," I found myself whispering, but I wasn't sure if I was apologizing for saying Kyle's name or for the thoughts rushing through my mind.

Lucas released me and rolled onto his back. The hand that wasn't pinned underneath me ran over his face again and again as he took steadying breaths, and finally flopped onto his toned stomach, the tips of his fingers barely grazing the muscles low on his abdomen that made me think of things I hated myself for.

I tore my eyes from his body and glanced at his closed-off expression before sitting up and scooting away from him. I froze when he gently grasped my arm.

"Where are you going?"

"The bathroom." I hoped he couldn't hear the waver in my words. I needed to get away from him. I needed to be alone to deal with the onslaught of emotions pouring through me.

As soon as he released me, I began moving away again.

I got as far as the end of the bed before strong fingers wrapped around my wrist, and I was hauled back. I hadn't even settled against Lucas's warm, firm chest before his mouth was on mine, and his other hand was cradling my neck, guiding the kiss that felt like a bittersweet goodbye. A goodbye I wasn't convinced I wanted.

When it ended, his dark eyes searched mine, and I knew he could see everything I'd tried to keep from him. He reluctantly released me, and nodded toward the bathroom. "Now you can go."

Chapter 21

DAY 25 WITH BLACKBIRD

Lucas

I had breakfast waiting in the sitting area of the main room and was pacing impatiently by the time Briar walked back into her bedroom after taking a shower.

She didn't notice me at first, completely lost in her own world as she sang softly to herself while tying a denim button-down shirt together at her waist.

Her dark hair was piled messily on top of her head—the first time I had seen it up—and something about it changed her features in an intriguing way. But I would always prefer her hair down. It made it easier to grab, and God knew I liked the way she moaned when I did.

My gaze traveled down, my blood heating as I took her in.

Briar was adorable, alluring, and sexy all at once. I doubted many girls could achieve that.

She looked like a ballerina in the full skirt that sat high on her waist and fell to her knees.

Pure. Innocent. Untouchable.

Damn if that didn't make me want to touch and tease her until she was begging for more again. Until she was shattering beneath me.

Then the look in her eyes from that morning flashed through my mind, making my hands curl into fists. I forced away the urge to grab her and take her back to bed, knowing that wasn't what she needed. Knowing it wouldn't do anything to help make up for the first three weeks.

She finally noticed me when she was a couple feet from me, surprise filling her eyes at finding me there. "You're here."

I knew we had a while before she would stop expecting me to disappear, or stop expecting me to *try* to give her lessons. But I had no intention of going anywhere, and I would never attempt to give her another lesson. And though I had a dozen things I needed to do for work, they could wait.

"I thought you would want to eat breakfast with me."

Her mouth curved up into a hesitant smile. "Okay."

I held my hand out to her and bit back a satisfied grin when she took it to walk with me. "You look beautiful."

She glanced up at me with a startled gaze before quickly dropping her head to stare at the floor. But the blush that stained her cheeks at my comment didn't match the pain I'd seen in her eyes.

I knew what had put that pain there.

Or rather, *who*.

I knew, and I kept telling myself not to ask her. But I hadn't been able to handle the broken expression in her green eyes during the first three weeks. After last night? I was walking that dangerous line, ready to fall to my knees and offer her anything as long as it took that hurt from her eyes.

"Are you going to tell me?" I asked when I sat in the corner of one of the large couches that faced the lake.

She gave me a confused look as she sat next to me, but didn't respond.

"What's on your mind?" I prompted.

"Oh." That blush was back and darker than before. "You don't want to know."

No, I don't. Because I hate the man you're thinking about even though I know I can't keep you.

"Blackbird," I said, my voice rough as I fought with myself over what I knew she needed and what I couldn't stand to hear. "Out with it."

With a resigned sigh, she repositioned herself on the couch so she was facing me but would only stare at my chest. "I have questions . . . I mean, I wanted to ask you something. Or tell you something, I guess." She looked up at me from under her lashes and waited for me to nod. "I was wondering because of last night—because of what you told me," she added quickly, "if I could speak freely with you?"

I laughed edgily. "Don't you already? How many times have you told me that you hate me?"

"Uh, no, not that. Now that I know that you might . . . that you might care about me. Maybe," she whispered, and looked to me for confirmation.

Words I had learned during training flashed to mind but I pushed them back and, after a few beats, nodded.

She let out a shaky exhale and seemed to think of how to word her next statement for a while before finally saying it on a rush. "I don't want to kiss you. I don't want to do anything with you. Last night—last night was . . ." Her anxious stare flashed to mine, her eyes tightening as if she was in physical pain.

I refused to admit that I understood and felt her pain. I refused to acknowledge that I was no longer seeing Briar's face as her words brought to life something that wouldn't stay buried.

As I sat there with my arms folded across my chest, clenching my jaw shut and trying to force that mask of indifference, I knew I couldn't keep lying to myself; I couldn't keep saying this wasn't the same.

Because I now struggled to find anything in this situation that was different.

"Well, I don't know what it was," she finally continued, her jaw trembling as she did. "But last night shouldn't have happened. I don't know if it was because there was still something lingering in my mind from when William came here, or if it was *that* mixed with you telling me everything you did last night. But for all I know, you lied to me last night to make me think I could trust you so I would progress, or whatever you and William keep saying I need to do."

My brow dropped low over my eyes. My tone was grave when I asked, "You think I lied to you?"

The pain in her eyes gave way to something else, something I couldn't understand, but her shoulders sagged as her eyes darted quickly back and forth between mine. "No," she admitted, her voice nothing more than a breath. "No . . . I don't know. I don't know what to believe right now—I can't even trust my own mind, Lucas."

My fingers twitched against my sides when that name poured from her mouth. William had to have said it in front of her, but watching those lips twist around my name, I didn't fault him for it.

She tucked her feet underneath her so they disappeared under her skirt, and nervously brushed back pieces of hair that had fallen in her face. When she spoke again, she wouldn't look up at me.

"Despite what happened last night, I'm engaged, and I love—"

"Briar," I growled in warning.

"You have the wrong girl," she whispered as if I hadn't said anything. "Why can't you see that?"

"I have the wrong girl for my life, not for me." The words were out before I could begin to filter myself. This girl would be the death of me. I had no doubt of that.

She shook her head. "I will never be okay with your life, Lucas. I will never be okay with multiple women in this house vying for your attention and your love that you won't give because you're incapable of feeling it—especially when all I want is to go home and marry Kyle."

I forced myself not to react to the pain of her last statement—to the fear that rose in me from old memories. But beyond the pain and my memories was a fear of something so much greater: William. He'd seen Briar's attempt to contact Kyle. It was crucial he never heard about her life in Atlanta again.

Because the women sold into this world usually came from places they didn't want to get back to. I didn't want to think about what William would do if he found out Briar *was* different. He was a dangerous man, and untouchable. And he'd already broken so many rules . . .

"Don't say that name in this house again, do you understand?"

She clenched her jaw and after a few seconds nodded stiffly. "As long as you understand that you will never make me into one of your mindless whores."

"Watch yourself," I warned. I studied her worried expression as seconds passed in silence. "Briar, I can't make you believe anything you don't want to, especially after how you came to be here, but last night wasn't a way for me to make you progress faster. Admitting any of those things to you is no different than putting a gun in William's hand, and pointing it at my forehead. I . . ." I shook my head as I searched for the right words. Looking up, I said, "I won't promise I'll never touch you or kiss you, but I promise I won't touch you again until you're ready."

"But I'll never be ready."

I didn't tell her that I disagreed. I just echoed, "Until you're ready."

More minutes passed, and with each one her body sagged more and more. As if I was breaking her without even trying. "I want to ask you something I have before, but I want you to answer as Lucas . . . not the devil." When I only raised an eyebrow, she stressed, "The Lucas who breaks rules for me."

"Ask your question, Blackbird."

Her chest hitched and her eyes watered, but she held the tears back. "Will I ever go home?"

A dozen thoughts begged to be voiced. A dozen thoughts haunted me. One louder than the rest: *It might just kill me when you do.*

Despite my thoughts, I forced my head to shake slowly, and I watched as agony crossed her face before she could hide it.

"You are home."

Her jaw was set in determination, but her voice shook. "You made a mistake buying me."

I nodded—hurt flashed through her eyes at my silent answer. I moved closer to her so I could pull her into my arms, holding in my relieved sigh when she came willingly.

Cradling her face in my hands like she was fragile and irreplaceable, I dipped my head close so I could hold her watery stare. "Buying you was the best decision I ever made in my life. It would only ever be a mistake if anyone learned how much you are beginning to mean to me and took you from me. I would unleash hell on earth if I lost you now, Blackbird."

Chapter 22

SIMPLE KISSES

Briar

My mouth pulled into a frown weeks later as I crumbled bacon over the chicken carbonara. One of the only precious memories I had of my parents from when I was little danced through my mind, tugging at my heart and putting pressure on my chest.

"We're gonna need more bacon than that."

"No, sir," Mom chastised and swatted at Dad when he went looking through the fridge for the package of bacon. "You shouldn't be getting any at all. You heard the doctor, you need to watch your cholesterol."

"Ah. What do doctors know? If it's my time to go, then I'll be ready . . . with bacon in my stomach."

I giggled between my parents while I crumbled the crispy bacon, letting it sprinkle over the bowls of linguine as they continued their playful bickering.

It was the only time I could remember cooking with them. Actually, it was the only time I remembered either of them cooking at all—usually my nanny was the one who'd cooked in our house.

She was the one who had done everything: cooked, cleaned, raised me, taught me how to face my fears . . . She'd been everything my mother didn't know how to be, until one day she wasn't. Until my mother decided she wasn't good for me and sent her away with enough money to ensure that my nanny wouldn't ever contact me again.

That was the day I learned how disgusting money—and people with it—could truly be.

I was so lost in my thoughts I didn't hear him climb the stairs. I was so wrapped up in the ache spreading through my chest I didn't realize he was even in the kitchen with me until he placed a simple kiss on the side of my neck and moved to lean against the counter so he was facing me.

"Smells incredible," Lucas murmured appreciatively.

My cheeks warmed and my eyes met his briefly before I focused on the food again. Every inch of my body was still tingling from that kiss, and a part of me was already eagerly anticipating the next.

A small part.

Because at the moment I was just trying not to cry over a bowl of spaghetti.

"Blackbird." His voice was soft and unsure, but somehow still demanding.

I glanced up again and found dark eyes searching my face.

"What's wrong? Briar, what's wrong?" he repeated when I didn't respond.

I lifted one shoulder and grabbed for a towel to wipe my hands, but I hadn't finished before Lucas pulled me against him. One hand cradled my neck, his thumb brushed against my jaw and tilted my head back so he could study me more intently.

"Talk to—"

"My parents." The words were barely a whisper, but they stopped Lucas's as if I'd screamed them.

He stilled against me for a few beats before his chest moved exaggeratedly. When he spoke again, his tone was dark, yet cautious. Always Lucas. Always the devil. "What about them?"

I let my eyes drift to the counter for a second. "I made this one time with them when I was little. It made me realize I only have a few good memories with them. And I just . . ." I didn't try to continue, and I didn't need to say anything more, judging by the way Lucas's body relaxed for the briefest second before he tightened his arm around me.

"We can eat something else."

"No," I said, then laughed softly. "Just sad when you realize you don't miss your parents at all."

Lucas hesitated for a moment, then pressed his lips to the top of my head, and lingered there when he spoke. "Go sit down, I'll bring the food to you."

I was so caught up in his warmth and understanding I didn't realize it was the first time he'd let me speak about any part of my life in Atlanta without immediately trying to put an end to it.

I exhaled shakily when he released me and allowed myself one more look into his eyes, then walked out of the kitchen before I could do something like fall back into his arms.

As he'd promised me a few weeks ago, he hadn't attempted anything sexual. The first time he'd kissed my forehead after that conversation, it'd taken a second too long to realize what he'd done and for me to jerk away from the touch.

Before I could reprimand him, he'd smiled sadly and brushed his thumb across my mouth as he said, "I will not kiss you, Briar."

I just hadn't realized during that first conversation that that vow had only included my lips. But more and more often recently I found myself craving those little kisses from him, getting a rush when I finally received them.

And as Lucas handed me a bowl of food and sat down next to me on one of the couches in the sitting room, pulling my feet onto his lap, I realized it wasn't just the kisses and random touches I craved.

It was him.

It was the routine we had gotten into. It was his words and the side of him I could see struggling so hard to break free.

It was odd knowing he was the reason behind my heartache, while also being the cure. Even more so knowing he was keeping me from life back home, and yet as time passed, if given the chance . . . I wasn't sure I would leave.

Chapter 23

DAY 55 WITH BRIAR

Lucas

Some might think my life was dangerous. The things I dealt with on a day-to-day, the people I encountered . . .

I guess, in a way, it was.

But I had never been in as much danger as I was in Briar's presence.

Fear, wariness, adrenaline. All that I should've felt on a daily basis in this life, and nothing I ever had until I first saw that girl.

Every moment with her in my arms, with her full lips so close to mine, teasing and begging me for something I knew she wasn't ready for yet, and with that tempting body curled against mine, that danger grew.

Solidified.

Became a living thing inside me.

As I thought about leaving her to return to work for the first time in the almost two months I'd had her, I realized I was terrified. Not because I worried what would happen when I was gone, but because I wanted more. More hours in the day with her. More of the light that now burst from her. More of her infectious smile. Just *more*.

But *more* when I'd already broken so many rules was like playing Russian roulette by myself.

Chapter 24

HOME

Briar

I woke to the feel of his lips against the back of my neck and his fingers intertwining with mine. A sound between a hum and a purr moved up my throat.

"Wake up, Blackbird."

My heavy eyelids slowly blinked open, and I stretched between Lucas and the plush carpet as I tried to orient myself.

I curled my fingers against his, locking our hands against the carpet, and pressed my face against his tan arm as my eyes drifted to the window.

The sun was setting. I was in my favorite part of my level of the house. I had been singing and it had been early afternoon . . . I must have fallen asleep.

I twisted around to look up at Lucas's smirk.

"Good morning."

"You're home."

His grin widened into a brilliant smile, and he dipped his head to kiss the top of mine. "I've been home, but I stayed downstairs to get more work done."

I held back my disappointment that he hadn't woken me up earlier. "Do you want me to make dinner, or did you already eat?"

Lucas's face fell, and he hesitated for a moment. "There's something we've been putting off, and William called me out during a lunch meeting in front of some other men today."

My stomach dropped at the mention of his twisted mentor. "What is it?"

"Since he's my mentor, I need to take each girl to visit him once I think she's ready. Really, it should've happened within a week from you moving out of the starter room, but I haven't wanted you near him."

I pushed the thought of Lucas having other girls out of my mind. I knew it would happen—but it might destroy me when it did. "And what happens in the visit?"

"Nothing," he assured me quickly. "It is *only* a visit for the mentor to make sure I'm not breaking any rules, and that you're progressing the way you should. What he did that day with you never should have happened and never will again."

"Not breaking any rules . . ." I mused. "So how do we act? What do I do?"

He smiled warmly. "I'll go over everything on the way, but I need you to get ready. We need to leave soon."

My eyes widened when his words finally registered, when everything finally clicked. "Wait . . . leave. We're *leaving* the house?"

"That's usually what happens when you go visit someone," he said dryly, but winked at me.

"Lucas, I haven't been outside in months." I couldn't contain the smile that spread across my face, and I hurried to scramble out from underneath him. I had only run a few feet toward my room before I turned back around and launched myself at him.

He stumbled back a step but still caught me in his arms. His head dipped and lips brushed against my neck for a second before he nipped at the soft skin there. "*That* will not be allowed there, but, by all means, greet me this way every day."

I giggled and pushed away from him, and as soon as my feet were on the floor again, I was running to my large closet to find something to wear.

I was so giddy that my entire body was practically vibrating with excitement.

Outside . . . I was going *outside*. I was going to breathe fresh air for the first time in months.

I still didn't know days as they passed by. And while some passed quickly where others felt like weeks, I knew it was sometime in early July from an e-mail Lucas had received a week or so ago.

I'd wanted a specific recipe and, as he often did for me, Lucas had e-mailed William's women. He normally wrote the recipes out, but that particular morning he'd been called in for a meeting and had just printed off the e-mail instead. It had been dated July 1st—exactly two months after I had been taken.

I had held the paper in my hand for nearly an hour just staring at the date, an all too familiar ache flaring in my chest as I did. And as that date and the rest of the words on the paper blurred, I knew why Lucas never wanted me to focus on what day it was, or how long I had been gone.

Because it hurt too much. Because then I was sucked right back into that pain and grief. Because then the *progress* Lucas and I had made—the progress he now so patiently waited for, but so obviously craved—seemed to vanish.

But for the first time, my tears hadn't fallen as I'd mourned Kyle and my life in Atlanta. My eyes had burned and my vision had blurred, but the tears had dried before they could fall. And I'd been left with nothing more than a hollow ache in my chest and memories that transformed into comparisons and denials.

Meaningless denials, because there was no denying what my heart and my mind now screamed.

I had tried . . . *God*, I'd tried to keep my distance from Lucas after that night with him. I'd tried to build up my hate again. I'd forced myself to think of Kyle constantly. I'd told myself repeatedly that what had happened and what I'd felt had been nothing more than a product of some sick, twisted savior complex from when he'd saved me from William.

I had told myself so many things . . .

But Lucas had stolen a piece of my heart a day at a time before I'd willingly handed over the rest. It was dangerous and stupid to do, I knew that, but I was helpless to keep it from him because I was already gone to him.

Wholly, irrefutably his. Our pasts and future and his darkness be damned.

My devil, who constantly fought against the darkness he was so wrapped up in, was still incredibly affectionate, considering he wasn't supposed to be.

He had gone back to working at the office a couple weeks ago, and while it made my days different, lonelier, I was glad for the distance. I'd wondered if constantly being in a house with Lucas was the cause behind my shift in my affection toward him—even if we did spend time apart—but had gotten my answer that first night he'd come back to the house.

I could still vividly remember the way my heart had taken off, trying to burst from my chest when those dark, dark eyes had sought and found me. In that moment, it'd felt like I was looking at what I'd been missing for months . . . *home*.

The only thing that had kept me where I'd stood in the kitchen when all I'd wanted was to run into his arms, was the devastating realization that I'd never had that feeling looking into Kyle's eyes.

Since that night, there had been a change between Lucas and me. A slow burn that was known, but not acknowledged, and with each passing day we'd gotten closer to giving in.

And now we had to play a role for William.

Once dressed, I finished curling my hair that we had re-dyed recently, sprayed myself with the perfume that Lucas had bought me a few days before, and checked my outfit in the full-length mirror one last time.

I was in a pair of torn skinny jeans with a black silk tank and white blazer, and one of my favorite things my shopper had bought: a pair of leopard-print satin, pointed-toe Louboutin stilettos that put me at the perfect height for Lucas to brush his mouth across my forehead.

As far as Lucas was concerned, I still maintained they were just clothes, but my closet did make for fun days as I put outfits together, and waited to see what Lucas did and didn't like.

He liked me in these shoes, as I had found out when I'd been breaking them in weeks ago.

When I was satisfied with the way I looked, I turned to leave and froze when I found Lucas standing in the doorway, his arms crossed over his chest, with a heated look as his eyes devoured every inch of my body.

My breathing deepened from the warmth of his stare, and I wanted to bask in the desire that swirled inside me.

When his eyes finally made it back to mine, his intense stare and gruff voice made my heart race. "You can't wear that."

My head jerked back in confusion. "Why not?"

"Because I will break every rule in front of William if you do."

The confusion melted away, and I bit back a smile as I walked toward him. "I'm ready then."

"Briar," he growled with a hint of a warning.

"Yes, Devil?" My lips spread into a smile, and I reached out to brush my fingers against his jaw as I walked past him. "Come on," I whined when he didn't move. "I want to go outside. We're going outside." I bounced excitedly as I waited for him to reach my side.

His worry faded as my excitement transferred to him. "Don't jump in those. I don't need William harassing me because I had to call the doctor during our visit."

"I've been practicing—"

"Jumping?" he asked with a laugh.

"No, running."

"In those?"

I lifted my foot and looked behind me at the superfine heel. "Of course. I need to be able to run away from you."

Lucas's dark eyes danced, and one of his large hands gripped at my waist, pulling me closer. "And where would you go?"

"Don't worry, I wouldn't get far," I promised softly, letting the tips of my fingers trail over the spot on his jaw I had touched just moments before. "I'm your blackbird. These wings are broken without you near."

His handsome face transformed into something like awe for bated seconds, and then his mouth was on mine for the first time since that night all those weeks ago. The force of his kiss sent us stumbling back until we were pressed up against the wall, and a moan crawled up my throat when he bit down on my bottom lip and tugged gently.

"Briar, I should warn you," he said against my mouth, his voice rough. "I'm gonna kiss you now."

I'd barely cracked a smile before he was kissing me again, taking and taking and taking in a way I hadn't known I'd been craving. And I was sure it wouldn't ever be enough.

And soon everything was forgotten except for Lucas and his lips and our kiss.

Chapter 25

DAY 70 WITH BLACKBIRD

Lucas

"We're almost there," I said into the phone, and locked my jaw when William demanded to know why we were late.

We would be five minutes late, seven at the most, because kissing Briar and showing her how incredible she was would always be more important than my mentor.

I could've lied and said we were late because I'd had to teach Briar a lesson or because there'd been more traffic than I'd expected, but I knew he would see through it. Whenever William asked about Briar and our home it was there in his tone, he was searching for something that shouldn't be there—and it was there now.

"I said we're almost there. Goodbye, William." I hung up before he could ask any more questions and looked over at where Briar was resting her head on her arm. Her fingers were weaving through the wind as we drove, and long tendrils of hair whipped around her . . . I had never seen her so relaxed.

"Are you ready?"

"Yes." She looked over at me, and her ease vanished. "Don't display affection at all," she recalled quietly.

"Good. And if I tell you to do something, you have to do it, Briar."

There was a pause before she nodded hesitantly. "You keep saying that, but what does that mean? What would you make me do?"

I pressed my knuckles under her chin, forcing her to look up at me. "I need you to stop thinking that way. I can see your fear, but there shouldn't be any. I've told you, William crossed a critical line that day he showed up at the house and tried to train you."

Her eyes darted away at the mention of my mentor, and though she relaxed at my words, she wouldn't look at me when she whispered, "But what are you expected to do to me while we're there?"

"Nothing, Blackbird." I waited until her worried stare met mine to continue. "You won't ever have to do anything that makes you uncomfortable in front of others—the helpers who come to the house don't count. They're there for you. Tonight . . . tonight would only be like telling you to go in another room if I have to talk to William, or telling you to get me something. Things like that. Nothing degrading, but you *can't* question it. *They* can't see you question me. They have to see you obey everything. But even if you don't, you don't have to worry about being taught a lesson because lessons are only ever done between the man and his girl, privately. And I already swore that I would never teach you another one. Understood?"

This time when she nodded, she looked more confident, and that peace was back on her face. When the car rolled to a stop, she said, "Lucas, what if everyone does this?"

I looked at her with confusion, and she gestured between us.

"This conversation, what we're doing now. How do you know they don't all have these conversations and just pretend in front of other people?"

Oh, my blackbird.

"They don't, Briar. You'll see a fraction of it tonight, but as you meet more of the men and their women, it will be very clear that those men follow the rules. Doesn't mean their women aren't happy. And you can't hint that there's anything different between our bond and theirs . . . even to the women. They're just as loyal to this world as the men are."

I knew she was disappointed that I had just shot down her hope for the other houses, but I couldn't let her think the impossible about them. I couldn't let her think that we were normal when we were the furthest from that. When I was living with the weight of what our life, and my need for her, would one day mean for the both of us.

"All right, let's go. And, Briar?" I waited until she was looking up at me again. "Don't say my name while we're in there."

She jerked back as shock touched her face. "Am I not supposed to? Is that a rule?"

"It's not. But in there? You need to mean nothing to me. And when you say my name, it makes me want things with you that I'm not allowed to have in my life, and I can't afford to not be your devil in that house." I got out of the car, leaving her there to follow me as crimson stained her cheeks.

By the time we made it to the front door of my mentor's large house, Briar's face was pale.

"You promise I look okay?" she asked under her breath.

My mouth twitched. Turning my head away from the window I knew William would be watching us from, I whispered, "Breathtaking," then rang the doorbell.

The door was wrenched open, and I was thumped on the back of the head with something solid before I could turn back around.

Briar's face fell, but I was already smiling despite the throbbing pain in my head as I turned to find Karina standing there with a glare and large wooden spoon.

Karina was my favorite of William's women. She'd been brought over from somewhere in Italy, and had never once thought of going back. She'd always claimed William and this house were a safe haven compared to the life she'd been in before.

I don't remember my mom—she'd left when I was young—and Karina had been the only one of William's women to never have children even though she was the most motherly. From the first day of my training with William, she'd claimed I was as good as hers by reprimanding me and hitting me with that wooden spoon that was practically attached to her hand. She was outspoken, loving, and the one most likely to let you know when you had annoyed her . . . like my blackbird.

"Karina," I said warmly and stepped up to kiss her cheek, but was stopped when she hit me again.

"I have been waiting for months, and you have ignored my wishes," she hissed. "*Months.*"

I crossed my arms over my chest and breathed deeply. "You know how this works, you can't just demand things like that. She wasn't ready."

Karina scoffed at me, but it wasn't the same as when William did it. Hers was affectionate, like her. "Well, *we* have been ready. The others are furious with you for keeping her from us. Now let me take her so she can avoid the wrath that is coming for you inside this house."

"Karina," I said in warning and received another whack.

"Don't you use that tone with me, Lucas. I am not afraid of you, boy." She pushed me out of the way and a brilliant smile lit up her face, making her look younger as she stared at my blackbird. "Briar," she said with admiration. "Oh, you are so beautiful."

Briar looked terrified.

I cleared my throat, and Briar's wide eyes snapped to me. "Briar, this is Karina. William's first. Go with her and let her introduce you to the others."

She nodded without hesitation and stepped past me to take Karina's outstretched hand.

Karina began pulling her away, already talking to her about how all the women had been eager to meet her.

As soon as I stepped inside the house and shut the door, he was there.

"She's quiet tonight," my mentor mused. "She also looked frightened. I thought you said she was progressing."

"She is, but Karina attacked me before we were even inside—of
course Briar's going to be scared now. I don't think she was expecting
any of your women to be so . . ."

"Like Karina?"

I laughed and nodded as the women rounded a corner at the end
of the long hall, taking them from my sight. "Exactly."

Unease pulsed through me, and I had to fight against the need to
put Briar in my sight again. I wasn't worried about how she would get
along with the women, none of them were cruel, but I was nervous
that Briar might accidentally say something she wasn't supposed to.
Something that would hint that there was more happening in our
home than should. Hearing it would put all of William's women in a
tricky situation, because even though they cared about me as a "son,"
they were loyal to William and this life.

The children born of most of these . . . *families*, for lack of a better
word, went on to school and to marry and never spoke of this life
to anyone. They also weren't allowed to come back once they left.
Some of the houses made the children think they were in a type of
extravagant orphanage with the women as caretakers, so the kids
never knew any better. Other houses, the women weren't allowed to
have children.

If any of the men ever took on an apprentice, it wasn't often that
the apprentices formed family type bonds with the mentor's women,
as I had with William's. But I had come in just as the last of their
children had left the house, and once Karina had claimed me as hers,
the rest of the women had quickly followed.

And for the next three years it had been a never-ending question
of when I would buy a *daughter-in-law* for them to spoil. It had been a
long three years of training, an even longer six months after the auction when I hadn't bought a girl, and an unbearable two months once
I'd bought Briar.

"Why has it taken so long for this visit?" William asked, pulling me from my restlessness.

"She wasn't ready," I said automatically and met his hard stare.

He seemed to think for a moment, but I knew he was just purposefully dragging out my time away from her to see if I would break and go after her. "Could that be because you're too soft on her? It seems the only time she made progress was when I went to—"

I took a quick step toward him until I was in his space, but he didn't flinch. "Do you have any idea what you did by showing up that day? She wasn't ready, William . . . for *this*. She's terrified of you because she thinks *you* will teach her another lesson that you never should've taught *my* girl."

"She needed to be pushed," he said simply, a wry smile pulling at his mouth. "And don't forget . . . I only did a little *bending*."

I straightened and looked down on him. "It's up to me to know when and how. You've already had thirteen of your own, but if you're so desperate to break another, go to an auction. Leave mine alone."

"You're in too deep, Lucas," he called out when I turned to leave.

I slowly looked over my shoulder and narrowed my eyes. "Why, because I don't want another man near what's mine? Because I don't want another man looking at a body I paid for? Your mentor never did anything like this, and none would ever dare to. You're breaking rules because you're worried about me embarrassing you, but you won't have a life to be embarrassed about if you cross me again."

He considered my words for only a second before nodding, as if I hadn't just threatened his life.

Then again, *he* had told me what to say and do to protect myself and my house. He thought he knew what was a show of dominance and what was to be taken seriously.

If he was smart, he wouldn't be so confident in his assumptions.

Facing forward, I blew out a harsh breath and went to find my blackbird.

Let's get this night over with.

Chapter 26

DEVASTATING

Briar

"We will send Lucas more recipes for you," Lisa promised.

"Yes," Jordan agreed, then swatted playfully at Lucas. "And we will see if Mr. Grouchy will allow us to visit you."

"And if not, make him bring you to us." That had been from Sahira, with a look daring Lucas to say no.

The rest of William's women hurried to add their goodbyes as I was engulfed in hugs.

I didn't want to let go of them, and I didn't want to leave. I hadn't realized just how much I'd missed talking with people other than Lucas until I'd been thrown into a room with William's women.

But as the last hug ended and I looked up into cold blue eyes, I was suddenly ready to go. William had made this night miserable.

When he and I had been in the same room, his eyes hadn't left me. Always studying, always waiting to see if I would do something I shouldn't. And even though he never said or did anything to make me uncomfortable tonight, I couldn't get that horrific morning with him out of my mind, and it made my skin crawl.

But it was clear his women adored him . . . and I now understood Lucas's words: it was also obvious they followed the rules.

The women were all close . . . the best of friends. There didn't seem to be jealousy between them, but then again, I had only been there for a few hours. They were loud and infectious with their laughter, and scolded Lucas as if he were their child, but the mood shifted when William was with them. They all seemed to wait for him to give them something to do and clung to his every word. There was a great deal of respect when they spoke to him, and yet they were always at ease with him and even made jokes at his expense in front of him every now and then— something I was sure came with living together as long as they all had.

I didn't know how to explain it, but I could see it.

And I hated it.

Hated that the women's friendships and their devotion to William had come from being stolen. Hated that they'd been bought by a man so cold and unforgiving and cruel. Hated that William and this life was so much better than what they'd had before they'd been kid-napped that they'd happily chosen to stay.

My heart ached knowing I would never understand the kind of suffering those women had gone through. Knowing they would never see the beauty that life and love had to offer.

"Until next time, Briar," William said in that elegant accent that made my blood run cold.

I forced a smile and murmured, "Thank you for dinner," before turning to follow Lucas, already walking toward the car.

Calm . . . withdrawn.

Liar.

His fingers had traced random shapes on the inside of my thigh throughout dinner. His large hand had gripped my hip possessively when I'd passed him in the hall on my way to help the women with dishes, his eyes conveying how hard he was struggling to keep him-self from me. He had followed me into the bathroom and shoved me up against the door to attack my mouth and neck for heated seconds before he'd abruptly stopped and slipped back out.

And I had been counting down the hours until we could leave so I could have another hint of how much he wanted me.

I'd never craved a kiss as much.

He slipped into the car after I did, and as soon as the door closed behind him, energy sparked between us. He held up a hand so it was hovering just above his leg in a silent command to wait, so I sat still with my head bowed as I fidgeted with my hands, waiting for the driver to take off.

I wanted to know how he thought the night had gone, and if William had said anything. I wanted his touch. I wanted so many things . . .

"Luc—"

He lifted my head and pinned me up against the door of the car, his mouth slamming down onto mine in a feverish rush after we turned out of the street. A rumble vibrated deep in his chest when I turned in the seat and pushed back until our positions were switched so I was now leaning on him.

He gripped at my bottom and pulled me higher on his lap, pressing me down where he strained against his pants. I broke from the kiss and tilted my head back—a silent plea of my own.

"You were perfect," he growled against my throat, and I smiled as relief filled me.

"You were bad," I accused.

He laughed huskily and tightened his grip on me as his mouth dipped lower on my chest, and his hands released me to push my top up.

I pressed my hand against the top of the car to steady myself and arched back, needing his mouth on me—needing so much more than what he could give me now when this already *was* so much more than I had allowed in over a month.

"Wait, no," I choked out through my heavy breaths just as the shirt passed over my lace-covered breasts. "Wait."

He dropped the shirt immediately but groaned my name in frustration as he ran his hands over his face and through his hair.

His dark eyes were fire.

They were need and want, seduction and frustration.

"I'm sorry I just need a second to—I just need to breathe." I scrambled from his lap and over to the door, rolling down the window to reveal the city covered in night . . .

And I forced myself to breathe.

I felt horrible for giving him the smallest taste before backing away, but my head had still been spinning from the teasing kisses and touches that had made the night such a sweet torture, and it had taken too long to realize I was afraid of what he could do to my heart if I gave him more of myself. If I gave in to him simply because my body ached for his touch.

Because the last month and those teases had promised everything I craved from him, but I knew he could easily turn into the man who just took, and I would be powerless to stop him. And after a night where he witnessed thirteen obedient women, I was afraid it would push him in that direction.

"Bri—"

"I just need a second," I whispered quickly.

I looked back into the car when the privacy window rolled down and then slowly over to Lucas when he said, "Stop the car."

"Lucas, I'm sorry."

His mouth lifted in a faint smile, but quickly fell. "You need some air?"

I hesitated before nodding.

Long seconds passed before he said to the driver, "Wait here. We'll be back."

I stared at Lucas blankly when he got out of the car and held a hand out to me. "What are you doing?"

He leaned back into the car to gently grasp my wrist and pull me out. "*We* are going to walk around the city for a little while."

Surprise made my eyes widen and mouth pop open, and I stumbled to keep up with him as we crossed the street. "We're what? You're not mad at me?"

His next laugh was low and throaty and laced with exasperation. "I'm frustrated, Blackbird, but it can be taken care of by myself when we get home." His eyes darted over my face when I flushed with embarrassment, and he pulled me into his arms to kiss my forehead. "But, no, I'm not mad at you. You needed air, and I needed out of that car before my training took over and I forced you onto your back, so we're walking."

I stared at our feet for a second when his lips lingered on my skin and asked awkwardly, "Is this allowed?"

When he pulled away from me, that same sad smile from the car briefly crossed his face. "No. Letting you walk around outside, especially in the city, is incredibly dangerous."

"Because you don't trust me." It was a statement, not a question. If he trusted me, I would be allowed on the main level of the house.

He faltered then shook his head. "I don't trust you not to run."

I didn't blame him. This was something I had longed for in the beginning—to gain his trust enough to be allowed outside. Even though he was with me, there were still so many things I could do.

Lucas leaned forward—his chest pressed close to mine, and his lips brushed against my ear when he asked, "You think I don't trust *you*, Blackbird? Look around. Look at all the people."

I didn't move from him as I let my eyes touch on the couples and groups of people near us. It wasn't too late, and this part of the city was filled with people. I could easily slip away from him or scream for help, and someone would actually be able to hear me . . .

"You want to know where you are?" he asked, his tempting voice edging on a whisper. "You're standing in downtown Houston."

Houston . . . Texas.

Oh my God.

I stumbled back a step to look around at the buildings and restaurants.

Knowing where I was made me feel steady for the first time in so long. Made me think it would be possible to get back to Atlanta and Kyle, like I had dreamed of doing so many times . . .

But that thought was fleeting.

Because those dreams were from before everything had changed—before I truly knew Lucas. That was before I'd understood that, despite how much I loved Kyle, it wasn't a fraction of what I was capable of feeling for someone.

Going back to Kyle, no matter how much I ached to see him, meant losing Lucas. And though it was ridiculous because it had only been a couple months, the thought of a life without Lucas made that ache of not being with Kyle seem like nothing. Like a paper cut compared to losing a limb. Or half of your soul.

"I told you earlier . . ." I trailed off, and finally looked into his worried eyes. "I wouldn't get far without you."

"That was before you were standing freely in the city, Briar," he argued.

"Then take me home," I pleaded, and tried to leave his arms to go back to the car, but he didn't let me go. "If you're so worried, then take me home."

"You and I both need this, and after tonight, you deserve this." One of his hands cupped the back of my neck, bringing my face closer to his until our noses were touching. "I need you to know that these months with you have been the best of my life, Briar."

Something like fear and heartache seized my chest. "Are you—do you *want* me to go?"

"No," he said fervently. "But in the chance that you do, I need you to know what I wouldn't be able to say after. And if you do, know that I will chase you until I find you again because I don't think I know how to live without you now."

Why . . . *why* did this man insist on making me fall in love with him when I would never be able to have him the way I wanted?

"Then come chase me . . ." I whispered, and a hard rush of air left him.

Lucas's arms fell limply when I pushed away from him, and I kept my eyes focused only on him as I backed away. Anger and agony swirled through those eyes and across his face as he watched me go until confusion replaced it when he realized *where* I was going.

He started in my direction, his steps hesitant at first, then surer as he closed the distance to where I was climbing into the car.

My decision had been made. There was no running . . . from anything anymore. He not only owned my body, he owned my heart and my shattered soul that he'd pieced back together.

By the time he slid in behind me and shut the door, my top was falling onto my jacket on the floor of the car.

"Briar," he said, his voice barely above a growl.

I swallowed roughly and reached for him. "Take us home."

The driver had put the privacy glass back up at some point, and Lucas leaned forward to pound his fist on it. "Drive," he called out, and then his mouth was on my neck as his hands went to my lace-covered breasts.

I fumbled with the clasp of the bra and then moaned when his mouth replaced his hands once he pulled the material away. He laid me back against the seat and knelt between my knees, and a part of me wished I had waited until home. The car was too constricting—but there was no stopping this now.

I wove my fingers in his hair and pulled his face up to mine, holding it back just enough so my lips brushed his. "Give me *more* . . . give me *everything*." My sharp inhale filled the backseat when he bit down roughly on my bottom lip, and my stomach heated when he made quick work of taking off my shoes and unbuttoning my pants.

His aggravation with how difficult it was to get those jeans off was clear in the look he gave me, and I failed at stifling my giggle just before he succeeded in yanking them and my underwear off me. My giggle turned into a loud moan when he pulled me to the very edge of the seat and pressed his face against my bare sex.

"Lucas," I breathed, and gripped at his hair, needing something to hold on to.

His fingers and tongue moved relentlessly against me, teasing and torturing, slowly and breathtakingly fast. When those dark eyes met mine, I couldn't look away. Completely transfixed, I watched as he devoured me, forcing moans and whimpers from my throat.

The heat that swirled through my belly intensified, and my core tightened. I dropped my head back onto the seat and tightened my grip in his hair, eager for the blissful death awaiting me, crying out when he suddenly nipped me and then replaced the same spot with his tongue again. I shattered into a trembling mess as pleasure surged through my body, over and over again.

His mouth moved in a broken trail of faint kisses over my hip and up my stomach, ending just under the swell of my breast. "Wait here," he said gruffly, then opened the car door.

I opened my eyes to see the garage just past Lucas outside the car door, then looked at the range of emotions passing over his face. Want, excitement, lust, worry, fear, worry, worry, worry.

Before I could ask, he was out of the car and rounding the door to talk to the driver. His voice was too low for me to know what he said, but it was in that terrifying tone that always worried me about what would come next.

Within seconds he was back and holding his hand out to me. "Come here, Blackbird."

"I'm not dre—"

"He won't be looking," he assured me darkly.

Heat rushed to my cheeks when I took Lucas's hand as I thought about what the driver had heard—I wouldn't be able to face him again. My feet hardly touched the ground. As soon as my toes hit the cool garage floor, Lucas scooped me into his arms and carried me into the house, keeping his back to the driver as much as possible.

His mouth fused to mine once we were inside the house, and I waited for the incline of the stairs, but it never came. Soon I was being lowered onto a bed in a room I had never seen, Lucas's body following mine so he was hovering over me.

"If you're going to stop me, you need to do it now," he murmured as he quickly trailed down my stomach with his mouth.

"Everything," I reminded him.

"More?" he asked darkly.

"Yes," I hissed when he nipped at my hipbone then placed a soft kiss there.

His weight left my body, and I watched in fascination as he slowly removed his clothes, his sin-filled eyes on me the entire time. He seemed to be waiting for the panic to set in and for me to decide I couldn't do this.

The panic was there, but so was my need for him, and it was greater. And even after everything we had been through, after every horrible day with him, there was no fear for tonight. Because the days that had come after—that had come from *Lucas*—had been tender, and I knew this would come from that same place.

I crawled to the center of the bed when he knelt on it, and reached out to cup my hand around the back of his neck when he settled between my legs. One of his hands ran up my leg to grip my hip, and I bit down on my bottom lip to hold back a whimper when I felt his erection press against me.

"You are beautiful, my blackbird."

My heart stuttered at his words. At his intense way of claiming me.

I gripped the comforter below me and moved restlessly when he teased my entrance with just the tip of his length, aching to get closer to him. Just when I thought I would go out of my mind, he slid slowly into me, filling me in a way that left me breathless.

Using the hand at his neck, I pulled him closer when he began moving inside me. His face was just inches from mine, his dark eyes burning with passion and his hands gripping me tightly, as if he was afraid to let me go.

So different than I'd ever had before. So passionate. More than I could have ever expected or wanted from him.

He passed his lips over mine, then dropped his forehead so it rested against my own when his pace quickened. Each roll of his hips had the warmth in my belly growing hotter and tightening until I was close to bursting. My breaths hitched and my feet dug into the bed as it got closer . . . closer . . .

"No," I yelled on a whisper when his body completely left mine.

Lucas's chest and shoulders were moving with exaggerated breaths. His arms were vibrating like he was anxious for something while my body was quivering with the need for him to come back to me. He grabbed my hands in his and placed soft kisses on each of my wrists, then intertwined our fingers as he leaned down to whisper in my ear, "Show me, Briar . . ."

I looked up in time to see his passionate stare darken, but my question died in a soundless cry when he slammed my arms out to my sides and drove back into me. The muscles in his arms tensed and flexed with his rough movements, his fingers dug into my hands where they were pressed firmly against the comforter.

I came with a breathy moan seconds later, my back arched off the bed and my hands clinging to his, as I tried to hold on to the reality that the force of all that was Lucas had blurred.

His head dipped, and pain shot through my body when he bit down on my nipple, prolonging my orgasm. My breaths were ragged and loud in the otherwise silent room, and just when I started to come off the high, another bite sent me spiraling through it again. The orgasm never seemed to end, and suddenly my body was rebelling against it. I wanted it to end—but I never wanted *this* to end.

Pain and pleasure, I wasn't sure I could distinguish them anymore, and I wasn't sure I wanted one without the other . . .

An agitated scream tore from my chest and I fought against his hold when another flash of pain shot to my core. *Too much, too much, too much.* I couldn't handle more. If he weren't gripping me so tightly I was sure I would fall into some abyss and never find my way back.

"There you are, Blackbird." His voice was filled with reverence as

I continued to fight to get away from the never-ending torrent of pleasure.

"Please," I whimpered, "I can't . . ."

He chuckled darkly against my breast, but his grip on my hands left and he pushed away until he was on his knees again. I groaned in protest when he pulled me off the bed and onto his lap and exhaled roughly when he pushed inside me again.

One arm stayed wrapped around my waist, helping in his quick movements, and the other hand gripped at my hair and pulled until I was staring at the ceiling. I gripped at his shoulders, digging my nails into his skin and earning a growl from him in my attempt to hold on. Each breath that came from me was rough and on the verge of being a moan, and my eyes fluttered shut as another orgasm slowly built.

"I can't," I cried, and continued to dig my nails into him even as my fingers moved from his shoulders to his chest.

He jerked on my hair, and a shiver moved through my entire body.

"Come on, Briar."

"I can't." A mixture of a cry and a moan left my throat as he moved deeper, harder.

The shaking started from my stomach and exploded to my fingers and toes. He freed my hair as soon as I cried out and drove into me harder still until he found his own release inside me.

Other than pulling me forward so I could tuck my head against his neck, we didn't move. I clung to him as our chests moved roughly against each other's in our own kind of perfect rhythm. I was his air, and he was mine. He gave and I took, and vice versa—so like our complicated relationship.

My body was still shuddering with little aftershocks long after our breathing had slowed—each one earning a faint brush of Lucas's lips against my head, each one a gentle reminder that our night had been real. One of his hands made light trails up and down my back, keeping my skin covered in goosebumps and lulling me to sleep when all I wanted was to make this night go on forever.

It felt like I'd run a marathon. I felt shaky, weak, exhausted, and like I'd never been more alive.

"You are incredible, Blackbird. Everything about you."

His words warmed my chest as my heavy eyelids finally slid shut.

I had given my heart to a man who had no intention of giving his to me. As much as I wanted to believe that he could, I wasn't sure he was capable of such things.

Because he is darkness.

He is the devil . . .

. . . and I love him.

Devastating.

Chapter 27

DAY 71 WITH BLACKBIRD

Lucas

This girl was going to be the death of me. Literally. I couldn't see an outcome for us that didn't end with me staring at the barrel of a gun—and I didn't care. I would take every day with her until that death came, and I would welcome it when it did because they *would* take her from me. And of everything and everyone that had been taken from me during my empty life, Briar was the only person I couldn't live without.

She stayed.

My eyes darted over her sleeping face as I replayed the night before in my mind, and my heart thundered in my chest. She'd been in the city, surrounded by dozens of people she could have reached out to . . . and she'd stayed.

The rest of our lives wouldn't be nearly long enough. Not after how much I'd come to care about her—and definitely not after last night.

I wanted last night forever.

My blackbird had been beautiful when she'd let go for me, and I would never get the image out of my head of her moaning and fighting against me when it had become too much.

This girl made me want impossible things.

I was disturbed and twisted in more ways than she would ever understand. She was fragile and so innocent to my world and the sickening darkness that touched it. But I embraced her life and she embraced mine even though each other's lives went against our very being.

I traced the line of her jaw and suppressed a smile when she curled closer and mumbled something in her sleep. Her full lips parted slightly, and I dipped my head to taste them, unable to stop myself.

When I pulled back, green eyes were watching me. "Morning," she murmured, her voice thick from sleep.

"Good morning."

She looked away from me for a second to glance around the room. "Are we in your room? That's against the rules," she said when I nodded, as if she were informing me.

My lips curved up into a smile. "So is everything else we've been doing for months."

A smile crossed her face before she hid behind her hands to cover a yawn. She giggled when I kissed her hands, pressing them to her face.

"I'm gonna call the driver, have him bring food."

"Okay, I need to go shower." But though she said the words, she didn't move from her place in my bed . . . and I didn't want her to. She stretched lazily for a few seconds before rolling over to climb out, and I pulled her back.

"Use my shower. Come find me when you're done."

Seconds passed as she stared at me. "Find you down here? Really?" Her excitement abruptly faded. "Was last night a test to see if I was ready to be down here? When we were in the city?"

"Briar, no. I was . . . *Christ*."

How could she not understand what she meant to me? What more could I do for her to not think everything was a test?

"I was sure I was going to lose you last night," I admitted. "But I was frustrated and you wouldn't even look at me, so I was trying to help both of us. I just don't always think about what I'm about to do with you until it's too late—and last night was one of those times."

I knew she wanted to believe me, but there was still doubt in her eyes and on her face.

"Come find me once you're done," I repeated, and kissed the corner of her mouth before climbing off the bed.

I had showered and put on a pair of sleep pants the night before, after Briar had fallen asleep, so I grabbed a shirt out of the closet then walked back through the bedroom to call my driver.

My smile couldn't be contained when I saw Briar lying on the bed playing with the ends of her hair, smiling to herself. It took reminding myself that we had slept until noon and I needed to feed my blackbird in order to keep walking instead of climbing back into bed with her.

I walked into my office to make the call and check a few e-mails even though it was the weekend. I had been expecting them the night before, but I obviously hadn't wanted to deal with them once we'd arrived home.

Everything was taken care of within a couple minutes, and I moved the cursor up to shut the computer down . . . and paused.

I hadn't checked in weeks, and even then, it had been sporadic for the two weeks before, but I had been thinking of nothing but that since last night.

Watching her breaths deepen, her body reveling being outside the house . . .

She'd looked free.

Full of life.

A side of Briar I'd only glimpsed, but a girl I'd seen before. In pictures from another time—another *life*. And that girl who'd stood before me? She'd wanted me. *Chosen* me.

I needed to know what updates on Briar had appeared on the news—if any—or if the media interest in her disappearance had died down.

I quickly pulled up the Internet and went to Facebook, and grinned smugly when I'd finished with Briar's page and went to Kyle's. His pictures were the same as they had been most of this time: The large banner about being old and gray, and the profile that matched Briar's—them together. No, his pictures hadn't changed, but the girl in them had. She was no longer the Briar who was trying to get back to Atlanta to be with him. She'd had that chance and had chosen me instead.

But as soon as that thought entered my mind, my grin fell as something all too familiar settled in my stomach.

Yes, Briar had chosen me . . . for now. But I couldn't fool myself into believing that a day wouldn't come when that would end.

I scrolled down his page to look for the articles I had missed and saw that there weren't many of them. Most were just updates of the updates. Scrolling back to the top, I opened the most recent two in new windows, read quickly through the first, then moved on to the second.

No body had been found. Reports had flooded in at the beginning of sightings of "Briar"—none had ended up being her—but were infrequent now. Detectives were declaring Briar a runaway, saying it seemed to be an elaborate set-up between her and the friend she'd gone in to cover for at work the day she "disappeared."

As always, the end of the article was filled with numerous links to other articles dedicated to Briar's disappearance, but now everything seemed to be twisted into some juicy bullshit story about why Briar would have run away rather than being focused on the seriousness and possibility of her being taken.

Jenna Frazier listed as possible accomplice in disappearance of GA woman, Briar Chapman.

Sources say Briar Rose Chapman was tired of living perfect life for sake of fiancé's mother, Gov. Armstrong.

Was GA Gov. involved in future daughter-in-law's disappearance to gain votes for upcoming election?

Can pictures lie? Kyle Armstrong and Briar Rose Chapman's seemingly perfect relationship was anything but!

And there on the bottom was the same picture of her smiling brightly that had been on most of the news articles. Despite the statement that she was a runaway, below her picture was a phone number to call, and if the information led to Briar being found, a reward amount.

I had paid eight times that reward for her.

"I can't figure out your sh—"

I clicked out of the window as I shoved away from my desk, whirling on Briar as I did. "Out!" I demanded harshly.

She was standing there in nothing except the button-down shirt I had been wearing the night before. Her face was as white as if she had seen a ghost—and I guess in a way, she just had. But she didn't move, and her eyes stayed on the screen even as I rounded my other desk and stalked toward her.

A horrified cry burst from her chest and she covered her mouth with a shaky hand as her knees gave out, but I caught her before she could hit the floor. That same cry tore through her throat but was muffled by her hand—her stare never wavering from my computer.

"Out, Briar," I said again, this time softer, but her fists started flying as soon as I moved her to the door.

"You knew! You *knew*! How *could you*?" She clawed at my face when I stopped one fist. Tears streamed down hers as she demanded, "How long have you been doing this? *How* could you do this?"

It was the first time she had cried in so long that I didn't know what to do. I wanted to pull her into my arms and comfort her, but I knew that wasn't what she wanted especially since *I* was the one she was trying to hit.

"We'll talk about it out—" My words cut off when I glanced behind me and saw Kyle's Facebook profile still pulled up—both of his pictures in clear view. "Shit."

"Let me talk to him. Let me tell him I'm okay," she screamed when I picked her up and forced her over my shoulder.

Her screaming didn't stop as I hurried up the stairs and across the upper level of the house. I passed her room and continued to a place

I swore I'd never see her in again, but I couldn't think of what else to do at that moment. As soon as I was in the starter room, I bent and shoved her off me and onto the floor then stepped back into the hall and shut the door. I barely had it locked before she slammed into it.

I pressed my forehead and palms against the door as agony, nausea, and guilt swirled in my stomach.

"Lucas!" she screamed as she yanked on the handle. "How could you? I hate y—" Loud sobs burst from her and filtered into the hallway.

I wanted to die. I had her . . . I'd *had* her . . . and I'd just ruined everything.

"Fuck!" I slammed my fists against the door and shoved away, leaving my girl broken and alone.

Chapter 28

PROMISE NOT TO CHASE YOU

Briar

"Blackbird fly, blackbird fly," I sang quietly, numbly, "into the light of the dark black night."

My mouth shut and eyes slowly traveled from the carpet to the doorknob when I heard footsteps outside the door. I had been in this painful room for hours and hadn't left where I'd crumpled into a heap just inside. I hadn't seen a reason to move. I'd felt numb, yet still completely aware of everywhere I was broken. Moving would just hurt more.

Lucas had researched me. My face had been on his computer screen. *Kyle's profile* had been on his computer screen.

Until we're old and gray, and then long after.

I couldn't get Kyle's sign out of my head. Could he still feel that way after all this time?

It had only been a little over two months, but here with Lucas it had seemed like lifetimes. Long enough for me to see the true Lucas and fall in love with him. Long enough for me to choose any type of future with him over returning to Atlanta.

Despite the unexpected and overwhelming reminder of my life with Kyle, I knew I would still choose Lucas. But knowing he'd researched me made me feel like the last months had been an act to get me to want him . . . and he'd just been laughing as he'd watched Kyle's pain.

He is the devil.

The door unlocked and opened, and Lucas stood there with his arms folded over his chest. He was struggling to maintain a blank expression, but other intense emotions kept fighting and winning with brief glimpses. His eyes were bloodshot and puffy, and it took me a second to realize it looked like he had been crying. But devils didn't cry.

"Do you still love him?" he asked, his tone sure and not showing any of the war playing out on his face.

"Yes," I replied after a brief hesitation. There was no falling out of love with Kyle and our past. He had been my best friend, and I'd planned on spending the rest of my life with him. I would always love him in a way.

Lucas stared straight ahead for a minute with a resigned look on his face, not seeing anything in that room. Unfolding his arms, he placed his hands in his pants pockets and hardened his expression. My chest tightened, and I wanted to cry all over again at seeing *this* man in front of me.

Hello, Devil.

"Go take a shower, Briar."

"Wh—"

"Don't question me." He turned and left without another word, and after a minute, I picked myself up off the floor and went to my bathroom.

I showered slowly and dried my hair the same. I wasn't in a hurry to spend the day in my room, and there was no way I could spend the day with Lucas while he acted indifferent, like nothing had ever happened.

After finding my comfiest clothes, I walked into my room and slowed to a stop when I saw what was on my bed. I glanced over to my shut bedroom door then hesitantly walked over to the bed to pick up the papers and a thick envelope underneath them.

The first was a printed itinerary with my name at the top. My eyebrows rose as I wondered if this was how things would be now, but then I paused and started from the top again, sure I had gotten it wrong when I saw two key words . . .

Atlanta, Georgia.

"Oh my God," I said on a breath. It was an itinerary for a one-way flight to Georgia. The flight was circled with Lucas's scrawl next to it: *Tonight!* Below, was a number for a cab.

I flipped to the next page, and my heart dropped to my stomach when I saw the two hand-written pages. I barely noticed myself sink to the floor.

My blackbird,

I don't know how to do this at all, but I know I can't do it looking into your broken eyes. While I watched you sleep this morning, I thought of a life without you, and knew I would rather welcome death than go through one, but I can't continue to force you to live this way.

You said your wings were broken without me near . . . if you stayed, one day you would realize that your wings are broken <u>because</u> I'm near. And watching them break over and over again because of something I do or say . . . I wish you knew how many times I've wanted to tear out my own heart.

You were never meant for this life. I mean that literally. I should have never looked you up. <u>Never</u>. I expected you to lie and say things about people coming to look for you, but when I saw the tan line on your finger and remembered the engagement ring you'd asked about, I wondered if you hadn't been lying—and that wouldn't have matched the girl the sellers had supposedly taken. The type of girls they always take. So I looked up your name.

From what I've pieced together, you covered a shift at work for the girl who was supposed to be taken.

I became obsessed with knowing what the updates were on your case, and that included checking his social media. I'm sorry for keeping it from you, but I was worried about what it would do to us if you knew.

I could force you to stay here forever—I'm supposed to—and I know we could be happy. Incredibly, if the past couple months are any indication. But a part of you would always hate me, Briar. Always. I can't give you everything you want, and eventually we both know there will come a time when I would break your wings all over again, and I don't think I can watch that happen again.

It's obvious he's still waiting for you, and like you said, you still love him.

Go. Run, Briar.

> *I promise not to chase you.*
> *Your devil.*

I choked on a sob and pressed my fist over my mouth, trying to force my tears back, but they poured from me as if my greatest love had just been torn from my life. Looking at the envelope, I saw it was full of money, and I wished Lucas was there so I could throw it in his face.

I hated him. I hated him for doing this to me. Why couldn't he see what *he* meant to *me*? Why couldn't he be the man who wouldn't shut down at the mention of me loving him too? And *why* would he give me this ticket after today—the hardest day I'd had in over a month?

Grabbing the papers and envelope, I went through the upper level and down to the street level, my steps slowing as I did. It still felt odd to be down there. Lucas never had said I could be there, or that he trusted me . . . there'd just been last night and then this morning—and then I'd been thrown in the starter room.

I went through every room looking for him in the off chance he had stayed, and finally went into his office. It was empty, but the large computer was a glaring reminder of what had happened, of what had stolen our moment of happiness.

I walked slowly to it and sat down in the chair, and stared at the black screen as minutes came and went before grabbing the mouse and moving it to bring the screen to life.

My shoulders sagged when it asked for a password, and I realized I didn't know Lucas nearly enough to guess at one. A life kept secret from the world. A mentor who had shaped and molded Lucas into the devil. Work. I didn't know if he had any friends, but it wasn't likely. I only knew about us, and that made me feel very foolish. He had to have a life outside of this house.

But I still leaned forward and typed *devil*, then *Briar*, and then finally *blackbird*.

In awe that his password was about me, I forgot to get excited over the fact that I *had* actually figured out the password. I immediately pulled up the Internet and typed in *Facebook*. Lucas had logged out, but his password was saved so it was easy to log back in.

I didn't think it would be a good idea to log into mine.

I went to Kyle's profile to look at the picture of the sign he was holding but was sidetracked when I saw a link for a news update. I scrolled down to see that most of his posts were about that, and wondered briefly if that was why Lucas used Kyle's profile, but soon my mind was consumed with the disappearance of a girl I was struggling to have a connection with.

For the next hour and a half I searched through news articles until I realized I was reading the same thing over and over again, and then I went back to Kyle's profile . . . then mine. Looking at the old pictures and seeing posts from friends made the ache in my chest grow and my eyes water more than once, but I never thought about the plane ticket.

I just thought about Lucas's letter and Jenna.

All I had wanted was to help the girl get away from her abusive father. All I had wanted was to save someone whose fear and desperation had sparked some protective instinct inside me. But, I'd been taken in her place.

A humorless laugh forced its way out of my chest at that realization.

But despite the countless times I'd wondered why this had happened to me, and begged to be freed, I knew being taken was a blessing in disguise.

No, I hadn't had a horrible life like the ones I'd heard about from William's women. I hadn't been beaten or raped or starved by family members or boyfriends. I hadn't been saved the way they had described—even if they should have been given the option to leave their previous lives rather than stolen from them.

But my life? It had been predetermined.

Rich parents with a need to flash their money and only child around like a show pony. I was put in classes and given lessons to be the best and be proper. I'd known I would marry into more money; that was non-negotiable. I'd just been lucky that Kyle had fit my *parents'* plan for me.

I'd grown up knowing what the next day, month, even year would hold. I'd grown up knowing how my adult life would turn out, and I'd been happy—excited about it even—and eager to begin it. And it had. Life had droned on exactly how I'd thought it would . . . until it didn't.

Until I came face to face with the devil who showed me a life I would have never known existed.

And a love I never wanted to live without.

Chapter 29

DAY 71 WITH BRIAR

Lucas

I didn't have the driver take me home until late that night, and because of the shit I'd put him through that day, I gave him a month's pay as an unspoken apology.

But as soon as I walked into the house, I almost called him back and asked him to take me anywhere other than that empty house.

Because all of it was too familiar . . . but still so different. Everything I'd sworn I would never go through again, I'd let repeat.

But this?

Briar?

I didn't know how to survive this.

I went to the upper level and walked slowly to her room. I flipped the lights on and looked over to the made bed, and my heart dropped when I noticed the papers and money were gone. I forced myself from the room, knowing it would only kill me slowly to stay in there longer, and went back downstairs.

It was dark and quiet, as it had been for years before she'd come into my life . . . but now it felt all wrong.

I swallowed past the tightness in my throat and headed for my office, only stopping on the way to grab a bottle of bourbon. I didn't need a glass. I needed to stop feeling.

My cell phone rang, and as soon as the distinctive ringtone registered in my mind, I stopped abruptly just feet from the office door. I stared straight ahead, not seeing anything in front of me, just listening as my phone rang and rang, dreading this call.

"Yeah?" I answered in a dark tone, and was greeted with silence. "Unless you're worried about a bottle of bourbon hearing you, you can speak."

"How are things progressing?"

Progressing. I hated that word. I thought about the girl who was in the air, on her way back to Atlanta at that exact moment, and blew out a harsh breath. "They're not," I admitted.

There was a beat of silence before he demanded, "What do you mean, *they're not?*"

I waved behind me with the bottle of bourbon, as if to show that my house was now empty, but otherwise didn't respond. Instead, I flipped the light on in my office and walked to the desk from memory as I focused on opening the bottle and fell into my chair with a huff. The bottle was kissing my lips when I turned toward the computer and saw the piece of paper taped to it.

You IDIOT!

Yeah, Blackbird . . . Yeah. I took a swig, and focused on nothing but the burn as the liquid slid down my throat.

I was stalling. The man on the other end of the call and I both knew it, and I wanted nothing more than to continue, because my next words would change so many things. And as soon as I told him I'd sent my girl back home, I would be putting my name on a bullet, putting him in a difficult position, and creating chaos that shouldn't be touching our world.

"You have ten seconds to tell me what you mean. Nine. Eight. Sev—"

"I looked into her," I finally said and knew the sound I heard was most likely a chair he'd just sent skidding across the floor.

"You now have five seconds to tell me why things aren't progressing," he growled.

"She wasn't ever supposed to be taken. She wasn't an unknown. Briar Chapman. Type in her name, dozens of news stories will pop up. The governor of Georgia's son was her fiancé."

There was a long pause before he hissed out a curse. "Even if all that is true, there is a reason you don't look them up. What the fuck did you do?" He didn't wait for me to respond; he already knew, based on his next question. "Do you realize this could ruin *everything*?"

I glanced down and drew in a slow breath, savoring it like it was my last. But before I could release it, I noticed a pile of shredded paper sitting on top of my keyboard. My brow furrowed, and I released the breath I was holding as I set down the bourbon bottle. I picked up strings of paper, trying to figure out what my broken girl had destroyed, and had just decided it was probably my letter when I realized everything I was seeing was printed, and the strip in my hand had Houston's airport initials on it.

"I have to go," I said quickly and tripped over the foot of the chair from trying to get out of it so fast.

"No, you need to tell me exactly what has happened and what you've done," he demanded as I took off running out of my office.

Apparently not what we both thought, I thought to myself as I flew upstairs. "I told you, I looked her up."

"You said—"

"Things aren't progressing right now, but they will. I have to go," I gritted out and hung up before he could respond as I rushed to the starter room and then back to Briar's room when she wasn't there. After looking through her bathroom and closet as well, I went to another room, and another. I was almost finished checking all the bedrooms on the top level when it hit me, and I took off in a dead sprint for the stairs again.

I burst into my room, my chest rising and falling harshly from the adrenaline, my heart racing as I stared at the small, perfect shape of my blackbird as she slept in my bed.

"Briar." Her name fell from my lips like a prayer, and some indescribable, overwhelming feeling filled and warmed my chest.

I stepped out of my shoes and socks as I walked toward the bed, and crawled so my knees were on either side of her, caging her in. Brushing her long hair away from her face, I said her name again, and watched her slowly wake.

Her eyes glanced at me, then widened. "Luc—you're h—you *idiot*!" she cried, and tears instantly filled her eyes.

"Yes, Briar, yes," I said on a rush. "For so many things I am that."

"I will always love him—I thought I was going to marry him." Her eyes were wild as she tried to get me to understand something I couldn't. "But can't you see that I can't live without *you*? Can't you see that I'm *in love* with you?"

I sat back, shocked at her words.

"I know, I know . . . it isn't allowed. But since when have we ever cared about what is allowed? I don't care if you will never be able to love me back. I knew that even when I gave you my heart." Briar wiped at her tears and looked up at me with a pleading stare. "I gave you my heart, stop trying to make me leave you."

Shock was replaced by awe as I looked at her. "You're mine." For the first time, it was a realization.

"Yes! You *idi*—"

I pressed my mouth to hers and wrapped my arms underneath her to lift her upper body off the bed. With a slowness that suggested we had an eternity, I pulled the shirt off her and dropped it over the side of the bed, then cupped her face in my hands to wipe away the remaining tears.

"I had to let you go, you have to see that." I passed my thumb over her bottom lip when her jaw trembled and searched her eyes. "You'll never be forced to stay here again, Briar, but please God, don't ever leave."

"I don't want to be somewhere you aren't," she said simply as she reached for the button on my pants.

I captured her lips in a slow kiss and groaned into her mouth when she freed me and curled her hand around my length. With the other, she pushed my pants and boxer briefs down and slowly lay back against the pillows.

She looked like a goddess with her dark hair spilled out around her and across her chest, her breasts full and waiting for me.

I climbed off the bed to finish removing my clothes then slowly pulled the lace off her hips and down her legs.

When I moved back between her legs, she pressed the tips of her fingers to my chest, and I paused to look at her. "For tonight, can you . . ." She trailed off and swallowed thickly. Even in the dark room I could see the way her blood rushed to her cheeks. When she continued, her voice was barely above a whisper. "Can you pretend that you could love me, too?"

"Blackbird . . ." I didn't tell her she was asking for something I would never be able to give her, she already knew.

Placing one hand over her chest, I memorized the feel of her thundering heart as I slowly pushed into her heat. Her sharp inhale mixed with my low groan as I filled her inch by inch. Incredible. I never wanted to stop being overwhelmed by the rush of emotions when my body joined hers. I never wanted to stop being overwhelmed by *her*.

Our movements were never hurried, and there was never any *more*. And as she whispered my name against my lips when she came, I found it all too easy to *pretend*.

Chapter 30

YOU'RE DANGEROUS

Briar

My eyes felt scratchy and raw when I woke the next morning. When I first arrived, I had gotten so used to days upon days of crying that I hardly noticed the feel of it anymore. This felt miserable, and I still felt emotionally exhausted. But memories of last night and how beautiful it had been had me eager to see how this morning would be.

I rolled over to an empty bed and frowned at the piece of paper that was propped up with my name on it. The last letter from Lucas had broken my heart, so I wasn't sure if I wanted to read this one.

I studied the offensive paper for longer than was necessary before grabbing it, and rolled my eyes when I read the few words there.

My blackbird,

> *I have some errands to run. I'll be back soon with breakfast.*
>
>> *Your devil*
>> *P.S . . . my shower isn't that complicated.*

I pulled on my clothes from last night then hurried to his bathroom for morning necessities, stopping at his shower to study it again on my way back to the bedroom.

No, it was definitely too complicated. There weren't any knobs, levers, or handles. There was a screen on the wall I couldn't get to turn on.

Once I was back in the room, I made the bed and took my note before heading upstairs so I could rinse off my body and change. While I waited for the water to warm, I went into the closet, pulled open the drawer that held the skimpy lingerie I still refused to wear, and dropped my morning note on top of the letter from last night.

I had decided the day before that if anything ever happened and this life was torn from me, I wanted to have something to know that it had been real.

That *he* had been real.

I was pulling on a pair of shorts not long after my shower when I heard Lucas's heavy steps in the bathroom, and I bit back a smile when I glanced at him over my shoulder.

His arms were folded over his chest and his mouth was curled up on one side in a smirk that made my heart beat harder. "Morning."

"Morning," I echoed when I turned and walked toward him, and let my smile broaden when he pulled me in for a soft, teasing kiss that made my knees weak.

"Hungry?"

"Mmm-hmm," I hummed against his lips. "What about work?"

He leaned back only far enough for those dark, dark eyes to search my face then said simply, "It can wait another day." He cradled my head in one of his large hands, securing his fingers in my hair as he did, and tipped my head back to brush a feather-soft kiss across my lips. "Some things are more important," he whispered, pulling me out of the closet. "Come on, breakfast is out back."

With the havoc he'd just inflicted on my heart and my body, I wanted to forget about the food . . . but I let him lead me through the house to the doors that opened up to the backyard and sent him an excited smile when he waited for me to go ahead of him.

I'd looked down on this yard from the top floor numerous times, but looking down didn't compare to this.

My breath rushed from me when we walked straight into a mini paradise, complete with palm trees, lush greenery, and a multitude of gorgeous flowers. A large pool was straight ahead with lounge chairs positioned on one side and an oversized cabana on the other. Before that, couches and tables with plush chairs littered an equally large patio, all covered by an extended wooden roof.

"Lucas," I said on a breath, "this is beautiful."

He wrapped his arms around my waist and pressed me to his chest. "I'm glad you like it. Maybe now someone will actually use it."

"I can come out here?" I asked, surprise lacing my words.

His laugh was silent, but his chest moved with the force of it. "Yes, Briar, you can come out here. You can go anywhere you want."

"You'll never be able to get me in from the backyard," I said excitedly, and he barked out a laugh.

"Come on, let's feed you."

We'd spent hours after breakfast talking about nothing and everything while lying on the king-sized lounger in the cabana. I was pressed close to Lucas's chest as I took my time studying his arms and his face for the first time, my lips twitching into little smiles every time he'd hum in appreciation when my fingers would trail over his tanned skin.

I paused over one of the many scars on the arm I was focused on and chewed on my bottom lip for a second before whispering his name.

One of his dark eyebrows lifted before his eyes slowly opened.

I started to speak but stopped before I could ask my question.

"Whatever it is, ask."

I searched his eyes for a few seconds, letting my gaze trail to where my fingers were drifting over his forearm. "I thought I knew you," I began, my voice soft and unsure. "I thought I had you so figured out . . . but your arms make me wonder if there's a part of you I don't know at all."

If I hadn't been pressed so close to him, I wouldn't have noticed how still he had become at my comment, because his face and his eyes gave nothing away. But I knew in the way he'd tensed I was right, and there was another layer to my devil I had yet to meet.

And as I lay there waiting for him to respond, I wondered if I wanted to meet him at all.

His brown eyes danced and his chest jerked from the force of his unexpected laugh. "My arms? What exactly are my arms telling you, Blackbird?"

I held his stare as I continued my slow dance up and down his arm. "You live in a multimillion-dollar home and have a driver. You wear suits ninety percent of the time and buy me everything, even if I don't ask for or want it. You aren't even thirty and you own an energy company—"

"I'm not the only owner."

"You own a fifth of it, but it's an equal share," I amended. "You live in a world where men buy multiple women who are stolen from their lives, and where rape is a form of teaching those women a lesson. But somehow you've all twisted your minds to believe that raping them is still better than what they had before."

Lucas's eyes had gradually hardened with each point I brought up, and when he spoke, his voice was tight. "What's your point, and what do my arms have to do with this?"

Without looking, I moved my hand down to where one of his tattoos began, the design wrapping around the inside of his left forearm. "These don't fit."

His eyebrows ticked up. "You don't like my tattoos?"

"I didn't say that. I said they don't fit with the guy I just described. Especially not *yours*." Before he could respond, I let my fingers slide up, tracing a long scar. "And neither do these. People have scars, Lucas, but you have so many," I whispered as I moved to another, and then another. I studied the scar I was touching high up on his arm, and asked, "What happened to you?"

"That one was a bullet."

My head snapped up at his reply. I hadn't expected him to answer me, and I would've never expected *that* response. "What?"

But no matter how much I silently begged him to repeat himself, hoping that maybe I'd heard him wrong, he just stared at me as a minute passed by.

"Why were you shot?"

Instead of answering, he turned the conversation around to me. "Why do you stop singing when I walk into the room?"

As it had so often with Kyle, my body tensed. And just as I'd known I'd had Lucas not two minutes before, he now knew he had me.

He didn't wait long for a response, and from the look he was giving me, he hadn't expected one. He curled his large hand around my neck and traced feather-soft circles against my throat with his thumb as he spoke. "You don't need me to tell you that your voice is beautiful; you already know it is. But you stop when you *know* I can hear you, and you sing when you're scared . . . like it's an involuntary reaction you can't stop even though I could tell in those first days that you'd wanted to." Another sweep of his thumb across my throat had my fear receding and my breaths growing heavy. "Now tell me, Briar, why would someone with a voice like yours be so afraid of it?"

Again, my body stilled, but it no longer had anything to do with the suspicion that crept through my body whenever anyone mentioned my voice . . .

Kyle had asked me countless times what I'd had to be afraid of when it came to singing, implying that I was good enough to do anything I wanted with my voice. But he'd never once in the years we'd been together noticed that I sang when scared, just as he'd never noticed I was afraid of my own voice.

But the man holding me . . . he missed nothing.

"There are parts of my life that you don't know," Lucas continued, "but there are parts of yours I haven't begun to understand."

I shook my head slowly, subtly. "You understand more than he ever did." I didn't have to say Kyle's name. Lucas knew who I was talking about. "I used to love singing."

When I didn't offer anything else, he asked, "Not anymore?"

"I want to. I'm trying to—I've *been* trying to. I've sung a lot more for the fun of it in this last year than I had in the five years before. But most of the time I feel like I don't know how to just *sing*."

His dark eyes searched mine for a few seconds before he nodded. "The night I was shot . . . a lot of people died and a lot of people lived. I'm just lucky that when it all ended, I was one of the latter."

I thought over his vague response as confusion flooded me. "Were you in the military?"

He laughed softly, but something in the tone changed at the end. The sound made me feel cold even though it was warm and humid outside. "No to the military. You see who I am now, Briar? Who I am here with you?"

I hesitated for only a second before nodding.

"You saw who I was when you came here?"

Another nod.

"I wasn't born into this. I had to fight to get into this. I had a rough life before I met William. The night I was shot was a live-or-die shootout within my family." When I looked up at him in horror, he dipped his head closer. "Not what you expected from your devil? It was a necessity for William to take me on."

This man wasn't just cloaked in darkness; he *was* darkness. I had feared him and that darkness, but I had never thought of him as dangerous. Panic slithered through me at his menacing tone, but I didn't shy away. Because even though the fear was there, I couldn't connect it to the man in front of me.

"You . . . did you kill someone?"

He released me and rolled so he was on his back and staring at the top of the canopy, but not before I saw his eyes. "I've killed a lot of people."

I knew from his steady words he wasn't lying, but I also knew in the heaviness of his tone and the pain that flashed through his eyes he hated himself for what he'd done.

And it was then that I knew I had been right: I didn't know this man at all. Because that look and that weight pressing on him wasn't the devil who'd bought me, or the Lucas who'd broken rules for me. He was someone else entirely.

I sat up so I was sitting cross-legged on the bed and forced myself to remain calm when I asked, "Why?"

As if he didn't realize he was doing it, his right hand passed across his left forearm a few times, just over the large, swirling tattoo. "It's easier to explain why I've killed people than it is to explain why I tried to break you, but that doesn't mean I *can* explain it to you."

"Lucas, I've given my body and heart to you, and you just told me you've killed people—including members of your family." I took a steadying breath when my voice took on a frantic edge and swallowed roughly before continuing. "You need to give me *something*."

He reached out for me, but he paused when I flinched. "I won't ever hurt you again." His hand stayed suspended between us for long, torturous moments before it fell to his stomach, and he looked at the canopy again. "Sometimes you don't have a choice, Briar," he said in a soft, haunted voice. "As for the family . . . like I said, it was a live-or-die situation, and my brother technically shot first."

I stared down at him as shock and confusion flooded and over-whelmed me. I didn't understand how he could talk about these things so calmly. I didn't understand how they could be true at all and wanted them not to be.

"How could a family enter into a shootout in the first place?"

"Because they wanted to hurt something I'd vowed to protect." Lucas's face had slipped into an emotionless mask, and his voice was a deadly calm when he responded, letting me know he was done talking about what had happened that night.

I'd wondered so many times how the women who were forced into this world would ever want to stay, especially when they would never have the kind of relationship that Lucas and I had. After meeting William's women and hearing their stories from their previous lives . . . in a way, I could understand. But only to an extent.

Even more, I'd wondered how these men had ever entered this world, and how their minds had been warped and twisted into thinking this life was okay. I'd been sure they'd all come from money—given what I'd seen of Lucas and William, and knowing that they paid for all the women—and had disturbing fetishes. But after being given the smallest glimpse into Lucas's past, I couldn't help but wonder how someone like him had stumbled into this life, and *why* his past had been essential for it.

"So, you're dangerous," I mumbled softly.

"Not to you."

"In general." I let my eyes gloss over the scars that littered his arms and wondered what all the other ones were from. "Why was that a necessity for William? What in this life would require you to be that way? The energy industry can't be so . . ." My words died when he laughed darkly.

"Not all of the men in this world work in energy. There are some in oil, gas . . ." He eyed me and dropped his voice. "The government, the police . . . which is why we're able to live the way we do. We control Houston and everything that happens in the surrounding cities. Police, weapons, drug—"

"Sex trafficking," I added bitterly.

Lucas made a face like he was going to deny it. "Human trafficking."

"There isn't a difference—"

"There is," he argued. "It's different than the sex trafficking that you hear about in the news. If you hadn't been bought at the auction, you would have found yourself in a situation like what you see in the news. The sellers would have just sold you off to a brothel, or taken you overseas and sold you to a whore house where they keep their women of all ages pumped full of drugs so they can't try to run."

My stomach churned. "Oh God."

Lucas nodded. "But I guess, in a way, we control that too. We don't outright say anything to, or against, the sellers, and they don't expose our world. But since we have law enforcement in our world and in our pockets, every couple of years or so we tip detectives off when we know they have a shipment of children coming in or going out of the Gulf, and law enforcement conveniently looks the other way when we bring in weapons. And the cocaine that runs along the Gulf and up through Houston? It doesn't get bagged or pass hands until it goes through William and then me, and it comes from an Irish-American mob."

"Comes from a what?" I choked out, my words nearly silent from the shock of his admission.

His eyes searched mine for a minute before he spoke again, his tone soft, yet urgent. "So now you see, my work is so much more than just going and sitting in an office, and I am surrounded by the worst kind of people. *That* is why William was so interested in my past."

My head shook absentmindedly as I tried to comprehend all that he had told me.

Knowing the man Lucas was behind the darkness, I couldn't grasp why he had ever fought to get into this life at all.

"I'd been wondering what had happened in your life to make you into the devil I saw so often at the beginning," I began, my voice soft . . . almost hesitant. "But now I wonder how you were able to remain you, instead of letting the devil completely consume you."

"Don't ever make the mistake of thinking that that part of me isn't there."

"I couldn't," I said honestly and huffed a small laugh. "He's always there . . . I see you fighting him all the time. Now, more than I have in a long time."

He held my stare, and his dark eyes burned with something I couldn't define. "You're afraid of me."

I wished in that moment for my room so I could have something to hide behind, at least for a minute, because I knew I couldn't hide any of the emotions coursing through me, and I couldn't lie to him. "Yes," I whispered and hated that he seemed to not only expect my answer but accept it. Reaching out, I traced around the outer edge of his eye, thankful I wasn't shaking. "I'm afraid of the eyes I'm looking into right now. I've been afraid of them for a long time. I'm afraid of what I know about you now, but I wonder if I haven't always known. If you haven't hinted at it before . . ."

"Briar—"

"But the things you see in your mind that force me to see these eyes? They've been there this whole time. They were there when I fell in love with you, and I knew when I fell that they would always be there." I watched as he fought with whatever haunted him and lowered myself back onto the bed and curled against his side. "The darkest part of your soul can terrify me, but it won't cause me to leave."

He gripped my hand in his, and mumbled, "Sometimes I wish it would." Before I could react or respond, he continued. "If you think I'm dangerous, maybe you understand what my life is like, and maybe you can grasp the danger in throwing out the rules for you. Eventually someone other than William will see what you mean to me. And with who we are and what we do, we all have so many enemies who've been waiting for a chance to get back at us—to hurt us." He raised our joined hands to kiss my wrist and let his lips linger on the skin there. "We don't have weaknesses, Briar, but you are mine. They've been waiting for *you.*"

Chapter 31

DAY 87 WITH BRIAR

Lucas

"Mr. Holt?" my driver called out in a reverent tone that bordered on terrified.

I paused from walking into my house, my fingers still over the screen of my phone from where I'd been responding to an email, and turned slowly.

His eyes quickly fell to the floor of the garage, and I rolled mine in response.

My driver was lethal and willing to die for Briar, or any other girl I would have in the future. That was why I had him, why I trusted him, and why I paid him as much as I did.

But he nearly pissed himself whenever he had to address me.

Maybe it was the product of him witnessing my behavior for the last three and a half years, having seen the man I became in order to do my job well. The fear I saw in his eyes and heard in his tone wasn't uncommon, and I'd had to prove myself to instill it in the men we dealt within our business, but it was irritating coming from the man I employed.

Especially one I saw daily.

He, of all people, should know if I was going to shoot him, I would've already done it long ago.

"Yes?"

"I'm sorry, Mr. Holt, it's just that I was wondering if you've noticed the date?" His eyes bounced up and down, each time holding my blank stare longer and longer before he eventually stopped looking away.

My mind raced as I held on to my calm, bored façade.

I knew it was the end of July, and a quick glance at the date on the email I was responding to confirmed that, but other than that, the date meant nothing to me. Briar had been there for almost exactly three months—and that was when I wondered if I'd missed her birthday since I didn't even know when it was.

Before I could ask my driver what exactly the date meant, he cleared his throat and said, "In all the time I've worked for you, you've shipped a package on the twenty-eighth of every month, Mr. Holt. That was yesterday, sir."

I stilled as I fought back memory after memory and wondered how I could've forgotten—

My blackbird. Of course she'd be the one to make me forget.

No one and nothing else had ever made me forget about *her*, but Briar had.

With one look, with one plea, she could have me forgetting the world.

I swallowed thickly and nodded. "We'll do it tomorrow." Without waiting for his response, I turned to walk into the house, and went back to tapping on my phone as I called out, "Take the rest of the night off."

But my mind wasn't on my driver or the email I was sending or the package I had to ship—all I could think about was the girl I could now hear singing from upstairs.

The girl who could make me forget.

The girl who made me want dangerous things I couldn't have.

I shrugged out of my jacket, draping it over the banister of the stairs as I headed up, loosening my tie, and rolling up my sleeves as I followed that voice.

Soft, but commanding. Full, with a hint of hesitation that made it alluring, made you want to follow that voice anywhere, even to your death.

As I rounded the corner into her bedroom and took in my black-bird, I knew I would do just that.

I knew the moment she felt my presence, knew it in the way the song abruptly ended, as it always did.

A siren terrified of her own voice . . .

I was a few feet from her when her words stopped me.

"My nanny taught me to sing." She turned to face me, a sad smile playing on her lips before falling. "I can't remember a time with her when she wasn't singing or teaching me. Her name was Nadia . . . she had such a beautiful voice." Her words were thick with emotion, and every instinct told me to pull her into my arms, but I didn't move.

Briar tensed if I mentioned her singing or her fear associated with it, and never volunteered anything about her past to help me under-stand that fear. Now that she was talking, I wouldn't do anything that would hinder that.

"One time when I was young—I think I was four—my parents decided to go on a vacation without her and quickly realized they didn't know how to be parents. We were at a park that had some kind of farmers market set up. There were vendors everywhere. And they . . . well, they didn't lose me . . . *I* lost *them* because they forgot I was there at all and just left." She laughed sadly and looked up at me. "They were so used to being alone, and so used to having someone else take care of me, they didn't even realize I wasn't with them for *hours*.

"I'd been so afraid when I couldn't find them that I'd found my way back to the parking lot and ran around it screaming for them. Whenever anyone tried to approach me to ask if I was okay, I'd run away and hide. By the time they came back to look for me, it was dark, and a police officer was already trying to get me to go to the station with him. I remember my parents telling the officer that *our nanny* had lost me that afternoon and had been too afraid to tell them until then."

My arms were folded across my chest to hide my fisted hands and the way my body was beginning to shake with anger at her parents— an anger I knew all too well. My mom hadn't been around, and my dad had destroyed his life, leaving me with the wolves without so much as a *"Hope you survive."*

"I was terrified of everything after that," she whispered. "Terrified of being alone, terrified of the dark, just . . . *everything* in a way I'd never been before. My parents left for business trips so often, and every time I would scream and scream, so sure they were never coming back for me. But Nadia was always there, and when I was completely inconsolable, she would hold me close and tell me to sing with her. And then she would start, and she wouldn't stop until my thrashing and screaming had ended, and I was singing too." Her downcast eyes held mine, and her shoulders lifted in a faint shrug. "And that's how it began. Any fear, no matter how big or small, she would scoop me up and tell me to sing until it became second nature.

"And then not long after I turned fifteen, Nadia woke me up in the middle of the night, and she looked so worried. I remember that look so clearly and the way it made me feel . . ." The corners of her mouth tipped up, but there was no amusement in her eyes. "I automatically began singing as soon as I registered her anxiety, and I didn't even know what was going on. And then she said to me, 'Every fear and every worry fades to nothing when you sing, Briar Rose. Your voice is your comfort and your security. Don't let anyone take it from you.'"

Silence fell between us, heavy and smothering. When a minute passed without Briar continuing, and then another, I couldn't take it anymore.

"Why was she worried that night?"

"Because she knew what was going to happen the next day." When Briar looked at me again, the weight that had been pressing down on her was gone, and her sadness had been replaced with bitterness.

"For the first time in . . . *years*, my parents were interested in me. Wanted to be with me, do things with me. They planned this whole day out with me. I remember being so excited, and then the next thing I knew, we were going from place to place, and my parents were making me sing for people. Telling me how they were going to make me famous, how I was going to make them rich—like they didn't already have so much money they were drowning in it.

"Suddenly my mother wanted me with *her* all the time. She didn't want me with Nadia even though Nadia was the one who kept our house running . . . the one who felt like a mom to me. And then my mother started grooming me to be the girl she thought I needed to be, the adult she wanted me to be. She told me how to act and what to say, who to see and not to see. She told me what I would need to look for in a husband one day . . . all while they constantly used me for my voice. Anytime we were anywhere, 'Have you heard Briar's voice? Briar, sing for this gentleman.'" That bitterness in her eyes burned as she continued. "And soon, men my father's age wanted to touch my hand or my arm, the small of my back or the back of my thigh. They wanted me to stand closer to them so they could accidentally brush my breast or tease my waist as they showed me pictures and made me read contracts while they caged me against the desk to *read over my shoulder*."

I was vibrating as white-hot rage coursed through my veins, as visuals I didn't want flashed through my mind. I already had a bullet for every single one of those men, and I didn't even know their names.

"'Just remember to keep smiling at him, Briar,' my mother would say. 'Don't wear those pants, Briar, a skirt is more fitting for this meeting—a shorter skirt. He didn't mean to touch you, Briar, he was just reaching for the paper. We could've had a record deal years ago if you would just keep your mouth shut, Briar.' It was endless for years, and I began hating my voice and my parents' money as they paid off man after man at these record labels so they wouldn't sue us because I'd thrown coffee on one or kneed another when they touched me.

"And throughout that time, Nadia was the only one on my side. She'd sneak into my room at night, lie down next to me, and sing until I was singing with her. Then she'd repeat the words she'd said to me before it had all begun. On my eighteenth birthday, I walked in on my mother handing Nadia a check and telling her not to contact me ever again. But Nadia was so much more than my nanny. She was my best friend, my mom, my teacher—she was everything. I didn't think she would give in to my mother's demands . . . but she did. I never heard from her again. And I've never let anyone use my voice, or intentionally hear it, since. I didn't sing for an entire year after that morning."

"Briar . . ." I said softly and began reaching out for her but stopped at the look she gave me. A look that told me she was just getting started.

"I never told Kyle any of that." She whispered so quietly the words were almost lost by the time they reached me, and I tried not to react to the mention of the man waiting for her in Atlanta. "I never felt like I could—I didn't think he would understand because he continuously pushed the issue no matter how many times I asked him to stop. He always wanted me to keep singing, and he always wondered why I wouldn't. But only because he was so sure that with my voice, I could have whatever I wanted. He never realized that I sang when I was scared, or that I was scared *of* my voice. He thought I was afraid of failing."

She closed the distance between us, each step slow and calculated. Once she was close enough, I slid one hand around her waist and the other around the back of her neck, using her hair to tilt her head back so I could study those eyes that captivated me.

"I hate that you have so much money that you buy women. I hate that you *bought* me at all, but mostly that you bought me *because* I started singing. I hate the circumstances that brought me to you, but I love you and am thankful I'm here with you all the same."

My chest ached and filled with warmth. I wanted to kiss her and thank her for trusting me with her past. I wanted to erase every bad memory and replace them with ones of us now, but she didn't realize what she'd just said . . .

As much as I wanted what she was saying to be true, it wasn't, and it never would be. It couldn't.

"You don't," I said thickly, forcing the words out through the tightness in my throat.

Confusion covered her face and her brows drew together. "I don't what?"

"You don't love me."

I felt the shock that went through her body, but she didn't try to pull away from me. Instead, she gripped my shirt in her hands like she was pleading with me in her touch alone.

"Lucas . . ."

My eyes slid shut, and I released a slow, weighted breath. "You *don't*, Briar."

"I know you think you don't know how to love someone, but you *do*, you *have been*. You know what love is, and I have never been more aware of how loved I am by someone than I am by you."

I ground my jaw and finally looked at her again. Instead of disagreeing with her, I said, "You can't love me, because you don't know me."

I hated the hurt in her eyes. I hated that I was putting it there. I hated everything I was, hated that I would never be enough for the girl I didn't know how to let go of. *Couldn't* let go of.

"Yes, I do," she choked out. "I've seen it, I've felt it, I've experienced your darkness and your monsters, and I'm still here. Haven't I proven myself yet? Haven't I proven I am not going anywhere? That you can't make me run?" Her gripping hands flattened and moved up to curve around my neck. "I knew to fall in love with you I had to fall in love with the devil, too. I am not as naïve as you think I am."

"But you have no idea exactly how heartless your devil is," I said darkly.

"Then let me see—"

"I won't let you into that part of my world," I said on a growl. Just the thought of her being in a situation to see me like that—to see that part of my world—chilled me in a way that made me feel sick. "All of *this* will change the minute you see it. Trust me when I say you'll never be able to look at me the same, and I won't be able to live with myself if that day ever comes."

"You can't know that," she argued, her words still sounding like a plea.

"Think of your worst memories with me, Blackbird," I ordered gently. "Think of what I told you about the shootout with my brothers. Think about what William did to you. Now try to grasp that all of that is *nothing* compared to what I have done, and what I do, without feeling a thing."

I waited for it to sink in, and after a few moments, it did. And there was that look in her eyes I'd come to dread and hate—fear and uncertainty. But I could still see her love for me.

Unfailing and undeserving.

"Didn't you hear me the first time?" she finally asked as tears filled her eyes. "The darkest part of your soul terrifies me, but, Lucas, I'm not going anywhere."

One day, she would. One day this illusion would shatter. And on that day? She would go running back to the man I knew was still waiting for her. Didn't she realize that allowing myself to fall in love with her only for her to be ripped away from me was something I couldn't let happen?

Losing *her* had broken me.

Losing Briar would destroy me.

Chapter 32

SHADOW

Briar

After making a sandwich, I downed a bottle of water as I padded through the house to the office then cracked another bottle open when I sat down in front of the computer.

I'd spent hours outside, alternating between swimming and just lying on one of the chairs, soaking up the sun. After the first morning Lucas had taken me out back, I had spent nearly every day out there. The days I didn't think I could take any more sun without getting heatstroke, I lay in the cabana reading.

Anything to be outside.

I slowly picked at my sandwich as I opened up Lucas's e-mail and started one to him.

He had given me his credit card number a few weeks ago, but I didn't want to have control of his money.

I'd shredded the paper that contained the number in front of him.

But I couldn't have a job, not without risking men from Lucas's world finding out—women working was *not* allowed—and sometimes this house and my life became very mundane when Lucas was gone during the day.

So I'd finally given in.

Now I e-mailed him the titles and authors' names of the books I wanted from his own e-mail address, and he bought them for me.

Once the e-mail for new books was sent, I scrolled through the list of his unread e-mails, looking for any he had flagged and unlocked for me to read.

I straightened in the chair and smiled when I saw three from William, the subject showed they were just a few of many replies in the chain of *Recipes for Briar* e-mails from William's women.

I scrolled through until I was at the beginning of the new ones, and printed out two recipes, then scanned the conversations from today.

Lucas, it has been weeks since we last saw Briar. Let her come over!
    We love you.
    All of us.

No. You can come see her.

I rolled my eyes at his terse reply. It wasn't any of their faults I couldn't stand being around William.

A chime sounded through the computer, and I glanced around the large screen until a small conversation window popped up in the corner after a delay. All it said was "**Hello?**" but I couldn't see who it was from. There was only a gray circle with an X through it as the sender, so I exited out of it and went back to finishing the e-mail.

Always so grouchy, Lucas! Karina has now grabbed the wooden spoon; you have been warned. If that is how you must be, let William know what day we can come see her. Sahira wants to know if Briar would like us to schedule a spa day at your house, and we all want to know if she is pregnant yet. We need a grandchild to play with now that all of the children are grown and gone.

I knew I had to look horrified as I stared at the e-mail.
Pregnant? Kids with Lucas?

Of course I'd wanted to be a mom. I'd wanted that for so long, to be someone as nurturing and kind as Nadia had been to me before she abandoned me. I thought that coveted future was going to be a reality sooner rather than later. But then everything I thought I'd known had been torn from me, and I'd learned that while I'd loved before, I'd never loved wholly.

And now I had that love . . . but I couldn't have children. Not with Lucas.

I was sure—I was so sure that he loved me too, even if he refused to understand he was capable of loving someone. But I knew that despite that love, and despite how different we were from the rest of the people in his world, he still had every intention of buying another girl. And another. And it would destroy me when that time came, destroy what we had.

If we had a child, it would just push my heart and my mind into thinking we could have more than *this*; that we could have everything. And I wasn't reckless enough to not take his words to heart; I knew we couldn't.

"No. No babies," I whispered numbly, and tried to ignore the aching in my chest as I exited out of the e-mail.

I took the last bite of the sandwich, and started to roll away from the desk as I dragged the cursor up to shut off the computer when two chimes sounded. After another delay, the same conversation window popped up.

X: Are you there?
X: Briar?

I jerked back in the seat, and stared at the screen like the words would attack me. After nearly a minute passed, I clicked on the box and let my fingers hover over the keyboard for another moment before responding.

LH: Yes.
X: Briar Rose Chapman?

The full name came within a split second of my reply. Fear coursed through me, making my heart beat faster. Part of me screamed to shut off the computer, but I was afraid of what would happen if I didn't address the name.

LH: No, I'm sorry, you have the wrong person. My name is Briar Holt.

I bit nervously at my bottom lip as I waited for a reply, but didn't have to wait long.

X: Briar is a pretty unique name. But it's okay. I know who you are and I'm here to help you.

Get off the computer, get off the computer, get off the computer! I screamed at myself.

LH: I don't know who you are, and I don't need help. Goodbye.
X: I can get you home. I can get you back to your life.

That familiar ache flared at the thought of returning to everything that was familiar but was followed by a stronger one. Because as I'd known for some time now . . . it wouldn't be much of a life without Lucas. Instead of responding, I clicked on random parts of the window to try to figure out who this X was.

X: You don't have to say anything. I know you're scared. I'll get you out of there, but I'm going to need your help.
LH: I don't need your help. You have the wrong Briar, and you are what's scaring me. Leave me alone.
X: Do you know what Stockholm syndrome is?

My eyes narrowed, but again, I didn't respond.

Of course I do.

I'd taken a psychology class in college, and while I didn't remember everything from that class, I remembered fragments. The lectures on Stockholm syndrome being one of them.

And what little I remembered of it was half of my reasoning on why I'd first let Lucas touch me all those months ago. It was why I'd tried to keep Lucas at a distance afterward, even when it became so clear that my feelings for him had been shaped from who he was as a person, and not because I'd formed some twisted bond with him because he'd kept me locked in a room or had saved me from his mentor.

I had finally found the e-mail address linked with X, which was really just a bunch of random letters that looked like a spam account, when he sent message after message of long definitions for Stockholm syndrome.

My eyes darted quickly over what he had sent me but nothing triggered. Nothing made me question my love for Lucas or my want to be with him. I was acutely aware of what we would look like to someone on the outside of Lucas's world. I knew what we looked like on paper, but this person didn't understand my relationship with Lucas at all.

Hostages express sympathy . . . have feelings toward captors . . . defend . . . identify with . . . mistake lack of abuse for kindness . . . strong emotional ties . . . one person harasses, abuses, threatens the other . . .

"William and his women," I mumbled to the screen once I finished reading.

That's who those words described. And even though I hadn't met anyone else, I had no doubt those definitions would fit the *bonds* between the other men of this world and their stolen women.

LH: Thank you for the lesson, although it wasn't necessary. Leave me alone.
X: Think about it, I can get you out safely.

I immediately pulled up Lucas's e-mail and started a new one to him. I flagged it as urgent, put nothing but exclamation marks in the subject, and only five words in the body:

Someone found me through you.

The landline rang a few minutes later, the shrill tone causing me to jump in the chair. I hurried to answer it and tensed when I heard Lucas ordering the driver to go faster. His tone had an edge to it that sent a shiver of fear through me even though his threats weren't directed at me.

"Luc—"

"Where are you?" he growled closer to the phone.

"In your office."

"Are you safe, yes or no?"

"Yes, but—"

"Don't stop," he snapped at the driver then came back to me. "We're headed back to the house, I'm only a few minutes away. I need you to open the bottom right drawer in my main desk."

I did as he said. "Okay."

"Take out the false bottom, then open that safe. It's the same code you use to call out on the landline."

"Is there anything in your life that isn't secret and locked up?" I asked, exasperated.

"Can't afford it. Now—"

"What am I supposed to do with these?" I yelled as I stared at the handguns and extra magazines of rounds.

"Grab one and go to my room. Lock yourself in there."

I shook my head quickly. "No, this isn't necessary. You're overreacting."

"Bri—"

"I've never even touched one of these in my life."

His voice boomed through the phone. "Briar, don't you understand what is happening right now?"

"Yes, but I'm not in any danger. It was just on the computer."

"Computer or not, if you've been found we're all in danger. Take a gun and go lock yourself in my bedroom closet. If anyone is already in the house, shoot them. If someone tries to get in the closet that isn't me, shoot them. Understand?"

"Yes," I whispered weakly. I felt nauseous thinking about holding one of the guns in front of me.

"And, Blackbird," he said, his tone lighter and with a hint of amusement, "keep your finger off the trigger. I don't feel like getting shot today."

By the time I finally grabbed the smallest gun in the mini safe and walked out of the office, Lucas was storming into the house with a murderous look on his face.

"What happened?" he demanded as soon as he saw me from across the hall.

"I don't want this." I held the gun out toward him with it between two of my fingers.

Lucas gripped the gun in his large hand to take it from me, and passed it to the driver as he came hurrying in behind him. "Stay with her after I'm gone. If anything happens . . ." He let the warning trail off and shoved his hands into his pockets. "Now tell me what happened, Briar."

My eyes weren't leaving where his hands were now hidden. I tried to tell myself it was just his fear and anger that had him reacting like this, but the sight of his stance still sent ice through my veins. "Um, I uh . . ." I shook my head and forced myself to look up into the fury in his dark eyes instead. "I was checking e-mails. This guy started messaging me. He knew who I was, and he was saying—well, I left it up there."

His jaw was clenched so tightly I thought it might shatter. In one quick movement he stepped forward and grabbed the back of my head to press his mouth roughly to mine, and then he was gone.

"This way, Miss Holt," the driver said once Lucas was gone.

I pointed down to the gun in his hand and asked warily, "Do you know how to use that?"

His face was all business when he responded, "Yes, ma'am. I wouldn't be Mr. Holt's driver if I didn't."

"Of course not." I let out a shaky sigh as I followed the driver into Lucas's room and then into the closet, locking all the doors behind us on the way.

The messages led to a dead end.

People had come over to help Lucas just minutes after he'd arrived—people who didn't exactly care about doing things legally, which had been one of the reasons Lucas had wanted me locked in the closet with the armed driver—and they had started investigating immediately.

Thankfully, it hadn't taken long before their investigations led the other men out of the house, and soon they were calling Lucas with updates.

The chat messages had been sent from an abandoned, dilapidated Internet café, and they had nothing else to go on.

A look had snapped into Lucas's eyes that had left me feeling cold for hours. He'd left immediately after, leaving his driver with me, and hadn't said anything about where he'd gone or what he'd done when he came home. Only that I needed to let him know if I was contacted again, and he didn't want me in the backyard unless I had someone else with me.

He also wouldn't leave my side or work away from home for two weeks because of it.

As much as I loved every second with him, those weeks had been uncomfortable because he'd been on edge the entire time, and it had left me unable to prepare for tonight.

Thank God there had been things at the office that needed to be taken care of in person today so he'd had to leave, but now I was running around Houston with the driver, trying to find the perfect gift for the man who had more money than he knew what to do with.

"What's this place up here on the right?" I asked the driver, who still refused to give me his name.

"Clothing."

I sighed and sank into the seat. I'd already been into seven stores—two had been clothing stores—and nothing had stood out to me. At least I'd finished Lucas's caramel banana cake before we left so I wouldn't need to worry about it once we got back to the house. I'd considered making a devil's food cake to be funny, but I'd paid enough attention to what he liked over the last months that I was sure he'd be happy with what I'd made.

"This one on the right?"

"Jewelry, Miss Holt."

I groaned in frustration. Lucas and jewelry did not mix. "What does he like?" I asked out loud, even though I didn't expect the driver to answer since he rarely answered any personal questions about anyone.

"Guns."

I glared at his reflection through the rearview mirror. "What about all of those coming up on the left?"

"There is a—"

"You know what, it's okay. Why don't we park and I can make my way through this strip? Maybe walking through these stores will help me think of something."

He nodded and slowed to find parking. "I pick up lunch just over there for you quite often. Would you like me to get you something to eat? You haven't eaten all day."

"I've been busy all day," I mumbled. "Thank you, but no, I just want to find something and get back to the house. But if you're hungry you can go."

"I'm not hungry," he responded easily.

"Of course not."

We were in the second shop on that strip of stores when it all got to be too much. I felt restless and anxious, and like I was going to scream if someone didn't give me some space soon. It had been like this ever since our first store that afternoon and had only gotten worse as the day had dragged on. Having someone by my side twenty-four/seven for two weeks, after months of mostly being alone, left me feeling suffocated.

"I will be okay if I walk to the other side of the store without you," I snapped, and immediately regretted it. "Oh God, I'm sorry. I'm so sorry. I just—I just want some space. You two are always hovering, and it's exhausting me and stressing me out, and now today . . ." I trailed off, shaking my head. "I'm sorry."

The driver smiled patiently, understanding covering his face. "It's okay, Miss Holt, but I can't leave your side."

"Nothing is going to happen. Please? Just for five minutes even, would that be so bad?" When stress caused the driver's eyes to crease and his lips to thin, I thought about Lucas's threats to him simply because he wasn't driving fast enough and realized it might be that bad.

"Five minutes. I'll meet you out front." He swallowed roughly, and I knew he wished he could take back what he'd just said.

"Thank you. Thank you. Just—thank you." I immediately turned from him and walked through the store. I wasn't even looking for a gift for Lucas anymore. I was just relishing in the feel of not having a shadow for the first time in weeks.

It was amazing.

After the first few minutes, I finally paid enough attention to know I wasn't going to find anything in that store anyway and headed toward the front. The driver visibly relaxed when he saw me headed toward him, and I sent him a small grin. "How'd you do?"

The glare he sent me was so unlike him that I barked out a laugh and turned toward the next store.

But five minutes hadn't been enough.

Before we'd even reached the doors to the next store, I felt anxious again. Like I needed to get away from my own skin, and I wondered if the driver would give me another five minutes alone.

"Excuse me," a woman called out, trying to get our attention.

"I can't find . . . uh, this place. I'm not sure I'm even pronouncing it right," she said with an embarrassed laugh as she pointed to her phone. "Can you help me?"

The driver looked at the phone for a second, looked down the street, and pointed.

That crawling feeling all over my body got worse as he started giving her directions and started over when she decided to type them into her phone. I rolled my shoulders and shook my arms out, trying to relax. But the feeling only grew until I felt so jittery that I worried there might actually be something wrong with me.

I need space. I need—I just need to get out of here.

I was about to tell the driver that I would meet him inside the store when an arm wrapped around my waist and pulled.

Chapter 33

DAY 116 WITH BRIAR

Lucas

"You are agitated," William stated when we finished with our meetings.

"Yes."

"Do you need to discuss whatever has you acting this way?"

My eyes darted to his. "No."

He seemed to accept the answer as we walked, but a minute later asked, "This couldn't have anything to do with a certain *First*, could it?"

I groaned and turned on him. "You clearly have something you want to say, so stop wasting my time and get on with it."

"You cannot keep her."

I ran my hand over my face and wasn't able to stop another groan from sounding in my throat. "I can't deal with your hypocritical bullshit today."

He continued on as if I hadn't spoken. "What I saw the last time you brought her over was far worse than the first time, and even that was worrisome. Christ, the first two times I saw you with her at your house concerned me. I gave you time to see an error in your ways, but I cannot allow you to have more. You cannot care about a girl the way you care about that one . . . you *cannot* keep her."

"Don't forget that whatever you *think* is happening between Briar and me, you have been doing for years with one of your women, and no one has tried to stop you . . . yet."

He casually waved his hand between us. "You cannot threaten me, boy."

I could, and for Briar, I would do so much more.

I stepped forward and dropped my voice so the warning was clear. "If you're going to threaten my house, expect the kindness to be returned."

William laughed like I was amusing him. "You cannot threaten me because there is nothing to threaten. I have told you time and time again that we do not care for our girls. We can't. It is dangerous and it shows weakness."

"And yet you—"

"And my weakness died long ago," he snapped. His eyes filled with rage and agony for half of a second before it died out.

"You talk about her like she's here, and you expect me to believe that?"

"Because I have not forgotten a single thing she did."

I shook my head and turned to continue walking. "I don't have time for this, William."

"I have had fourteen girls in all . . . she was technically the fourth, but I kept her on a pedestal as if she were my first," he called out to my back. "From the beginning she captivated me, and I didn't care to hide it even though I knew it was against our way. She had just told me she was expecting a child the night the house was attacked. I wasn't home to protect her."

I stopped and looked at him but didn't know what to do when he was so close to losing his grip on his calm. In the years I'd been with him, I'd never seen him like that.

"They didn't go after anything in the house or anyone else. Just her. They knew what she meant, and I knew it was one of our own. They announced themselves by heartbeat," he said on a growl.

I blinked slowly and had to force myself to ignore the pain in my chest for William . . . for an innocent girl none of us had protected.

Knocking on a door in the rhythm of a beating heart was something I'd quickly learned the men in this world used to announce themselves to those who broke too many rules and were becoming threats to the way we lived. Whether it was torture or death— usually the latter—nothing good ever followed a heartbeat.

"Who was she?" I asked. "What was her name?"

"We do not speak it."

I nodded, knowing I should have expected that.

"You reminded me of her—you could have easily been her son for how much you look like her. The first time I saw you, I wondered if you had been sent to torment me. But the more I saw you, the more I realized what an asset you could be to me. Then you proved to be valuable in this life and in the company, and were a reminder of the time I had with her . . ."

"Watch your words, William, you're sounding like you could actually care about something other than yourself, and dying isn't something I want to do today."

Again, he continued like I hadn't spoken. "I just hadn't realized you would screw everything up so greatly with a girl."

My lip curled and my tone darkened. "Not as bad as some, apparently, considering my house hasn't been raided, and my girl is still alive."

His eyes narrowed, and he sucked in a breath through his teeth so quickly that it sounded like a hiss. "You cannot keep her," he barked when I began walking away, and hurried to catch up with me. Grabbing my shoulder, he flung me back and stood in my way. "Do you see what they will do to her, and in turn, to you?"

Fear of something happening to my blackbird swirled with my anger, but I didn't know how to live without her—didn't know how to let her go.

Ice-cold fear had gripped my spine the day someone had messaged her, and I knew that wasn't the worst we could face . . . not by a fraction. But all that day had done was force me to keep her closer rather than push her back like it should have.

Holding William's glare, I stated, "It's not your decision to make at this point. Briar isn't going anywhere."

And like his pain had never been there, suddenly his blank, indifferent stare was back. "Well, I'm not so sure about that."

My heart skipped painful beats, and when I spoke again my tone was lethal. "Care to explain?"

"Curious to find she uses your computer," he said casually. "That shouldn't be allowed in the first year, maybe not even in the second or third."

I stilled with my hands in my pockets as my mind raced. Briar knew not to respond to the e-mails to William's women, and I knew she hadn't before today. I had the urge to grab my phone to see if the conversation with them had continued but didn't move as I thought of the last time Briar had been around the women and what she might have said, and then the man who had found Briar . . .

Suspicion and rage made my chest rise and fall roughly while my heart took off in a dead sprint as I studied William's knowing look.

"I'll give it to you that she is loyal, Lucas, but we both know it isn't for the right reasons. That girl fell in love with you and would have eventually been used against you. Best to end things this way before it went too far with a certain miss Briar Rose Chapman."

My blood ran cold as those words—her name—left the man before me. A full name he shouldn't—*couldn't*—know.

"How do . . . wait, *would have* . . ." My stomach dropped. "William, what did you do?"

"You will thank me one day," he assured me.

"What have you done?" I roared, my voice echoing back at us in the long hallway. Gripping the collar of his shirt, I slammed him back against the wall. "What have you done. Tell me *now*!"

"Once you've had time to think—"

I punched him with every ounce of anger and fear and anguish swirling through me, letting him drop to the floor because I was already running, my fingers already grabbing for my phone and dialing the landline at the house. But no one picked up. I let out a roar of frustration when my driver didn't answer his phone either, but I answered on the first ring when he called back less than a minute later.

"Where is Briar?" I yelled into the phone, my calm completely gone.

Sirens and too many voices filled the other side of the phone. I slowed, unable to continue moving, and then staggered back before falling to my knees when I heard his worried voice. "I'm sorry, Mr. Holt, I'm so sorry. It was my fault."

Chapter 34

KISS OF FIRE

Briar

My breath whooshed from my lungs as I was ripped away from the driver, and it only took me a second to realize it wasn't Lucas coming to meet us and surprising me. The person pulling me was pulling too fast and wasn't stopping. And when his other hand clamped down over my mouth immediately after and he started whispering my full name, I realized this had to have been the person responsible for my anxiety.

I screamed against his hand and thrashed; people stopped to look with dumbfounded expressions as he pulled me through a small gap between the two stores.

No, no, no! This isn't happening!

"I'm going to get you out of here, Briar Chapman," he whispered again on a rush. "It's going to be o—" He cut off with a grunt and stumbled when I snapped my head back against his face.

I regretted it instantly. Black spots danced across my vision and the cramped alleyway tilted although he was still holding me straight up. I struggled to get out of his hold, but my pathetic attempt at an escape had only caused him to tighten his arms.

People began screaming and running away from the storefront sidewalk seconds before gunshots tore through the air.

The man started running backward again, and I screamed against his hand and doubled my efforts. I dug my nails into the man's arm and tore as hard as I could and bit down on the meaty part of his palm covering my mouth.

A growl sounded in my ear, and he dropped the hand from my mouth.

I screamed as loud as I could for help, but my voice was lost in the chaos on the street. Turning in the arm still holding me tightly, I shoved against the man's chest and clawed at his face as I yelled for him to let me go.

But he was large with thickly muscled arms, and every few seconds his arm constricted tighter around me.

He grabbed my waist and lifted me off the ground as he started running again, but before he could get me over his shoulder I shoved my knee into his groin and scrambled to my feet when he dropped me.

"Bitch!"

"Someone help me!" I shouted as I ran past him toward the storefronts. I'd only made it halfway up the alleyway when I was yanked backward by my hair, forcing a cry to rip from my chest. I screamed for help over and over as he gathered my fists into one hand across my chest to restrain me from another attack, then slammed his other hand over my mouth again.

Another gunshot rang out, this one deafening as it echoed through the alley. The man holding me whirled around and forced me higher up on his body to use me as a shield for his chest and face, and I cried with relief against his hand when I saw the driver walking toward us with his gun raised.

He didn't say anything, just walked quickly as his eyes darted over me. When the man began matching the driver's steps with his own, the driver's eyes found mine and locked. After a few steps the driver's eyes flickered down to the gun and then back up . . . a few steps more and his eyes settled on something near my feet.

I didn't know what he was trying to tell me and I was shouting against the man's hand for the driver to just do or say something. The man holding me laughed.

We were nearing the other end of the alleyway, and the driver finally barked, "Lift your feet!"

I lifted at the same second the man holding me turned to run, but the driver fired, and the man holding me stumbled and roared in pain. His knee buckled, and we started falling, the ground coming up fast when another deafening shot filled the alley.

"Miss Holt!" The driver was suddenly there, yelling, but his voice sounded off with how loud my ears were ringing.

The driver ripped the man's hand off me and pulled me from his body, and I turned to see blood pooling from a hole at his temple.

A horrified cry left me and my body trembled uncontrollably as I scrambled to get farther away.

"Miss Holt, are you okay? I need to know if you are okay. Miss Holt, please say something. Miss Holt. Miss Holt!" The driver wrenched my face toward his, away from the dead man. "Have you been hurt, Miss Holt?"

I think I shook my head, but it could have been from the way I was already shaking so violently. "H-h-h-h-he . . . oh my—he's dead," I screamed.

The driver quickly pulled me toward the opening of the alleyway. Sirens could be heard in the distance, and the sidewalk that had been filled with shoppers was now empty.

A shuddering breath left me and I covered my mouth to mute my next scream when I realized it wasn't.

The body of the woman who had stopped us to ask for directions lay unmoving on the sidewalk. Blood pooled from her head.

"She was a decoy, she tried to kill me," the driver explained calmly. He sat me down on the sidewalk, facing away from the woman and alleyway. "Miss Holt, are you okay?"

"I don't know, I don't—people are dead!"

"Are you *hurt*?" he clarified, and breathed a relieved sigh when I shook my head vigorously. "I am so sorry I allowed this to happen. I will never forgive myself for—"

"Stop! Please stop," I pleaded, and focused on breathing for a minute. Fighting to find the calm that Lucas exuded. "It's not your fault. You and Lucas were right about everything. We should have never left the house."

Fear flashed through his eyes. "I need to call Mr. Holt," he said with a determination that didn't match the resignation on his face. With a sigh, he helped me to my feet when police started pulling up, and led us over to where the first officer was getting out of his car.

A look of recognition passed over the officer's face, and he walked up to us to shake the driver's hand, as if there wasn't a dead woman just a few feet away. As if the driver hadn't shot her.

I had the urge to look at where the woman lay, to make sure I hadn't made it up in my mind, but forced myself not to turn.

Because then I remembered what Lucas had said about owning the police, and I wondered how many times this particular officer had come in contact with Lucas and his driver—if that was the reason there wasn't an ounce of suspicion coming from him.

They spoke quickly to each other, but I wasn't able to focus on the words or most of what was happening around us. The only word I caught was when the driver said *Holt*, and the police officer looked down at me with fear and . . . was that awe?

"Please go with him while I handle this," the driver said, and handed me over to the officer.

"Mrs. Holt, please, come sit in the car so we can keep you concealed from the public." The officer's voice wavered with fear, and his movements were jerky as he led me to the back of his car. "Anything you need? Water? It's warm out, but do you need a blanket? You're shaking."

I was so thrown off by the way the officer was reacting and what he'd said, that I wasn't able to answer right away, and I never corrected him on the *Mrs.* "Um . . ." I looked over to the driver to see him talking on the phone with his back to us then back to the officer. "It wasn't his fault," I said quickly. "He saved me."

"Yes, I know. Can I get you anything, Mrs. Holt?"

I blinked slowly, trying to sift through the fog in my mind. My ears still had a dull ringing in them, and my mind was a blur of dead people, gunshots, and consuming fear of being taken again.

Lucas.

It would have been Lucas I'd been taken from. The thought of never seeing him again devastated me.

"I don't know," I finally said, my voice barely audible.

By the time the driver came to where I was sitting in the back of the police car, the area was flooded with officers and people trying to see what was going on.

I lifted my head off the back of the seat and took the food and bottle he handed me.

"Please eat, Miss Holt. We need to get something in your system. Mr. Holt should be here shortly."

I stopped trying to open the bottle of water, and said, "He's coming?"

My relief was met with worry from the driver. "Yes, Miss Holt." He took the bottle from my shaking hands and opened it before handing it back.

"It'll be okay," I promised. "You saved me; it'll be okay."

He nodded but didn't look convinced.

"I don't understand, why aren't they questioning you? Why aren't they questioning me? Why wasn't the officer suspicious of you or us when he pulled up? Why aren't they—?"

The driver shook his head once, and gave me a look that made me stop talking. "Don't ask questions you don't want the answers to, Miss Holt."

"But—"

"We're fortunate which officers arrived today." And I knew from his tone that he wouldn't say any more.

The sound of screeching tires drowned out the noise from the crowd that had gathered, and I tensed in preparation for the impact that would follow. Officers turned, and the driver reached down to his hip as he watched for the threat. But the impact never came, and the driver relaxed his stance. I sat up to look through the back window, and saw the devil himself storming out of a car, barely taking the time to slam the car door as he tore onto the scene.

I scrambled to get out of the police cruiser but was stopped by the driver.

"Please, Miss Holt. You need to stay—"

Whether it was his fear of what Lucas would do if the driver actually used any force to keep me in the car, or if the look on my face made him relent, I wasn't sure, and I didn't care. I squeezed past him, and as soon as my feet were on the ground, I was running toward my devil.

His darkness cracked the moment his eyes found me, his body sagged with relief, and his pace quickened. For the first time since everything had begun that afternoon, a sob burst from my chest and tears filled my eyes.

I thought I'd never see him again.

Lucas caught me easily when I launched myself at him and crushed his mouth to mine in a searing kiss.

"I thought I'd lost you," he said against my lips, and then kissed me again. "Damn it, Briar . . . what are you doing out of the goddamn house?" His voice was demanding, but his ragged breaths and the ache in his words softened his tone.

"I'm sorry. I'm sorry, I was trying to get you something for your birthday, and—"

He barked out an incredulous laugh before his mouth was moving against mine again. "You stupid girl," he gritted out, but the words were full of affection. "You stupid, stupid girl. I thought I lost you, I can't lose you."

"I know, I'm so—"

"I love you, Briar." The words came out so suddenly, so effortlessly, that I was sure I'd heard them wrong until he repeated them against my lips.

Our next kiss was fire.

I forgot about the people, the officers, the death ... all of it. I could've forgotten about the entire world in that kiss if an officer hadn't come up and interrupted it.

I hadn't heard whatever he'd said, but his hushed words made Lucas tense. His arms tightened around me as a curse slipped from his lips. "Briar," he said so low I barely heard him above the ringing in my ears. "I'm going to put you down and walk you back to the police car."

"Wha—"

"There are people taking videos of the scene on their phones. If you were just a girl who had been sold at an auction, I still wouldn't be able to risk a video of you ending up online. But you and I both know there are a lot of people looking for you." As soon as he felt me stiffen, he placed one more soft kiss against my lips, then let me slide down his body.

He curled his arm around my shoulders, pulling me into the safety of his body and allowing me to bury my head against his chest in an attempt to shield my face from any cameras or phones.

Once he had me in the police car again, his large frame blocking anyone from seeing in, his haunted eyes locked with mine. "When we get home, we need to talk."

I searched his expression, and asked, "Is everything okay?"

"After this, nothing's okay. But we can't talk here. I need to get you home right now."

"But what about the police? Don't I need to tell them what happened?"

"Blackbird," he said in an amused tone. "You're mine. They won't ever need anything from you, and they'll take the driver at his word."

"The driver . . ." I mumbled, and looked around until I caught sight of the driver from out the back window. Looking back at Lucas, I said, "I don't know what you've said to him, but you will not fire or threaten him." I tried to have the same sure tone Lucas always had, but my words came out as more of a plea.

Lucas's eyes were dark when he glanced back to the driver, but his tone was still amused. "Won't I?"

"He saved me, Lucas," I whispered. "I was standing right next to him when it happened. He did what he was supposed to."

After a brief pause, Lucas nodded and blew out a harsh breath as the driver approached us.

"Mr. Holt, I am—"

"Take Briar home for me. Keep her in this car so she won't walk in front of any more cameras. Make two officers check the house before you let her inside. I need to take William's car back to him and discuss some things. I'll be home soon." When Lucas bent close to kiss me, my disappointed look had his eyes narrowing. He straightened out of the car to look at the driver, and his voice dropped low so it wouldn't carry, but there was no mistaking the honesty of his words. "Thank you for saving her."

The driver looked stunned. "Of course, Mr. Holt."

Lucas was gone after giving me a short, passionate kiss, and within five minutes, so were we.

Once we were settled in the house and the police officers were gone, I turned to the driver. "I think I'm just going to go soak in the bath for a little bit."

"Okay, Miss Holt."

I stopped on the way to the stairs. "You know, after today I feel like I should be allowed to know your name."

His head shook. "I am your driver, that's enough."

"Of course it is," I mumbled.

"Miss Holt?" he called out when I was about to turn the corner. "I have never heard him thank anyone in the years I've worked for him."

Why didn't that surprise me? "Well, you've more than earned it."

Chapter 35

DAY 116 WITH BLACKBIRD

Lucas

I stepped out of William's car slowly, my face a carefully composed mask of peace that promised so many things that were far from that. Glancing at his house as I rounded the back of the car, I lifted the trunk and let my eyes roam over things that my mentor always kept in his personal car.

Golf clubs, blankets, water, baseball bat, shotgun . . .

I grabbed the bat and stepped around the car again, letting my gaze trail back to the house as I tested the weight of the bat in my hands. I knew he would be watching, because I knew he would have been waiting for me from the moment he'd had his driver bring him home.

At the last second, I dropped the hold on my façade and smashed both driver side windows, then the windshield. By the time I had rounded the car and was smashing both passenger side windows, the door to the house was thrown open and a handful of his women ran outside.

They yelled for me to stop as I dented the frame and hood of the car, but never made a move toward me. Smart.

I stepped back to look at the car, nodding as my calm slipped back into place.

"Done," I told them, letting the bat fall to the ground as I headed back to the trunk.

I didn't stop walking, only slowed enough to snatch the shotgun out as I headed toward the house. The rest of the women lined the entryway with looks of shock, disappointment, and fear.

"Lucas, stop this at once."

"What is wrong with you, child?"

"What are you doing?"

"Have you gone mad?"

"Don't hurt him."

They all continued their yelling and questions, but I never stopped walking until I was standing outside William's office doors.

"It would be best if you stayed out here," I murmured in a bored tone.

I didn't pay attention to anything else they said, I simply stepped calmly inside.

"That was quite a temper tantrum," William bit out from where he stood at his window, overlooking the driveway.

"How brave of you to let your women try to stop me."

He loosened a long, slow breath through his nose, and *tsked*. "That's my favorite car, Lucas."

"You won't be needing it anymore," I assured him.

He turned slowly and looked me over from where I stood with his own shotgun aimed at his stomach. The expression on his face was one I had seen numerous times since I'd bought Briar. He was disappointed.

I didn't give a shit.

"One day you will thank me. You'll realize it would have turned out badly. You were way beyond the bond the two of you were supposed to have. She would've become a ransom, or a target for a grave."

I didn't respond.

"Put the gun down, Lucas. You're acting like a spoiled child who had his toy taken from him. You're mad now, but it wouldn't compare to the pain later."

"Her name . . . how did you find it?"

The corner of his mouth twitched wryly. "I have my ways."

I nodded absentmindedly. I should've never put it past someone like William to break every rule he enforced without a care for the consequences. Because he knew he was untouchable.

At least, he had been.

"I've let you get away with too much because of who you are," I said darkly. "That ends today. If you ever touch, or try to take Briar from me again, I promise you won't live another day."

Shock flashed through his eyes, but he composed it quickly.

I smirked. "What is it we say? Oh. Right. Because she's still breathing . . ." Dropping the barrel a few inches, I aimed at his right knee and shot.

Like for like.

Screams sounded from outside the room, but they didn't compare to the blood-curdling cry that came from William. His knee was completely blown out, and he just continued yelling over and over again as I walked slowly up to him.

"It's a good thing we have drivers to take us everywhere, isn't it?" I sneered. "Looks like you'll be needing one for the rest of your life." I turned and walked over to open the doors and searched the horrified faces of the women who'd been brave enough to stay outside. "Call the driver, get William to a hospital. He'll probably lose the bottom half of his leg, but he'll be fine," I assured them.

"Lucas, what is wrong with you?" one of them cried when I walked past them. "How could you do this to him?"

How could I not?

He'd tried to take Briar from me.

My hand twitched on the shotgun, and I had the urge to go back into the office and aim the next shot at his chest. But in *this* world, it was like for like. My girl continued to breathe, so the person responsible for her pain would as well.

I gritted my teeth and forced myself to continue moving. "Ask him yourselves."

I walked through the house to the garage and took the keys to another of William's cars.

He wouldn't have use for that one either.

My driver had positioned himself so he could see the front, back, and garage doors, and was standing still as a statue when I walked in from the garage not long after that.

"Briar?"

"Upstairs, Mr. Holt."

I thought about what that could mean. "And how is she?"

He thought for only a second before saying, "I believe she will be fine. She is strong where it matters."

That she is. I nodded down the hall and walked in that direction. "Come with me." Once I was in my office, I went to the large safe in the corner and opened it while I waited for my driver to follow me in. I glanced over my shoulder as I pulled out a thick stack of cash, and smiled at the fear he was trying hard to conceal. "You have a protector, you know."

"Mr. Holt?"

"I don't think Briar would ever forgive me if I fired you—never mind hurt you—and I can't have Briar mad at me," I explained as I shut the safe and twisted the two-part lock.

Relief washed over his face, and he dipped his head in thanks. "She is a great first."

She's a great only.

I handed the cash to him when I reached where he was standing just inside the doorway. "For saving her today." Reaching into my pocket, I grabbed the keys to William's car and placed those on top of the cash. "Think of that as an apology from the man who caused all of this."

The driver's eyes widened as he took it all in. "Thank you, Mr. Holt . . . thank you." He was barely hiding his shock when he asked, "You know who was behind this?"

"Yes, and I have no doubt it was the same man behind the messages to her. The threat's gone . . . at least for now. You can go home for the night; your new car is in the driveway."

He nodded again as he backed away. "Thank you again. Good night, Mr. Holt."

I went looking for my blackbird as soon as the driver was gone and the house was locked up and found her walking out of her bathroom.

She was wearing that damn skirt again that made her look so pure and untouchable.

My fingers twitched with the need to touch her. Taste her. The need to hear her scream my name threatened to consume me.

She stopped walking abruptly when she saw me. "Hi," she said softly, her tone almost reserved.

After the way she'd jumped into my arms earlier, it wasn't what I'd expected. "How are you doing now that some time has passed?"

"Better," she said after a second of hesitation. "How are *you*?" The way she asked was as if she was worried about my answer.

"I'm fine. What's—?" The question died in my throat, my hands clenched into fists inside my pockets.

I should have asked the driver if any of William's women had called.

"Why are you standing like that?" she asked suddenly, prompting me to look down at myself.

"I always stand like this."

Her head was shaking before I finished speaking. "My devil stands like that. *You* stand with your arms folded over your chest. After today . . ." She trailed off and her shoulders sagged. "I'm sorry but I don't think I can handle the devil tonight."

An edgy laugh forced from my chest. "You can't tell something like that from the way I stand, Briar."

She smiled sadly and walked closer, but stopped a couple feet away. "I don't know what happened between the time you left me and came home, but even if you are fighting that side of you, *he* is winning if you are standing that way. And your darkness will only break my heart after that bliss you gave me this afternoon." Briar stepped forward and placed a kiss on my chest but moved away from me before I could wrap my arms around her.

I let her walk past me without trying to stop her, continuing to stare in the place where she had been standing.

It was stupid to think that the way I stood said anything about me, but she had come to fear everything about that side of me, and I wondered if she could recognize it better than even I could.

All I had wanted was to get home to her, but it hadn't been easy to get past the bitterness and hatred that had swirled through me from William's betrayal. Just like it wasn't easy to go from carrying out threats to coming back to my blackbird—that was what the calm was for.

"Let it wash over and through you until there is nothing left," William had always said about that calm.

Like I'd done before I'd arrived home.

I would never trust William again, but the hatred wasn't pounding through my veins anymore. The adrenaline from smashing his car into a shattered and dented mess had left as though it had never been there, and the thrill of vengeance had long gone. Now there was nothing.

And now Briar didn't want me near her.

But I needed her. I needed her in my arms. I needed her body pressed against mine.

I was wrong. There was something. My blackbird was there, as she always was, trying to pull me from something I couldn't see.

I turned and left the room and eventually found her in the kitchen on the main level of the house, looking in the pantry.

Her body tensed and she stopped breathing when I stepped up behind her, but her skin covered in goosebumps when I wrapped an arm around her waist to pull her close.

Lifting her right hand, I passed my lips across her wrist and said, "Darkness can only ever remain that way without light, Blackbird."

"And what happens when darkness consumes the light?" she asked as she continued to stare straight ahead.

I tilted her head back so she was looking up at me and shook my head. "That will never happen."

"That side of you is darkness incarnate," she whispered.

"Then what does that say about how bright you are when you look at how much you've changed me? I may have . . . *dimmed* you, but you still have the ability to change the way I look at life."

"Just dimmed?" she asked somberly.

"Dimmed," I confirmed. "You can't attempt to touch me with your light and not expect me to darken your soul. I'll always try to consume your light just as you'll always try to consume my dark. It's who we are, but it won't *change* who we are. It's those pieces of colliding that make us incredible."

Briar twisted in my arms and pressed her head against my chest, her arms wrapped tightly around my waist. "When I couldn't get away from that man, all I could think about was that I would never see you again," she admitted softly. "I fought so hard to get away from him, Lucas, but that thought—" Her breathing hitched, and she waited a second before she spoke again. "It was crippling."

I gripped her closer and pressed my mouth to the top of her head. "I know, Blackbird . . . I know. I've never had fear devour me like that. I knew someone was coming after you, and I couldn't get ahold of the driver. Those seconds before the driver called me back were torture. But when he called . . . the way he apologized made me think they had succeeded. It felt like someone had torn my life from my body."

Briar's fingers brushed against my jaw and down my neck slowly, like she was proving to us both that she was still there.

"I meant what I said this afternoon."

Her fingers stilled on my chest, her eyes widening as they locked with mine.

"I love you, Briar."

"I love *you*," she whispered back as her eyes misted, her words sounding like a promise.

No, you don't. And soon you'll see why.

But I was selfish enough to take those last minutes with her when she thought that she did—when I thought that she *could*.

I pulled her back to the large island in the middle of the kitchen, caught her mouth in a teasing kiss as I lifted her onto it, and pulled her hips to the edge of the granite countertop. Lifting her shirt from her body, I let it fall to the floor as I tried to savor every moment, every look, and every touch.

I claimed her mouth again and swallowed her moan as she pulled me closer to wrap her legs around my hips. She loosened my tie and pulled it over my head slowly, but as the kiss heated, her hands started moving faster. My belt was off within seconds, and her fingers worked quickly through the buttons on my shirt as I pulled it out of my pants.

Her hand paused where it was pushing my pants and boxer briefs down, and a needy moan sounded in her throat when I trailed my hand up the inside of her thighs, pulled the lace aside, and slid a finger inside her. Her toes curled against my hips and her breath came out in a shuddering moan when I added a second. I pulled back to look at her, completely captivated as her eyes fluttered shut and she arched back.

"This skirt . . ."

"I know," she breathed, and her mouth twitched up into the faintest of smiles. "Happy birthday."

"Lean back," I ordered and finished stepping out of my clothes as she did. Grabbing her thighs, I pulled her away from the island until only her back was touching the granite. "Hands under you."

Briar's eyes flashed and her cheeks filled with heat.

Once her fingers were wrapped around the edge of the counter, I placed her thighs on my shoulders and growled, "Don't let go."

Chapter 36

HAUNTED

Briar

We were sitting on the floor of the kitchen sometime later picking at the cake I had made for him, mostly dressed. Lucas was in his slacks, and I had managed to find my skirt that had come off at some point during the transition from the island to the hallway wall since we hadn't been able to make it to his room. By the time I had finished putting it on, he had handed me his button-down shirt. Everything else remained scattered around the floor, and the sight made me smile as I stabbed a small forkful of cake. Lucas hadn't bothered to cut a piece or get a plate. He'd just grabbed a fork for us to share and had brought the entire thing down here with us.

He pulled me closer into his body, and I curled against his chest as I handed the fork back.

He groaned in appreciation around the bite, as he had the others. "This is perfect, thank you."

"Happy birthday. I'm sorry it was horrible and I didn't get you anything."

He huffed through his nose and set the fork down. Pressing his knuckles under my chin to lift my head, he studied me intently for long seconds before saying, "You have."

I rolled my eyes.

"Blackbird, you've given me more than I deserve, and I'll be thankful every day for you."

My chest warmed, and though I tried to hold it back, my lips kept curving up into a smile.

But the look that suddenly filled his eyes didn't match his words or the warmth that had filled me, and was now quickly receding from me.

"I told you this afternoon that I needed to talk to you when we got home." He swallowed thickly, and something like fear flashed across the devil's face. "Briar . . . it's time . . . it's time we talked."

I nodded hesitantly. "Okay," I said slowly, drawing the word out.

He gently pushed me away until I was sitting on the floor a foot away from him, and no matter how much my body begged me to reach for him again, I worried that the distance he'd placed between us wouldn't be enough.

"Lucas, you're scaring me."

His head tilted, and a small laugh of frustration forced from his lungs. "I want to tell you that you shouldn't be scared, because of everything I've done to you, this will only be talking. But out of all the conversations we've had, this is the one I was sure I would never have with you, and it's the one I'm positive will make you run back to Georgia."

I pulled my knees up to my chest and wrapped my arms tightly around them but didn't speak again. Just waited.

"You have to understand that telling you any of this isn't allowed, and I don't mean for *this life*. This is so much more dangerous than breaking rules with you, Briar. But after today, I can't continue to let our life go on without you knowing."

"Lucas, I've told you nothing will make me run. Just tell me," I begged through clenched teeth and fisted my hands in a vain attempt to hide my shaking.

His head shook sadly. "That was before. If you need me to stop, say it. If you need a break, tell me. If you need to leave . . . know that

I love you, but I won't chase you," he choked out, and dropped his gaze to the floor.

I waited as an eternity passed in silence, my heart racing as those fated words played in my head again and again.

"I won't chase you."

When Lucas looked up at me again, my faint gasp at the haunted look on his face tore through the silence in the kitchen.

"My name isn't Lucas Holt. I will tell you everything you want to know, answer every question you have, as long as the answer isn't something that will hurt you, but I can't tell you my real name. It's safer if you don't know it, because I *have* to remain Lucas Holt. I can't be anyone else right now."

I had already gone completely still. Confusion and denial were swirling so deeply inside me, mixing with the intense ache in my chest.

Not Lucas Holt. Not Lucas Holt.

When he'd first spoken, I'd wondered if all the men in his world changed their names in a way to protect themselves, but that thought had abruptly died when he continued.

"I've given you glimpses and hints at what my life was like up until just four years ago," he went on, "because I knew I was falling in love with you, and I wanted you to know me, to try to understand *who* you were falling in love with instead of this illusion I've created—but the real me shouldn't be allowed to even have this chance with you." He ran a hand roughly through his hair, and a muscle ticked in his jaw.

When he spoke again, everything was rushed and said so softly it was almost too hard to keep up with him. "I told you I had to fight to get into this world . . . but that's only a small part of it. For almost six months, I was repeatedly put in situations so William and I would run into each other when he was dealing with the darker side of this world. All for the slim chance that he would see something in me that could be of use in his business. But every single one of those meetings was planned and monitored by the FBI. They had tracked multiple shipments of drugs going from the mob to William and thought he was the head of a drug ring in southern Texas. But that's *all* they thought he was involved in. They needed me to get close to him, gain his trust, and learn everything I could about him so we could take him down. But I knew I would have to do things I would hate myself for just to prove to William that I would be useful for him. So I did. And I got in close with him—too close.

"No one had expected what I found. None of us had even imagined it went so far beyond drugs—that the drugs were the least of the worries. And by that point, William had already begun mentoring me, had already begun testing and training me to see if I could become *this*. I've been forced to continue with the cover and go deeper and deeper so that one day the FBI and other non-government agencies can take down this entire ring. What you now know as *my* world."

I wasn't breathing or blinking, I wasn't sure I was even processing what he'd told me. This was . . . well, this wasn't real. I must have fallen asleep after coming home from the disaster in the city.

But as minutes came and went, my lungs started aching from lack of oxygen, letting me know this was in fact real.

The faintest flicker of relief sparked in my chest—knowing he wasn't really this man who'd bought my hatred . . . wasn't a man who chose to be in this life—but that relief died as fast as it had formed. Tiny cracks raced through my heart, spreading out like a spider web as memories from my first weeks with Lucas flashed through my mind. Tears pricked at my eyes and betrayal burned deep.

"Why didn't you tell—how could you—you *hurt* me! You let William touch me."

"I never *let* him touch you," he snarled, his voice dark.

"You were going to rape me. Why didn't you tell me from the beginning? Why didn't—"

"Because I don't know how long I have to be in this fucked-up life, Briar. I am undercover; this *has* to be my life. I *have* to play my part.

Until you, I'd done my job flawlessly. Since you, I have *failed* every goddamn step because I couldn't stand the thought of hurting you. But if William or any of the other men suspected anything, it would ruin *everything.*"

"You should have told me," I cried out.

"Do you think I haven't wanted to? Do you think I wanted to do any of that to you?" He was breathing roughly, and his eyes were wild.

I didn't know what to think.

This was destroying him . . . I could see that—I wanted to *believe* that. But it had been a lie. Every part of the last four months with him had been. He'd been playing me from the beginning—*using* me. Once again, I'd been a pawn to someone else's gain. And it hurt. It hurt so much.

"When I was approached by the FBI four years ago, they told me they needed help busting a drug lord. Easy. I never wanted to be part of that world again because I had just spent years trying to escape it, but fucking *easy.* And then I was thrown into this. I was told I had no choice but to keep going deeper and deeper, and then I bought you . . . and no matter how much it killed me, I knew I had to do what William had trained me to. Even though it's against the rules, my biggest fear was that at any moment, William would show up unannounced. I knew if that happened I had to be prepared; I knew my life and my house had to be convincing, including my *bond* with you.

"And then that morning happened, and I realized what he was doing, how he'd tricked me into leaving you alone so he could get to you. I fucking panicked and nearly ruined everything with the way I reacted when I found him in that room with you because you—" He let loose a harsh breath, his chest rising and falling quickly as he gripped his hair. "Because you'd already buried yourself so deeply under my skin, and I didn't know how to do my job anymore. A job that I'd more or less been doing my entire life," he whispered, his voice dripping with exhaustion.

My head was shaking absentmindedly. Whether to try to block out and deny what he was saying, or because I couldn't understand, I didn't know.

"I don't understand," I said numbly. I didn't recognize my voice, and felt so detached from it. "How was it a job you'd been doing your entire life if you said it had just been a few years, and what did you mean that it was a world you never wanted to be a part of again?"

He grimaced then glanced at me for only a second before looking down again—his hand immediately trailing over the tattoo on his left forearm. "I'm not a good guy, Briar. I'm not a cop, or detective, or someone who saves women and children from this kind of stuff. But because I'm none of those things, that's why I was able to slip in with William." He stretched out his legs in front of him and blew out a deep breath before continuing. "They'd been trying for years to get someone in, and no one had ever been able to. I . . . I was supposed to go into witness protection but was stopped before I was transferred. They came to me with the situation and why they thought I might work, and I agreed to try."

When he didn't continue, I asked, "But *why* did you work, Luca—or . . . what's your name?"

"I can't tell you," he mumbled. When he spoke again, there was no emotion in his voice. "I'd been in a gang most of my life, and after years of trying, I had finally escaped. That was when the FBI came to me. I felt like I couldn't say no to helping them because I was getting a chance at a new life when I should have been rotting away in a cell or in the ground. Half of my crew made and sold drugs. *That's* why they thought I would work."

His mouth curled into a wry smile, and he gestured to the large tattoo that twisted up his left forearm. "That's why my tattoos don't fit with this life, as you said, because they're from a different life. This one covers the symbol of that gang I was in. And my scars? That's where they're all from. I'd been forced into the gang, and I'd been forced to do all the dirty work for my leader for *years*. *I* was the one who sent messages to people or other crews if they messed with us. *I* was the one they were afraid of showing up. *I* was the one who had to carry out the hits. If I'd refused to kill someone, my leader would've killed me. That's just how it was. But in our crew, we did drugs and passed around women, even if the women didn't necessarily want to be there. Again, something that *had* to be done if we wanted to stay in the crew—stay *alive*." When a shuddering breath ripped from my lungs, he said, "Before you ask . . . I'm clean. I've been tested numerous times, and I haven't had to use in almost five years."

My mouth slowly fell open as another wave of denial crashed over me.

Everything he was saying—the man he was explaining—couldn't be *real*.

He finally looked up and nodded when he saw the horror on my face.

"They needed someone to take down William—not realizing the extent of what he was involved in—and found a guy who had been perfectly groomed for this world. I've been trying to escape it for just as long." He smiled, but there was no amusement behind it. "Guys like me don't get second chances, Briar, and I've gotten third and fourth and fifth chances. But guys like me also don't fall in love." He dipped his head toward me, and said, "It wasn't that I thought I couldn't love anyone, it was that I didn't deserve to, and because I didn't think I could handle letting myself. Because I knew one day I would break your heart when I was forced to buy the second girl, or it would come down to this, and you would hate me. And because I refused to go through the pain of losing the girl again."

Through my confusion and horror and heart ache as he slowly, *slowly* broke it, my chest seized as something new gripped at my heart and refused to let go. It was as if the man in front of me was holding my heart in his hands, shattering it to find and tear out the love and happiness he had given me. Because I was positive I hadn't heard him wrong, and after the high of finding out that my devil loved me, the low of knowing he had loved someone else was a long fall.

"W-what?"

"I'd been charged with taking a girl hostage. I wanted no part in it, I'd never wanted a part in any of that life, and I swore to protect her because I'd fallen in love with her. Only problem was, we were holding her hostage because her *fiancé* was an undercover detective who had infiltrated our crew years before. She only ever wanted him and went back to him when we got her out. But she made sure her fiancé and his partner got me into witness protection because of what I'd done to the remaining members of my crew to get her out—that shootout with my brothers. After her, I never wanted to put myself in the position where I could lose the girl again. Then I ended up here, undercover, in another place and life I didn't want to be with a girl I want more than my next breath. And she's engaged, and I'm not supposed to want her." One of his eyebrows ticked up. "Ironic, isn't it?"

This wasn't ironic; it was a morbid joke.

It had to be.

But as I pushed myself back until I was pressed against the cabinets and watched as acknowledgment mixed with a pain so great on his face it made the ache in my own chest magnify, I knew it wasn't.

"As I've said, Blackbird. You do not love *me*." Each word was laced with pain and seemed to take all of his strength.

I wanted to deny it, but I didn't know how to. I didn't know who was sitting in front of me anymore. He'd told me—he'd tried to warn me, but I couldn't take the stories he'd told me when I'd thought of him as Lucas and connect them to what I'd just heard.

Everything I knew now felt so heavy and hard to handle.

And it was painful . . . *so* painful knowing I'd been sleeping with a man I didn't know at all. That I'd fallen in love with a façade. And he'd allowed it.

"How many people have you killed?"

His eyes darkened, and his right hand once again moved to the large tattoo on his forearm while his head moved in the faintest of shakes. "Enough that I refuse to tell you."

"One would be more than enough, but you said you would answer my questions," I said tightly as I wrapped my arms around my waist, trying unsuccessfully to calm my churning stomach.

Nearly a minute passed without the devil responding, and I wondered if he was counting or avoiding answering when he suddenly said, "I remember every single person, and I'm haunted by their faces every day. I won't haunt you with a number."

I wanted to tell him that I might have preferred a number over the answer he'd given me—because his answer left a chill deep in my bones and my stomach rolling with unease as terrifying images and thoughts filled my mind.

I watched as he trailed his fingers over his arm and wondered about the other person who haunted him. "Do you still love her?"

His hand stopped, and his unnerved gaze met mine. "No, but I still care about her. I always will. Of anything, you have to understand that."

I did.

Images of Kyle assaulted me. Flashes of a disastrous morning burned behind my eyelids.

A fleeting moment of bliss ruined by agonized cries and pleas and one weighted question . . .

"Do you still love him?"

"Yes."

A devastating day filled with handwritten notes and misunderstanding. A night mended by the most beautiful connection—and the first time I'd told Lucas I loved him.

And now even *that* memory felt tainted.

My throat tightened as every emotion overwhelmed me and threatened to suffocate me. My vision blurred, and I hated how weak and pathetic I sounded when I asked, "Did you ever love me?"

Pain tore across his face, and I watched as he struggled to replace it with that infuriating, cold indifference. "If you have to ask, then you won't hear my answer."

He was right. It didn't matter what he said then. I already felt so shattered. If he'd said he hadn't loved me, my heart couldn't break any more than it already had. If he told me that he had—that he did—I doubted I would believe him.

I had looked past the man the devil was supposed to be and had fallen in love with him. I had looked past his cruelties to his kindness and love and had thought I'd shown him he could have more than *this* life. I'd looked his darkness head-on and embraced it.

The darkness of the man before me was all new. Something *he'd* wrestled with but *I* hadn't been prepared for. Something I hadn't been forgiving and fighting against all these months. And despite how much I wanted to believe that the Lucas I had fallen in love with was really the man before me, I didn't know how to. I wasn't sure I could.

I couldn't differentiate between the lies to find the truth.

"I need . . . I'm sorry, but I just need time," I whispered, then staggered to standing.

Without seeing him or the kitchen that just an hour before had held our passion and our fabricated bliss, I walked blindly up the stairs and to my room, and had barely made it into the shower—clothes and all—before my sobs broke free.

Chapter 37

DAY 119 WITH BRIAR

Lucas

Briar hadn't come back downstairs that night, or the next, or the next . . . And despite my panic and my restlessness and my overwhelming need to beg her to understand, I hadn't gone searching for her.

I'd told her I wouldn't chase her.

I'd been so sure she would be gone as soon as she knew the truth, and even though she'd walked away from me, she was still inside the house and had only said she'd needed time.

I wanted to give her my life . . . *time* seemed like nothing in comparison.

But as that time had stretched on longer and longer without any word from her, or a song floating from the top floor of the house, my panic had turned into regret and frustration.

I refused to leave the house and hadn't slept for more than an hour or two each of the last three nights. I tried telling myself I was stressed about William, and having told Briar about who I really was—but I didn't believe my own lies.

I was terrified that if I left, or allowed myself to sleep, that would be when I lost her.

I glanced up from the kitchen table when my driver entered the house from the garage and eyed the bag hanging from his hand for a second before a miserable-sounding laugh forced from my chest.

"I'm sorry, Mr. Holt, but with you not wanting to leave the house, I thought it would be best if I chose and shipped the package this month."

I stood and accepted the coffee from his other hand, and wordlessly walked into my office to grab a blank card and a pre-addressed bubble mailer. When I walked back into the kitchen, my driver was standing with terror in his eyes, as if he'd made a colossal mistake by choosing for me.

Knowing the look my blackbird would have given me if she were there, I held back an eye roll and forced myself not to growl when I said, "Thank you for doing this."

Like he had just days before, my driver looked like my thanks had floored him as much as if I'd moved a mountain. It didn't matter that the man worked for me or that I trusted him with Briar's life.

I didn't become *Lucas Holt* by thanking men, and I wouldn't be able to hold on to the image I needed to if I continued to.

"O-of course, Mr. Holt." His gaze darted nervously around the room before he asked, "Do you want me to pick up breakfast?"

I held up the coffee he'd brought, let my eyes dart over to him then back to the table. "No." I took a long sip of the black coffee, and pretended that I could taste it, feel the heat as it slid down my throat.

But there was nothing other than the last shred of my sanity I was clinging to.

I glanced at the bottle of nail polish my driver had picked up, then to the blank card I was trying to write on.

Two words. Just two words I'd written over and over again, every month, for years. And now I didn't know how to, because all I wanted to say was I'd found her—that girl she'd said I would find—but I'd destroyed everything by trying to keep her . . . because of who I was. But I knew I couldn't risk that, not right now.

I'm fine.

I stared at my written words, dropped the pen, and grabbed for my coffee again. I had the cup halfway to my mouth when she entered the kitchen, and everything inside of me faltered.

"Briar." Her name was as soft as a breath and sounded like a prayer coming from me.

A sad smile pulled at her lips for a fraction of a second before falling, and then confusion took over that beautiful face when she looked at the table.

"I'll take care of this, Mr. Holt," the driver murmured and hurried to collect everything off the table before disappearing.

I didn't watch him go. I couldn't stop staring at the girl in front of me as she watched me.

I wanted to pull her into my arms. I wanted to beg her to tell me what she'd thought about and decided over the weekend. I wanted to tell her I understood and didn't blame her, because I'd been preparing for this day from the first moment I'd watched her sing. But I didn't move. I didn't speak.

After a minute of heavy silence, her gaze dipped back to the table that was bare except for my coffee. "What was that?"

I leaned back in my chair and folded my arms over my chest, trying to hide my shaking as I forced myself to stay there—forced myself not to say that after two and a half days of silence, this wasn't what I wanted to talk about with her. "Nail polish and a note." As if she hadn't already seen it.

"Right. What for?"

"For her." I waited for her to understand—waited until those eyes flashed to me again and hated the hurt and uncertainty that filled them. "I send both every month so she has a way of knowing I'm still okay. She knew a lot of people wanted me dead, and prison can't stop them from making it happen—which is why I was supposed to go into witness protection. Once a year I send her a journal because she always wrote in one. That's why I put one in your room." One corner of my mouth quirked up. "Obviously wasn't one of my better decisions."

Another hint of a smile, this one at least held some amusement behind it. She took the few remaining steps toward the small, square table and pulled out the chair on my left. Once she was sitting in it, she rested her elbow on the table and her head in her hand, letting her eyes slowly take in every part of me she could see.

I thanked God for another chance to have this girl so close to me. I knew I would never forget her—would never forget this moment or her pure, composed façade.

I hadn't wanted to fall in love again after what had happened all those years ago, hadn't wanted to feel that pain. Watching Briar, I knew if she walked out of my life, it wouldn't be a matter of wanting to avoid the pain again . . .

There wasn't a possibility of loving anyone else after having loved the girl who tried to consume my darkness with her light.

Once she finished her inspection and those eyes were locked with mine, she asked, "What do I call you?"

"Lucas. Devil. Whatever you want."

She hesitated for only a second before altering the question. "What do you *want* me to call you?"

A name tore through my mind, screaming and thrashing, trying to claw its way out. I shoved it down with every other memory I kept buried. "I *need* you to call me Lucas."

"Until when?"

"I don't have an answer for that," I said honestly. "I don't know how long I'm here—how long I'm in this life. I'd already been in it for three and a half years before the auction."

"And then what happens when it's over? When your job as Lucas Holt is done. What happens to us?"

My heart clenched painfully, then steadily beat faster and faster, each thump more uneven than the last, until it felt like my chest wouldn't be able to contain it anymore. *What happens to us?* I wanted to reach inside and tear my heart out just to be done with the pain. "Then you go home. Then, hopefully, all the women go home . . . or somewhere where they can get help."

"You want me to go back to Atlanta?" Her face gave away nothing, and despite struggling so hard to find the required calm, I knew mine gave away everything.

"I want you to be where you need to be. I want you to be wherever *home* is."

She seemed to nod distractedly for a few seconds and continued to, even as the first few words left her lips. "I don't know why it seemed so much easier to accept the story of *Lucas*, and to forgive it, but it did. Maybe because I kept seeing you fight the dark and believed, deep down, you never wanted to be this man—be the man who bought stolen women and terrified them the way you did me. Maybe because I believed something about *me* made you want to not be that man. Only to find out that you had never been that man at all, but someone else entirely. Someone just as awful, just as terrifying . . . someone people turned to in an attempt to tear down this horror-filled world, because you had already lived in a similar darkness. Breathed it in and let it fill your veins until you became darkness, and darkness became you."

I wanted to deny everything she was saying, tell her that I wasn't the man she was describing—but I was. I always had been. If Briar knew half the things I'd done in an attempt to keep myself alive, she wouldn't be sitting at this table with me.

She was too pure. Too unsullied. Too . . . light.

Wives and girlfriends of the men I'd killed had called me a monster as I'd walked from their homes.

Even though my brothers had only ever called me by name, other crews had called me *Reaper* since death followed in my wake.

The name *Devil* had summed up my entire life all too well . . . summed up everything about myself I'd hated and hadn't been able to escape. But being *Briar's* devil? It had never felt like something I'd wanted to escape but rather something I'd wanted to cling to. Be redeemed by.

"I told you your darkness scared me," she said, her tone and expression thoughtful. "But for the first time in so, so long, I was afraid of *you*. I was terrified just being near you. I felt sick knowing I'd given my heart and body to someone who *wasn't* the man I'd thought I'd fallen in love with. I'd given my heart to a man who could so easily slip into the role you've been playing, because you've done worse."

My jaw was clenched so tightly it felt like it would break, and my blackbird . . . she studied me like she wasn't about to annihilate me in a way nothing in my life had ever been able to.

"And then last night I realized I'd fallen in love with a man who *should've* been able to slip into that role like it was second nature . . . and couldn't." Briar stood slowly from her chair and took a step toward me, and then another—tears filling those beautiful, beautiful eyes. "And that thought just kept turning over and over in my mind, and I couldn't figure out *why* a man like you hadn't wanted to hurt me. Or why it had clearly *killed* you to be the devil in those first weeks." Tears were now slowly slipping down her cheeks as she slid between the table and me and crawled onto my lap.

My heart thundered as I gripped her waist, pulling her closer and trying to memorize the feel of her and praying this wasn't about to be goodbye.

"And then I understood," she whispered, her voice thick with emotion. "I saw the role you tried to play, and I watched as you failed, and from that moment on you never truly hid who you are from me. There are so many things I still don't know about you—including your name—and who knows if I'll ever know it all, but there are five things I do know with absolute certainty . . ."

She placed her hands on either side of my head, her fingers gripping at my hair as she pressed her lips to my forehead. "One. You've had so much darkness in your life that you've *become* it." Her lips swept across my forehead, and pressed gently to my temple. "Two. You hate it and what's in your mind from it." She lifted one of my hands from her waist, and passed her mouth across my knuckles. "Three. You fight it and fight to keep others from it." Keeping my hand in hers, she interlaced our fingers and kissed the tips of them before pressing them against my chest. "Four. You are *good*—"

"Briar, no," I said softly, cutting her off. "Didn't you hear anything I told you?"

She slipped her hand out from underneath mine and placed the tips of her fingers over my lips. "Every word," she said through her tears. "I've seen your heart, Devil, and I know who you are. And you *are* good, even if you can't see that about yourself."

"Oh, Blackbird." I pulled her hand up higher to kiss her wrist and felt the shiver that went through her body like it was my own.

"Five," she murmured as she leaned forward and paused with her mouth so close to mine that they brushed against each other with each word. "I love every part of yo—"

I captured her mouth with my own, swallowing her surprised whimper, then backed off enough so the kiss was nothing more than a tease until she opened to me. And then I took and took from the girl in my arms and tried to show her with every brush of my lips and sweep of my tongue how she had come to mean everything to me.

"I love you," I whispered against her mouth.

"You are my home," she said, stopping my heart with her confession. "If I ever find myself back in Atlanta, it will be to say goodbye to Kyle and those waiting for me."

Then she was pressing her mouth to mine again and trying to get her body closer just as someone began banging on the door, and didn't stop.

It took three seconds for my mind to register that the ominous knocking was similar to a beating heart, and another half a second for my body to lock up and my blood to run cold.

"Ignore it," Briar pled, but I was already moving.

"Get in the closet," I demanded in a low, urgent tone as I gently pushed her off and reached under the kitchen table. "Lock the door and call the driver. Tell him someone came to the front door with a heartbeat."

"Wait, what?"

As soon as I had the gun freed from the holster secured under the table, I stood up and cupped Briar's neck with my free hand.

"Oh my God, Lucas! What—?"

I slammed my mouth down onto hers to quiet her, then said, "That's not just someone at the door, Briar, it's a warning and a goddamn trap. And I can't go out there if I'm worried about you." When it looked like she was about to argue, I begged, "*Please.*" I took one of her hands, placed the gun in it, and held her stare. "If it isn't me or the driver, don't wait . . . just shoot. Now go."

I only waited long enough to make sure she was running toward my bedroom before I took off for the backyard. I rounded the house and slipped silently through the side gate, and only slowed as I neared the front of the house.

The adrenaline and the rage and the fear melted away, and I found my calm was all too easy to reclaim, knowing someone had come for Briar.

And I knew it was *her* they had come for.

It was a Monday. I was supposed to be at work. Briar wouldn't have understood the warning in the knock.

I stuck to the side of the house as I searched the empty driveway and the street. A bubble of rage started to form, but I was quick to push it away when I saw the empty car sitting in front of my house.

I stayed silent as I moved closer and closer to the front door. My eyes swept along the street for any other cars or people who might be outside—people who might be watching—but it was quiet, save for the man waiting expectantly at my door with a gun in his hand.

Suppressor screwed on. Finger already on the trigger.

Whoever gave this trigger-happy bastard a gun needed a bullet with their name on it . . . right after I thanked them for making this so easy for me.

I stepped up behind the man without him ever realizing I was there, and in a deadly calm tone, asked, "Planning your funeral?"

Chapter 38

DAY 119 WITH BLACKBIRD

Lucas

Before the man could turn, I slammed one hand over his mouth and, with the other, grabbed his hand holding the gun and squeezed.

He bucked and roared against my hand when the bullet lodged in his foot, but I held tight to him as I pried the gun from his hand.

"That's why you never leave your finger on the trigger," I said in the same tone as he continued screaming against my hand. "Now I'm going to give you three seconds to stop yelling, or I'll do it again. Three, two . . ." I let another beat pass as a few cries left him before he controlled it enough so they were only whimpers. "If you try to run, I'll aim for your head."

I released him so suddenly that he rocked backward, crying out in pain when he tried to balance himself with both feet.

"Do you really want to see if I was just making empty threats?" I asked as I glanced behind us for anything and anyone that shouldn't be there, then gripped his arm. "Walk."

He hissed and cried out in pain with every step, but was smart enough not to try to run or yell as we walked to the garage. I entered the code to open the door, spared one last look at the street and the houses around mine, then shoved him inside.

"Who?" I demanded to the pathetic man next to me once we were halfway into the garage, but he only kept crying. "Who?" I asked again, my voice dropping lower, taking on a more lethal edge.

I heard a car racing up the street not long before my driver flew onto the driveway, but I only spared him a glimpse as he ran from the car into the garage. I focused on the man in front of me again. "I asked you a question, and it wasn't rhetorical."

I slammed my foot down on his injured one. As soon as the pain registered and he screamed, I lifted my foot and shoved it into his knee as hard as I could.

The roar that tore through the garage would've had my neighbors calling the cops if my driver hadn't already shut the door. My house was as soundproofed as they came.

The men in this world ensured their houses were. It was a necessity for those first weeks after buying a woman since they tended to scream and beg for someone to save them.

This man should've thought of that.

Should've known that even if I hadn't been here, I would've brought him back and made him scream, and no one would've heard him or come to save him.

I watched where he lay, crumpled on the ground and yelling as he tried to grab at his unnaturally bent leg, and forced myself to hold on to that calm. I had to feel nothing.

He'd come for Briar.

"Last time. Who?"

"W-wuh—" He broke off on another sharp cry and gritted his teeth against the pain for a few seconds before he bit out, "William."

A rage unlike anything I'd ever felt—even last week's horror when William had tried to have my blackbird taken from me—built in my chest until it felt like that was all I was, and all I would ever be.

He isn't going to stop, I realized.

And knowing William's mind . . . *Fuck*.

William's threats came in twos. Always. This man wouldn't be the only one here.

I looked over at my enraged driver, and horror coated my voice as her name left me. "Briar."

The man on the floor started laughing manically between his hisses of pain, and I ran for the house, barking at my driver to stay with him.

I vaguely registered someone telling Briar it was over as I tore down the hallway to my bedroom. Vaguely registered that he sounded like me as he coaxed her to open the door.

But my rage and my fear were choking me, and making it hard to focus on anything other than Briar, Briar, Briar . . .

"That's my girl," I heard the man say, and my heart sank, my feet stumbled, as I thought about Briar—my *world*—about to face whatever William had sent for her.

I ran into the bedroom in time to see the man take a step away from the closet . . .

In time to see him raise a gun identical to the one in my hand at its door that was opening . . .

In time for him to repeat, "That's my—"

"Briar, *stop*!" I yelled.

The man began turning toward me, but I fired before he could react, adding his face to all the others that haunted me as his body fell limply to the floor.

I slid my gaze up to see Briar standing just out of the doorway of the closet with one shaking hand covering her mouth, another gripping the doorjamb, supporting her. The gun I'd given her lay at her feet, as if she'd dropped it.

"I didn't realize . . ." I began as I looked back at the man, my borrowed gun still aimed at him. "I didn't know who had sent the other man. I'd thought it was just him. When he said who—" I broke off and shook my head, trying to shake off the lingering fear. "I knew there would be another." I glanced back at Briar, took in her trembling body, and said, "Stop looking at him, Briar."

She tore her eyes from the man lying on my bedroom floor and gave quick jerks of her head. "I don't—I don't und—why does this keep happening? *What* is happening? Why are they coming for me?" she asked, each question louder than the previous as panic gripped her.

"I'll explain once we leave this room. For now, close your eyes and try not to listen," I said gently.

"W-what?"

"Blackbird," I said in a soothing voice, even though I felt anything but, "trust me. Close your eyes and try not to listen." As soon as her hands were over her ears and her eyes were squeezed shut, I walked up to the man and shot him one more time just to be sure.

Even with the suppressor, Briar still flinched.

I grabbed the gun from his lifeless hand and tucked it between my arm and ribs with the barrel facing behind me as I took slow steps toward my blackbird.

"Lesson one," I said softly as I bent to pick up the gun she'd dropped and slid it into the waistband of my pants. "Never keep your finger on the trigger. Lesson two, if someone is trying to kill you, kill them first. Then shoot them one more time to be sure. I've seen a lot of people die because they *didn't* make sure. Lesson three, stop looking at the man on the floor, Blackbird."

Her head shook slowly at first and then faster and harder until a sharp sob burst from her chest. "Tell me why this keeps happening, Lucas, *please*."

I took her chin between my fingers and tilted her head back so I could brush my mouth over hers, trying to pass a different kind of calm to her. "I'll tell you everything I know, but we have to get the rest of the story from the man in the garage. Walk with me, and keep your eyes off the floor." I released her chin but placed my free hand on the small of her back as I led her out of my bedroom.

As we walked, I told her everything about Friday—from my entire conversation with William, to what I'd done at his house. When she began shaking, I pulled my hand away from her, trying to give her the space she might need after getting a glimpse of how evil her devil really could be.

"William," she said on a breath, but the softness of the word didn't cover the shock or the horror of her tone. She stood with her back pressed to the wall just outside of the garage, her head shaking slowly as everything I'd told her sunk in. "And he sent these men?"

I nodded when she looked up at me for confirmation. "I don't know what they were supposed to do though. William wouldn't try to have you taken again, he would want to send a message to me." I forced down that paralyzing fear that tried to resurface and tried to tell myself that Briar was there, standing in front of me, whole and unharmed. "He's either retaliating because of his leg, or he's trying to do to me what happened to him."

"Which part?"

"The only woman he ever loved was killed because he loved her, and he knows I love you. I'll keep you safe," I added when raw terror filled her eyes.

She only nodded.

"When I go into that garage, I'm going to be someone I never wanted you to see—*all* of this is a part of me I never wanted you to see. If you don't think you can handle it, please don't walk through that door with me."

Briar's body began trembling harder. "Like what you did to William?"

I cocked my head to the side hesitantly. "I had to find out who sent them."

Her full lips parted and a shuddering breath rushed from her when she realized what I was saying—that I'd already done something similar to the man in the garage.

Seconds passed in weighted, pressing silence before she asked, "You'll be Lucas Holt?" When I dipped my head, she continued. "Will you feel anything?"

"In there? No. When it's over . . ." I trailed off but held her stare.

"*Every* one of them haunts me. I would destroy every last man in the world to keep you safe, Briar, but they would all still haunt me."

She closed the distance between us in the small hallway and placed her shaking hands on my cheeks, tilting my head down to hers. "Your soul is beautiful, Devil. Please don't forget that," she whispered, her lips brushing against mine. "I'll stand by you—*you*, whoever you have to be—and I'll wait for my devil to come back to me. Finish this."

I wrapped my arm around her waist and caught her mouth with mine, deepening it for only a moment before saying, "You brave, brave girl." After another pass across her lips, I pulled away, forced that calm to pour over me, and stepped toward the door. In a low, cold tone, I gestured for her to go first. "Blackbird . . ."

The look of shock on the man's face when he saw Briar only lasted for a second before terror took over as he focused on me.

I looked over at the driver and noticed his relief when he saw Briar.

"Look at the driver," I said in that same detached tone to Briar, but I spoke loud enough that the men could hear me. "Look how he's standing. How he's holding his gun."

He was a handful of feet away from the man lying on the floor, feet shoulder-width apart, both hands on his gun . . .

"Finger off the trigger."

"You've mentioned that," she murmured back, making her response sound like a question.

"Because it's important." I let a savage smile pull at my mouth. "Ask the man on the floor how I helped him shoot himself." I ignored Briar's sharp inhale and walked over to the hitman, passing off his partner's gun to my driver as I did. "*Why* did William send you?"

The man's fear-filled stare darted between Briar and me over and over, and I noted that my driver was slowly backing away from me. Smart.

But I knew what his face would look like, what Briar would see when he went to go stand near her: a grown man who was intimidating in his own right, who had saved her, unable to stand near me when I turned into this. And for a second, I almost lost my hold on who I needed to be.

"The body's in my room," I said as I forced myself to remain in control, knowing my driver would be relieved for the distraction.

I heard him try to get Briar to leave, but I knew without having to turn around that my brave blackbird wouldn't go anywhere.

"I thought you would've learned earlier that I don't like repeating myself," I stated darkly and stepped onto the man's destroyed knee with all my weight.

His screams filled the garage immediately, mixing with his stuttering of William's name over and over again. Before I could tell him he was answering the wrong question, he yelled, "S-s-send a m-message. H-he wanted us t-to send a message. That's all."

"Is that so?" False amusement slid through my voice, and without taking my eyes from him, I reached behind me and shot his uninjured foot. When the new screams began, I kept my voice calm, steady, dark. "You think I hadn't figured that out the second you announced yourself?"

The door to the house opened, and my driver came shuffling in with the body of the other man slung over his shoulder.

I waited until he dropped the body next to the man I was still standing on before asking, "What was the message?"

But the man was now shaking so hard I wondered if he would go into shock from the pain before he could answer me.

"Last time," I growled. "What was—?"

"H-he—he h-h-has . . ." He pointed at the other man when talking became too difficult.

I stepped off his knee and bent over the dead man next to him, checking his pockets with my free hand until I found a small, thick envelope. I pulled it out and opened it, and had only read the first cardstock before everything inside me went numb.

This wasn't like for like.

He'd lost his goddamn mind.

I looked at the man on the floor from under my eyelashes, and growled, "Kill her."

He nodded slowly as a sob burst from him, and the front of his pants became wet. "J-j-just do it. *Do it.* K-kill me!"

I bent down to drop the second cardstock on the chest of the dead man, and then placed the first on the quivering man. I stepped back, pulled out my phone, and took a picture of the men and sent the picture to William with the words:

Because she's still breathing, one of them will continue to . . .

William's cards were in plain view, both with bold, swirling letters.

Now you know how it feels. . . .
I hope you enjoyed her. . .

After the message was sent, I squatted so I was near the man still alive, but getting closer and closer to losing consciousness with each passing minute, and let my calm slip just enough so he would never forget me, never forget my next words, and would never think to come after what was mine again.

"Three people have lost their lives because they've tried to take that girl from me, and another will never walk again. The only reason I'm not going to take my time killing you is because she is still breathing. Consider yourself lucky that you can be a message to anyone else who thinks they can tear her away from me." I leaned closer and growled, "I would burn the world to keep her safe."

I stood as I let my calm take over again and walked slowly away from the men.

When I reached my driver, his stare was bouncing from the floor to me, and he was cringing, like he was waiting for something else.

But I'd done enough.

"Get someone over here to dump these men on William's driveway, and someone else to fix the carpet in my room."

He dipped his head in a faint nod and avoided meeting my eyes. "Y-yes, Mr. Holt."

"But don't enter the house until I contact you."

"Yes, Mr. Holt."

I ushered Briar into the house and gave her a look, begging her not to say a word until the door was shut behind us and we were walking up the stairs. "Bla—"

"Why can't he come—?"

"Listen," I said softly but urgently as I lifted my phone and shot off a message I knew would be received immediately. "I told you I was going to keep you safe, and I will. I'll do everything I can so that nothing like this ever comes near you again. And the phone call we're now waiting for can't be heard by anyone—even the driver."

She went still at the top of the stairs. "Is William going to call?" she asked breathlessly, her face pale, and her wide eyes terrified.

My eyes narrowed and lips thinned as I tried to push back my anger. "I have a feeling we won't hear from William for a long time."

"Then who . . ."

I brushed Briar's wild hair back from her face, and continued to cradle her head in my hand in those last seconds before that distinct ringtone went off. My heart was beating so hard I knew she could hear it, knew she could understand the urgency and anticipation in the hard pounding. "My handler at the FBI," I answered. "I'm going to get us out of here."

Chapter 39

RUN TOWARD DEATH

Briar

Lucas dipped his head close, sweeping his mouth along my jaw to whisper in my ear, "Don't say a word." He pulled away then, answering his ringing phone and putting it on speaker. He placed his hand on the small of my back, leading me deeper into the living area of the top floor. "David."

Seconds passed in silence, and Lucas's eyes narrowed, triggering the most incredible change . . .

The wrath in his eyes since the knocking began burned darker until Lucas transformed into someone I'd never seen before.

He wasn't the man our driver feared. He wasn't the man who'd enjoyed torturing the hitman in the garage. This man was truly what nightmares were made of. This was *him*, whoever *he* was, and he was beautiful.

As I studied the fury that swirled with his darkness, I realized I had been right all those months ago. He was an avenging angel, even more lethal because he had fallen . . .

That was who this man was, and he loved me.

"I didn't send that message lightly," Lucas said darkly, his voice rumbling deep within his chest. "Speak."

"What happened?" the man on the phone asked immediately, a tremor of panic woven throughout his words.

"William just sent men to kill Briar because he failed at taking her from me last week."

"What do you mean *failed at taking her*?" the man demanded, his voice rising with each word. "What happened, and why didn't you contact me?"

Lucas didn't answer him, only continued. "I'm done; *we're* done. We're leaving today, and you're providing that."

Silence greeted us for nearly a minute before the man said, "No," in a dull, reserved tone.

Lucas slammed his hand down onto the table the phone was now on, and bent to lean close to the phone as he yelled, "Did you hear me? He tried to take her from me. He sent men to kill her. I *need* to get her out of here, so tell me how we do this."

"*We* don't. *You* can't leave. You will stay there and finish—"

"If I stay, they won't stop until she's dead."

A chill so cold it couldn't be described spread through my body, and I swayed on my feet. The day—the last few days—were catching up with me. My fear was becoming a living, breathing thing as I listened to my devil's voice twist in agony.

His head snapped in my direction, and he quickly pushed away from the table to wrap me up in his strong arms, steadying me as he pulled out a chair and sat in it, keeping me in his lap.

The adrenaline had faded from me, leaving an exhaustion so deep, I couldn't fight it. I let my head fall onto Lucas's shoulder and my body go limp as he held me close—trying to protect me from things I couldn't push from my mind.

"My hands are tied. We can't jeopardize everything, all these years, for one girl."

Lucas went still as stone. After a few seconds, his chest expanded with a deep, shuddering breath. Without moving my head, I looked up to find his jaw clenched and eyes murderous.

"*You* can't," he said calmly, but no less terrifying. "*I* will."

There was a crashing sound that came through the phone before the man yelled, "Two months. We have spent years preparing for this, and we're two months away. You can't ruin this."

I felt Lucas's shock, but his voice didn't give it away. "Two months. It's happening in two months? Didn't you think I should kno—?" He cut off with a hiss, then said through clenched teeth, "The celebration. Were you going to warn me?" More silence. "Were you going to warn me?" he roared, the loud boom of his voice causing me to flinch.

He flexed his arms, tightening them around me for a second before relaxing so he could look down at me. His dark eyes searched mine as one of his hands released me to cradle my face, his thumb making soft, sweeping motions along my cheekbone.

The man on the phone cleared his throat. "It would've been better for you not to know, that way nothing could have been compromised. We worried that if you knew, you would do what you're trying to do now. You would try to get Briar out before we came in—"

"Of course I would," Lucas whispered, and made another sweep.

"—or you would tell her what was happening to prepare her, and we couldn't risk that. We can't risk other people knowing what's happening—especially one of the women. They could ruin everything. *She* could ruin everything."

I opened my mouth to try to assure Lucas that I wouldn't, but the thumb that had been lazily brushing against my cheek rested on my lips in a silent reminder not to speak.

"She won't," Lucas said gently as his eyes searched mine. "She knows the risks, David, but I still need to get her out of here."

"What do you mean, *she knows the risks*?"

"I hadn't been able to continue doing my job with her," he began, and David swore. "That's why William tried to have her taken from me. He knew she meant too much to me and would be used against me. So I made sure William would never forget the day he tried to take her from me, and that night, I told Briar everything. *Everything* except my name."

"Do you realize what you've done?" David yelled, and another crash sounded through the phone.

"For the last four months, I've thought she would be smart enough to leave. But even after finding out all of it, she's still here," he said with an amused grin. "So . . . yeah, I do."

"You haven't just put Briar's life at risk, every woman's life in one of those houses is now threatened. When those men find out who you are—and they *will*—they will take Briar from you. She will be tortured just to ruin you."

Lucas's head snapped up so he was looking at the phone. "You think I don't know that? You think they haven't already tried? Didn't you hear me? They *tried* to take her. They *tried* to come to the house and kill her. Bodies are piling up because William wants to send me a message, and I can't let Briar stay here when there's a chance that someone else will come for her. I need to get her out."

"And what about the other women?" David asked. "Who's going to protect them when the men send their rats to dig deeper, and they finally work out who you are? Because those men will kill their women just to keep them from being able to talk—just to destroy evidence."

Lucas's face fell, and his tanned skin suddenly looked pale.

"Did you not think of any of these things before you told Briar who you are? Before you forgot your job because of the way a girl makes you feel, and declared war on William for—"

"*I* declared war?" Lucas repeated in a dangerously low tone, cutting the man off. "He tried to steal what was mine. In William's world, that *is* a declaration of war. I retaliated exactly as any of the men would've. If it weren't for *their* rules and *your* goddamn need to keep him alive, I would've ripped his heart out of his chest that day he touched Briar. I may not have kept to the rules with Briar, that doesn't mean I've stopped doing my job."

"If you've sent me a distress message, you have. If you have people trying to kill Briar, you have. You have threatened everything when we are so close. We went in looking for William, and now what if he starts backing off because of what you've done? What if that entire ring starts dispersing because of your actions?"

"Stop trying to give me so much credit," Lucas said dryly.

"What if he has you taken out for it?"

Despite everything from the day, from the conversation, Lucas smirked. "He's going to have to get in line."

"This isn't a joking situation; you have possibly ruined hundreds of women's lives."

"You've ruined *mine*," Lucas sneered, all traces of amusement now gone from his face. "We've ruined *hers*. This isn't what I signed up for. None of this was supposed to ever be my life—my reality. I was never supposed to become this. I did all of this for them on *your* orders. I have sacrificed my life, destroyed something good, and torn out my goddamn heart for every one of those women. So don't fucking tell me what *I* have ruined."

Seconds passed without a response, but when David spoke again his voice was placating. "If you get Briar out, those women are as good as dead. If you leave, all of this will have been for nothing."

Lucas looked back down at me then, jaw clenched like he wanted to keep fighting, but he sounded resigned when he said, "If something happens to this girl, I suggest you run . . . and pray I never find you." He reached out and ended the call before David could respond, and then his hand curled around my neck, gentle and soothing. "Tomorrow I'm going to start teaching you how to shoot and start working with you until you're comfortable holding a gun," he said quickly, quietly. "I'm going to teach you how to defend yourself if you're unarmed . . . because I won't have you defenseless if anyone dares to come after you again."

But with each second that passed, and with each promise he made, an invisible weight seemed to press down on him, heavier and heavier until he couldn't continue fighting against it. His head bowed low, pressing against my chest, and the hand gripping my waist tightened—as if he was trying to hold on to me.

An ache so great pierced my chest, seeing this man so vulnerable; it stole my next breath. I wove one hand through his dark hair, placing the other on his shuddering back, and silently struggled as I tried to think of a way to help him.

"If anything happens to you . . ." he trailed off, his voice tight. His body tensed, then began vibrating. "I just keep seeing that closet door opening," he admitted softly. "I was sure I was going to watch him kill you because I hadn't been there to keep you safe."

A dozen responses swirled through my mind. A dozen reassurances were on the tip of my tongue that would have meant nothing to Lucas in that moment.

Because even though he had done more than most men were capable of in order to keep me safe, I knew he would only see everything that happened to me as his fault.

I placed a soft kiss to the top of his head then made slow passes up and down his back as I tried to ease some of his fear and grief the only way I knew how.

Lucas's rough breaths halted with the first melodic words that fell from my lips, and his tense shaking slowed and steadied by the time I started on the first chorus. But he didn't move from his position. His head stayed pressed close to my chest, one hand gripping me tightly while the other cupped my neck like I was fragile.

Our position made me feel safe and cared for, and I felt his love for me pouring from him in waves. But as I sat cocooned in his arms, letting a song flow from me soft as a whisper, I realized I'd never felt more free.

When the last words of the song trailed off into nothing, silence engulfed the room and time passed without measure.

His thumb eventually moved to make lazy circles along my throat, and a few moments later, he straightened his body to look at me. His dark eyes were full of wonder, his voice low and rough when he said, "You're not shaking, Blackbird."

I lifted a shoulder and held his curious stare as his unspoken question lingered in the air.

I'd only ever sang in front of him if I was shaking—if I was afraid . . .

"I wasn't singing for me."

His mouth met mine in a gentle, but searing kiss. And without breaking contact, he stood and walked us into my bedroom and laid me on the bed. His lips moved down my neck and stopped at the base of my throat. His teeth grazed against the soft skin there, followed by a whisper of one last kiss before he curled his body around mine.

A corner of his mouth twitched in amusement when I turned in his arms and reached for him, but he stopped me.

Grabbing my hand in his, he lifted them so he could pass his mouth over my wrist then said, "After everything you've been through the last few days, you need to sleep. Your body is crashing." His eyes darkened with need, and his voice dropped to a rough whisper. "When you wake up I'm going to devour every inch of you and bury myself deep inside you, because I need to taste and feel you to know you're here—you're safe. But for now, sleep."

But I was afraid to. I was afraid of what I would see when I did. I'd been trying to escape the horror of it all, and I knew I wouldn't be able to once I gave in to exhaustion.

The fear of losing the man holding me, the smell of blood and sight of dead people around me, arms that ripped me away and knocking on doors that meant horrible, horrible things. All of it would be too much, and I wouldn't be able to get away from it.

"How did that man know where I was today?" I asked, trying to prolong the inevitable.

His grip on my hand tightened, a rumble sounded low in his chest. "William. He knows my house, and where I'd hide you. When you didn't answer the door . . ." He lifted a shoulder in a jerk of a shrug, that fury from earlier clouding his eyes again.

I tried to wrap my mind around all that had happened and quickly shook my head. "You knew . . . that man started knocking and you immediately knew it was a warning and a trap. How?"

"It was a trap, because if I hadn't been home, you would've gone to the door and answered it," he explained, his tone laced with barely concealed rage. "In the world I grew up in, there was never any warning; we would just go in with guns raised. In this world? It's all about games and threats and sending messages and instilling fear. The men in this world are so confident they want to terrify whoever they're going to torture or kill before they even come into the house. Knocking in the rhythm of a heartbeat is as good as announcing death."

My lips slowly parted, but it wasn't from the shock of what he'd told me. I'd either experienced enough in the last few days or was too tired to be shocked by the audacity of the men in this life. All I felt was wonder and awe as I studied him. "And you ran toward death . . ."

"The Reaper doesn't run toward death, Blackbird. He brings it."

"Reaper? Don't call yourself—"

"I didn't give myself that name," he said in a hollow tone, and I knew in the haunted look he was talking about something from a lifetime ago.

And I hated it. I hated everything that haunted my devil, this man who had continued to destroy his soul to keep himself alive and to help others—to keep me safe.

Threading my fingers through his hair, I kept my eyes locked with his and let my lips twist into a coy smile. "So . . . you're dangerous?"

Chapter 40

PROMISE

Briar

I woke up sometime that night to an empty bed, covered in sweat with tears staining my cheeks. I nearly screamed Lucas's name, but was thankful when my scream came out as nothing more than a hushed song when I heard deep voices talking outside my room.

After using the bathroom to freshen up and changing into a clean set of pajamas, I walked back through my room and slowed as I reached the hall that led to the living area of the top floor. I didn't know if I was supposed to hear the conversation, but I couldn't stop from going toward the voices.

I could hear him, but I needed to see him.

Lucas couldn't lose me—he'd made that clear. However, he didn't seem to grasp that the thought of losing him crippled me too. And after enduring nightmare after nightmare of *him* being the one I'd watched die this afternoon, I needed to feel him.

Both he and the driver looked up when I walked into the large room, and their conversation immediately stopped.

I tried to stifle the relieved sigh that rushed from me, seeing my devil alive instead of lifeless on his bedroom floor, and cleared my throat. "Um, I can—"

"Leave," Lucas demanded, and my heart clenched at the cold tone.

But before I could move or let the ache in my chest spread, I realized the order had been for the driver when he turned and headed for the stairs, and Lucas strode toward me.

He hauled me to him, pressed his mouth to mine in a firm, possessive kiss, then leaned back to study my face. "Are you okay?"

Not wanting to go into the nightmares I was trying so hard to push away, I just said, "You weren't there."

"I'm sorry," he said gently, his eyes tightening as he took in the redness of mine. "Tell me what's going through that mind of yours."

"You weren't there," I repeated, my words now forced as my throat tightened. My eyes burned and tears threatened as I tried to push back the image of his lifeless eyes.

"Blackbird . . ."

"You weren't there. I can't lose you."

Shock and confusion swirled in those dark, dark eyes, and I tried to focus on the mass of emotion in them, tried to focus on the fact that he was holding me, and he was warm. "Lose me?"

"I thought it was you," I choked out. My next words were rushed and frantic as I explained everything to him while trying to force my tears back. "I know I didn't imagine your voice, I thought you were on the other side of that door. Then everything happened so fast that all I could comprehend was I had heard your voice, and then I heard a gunshot, and there was someone bleeding out on your carpet. And it took too long for me to absorb that *you* were standing in front of me and not on the floor. All I could see when I slept was you where he had been, and *I can't lose you.*"

One of Lucas's hands moved to cradle my cheek as he tried to quiet and soothe me, and by the time I had finished talking, he was fighting a smile.

"How are you finding this funny?"

"I'm not," he said honestly. "What you saw today, what you thought and your fear . . . I would do anything to take that away, Briar." His mouth suddenly pulled into a devastating smirk despite how serious his tone had been, and humor danced across his face. "I'm just trying to decide if I should be offended that you think I'd let someone kill me."

"Lucas, if this is truly the world you've put yourself in—if you *really* lived this growing up—you have been so incredibly lucky. You've been shot and you've been stabbed numerous times, that luck will eventually run out . . . especially if you think you're untouchable."

"Untouchable? I'm good at what I do. I've had to be. But, untouchable? Hardly. There have been times I was sure it was my last day. My last hour." His humor faded, and his warm eyes pierced mine. "But I would never let someone take me from you. Not while you're mine."

I trailed the tips of my fingers down his cheek and across his full lips. My voice wavered when I asked, "Promise?"

He kissed my wrist then whispered, "Swear to you." His head dipped, leaving a trail of feather-soft kisses to the sensitive spot behind my ear while chills skated along my skin. "Forever, Blackbird."

My heart soared as those two words echoed in my mind over and over again. Yes, I wanted forever with this man. I wanted an eternity with his beautiful, clashing heart. I wanted the darkness and light that fought within him. I wanted it all.

"Get us through these two months," I whispered breathlessly as he nipped at that spot on my neck. "Let me help you destroy this world, and then let me have that forever with whoever *you* are."

His hands went to my thighs and lifted me into his arms as he walked us back into my room. His lips brushed my ear when he said, "Our forever started that first night you decided to stay."

The heat that filled his eyes sent a warm shiver down my spine when he set me on the center of the bed. The possessive way he held me and the predatory smirk that covered his face already had my ragged breaths deepening and a warmth pooling low in my stomach and spreading through my veins.

"Need to feel you. Need to convince myself you're here the same way you need to." He tipped my head back and kissed me softly, teasingly. Then his voice dropped, the tone so carnal I nearly came undone right then. "Show me, Briar."

Lucas's fingers tightened around my chin as his mouth devoured mine. Taking and taking in *his* way that always felt like too much, yet not nearly enough. Swallowing each whimper and moan and leaving me with the word "more" on the tip of my tongue when he bit down on my lip, only to back away so he could slip my shirt off my body.

Eyes dark with need and lust met mine before taking in my body again as he laid me back on the bed—the look in them making me feel beautiful and powerful and sensual all at once.

His large hands drifted down my body to grip at my shorts, a moan sounded in the back of my throat when his mouth pressed low on my hips. And in one slow, torturous movement, he pulled my shorts and underwear over my hips and down my legs—his mouth following the material with hot kisses and teasing bites. Each kiss had my thighs clenching, my hands gripping at the comforter, my back arching, and my body aching . . .

"You're so beautiful," he said quietly as he leaned forward to press one last kiss to my stomach.

I watched in fascination as he stood and began undressing himself—as if it was the first time he was baring himself to me. Because I had never seen *this* man before. His scars and tattoos were stark against his tan skin, and now that I knew more about the man behind them, they *fit* him. The muscles that tensed and rippled with every movement now screamed dangerous and protector—exactly like the contradiction that Lucas was. The good that fought with the bad within him now meant more than ever. Anyone less would have abandoned the good inside themselves long ago if they'd lived his life, but Lucas only gripped tighter to it. *Fought* for it.

He knelt on the bed and settled between my knees—a wicked, knowing grin tugging at the corner of his mouth when I tried to get closer to the tip of his length, barely brushing against where I ached for him.

I reached for him, needing to feel his body on mine, his mouth taking from mine in a synchronized dance only we knew, but I paused and shuddered when he fisted himself.

With his free hand, he intertwined the fingers of both of my hands and softly passed his lips across each of my wrists as he slowly pumped up and down his long length—his heated stare on mine the entire time.

My eyes fluttered shut as each stroke from him brushed against my sensitive skin, and my voice came out as nothing more than a breath when I begged, "Please."

Instead of the immediate, hard response I'd come to expect from him, he took his time leaning his body over mine—my hands still in his—and pressed our joined hands on the bed above my head. "Please what?"

I tried to lift my hips, but he only released himself long enough to push my hips back down onto the bed before resuming what he'd been doing. I forced my eyes open, frustration and need leaking through my next *"Please."*

His answering smile was pure sin, and I wanted to scream at the torture he was putting me through.

He bent his head to tease me with a barely there kiss, and when I tilted my head higher, he backed away. His eyes grew darker and darker with every soft whimper that sounded in my throat from each faint brush from him, and then the brushes were gone altogether, and he was leaning back to place kisses down my chest.

When he spoke, his voice sent warm shivers down my spine.

"I like the way you crave that bite of pain to bring you higher and higher and beg for more," he said as he bit the underside of my breast.

When I gasped, he growled in appreciation, and the hand that had been the cause of my previous torture began teasing where I was aching.

"I like the way you shatter beneath me." He slid a finger deep inside me and placed a kiss on my stomach as he removed it, then pressed two in.

"Oh God," I breathed, writhing against the bed.

"I like bringing you to the height of another orgasm even when you think you can't give me another." He left a trail of warm, teasing kisses up my body until his face hovered above mine, and the hand holding mine to the bed tightened. "I like the way you fight me," he said in a dark, seductive tone, and dropped his head to give me another barely there kiss—to bring us back to where we'd begun—and his eyes locked with mine. "And I love the way you look at me like it will never be enough."

"Luc—oh!" I gasped when he suddenly pinched my clit then slid his fingers back inside me, driving them in harder and harder as he kept his thumb pressed against that sensitive knot.

I ignited, immediately responding to his touch and craving more—just as he'd said. I gripped the hand holding mine down as my stomach warmed and twisted, and my body begged for the release that was so close.

As the tremors began, Lucas backed off. His movements slowed, the pressure lessened, and that wicked smirk grew more and more profound until I was ready to beg him for the bliss he kept just out of my reach.

Just before I could cry out in frustration when he backed off again, he said, "Tell me what you want."

"Mor—" The word died in my throat, got lost in the nothingness when he pinched down on me again, and I was immediately wrapped up in warmth and darkness as wave after wave of pleasure rocked through my body.

His fingers rode me through my orgasm, tormenting and pleasuring until I no longer felt like I was floating but was trembling as he pushed me toward another.

And it was too much . . .

And everything felt too sensitive . . .

And my body reflexively shied away from his touch while I thrashed against his strong hold. But for the first time, I was also begging him not to stop.

"There you are," he rumbled, and his mouth fell onto mine.

His tongue moved against mine slowly but surely. The pacing and the sweetness of the kiss was so opposite from what his hands were doing to me, but so perfectly him—so perfectly *us*.

Light and dark.

I came with a silent moan and cried out against the kiss when he suddenly grabbed my hip and forced his thick length inside me.

His hand tightened against mine as he drove into me, the muscles in his arms straining, his hips rolling with each fluid, forceful movement. He released me suddenly and sat back on his knees, gripping my hips as he moved deeper and deeper, each stroke slower, but no less powerful, than the previous—and my heart clenched watching the man above me.

So beautiful and destructive and dark . . . the look in his eyes so raw I wanted to cry.

Every scar and every haunting memory that made my devil was on full display, every dark part of him so beautiful it hurt. And he was looking at me as if he'd found the only person who could make it all go away . . .

Tears burned my eyes, and he bent toward me at the same time I reached for him, needing to feel all of him. Because this was it—that moment I had craved all those months ago but hadn't been able to comprehend before now.

This was the wake of our war.

And I did—I wanted to stay in the moment forever.

"I love you. I love you," I whispered over and over again when he found his release inside me.

"Forever, Blackbird," he vowed against my lips. "Forever."

Chapter 41

DAY 125 WITH BRIAR

Lucas

Briar looked around the workout room that weekend, her expression confused when she realized no one else was joining us. "Is the driver picking someone up?" she asked as she continued to look at the large, open space in the middle of the room I'd created for today.

"No, but he'll be here eventually with lunch and to see how it's going."

She rubbed at her sore wrist from the other training we'd been doing the last two nights as she finally looked up at me. "I thought you said someone was training me how to defend myself."

I glanced down at myself, letting my gaze flick back up to her. "I'm training you."

She immediately stopped rubbing her wrist, her eyebrows shooting up as she realized the depth of what I was saying. "Are you afraid the other men would find out if you hired someone?"

"No."

With William probably hiding out in his home now, plotting out his next attack, I wasn't worried about anyone bothering to pay attention to our home life.

"Then why?" she asked, drawing out the last word.

The corner of my mouth tipped up in amusement. "Why not me?"

Every night that week, Briar and I had been training in other ways. We'd sat on the floor talking about anything to keep her mind off what I was trying to do—get her comfortable with guns. As we talked, I made her load an empty magazine into a handgun I'd given her, only to drop it, over and over again until she was no longer holding the gun between two fingers or cringing whenever I placed it in front of her.

The night I'd handed her the gun with a loaded magazine, the cringing had returned, and it had been even worse when I'd made her rack the slide to chamber a round. But I'd just kept talking to her about mundane things, every now and then prodding her to continue until she was doing it without thinking.

Load. Rack. Drop. Rack. Load. Rack. Drop. Rack.

Finger always off the trigger. Barrel always aimed away from both her and me.

Along with working to get her comfortable holding and loading a gun, the past two nights we'd spent hours at a range, teaching her how to shoot. She wasn't the best, but I hadn't expected her to be, and I didn't need her to be. I just needed her to be able to defend herself if it came down to it, and now she could. I needed her not to be afraid to hold and use the weapon that might save her life, and now she wasn't. After less than a week, I couldn't ask for more.

When the adrenaline had faded from the first night at the range, she'd broken down in the back of the car. Tears had streamed down her face, her body shaking so badly I'd had to hold her tight against me to calm her.

Once she'd finally been able to speak, she'd started rambling about the smell and the sound, and seeing people bleeding out in alleys and on sidewalks and in bedrooms. But the next night, she'd been ready to go again and had done better than the night before. On the way home, I'd massaged her aching wrist from the recoil of the handgun and had frozen when she'd mumbled, "I don't think I could shoot someone. I wouldn't know how to live with myself after."

I hadn't responded . . . partly because she'd seemed to be talking to herself, but mostly because the answer was that every day was a struggle, and she didn't need to be reminded of that.

But now Briar stared at me with a mixture of confusion and surprise, like she didn't understand how I didn't already know the answer to my own question. "B-because," she finally said, stumbling over the word, "how am I supposed to learn anything? I won't be able to concentrate with you, and I won't feel comfortable hitting you—don't you have any padding?" she asked suddenly and looked around the room again.

"An attacker won't have padding, Briar. Besides, I'm not worried about you hitting me." I took a few steps toward her, closing the distance between us so I could grab her hand and start massaging the wrist she'd forgotten about. "If you want me to hire someone, I will. He'll teach you techniques that would make a drunk man who doesn't understand the word 'No,' stop and think twice about coming after you. But if someone really wanted you, they wouldn't care what techniques you know. And they won't coddle you and release you when you land the correct hit."

I hadn't asked before because I knew I wouldn't have been able to handle the images it would give me—of someone trying to take this girl from me—but I needed to know.

"What did you do when William's man tried to take you?"

She flinched, and her eyes slipped closed like she was trying to block out the memory, but after a few seconds, she started talking in a numb voice. "I bit the hand that was over my mouth. I slammed my head back into his face."

My hands paused on her wrist, and my chest filled with shock and pride.

"When he didn't let me go, I turned in his arms and started clawing at him. I kicked him . . ." She trailed off then and shrugged.

"You're incredible," I whispered in awe.

"Did I do it right?"

I fought back my smile and continued to massage her wrist. "You *are* incredible, and you fought harder than I expected you to." The excitement in her eyes started fading, so I hurried to add, "Briar, you fought for your life, there's never a wrong way in fighting. I'm proud of you. But tell me what the man did when you did those things."

She only thought for a second before answering: "He tightened his arms around me. I got away once, but he grabbed my hair and pulled me back."

Rage flooded me instantly, and something like a growl sounded low in my chest—but the man was already dead, so I couldn't do anything about it now.

I swallowed thickly, pushing back that anger and need to hurt a man for hurting her, and nodded. "What you did when you fought is a lot of what an instructor would teach you. He would add in a couple stomach jabs and foot stomps, but the result would be the same—if the attacker *really* wanted you, he would tighten his hold instead of releasing you."

"Then what's the point of training?" she asked softly, her shoulders lifting in the barest of shrugs.

I dipped my head so my face was directly in front of hers and held her eyes. "Because *I* know exactly how someone would attack you, Blackbird. I've been that man."

Her face paled and a shuddering breath fell from her lips. "Right," she said, sounding breathless. "Right."

"I know exactly how someone would fight, and I know exactly how the attacker would respond." I forced back the memories that threatened to resurface. "And I know how to get away."

Briar was silent for so long that I started to ask if she was okay before she suddenly asked, "You mean *her*, don't you? The other girl you loved?" There wasn't a hint of jealousy in her voice now, just numb curiosity.

I stilled then nodded slowly.

"Tell me how she fought."

"Why, Briar?" I asked warily, worried that knowing would only scare her.

"I need to know." Her head was shaking, almost absentmindedly. "I need to know how she fought."

I swallowed past the tightness in my throat as those memories pushed through and swallowed again. "She kicked," I began, releasing Briar's wrist to fold my arms over my chest. "I was dragging her out of a closet, and she was clawing at the carpet, trying to stay in there. She just kept kicking, even when I forced her onto her back so we could knock her out. I dropped onto her to make her stop, and then one of my brothers brought a rag covered in chloroform. When she woke up, she fought harder. She punched and kicked and bit, so I sat down and held her in my arms. With each hit and bite, my hold tightened until she wore herself out."

Nearly a minute passed in silence. Unease slowly crawled through me as the girl in front of me continued to watch me thoughtfully, before she whispered, "My first day here with you . . . it was like your first day with her."

I hesitated for only a second before reaching out to cup her cheek in my hand. "In the beginning, I hated myself. I hated that I couldn't continue carrying out my role with you. I hated that the time with you felt too much like my time with her—that it had all felt the same. I tried telling myself over and over it wasn't, until I finally accepted it was. Then I fell in love with you and realized only the situation was similar—not *you*. And then you decided to stay . . ."

The corners of her mouth curled in a soft smile, and she turned her head to kiss my palm. When she looked at me, that smile had transformed into a smirk. "I'm glad she hit you."

A surprised laugh burst from my chest.

"You deserved it."

My amusement immediately drained from me, and my hand fell away from her. "For all I've done, I've deserved a lot more than that." I took a calming breath and said, "But like I said, she fought, and my hold tightened. You fought, his hold tightened. I need to make sure that never happens again."

Her eyes widened, and she looked lost in that moment. "I won't be able to do this the way you're hoping I will. I'll be afraid of hurting you."

"Don't." I turned and walked back toward the door of the room to flip off the light, talking as I went. "I want to start by seeing how you react when I grab you—to see what you do instinctively. Then I want to go over all the different ways someone will come after you. Running with you, dragging you, walking with you—all of it. I'll teach you multiple ways to get away."

"So no biting?" she asked as I walked back to her.

"If you bite, you don't bite to hurt. You bite to rip out flesh."

Briar shuddered then held her hand up to stop me when I neared her and pulled a bandana out of the back pocket of my jeans. "Wait, what are you doing?"

I paused from reaching up to place it over her eyes and lifted an eyebrow. "If I grabbed you right now, would you defend yourself?"

"No," she said with a laugh that hinted at her frustration. "That's why I think this is pointless."

"You were abducted four months ago," I began gently, "and someone attempted to take you just last week. If you can't see me, those memories are going to resurface and that fear is going to grip you, and you're going to react. Trust me," I said, the word almost a plea as I placed the material over her eyes, wrapped it around her head, and tied it in a knot. I pressed a soft kiss to her cheek, and then her lips, and whispered, "I'm sorry I have to force you to relive those days, but I'll do whatever it takes to keep you safe."

I stepped away from her and moved soundlessly to stand at the opposite side of the room so I was lined up with her shoulder.

I watched and waited as minutes passed, until her body began trembling and her lips began moving, like she was trying to keep a song from leaving them.

"Briar," I murmured, just loud enough for her to hear me.

Her head whipped to the left, but I was already silently slipping up behind her.

I forced myself to be calm, telling myself repeatedly that she needed this, until neither Lucas Holt or her devil was standing behind her—but a man I swore I would never be again.

Her trembling was increasing and her song was now a whisper when I leaned closer so that my breath stirred against her neck.

And it was the Reaper's voice that demanded, soft and low, "Fight me."

Chapter 42

SHATTER IT ALL

Briar

A tear fell and hit the marble countertop of my bathroom. Another dull splash. And then another.

Each tear heavy with every emotion I couldn't comprehend in those minutes.

Happiness, worry, love, denial, joy, terror . . .

I had thought I'd known fear. In the last five and a half months, I'd experienced more than most people were ever plagued by in their nightmares.

I'd been stolen from my life. I'd been sold to a devil. People had tried to take me from the man I loved and then more had come, looking to take my life.

But this? *This* made those moments seem like childish fears. *This* made those moments seem like nothing more than being terrified that my parents would abandon me, or that I would be forgotten somewhere again.

Two weeks until the celebration. Two weeks until the raid. Two weeks until this world would be nothing but a nightmarish memory.

My hand dropped to my stomach as a strained sob tore from my chest.

Because those two pink lines could potentially shatter it all.

Chapter 43

HELLO GIRL

Briar

"Hello, girl," an odd, familiar voice called out from the doorway to my room.

I straightened from where I was making the bed and looked over my shoulder slowly. Surprise and confusion swept through me as I took in the woman standing just inside the room with a smug expression on her face.

The shopper.

"Hello," I replied, my tone giving away how stunned I felt seeing her there. I hadn't seen her since the beginning of my time there. I turned to face her fully, my head tilting as I did. "No 'stupid' this time then?"

The woman just sent me one of her challenging grins, and lifted a slender shoulder. "You tell me."

"I don't know why you continued to call me that in the first place," I responded gently as her gaze swept the room—every now and then resting on something for an extra moment before continuing.

"Don't you?" she asked as she stepped up to me so she could search my eyes. "Where do you belong, girl?" When my brows only drew together, she *tsked* in that way I remembered. "Are you still trying to run away?"

I knew immediately what she was asking and what she wasn't. She didn't—*couldn't*—know about our plans or about Lucas's work with the FBI, but she remembered clearly from my first weeks that I'd wanted help to get back to Kyle. She had told me that by not helping me, she was saving my life . . .

My hand automatically fell to my uneasy stomach, and I prayed that it would stop churning so my answer wouldn't be mistaken for anything but honest.

"From him?" I asked softly, then shook my head. "Never again."

"Hundreds of women," she said with a twist of her lips. "I told you I've encountered *hundreds* of women and *dozens* of these men. Never once has there been a man's watch on the woman's nightstand—even a *first's*."

I stilled, then looked over my shoulder at where Lucas's forgotten watch lay.

"Never once has there been a jacket and tie resting on the chair of the woman's desk," she continued.

But this time I didn't need to look. By the time I faced her again, I could see the articles of clothing from the day before out of the corner of my eye.

Even though the carpet had been replaced in Lucas's room, he'd known I hadn't wanted to be in there again—hadn't wanted to continue to see the place where that man had died. Lucas had his clothes in his own closet, but we'd been using my room ever since, not that I could tell the shopper that. I knew even if I explained the dead man, it wouldn't matter. No man in this life would've shared a room with any of his women, no matter the circumstances.

"I knew from that first day, from the time I was measuring you, that there was something different between the two of you," she said. "To know that love can form in one of these houses gives me hope that anything in this world is possible."

I wanted to deny it, to try to protect Lucas and myself now that we were only days from the celebration. But this woman had had months to say something, and hadn't. William had figured it out before this woman had even come into my life.

We'd never fooled anyone.

My head had been shaking slowly in preparation of my denial and stopped suddenly when I realized what she'd said. "We didn't love each other then."

"Oh, stupid girl," she said affectionately, followed closely by another *tsk*. "You didn't realize what would happen because you were clouded by your fear and your sadness, and he did not *want* to realize it. That does not mean you didn't love each other, even then."

"But—"

"Why do you think I gave him the phone number, girl?" She lifted a brow and waited for my answer, but I didn't have one. "Because I knew. Because I could see it. Because I knew that one day you would recognize that your soul belonged with his."

I blinked quickly, shock filling me at her words.

I had thought she was just doing her job. I'd had no idea she was seeing something we couldn't.

At that time, I'd been in love with Kyle and was desperate to get back home. Now? Lucas was my home. And all I wanted for Kyle was a chance to grieve for the girl he'd known and accept that I was gone forever.

Tears filled my eyes before rapidly slipping down my cheeks, and a strained sob caught in my throat.

"Oh, girl," she scoffed. "No one has time for your tears. We need—" She broke off when I threw my arms around her neck and pulled her close to me.

She was the oddest woman I had ever met.

And I was so thankful for her.

"This shirt cost a fortune; do not ruin it with your tears."

I laughed through my tears and pulled away from her in time to see her give me a kind smile before her face fell into that look she wore well—like I was nothing more than an annoyance.

"Now, allow me to bring in the gowns. We need to find one for you to wear to the celebration."

Confusion flooded me as I gestured toward the bathroom that hid my enormous, too-full closet. "I have dresses."

Another lift of her brow and twist of her lips. "Not for the celebration, you don't."

Hours later I had my dress picked out and hanging in my closet in a garment bag, and something about knowing it was there added an ache in my chest to the fear that had already been gripping me.

I hadn't been able to say goodbye to the shopper. Not in the way I wanted to. I hadn't been able to thank her for helping me see that everything I would ever want had been standing right in front of me.

Instead, I'd bit down on my lip and held back more tears as she'd left, stating, "You will still, above all, be the one I look forward to seeing most."

I was lying on the bed, trying to force back the nausea and dizziness that never seemed to go away lately when the bed dipped from his weight and immediately cursed myself for not hearing him before he'd reached the room.

"Blackbird," he said softly, worry dripping from the word.

I didn't have to force the relief that poured from me when I said, "You're home."

But his dark eyes were searching my face, looking for everything I was trying to hide. "What's wrong?"

I shook my head quickly. "I've just been worried," I whispered, at least giving him that truth.

Every day he left had been agony, knowing he was willingly surrounding himself with other men from his world—men who could potentially be on William's side. Every day had left me unable to fully breathe until he came home.

But he had to keep up pretenses.

In the last two months, I'd only been alone while the driver took

Lucas to and from work or anything else business related. The driver returned to the house to protect me, making himself invisible while I stayed inside and trained or read, so I wouldn't feel suffocated—as I had before.

Today had been the last day Lucas would go into work. Today had been the last day he would have to leave me for any reason. And even though I was so thankful for that—so thankful I wouldn't have to worry for hours upon hours—I dreaded the next two and a half days.

It had felt nearly impossible to keep what was happening inside me from this man the last two weeks, but he'd been distracted enough with work and all the planning with David that it had been doable. But I could feel the anxiety and restlessness that these remaining days created. I could feel his need to spend every second with me as if it might be our last, because it was just doubling my own anxiety and reinforcing my decision to keep this from him.

He would do anything . . . *anything* to keep me safe.

But he wouldn't be able to think clearly if he knew, and he would get himself killed.

His fingers trailed lightly over my cheek, then he cupped my face in his large hand. "Briar, I've been thinking . . ."

My heart fell into my stomach at his tone and the defeated look in his eyes.

"I don't want you to go to the cele—"

"No," I said quickly. "Lucas, no."

"Briar, listen—"

"No, don't tell me to listen," I said through gritted teeth, and pushed him away so I could sit up on the bed. "I know what you're doing, and you can't do this to me. Not after all we've been through to make it here." Tears were already falling down my face, but I didn't bother to try to stop them. He was breaking my heart.

"Blackbird," he said in a soft, soothing tone as he reached for me again.

I stopped him from touching me and kept my shaking hand in the air. "I've heard every conversation you've had with David over the last two months. I *know* what this would mean."

Lucas's face fell, but he didn't attempt to placate me.

"You told him that once one of you buys a woman, you're not just allowed to go to this annual gathering, but you *have* to. Your entire house *has* to—which means me. I know why David wouldn't let you get me out of here. It was because of this night. If I'm not there, I know it will make a statement you can't afford to make."

"I can take care of myself," he said in a calm tone that grated on me.

"I can't let you die."

My words snapped something inside him, and he reached for me quickly, cradling my face in his hands. "I can't save you from something I can't see coming," his deep voice boomed. He looked like he was being tortured, but he was holding me as if I was precious. When he spoke again, his words were rough, his breaths uneven. "Don't you understand, Briar? If you're there, he *will* try to kill you. He knows I'll be watching you, and watching every move he makes. So he'll do it silently, without ever coming near you."

"You don't know that."

"I do," he said, his words twisted with grief. "And I'd rather die than live without you." He sat back, releasing me so he could reach into his pocket. He pulled out an envelope and slowly handed it to me.

My eyebrows pulled together when I pulled out a black, square card. It looked like a paint chip, but was so thick it would've taken an actual effort to bend it. "I don't . . ." I trailed off when I turned it over and saw the writing.

"The second auction of the year always immediately follows the celebration. I had to buy a ticket for appearances."

I already knew what he was telling me, but that didn't explain what I was holding in my hand. "What is this?" I asked, my voice barely above a whisper.

"It doesn't look like much, but that card you're holding is worth ten thousand dollars . . ." he began.

My stomach rolled, and I had to swallow back my hatred and disgust for the men who lived in this world—who spent this kind of money just to sit in on an auction.

" . . . and the chip inside it is how we get into the auctions. It was delivered to me today." Lucas tapped a finger on the silver-written note and growled, "That was already there."

I didn't need to ask who the message was from. The writing was exactly like I'd seen on the cards from the men who'd come to kill me.

Time to start over . . .

"I figured we wouldn't hear from William because he'd failed at both attempts to take you, and he would be recovering. I had no idea he'd plan something for the celebration."

I read the words over and over again, not realizing that my free hand had gone to my stomach at some point. But Lucas didn't say anything. If he noticed, he probably guessed it was due to my fear.

"Maybe he means the two of you . . ."

"You know he doesn't," Lucas said as frustration seeped from him. "William doesn't do anything without thinking it through. He could have called or put the message on the invitation to the celebration. He chose this—he's sending a message. He's knocking in the rhythm of a heartbeat, Briar."

"Let him." I dropped what I was holding and crawled onto his lap so I could cradle his face the way he had done mine earlier. His face blurred, so I shut my eyes and pressed my forehead to his, whispering, "Only a man who wants to die would knock on the Reaper's door."

Chapter 44

DAY 182 WITH BLACKBIRD

Lucas

I stood in the doorway of the bedroom and time seemed to get lost around me. It felt like days and seconds all at once as I watched my blackbird sleep, unaware of the war that raged inside me.

I wanted to scoop her into my arms, press my mouth to hers, and beg her to let me take her away. I wanted to wake her so I could spend one last hour worshipping her body, committing it to memory. I wanted to run before she woke so she couldn't try to talk me out of what I knew I had to do.

She'd asked me to finish this—and that's what I was going to do. But there was no way to win.

There had been times in my life I was sure I was going to die, but in that moment, I felt it in my bones. This was an end I was walking toward. My *luck*—as Briar had called it—had run out.

Because whether or not I physically lived, I wouldn't be *alive* after tonight. Not without her.

I pushed away from the frame, and let every emotion overwhelm me as I approached the bed I'd loved and cherished her in during these last months with her, and I pressed my mouth to hers.

"I love you," I whispered against her lips. "Forever. Forgive me."

An ache so profound it nearly brought me to my knees tore through me, but I forced myself away and somehow made it out of the room and downstairs where the driver was coming in with breakfast.

"I need you to do something for me. Do not question me, and do not alert anyone—especially Briar."

His worry was blatant as he looked quickly from me to the stairs. "Anything, Mr. Holt."

"You know her life will be in danger tonight. If something happens, do everything to get Briar out of there alive. Force her to leave," I said, my voice sounding strained.

He didn't move from his spot, and for once, his stare didn't waver from mine. "Mr. Holt?"

"Do everything to get Briar out of there alive, and force her to leave," I repeated in a low tone. Reaching into my pocket, I grabbed the folded paper and shoved it in his direction. "This man will find you. Make sure she goes with him."

"Of course, Mr. Holt," he said automatically and flinched away from me when I stalked past him on my way to my office.

He didn't look toward the stairs or notice the way each step away from where I'd left my heart was destroying another piece of my soul. He was too focused on not pissing me off. I knew I needed to keep it that way.

Because this was for the best.

As soon as I was seated at my desk, I took out my phone and pulled up the number that had been sent to me over Facebook an hour before. My thumb remained hovering over it as I stood on a cliff that my entire being was trying to recoil from—thrashing and writhing in an attempt to get back to that girl who held my heart.

I pressed down and lifted the phone to my ear.

One ring.

Two.

"Hello?"

Breathe in.

Chapter 45

BREATHE

Briar

Years of planning wouldn't have been enough to prepare me for what we'd walked in on late that afternoon. And I'd only had *months*.

I'd known how many men were in this world that I'd been sold into—this *world* that my devil had been taking part in for years in order to take it down. Lucas and David had said the number so often that it continued to bounce through my mind even when I tried to sleep.

Thirty-three. There were thirty-three men, including Lucas.

The number had only shocked me for half of a second before I realized that I'd already known. My shopper had said *dozens* on more than one occasion, and I had a feeling I'd known from that very first day.

I had stared down what had looked like dozens of one-way mirrors while dozens of lights flashed on and off as the men hiding behind them had bid on me.

No, that number didn't shock me, but maybe it was because I couldn't grasp what it really meant.

Standing in the enormous hall where every one of those thirty-three men were gathered for their annual celebration, I was beginning to understand just how terrible the number *thirty-three* was.

Because each of those thirty-three men had anywhere from one to fifteen women standing close by their side—most had the latter. One to fifteen women who had been stolen from their homes and sold in an auction like I had.

All of those stolen girls . . .

And they hadn't had a Lucas.

What was worse, nearly all of the women looked deliriously happy with their men—just as William's did.

Lucas had told me that, at some point, nearly every woman had a chance to leave and go back to whatever life she'd had before she'd been kidnapped, and none ever did. From the stories that William's women had told me of their previous lives, and from the little I'd heard from Lucas, I was sure I knew why . . .

The women only came from the worst of lives—lives that the women would be thankful to get away from.

Like Jenna would've, I'd thought numbly when I realized why they'd targeted her in the first place.

It was a way for these men to feel like they were saving their women from awful lives, and in turn, it was why most of the women thought they were in love with this life. Because even if the beginning was terrifying, it nearly always turned out better than what they'd had.

And now we were about to tear this life away from all of them. We were about to tear away a world where they'd grown comfortable with their brain-washing men and send them into a world full of therapists and agents in the hopes they would one day live the normal lives they always should've had.

Looking at the hundreds of women filling the hall, it terrified me to know that some of them would never adjust—to know that most of them didn't *want* to get out of this world—to know that being freed from these disturbed men would be harder for them than being torn from their homes had been.

I'd already been queasy before the event had begun, but my nausea had worsened since we'd arrived a couple hours before, and I felt close to fainting as I stood in the sea of lost women.

Lucas murmured a low curse under his breath, and I lifted my heavy head to look in the direction he was facing.

A couple of men and their women were walking in our direction and I instinctively backed up against Lucas's side when I noticed who one of the men was.

I didn't know his name, and I didn't want to. All that mattered was that when I looked at him, I remembered Lucas's words from my first weeks with him, and I understood just how badly this all could've gone for me when I was first sold at the auction.

"It's possible that if you'd been bought by someone else then you would have ended up as a sex slave."

This is what Lucas had meant that day. He was one of two men I'd seen at the celebration like this—and he made my already weak stomach churn until it felt like I would lose the remaining contents right there on the floor. I felt sick as I watched the man approach us, and I suddenly couldn't swallow anymore. My tongue felt too thick, my mouth too dry. I needed to get out of there.

The man was tall with a large, drooping belly. And in one of his meaty hands, he held the ends to leashes. Leashes that were attached to his women. Women who were crawling after him on the floor like they were dogs.

Lucas flinched away from me so quickly that I stumbled toward him, only catching myself when he gripped my upper arm and made me face him.

"Sorry," I whispered automatically. I knew I couldn't touch him. I hadn't meant to; I'd just wanted to get away from what I was seeing.

Lucas's head dropped so he was eye-level with me, and he pinned me with a cold stare. His lip curled into a sneer, completing the expression, and not matching his breathless words. "I've got you. You can do this."

To anyone watching, he was a man disgusted with the way his

woman had just acted, and was giving her quiet commands. To us, he was steadying and comforting me the only way he could while he played his part.

"Remember that we're taking them all down. Remember that we're freeing the women," he whispered then released me roughly, straightening just in time to greet the men as they approached us.

By the time I turned toward them and lifted my head, every emotion was locked up tight inside me—betraying nothing of what I felt. None of the fatigue or nausea from what was happening inside me. None of the revulsion or horror from what I was seeing in this massive hall. None of the anticipation or eagerness of what was to come before the night ended.

None of it.

For all they knew, I was a woman who had just been scolded in public by the man who owned her, and I was trying not to show that I was embarrassed.

"Lucas Holt," the man with the leashes called out. "I've been looking forward to speaking with you. It has been going around how well you have done with your *first*."

Now that he was closer, I could see him more clearly. He was sweating profusely, forcing his sex slaves to crawl through what was dripping from him onto the floor.

Bile rose in my throat, and I tried to force it back.

His eyes slowly raked over me, and I lost my hold on my neutral appearance when he licked his teeth and said, "And might I say, she is lovely."

I dropped my head and saw Lucas stiffen from the corner of my eye before his hands slipped into his pants pockets. I knew who was now facing those disgusting men, and I knew what he was imagining doing to them.

And for once it didn't scare me. I wanted it.

The floor swayed below my feet, and I squeezed my eyes tight as I blew out a slow breath, trying to calm my stomach. But my head felt light—too light.

I swallowed thickly and tried to open my eyes, but shut them again when it felt like the entire room was spinning around me.

When my devil spoke, none of the wrath I knew he was feeling could be heard. Only that unnerving calm, with the slightest hint of arrogance. "She was a challenge at first, but I found her out soon enough, and then she was easily broken."

The sweating man laughed loudly, and another man on my left spoke up, making me feel even more off balance. "You should buy tonight, Lucas. It's not often we find one who will do what we need them to so quickly, so you should take advantage and start on your second."

"I plan to," Lucas responded coolly.

"Would you look at that," the sweating man said with a snarl. "Your first can't even stand the thought of it. Jealous bitches they are in the beginning."

I knew he was referring to the way I wouldn't look at any of them, but I was afraid of what would happen when I opened my eyes. I was shaking and felt cold, as if someone had just shoved me in an icebox. I was also sweating as badly as the man with the leashes.

"Briar," Lucas said in warning, but I knew the tone was more for the men than me.

With another steadying breath out, I forced my heavy lids open—but I was only able to take in the scene in front of me before everything went black.

Silence that felt impossibly loud sounded in my ears, and I felt very aware of everything and nothing all at once.

I knew I was standing. I knew I was trying to breathe calmly. I knew I was staring blankly at nothing, because I was *seeing* nothing. I knew I was leaning too far forward, and I needed to stop myself.

But I couldn't see or hear anything other than that deafening silence, and I couldn't discern the time that was passing, because this horror felt like an eternity.

I threw my hand out to my side, to where Lucas had been. The force of my movement caused me to stumble backward. Before I could attempt to right myself, everything came rushing back to me all at once, and I slammed into Lucas's side as the light and the noise became too much.

Lucas caught me automatically, but I only had a moment to rest in his arms—my head falling heavily to his chest—before he was gripping my shoulder and shoving me away.

I could only imagine how I looked from the panic that flashed across his face before he was able to control it, and then his face was twisted with practiced anger.

"I need something to drink."

Surprise and worry filled those dark, dark eyes before he forced it away, and sneered, "You can wait until I'm finished talking with these men. Don't int—"

"No. Now," I said sluggishly, and blindly reached for him again when I swayed in his direction. He batted my hand away, but his other hand on my shoulder tightened to keep me from falling.

"What is wrong with her?" a man asked. His tone showed how shocked he was with the way I was acting.

"I need water," I said to Lucas as my shaking continued. "Something. Please."

When he spoke, his voice was low, dangerous. "You can wait. Do not interrupt us again."

The sweating man scoffed. "Am I right to assume all those rumors of your success have been just that?"

"Lucas, I'm—"

"Briar!" he snapped, shock and anger playing on that dangerous face as he forced me closer and dropped his head to whisper in my ear—but Lucas stilled when one of the men spoke.

"Is your mentor aware of your girl's disobedience?"

It felt as though the entire hall had gone silent even though it was just the group surrounding us waiting for Lucas's response.

My devil leaned away from me, a cruel smirk pulling at his mouth.

"Her disobedience?" he asked in a dangerous tone. His eyes left mine and flashed toward the men. "Her disobedience is nothing a night of lessons won't fix."

The men laughed loudly, and Lucas used the moment to dip his head so his lips were at my ear again.

"Breathe, Blackbird," he whispered in a calming tone. "Slow, deep breaths. Stand here and breathe. I can't let you leave, and I can't let you push me to stop the conversation. I promise I'll take you somewhere so you can sit down soon. Just breathe." He looked every inch of the Lucas Holt he needed to play when he pulled away from me, and he sent the men a frustrated look when he turned toward them again. But even though he released my arm, he was standing closer to me than he'd originally been, and I knew he was ready to catch me if I started to fall.

Which still felt like too real of a possibility.

"Ah. Jealous bitches," the sweating man said again, then searched through his leashes until he found the one he was looking for. He held it up, shoulder-height, and one of the women sat back so she was sitting up on her knees instead of kneeling down on all fours. "This one did the same—my first. We were at this very event when she realized I would be buying my second. She started crawling all over me like a bitch in heat. I didn't wait until we got home, I took her into the bathroom and taught her a lesson right then."

A shuddering breath left me, and my eyes fluttered shut as the room once again spun—as my hatred and disgust for the man grew so strong that I wanted to scream and claw at his face, wanted to yank the leashes from his hand and use them against him.

Lucas made some sort of humming noise in the back of his throat, but I was struggling too hard to stay vertical to focus on it. "That's not a bad idea," he said, his tone filled with amusement. "After the show mine just gave you, I think I'm going to have to do the same."

"Don't let us stop you," the other man said, and the sweating man laughed loudly, yanking on the leashes as he did.

Lucas said brief goodbyes, then turned and started walking away from me, and I struggled to follow.

It wasn't until we were out of eyesight of that group that he slowed and grasped my arm, gentle enough not to hurt, but firm enough to help me stay standing—firm enough for anyone looking to think he was dragging me rather than helping me.

"Are you okay?" he asked under his breath as he led me toward a table filled with drinks.

"I feel like I'm going to faint."

His grip tightened, and his steps faltered, but his face stayed cold and indifferent. "Did you? Back there?"

I clenched my teeth against another wave of nausea, and tried to breathe through it when it made the outer edges of my vision darken. "I don't know what happened," I responded honestly, then focused on taking calming breaths for a few seconds. "I might have blacked out."

I hated that I was doing this to him when we had hours or minutes or seconds until this was all over. I hated that I couldn't be stronger for him on this night when he was playing his part so well. I didn't know if it was the dress or the overly crowded hall or the knowledge of what would soon be happening. I just knew I needed to fight through the nausea and the fatigue until the night was through.

Lucas didn't respond until we were at the table and he'd grabbed a glass of iced water and handed it to me. "Blacked out. Wh—" He cut off, and looked blankly ahead for a few seconds before pulling his vibrating phone out of his pocket. He only glanced at the screen for a second before his pained eyes met mine as he answered the call.

"Yeah?" he growled in greeting, and then his eyes slid shut. "Right . . . okay."

The call was over before it began, and then Lucas was standing there with his eyes closed and his hand in front of him, like he didn't know what to do with it or the phone he was still holding.

"Who was that?" I asked softly, in case anyone close enough to us was listening. The women here weren't allowed to ask questions as simple as that one. When Lucas didn't respond, I asked, "Is it time?"

But I should've known that answer before Lucas shook his head. David wouldn't tell Lucas what time they were storming in—only that it was tonight.

"It was the driver," he finally said, and then released a slow, weighted breath. "Briar, I think you should go lie down."

I wanted to. I wanted to so badly that I was ready to cry just at the thought of the relief that would come from lying down. But I didn't know where I could in this hall, and with William's threat, I knew I wasn't supposed to leave Lucas's side. "I don't—I wouldn't know where we could go, and—"

He looked up at me then, and his voice was tight when he said, "Briar, you don't feel well. It's time you lie down."

My head tilted to the side as confusion filled my already exhausted mind, but I couldn't force it to continue shaking when I realized what he was saying. "What?"

"The driver will be waiting for you, go lie down in the car. I'll be there—"

"Lucas, no," I whispered, and started to reach for him, but managed to stop myself that time. "Don't do this," I pled, not caring if anyone could hear me.

He and I both knew women weren't allowed to leave the celebration until it was over, just as I knew I couldn't disobey an order from him if anyone else was listening. He was trying to get me out before everything could happen. After the extensive planning and all the lessons in defense, he was still trying to get me out. He still planned on putting himself in a dangerous position by making me go and leaving him here alone.

My head spun, or maybe that was the room again.

"Luc—" I swayed forward, but managed to steady myself. My hand automatically flew to my stomach when it rolled.

"Briar," Lucas said in a soft, pleading tone. I looked up to find his eyes locked on my stomach—his expression revealing his panic and denial. "Briar, tell me what's happening."

"Lucas, Lucas, Lucas . . ." a cold, charmingly accented voice said from beside us.

A chill rushed up my spine as Lucas's panic morphed into unrestrained shock and dread, then I looked down to a pair of pale blue eyes.

Chapter 46

BETRAYALS AND SACRIFICES

Briar

Lucas had been so sure that William would avoid us during the celebration since he had already announced his intent with the ticket. To see Lucas so rattled scared me more than I ever had been for this night.

"Ah. Briar, how lovely to see you again," William said with a knowing smile from where he sat in his wheelchair.

I didn't respond. I couldn't. I'd never heard him say my name before. It felt like the floor was rising up to meet me, but I hadn't moved.

"I'm sure you're wondering what happened," William continued, and rubbed his right thigh roughly to bring my attention to the limb that ended just above his knee. "Nothing but a hunting accident."

A woman scoffed, and I pulled my gaze from William's leg to see Karina glaring at Lucas. Sahira and the rest of the thirteen women wore equal looks of hatred for the man beside me.

I wondered if they would feel the same if they knew what William had attempted before *and* after Lucas shot him.

"Hunting," Lucas finally said, and even though I couldn't tear my eyes from the women or William, I was surprised to hear the cool tenor of his voice, and the humor in that single word. "I guess that's accurate. How did the surgery go? Sorry I didn't care to stop by and check on you."

"And why would you?" William asked as his smile broadened into something that made my blood run cold.

"Exactly."

I didn't know how William and Lucas were talking to each other so calmly. I didn't know how Lucas hadn't attacked him yet, or why I wasn't screaming at him for trying to have me taken away or killed.

But then I remembered what Lucas had said, and I knew what William was doing.

He'd made his intentions known, and now he was going to torture us slowly until he decided he was ready to make good on his threat against me.

William was playing a game . . . and Lucas was stalling as he tried to find a way to beat him at it.

"It is quite funny though," William mused, "the things you want as soon as you can't have them. I cannot remember the last time I just went for a drive, but that's all I want to do lately. Sadly, I cannot." His calculating gaze went from me to Lucas, and he cocked his head to the side. "Do you ever have the urge to go for a *cruise*, Lucas?"

Lucas was studying William intently, his eyes just as calculating, but his face looked oddly bored. He lifted his shoulders slightly. "Not lately. It's nice to have someone drive you around. I'm sure you'll get over your *urges* soon enough."

"Perhaps. Perhaps not." He shrugged, just as Lucas had. "I have been having these dreams of being back in the UK, cruising over the River *Trent*." He trailed off, seeming to get lost in those dreams—but I noticed how still Lucas became. "And then I wake up and realize that I am here, and I won't be driving again. It's quite devastating, let me tell you. Almost feels like a betrayal."

Despite the tension radiating from Lucas, he forced a smirk. "You're so dramatic lately, William."

"William. Lucas," someone called from behind us, but I was only able to glance over my shoulder at the stranger before my gaze snapped back to the man in front of me.

I was too focused on Lucas's reactions, and the way William was now pinning me with a victorious stare, to do more than that.

Lucas twisted to greet the man who had come but remained facing both William and me as he did. I knew I needed to turn, but I was afraid to have my back to the man in the wheelchair. I took a shaky step away, and shuddered when William's hand snaked out to grip my wrist.

Lucas's voice abruptly halted, but William smoothly said, "I'm sorry, Briar dear, I cannot hear you. Can you lean closer?"

I glanced at Lucas, noting the panic he wasn't able to keep from his eyes even though his face remained impassive.

Men weren't allowed to touch another's woman, but a woman also couldn't be the one to stop the man if he happened to—*her* man had to. But this wasn't just any man, this was Lucas's mentor, and William had just tied our hands in making it seem as though I was in the middle of a conversation with him.

Lucas dipped his head in the slightest of nods, but his arms slowly uncrossed from where they'd been against his chest, and he held them at his sides.

I shakily leaned closer to William, and he said in a low tone, "Look at him, *First.*"

I didn't.

"Fine, don't. I've already seen enough in the times that you have." He laughed darkly, softly and continued on a whisper so neither his women nor Lucas would hear him. "You thought he cared for you, and in turn you fell in love with him—but you only fell for what he wanted you to. Anything he may have told you or promised you were lies to keep you here and happy, to help you progress. And progress you have. To be where you are in six months is remarkable, most take double the time. But let me assure you that it has *only* been a ruse. Every word and every touch has been to ensure that you would end up here. All of this was one giant lesson, and Lucas taught you well."

Months ago, I might have believed what William was saying, but not now. I knew Lucas too well to let William try to make me second-guess everything now. It was what he wanted, but it wasn't going to work.

"Is that why he shot you?" I asked through clenched teeth, forcing myself to hold his cold, blue-eyed stare.

One of his eyebrows lifted, but he didn't look surprised I knew it had been Lucas, only surprised I would say anything to him at all. "Sometimes we have to make sacrifices in order to better this world."

"And I'm one of those sacrifices?"

William sent me a look that was so fatherly it shocked me. "Another ruse, my darling. Do you think you would still be alive if it hadn't been?"

"Do you think you'll still be alive if you try again?"

That fatherly expression immediately slipped from his face, and something so evil flashed through his eyes before everything went blank. That unnerving calm he and Lucas seemed to have mastered was all that was left when he promised, "You won't be around to find out."

"Time to go, Briar," Lucas murmured. His panic was clear because William grinned wickedly.

"No, Lucas, I think you should stay with me," William said coldly, and my stomach sank when he waved off his women.

After a few confused glances at each other, they turned and walked away as a group.

"There are some people I need to introduce you to," William continued.

"I've done fine without you so far, and I'll continue to. Briar, let's go."

I stood and tore my hand from William's grasp and tried to force the chill from my body when he said, "I told you to stay."

I turned toward Lucas, taking a step in his direction, but froze when I took in what was happening. "Lucas . . ." I breathed, horrified.

The calm and panic were both gone, but had been replaced by a silent rage that was terrifying to be in the presence of. But those eyes—those dark eyes I loved so much—were saying so many things he couldn't in that moment.

He loved me.

He was going to protect me.

He was sorry.

I dropped my gaze to where the gun was aimed at Lucas, then followed it up to the man holding it. The same man who had just greeted William and Lucas like long-lost friends.

"As I said . . . *stay*." William laughed softly then clapped his hands twice.

I didn't understand why people weren't reacting. I didn't understand why people weren't trying to figure out why this man had a gun aimed at my devil. But then I realized that what seemed so big to me was nothing more than a tight circle of people talking to everyone else at this crowded, crowded celebration.

I felt the presence behind me before I felt the actual man. He had to have been as tall as Lucas and just as wide.

"Briar," Lucas began softly, but whatever else he'd been about to say died in his throat.

I stiffened when something sharp pressed against my inner arm, and Lucas started, like he was about to lunge across the small space toward me.

"William," he snarled, but William only laughed.

"I suggest you both stay quite still."

Without moving my head, I looked down at the needle pressed to the crook of my elbow, and the clear liquid that filled it. I had a feeling it wouldn't just knock me out for a few hours. When I looked back up at Lucas and saw the soul-deep pain in his eyes, I knew I was right.

"I had planned to do this differently," William said cheerfully. "Poetically even. Something that people spoke of for years to come. That way you would never forget her, and this celebration would haunt you every year, *Lucas*. But then I received disturbing news a few days ago, and well, those plans no longer mattered to me." William's head tilted to the side as he studied Lucas. "Tell me, *Lucas*, what is your name?"

Fear gripped me, squeezing me tighter and tighter until it felt like I couldn't breathe anymore.

David had said they would find out the truth about my devil, and we'd been naïve to think they *couldn't* in the time we had left.

Lucas's chest was rising and falling roughly, unevenly, and his hands were clenching into fists. But he didn't move, and his eyes didn't leave me even as he spoke to William. "Don't ask questions you already know the answers to."

"But it's so fun," William said with another clap. "Really, boy, tell us. Humor me. You owe me that, at least. I just want to hear it come from you before I force you to watch as I tear your heart from your chest." His words were even more sinister in that lighthearted tone.

"Briar . . ." Lucas whispered, and William sighed heavily.

"Sometime tonight."

Lucas swallowed roughly, his head shaking slowly as he searched my face—like he was trying to memorize it. His gaze dropped to my stomach for a few seconds, longing and anguish flashing through his eyes before they met mine again. "Forever," he breathed, and I nodded, because I couldn't make my voice work.

My throat was tightening and tears were blurring my vision.

With one last ragged breath in, he held it for a moment, and then released it with a name. "Trent Cruz."

I only had one second to let that name wash over me.

I only had one second to realize what William had been saying earlier—how he'd been taunting my devil with his real name.

I only had one second, and then the hall erupted into chaos.

Chapter 47

DAY 182 WITH BRIAR

Lucas

William thought she didn't know. He thought Briar would look at me with the betrayal he had felt when he'd found out about my true identity. And I knew he was counting on that look—counting on the hurt to register on Briar's face once I confirmed my name—before the man standing behind her stabbed her with that needle and injected her with whatever poison was waiting inside.

I'd wanted to keep my name from her until this was all over, until this world had been brought down and I could finally give her *me*. But William wasn't going to wait forever, and I was running out of time before he snapped and did something rash.

I looked from her flat stomach to the tears building in my blackbird's eyes, then said on a breath, "Forever."

She nodded quickly. The resignation and devastation on her face threatened to destroy me. But I wouldn't go down without a fight—I never had before, and I wouldn't now. Not when her life was being held in the hands of another. Not when I was so sure she was keeping something from me—had *planned* on keeping it from me until we were through with this night so I wouldn't hide her away like I'd wanted to.

I swallowed past the thickness in my throat and chanced one last glimpse down at the gun aimed at me before I was looking at her again.

Finger off the trigger. Loose hold.

In the space of one second, I already knew exactly what I would do, and I was ready.

I took in a deep, ragged breath, and held it as I studied those green eyes for what I hoped wasn't the last time.

I love you, Briar. I'm going to get us out of this, I vowed, then released the breath I'd been holding, and let the name I'd kept secret for the last four years fall from my lips. "Trent Cruz."

I vaguely registered the sound of screaming coming from behind me—from the front of the hall where the celebration was being held—but didn't turn to look as I grabbed for the gun aimed at my stomach.

The man holding it had glanced up at the screams but jerked and fought against me when I tried to wrench the gun from him.

I forced his arms up so the gun was aimed above Briar's head and struggled to reach the trigger.

Briar cried out a split second before I fired at the man holding her, but my arms suddenly felt like dead weights, and my heart dropped when his head snapped back and he sagged to the ground. Because instead of falling with him, the needle was still there, sticking out of Briar's arm. Her face was pale and emotionless, and she swayed as she stared blankly ahead.

"Bri—"

The man I'd been wrestling for the gun slammed me into the ground, sending the gun sliding away from us toward the girl I'd failed, just as Briar fell to the floor.

I'd promised to protect her. To keep her safe. To get her out of there alive . . .

I'd fucking failed.

I pushed up from the floor and lunged for her, her name ripping from my chest and ending in a roar as something pierced my shoulder and was roughly ripped back out. I turned toward the man who'd just tackled me and caught his wrist as he brought his hand back down in a sweeping arc, the knife in his hand covered in my blood.

Keeping his wrist tight in my grasp, I yanked his arm toward me—straightening it—then slammed the open palm of my free hand into his locked elbow, forcing it to blow out in the opposite direction, and savoring the sound of his scream as the knife clattered to the floor between us.

Throwing him down onto his back, I gripped his tie in my hand and brought his head a couple inches off the floor so it would snap back against the hard surface as I drove my fist into his face again and again.

I could only feel rage and my suffocating agony as I hit him. He needed to feel a fraction of the pain I was in. I hadn't been able to make the other man suffer for taking my blackbird from me, and I needed someone to.

My fist halted mid-air when a gun pressed to the top of my head. I exhaled a strained, *"Fuck."*

"I will admit that even with what I knew of you, I did not see this one coming," William said through clenched teeth, and it was then that I focused on the screams that were being drowned out by deep, commanding yells for everyone to get on the floor.

The raid had begun.

William's finger moved toward the trigger, and I locked my eyes with his.

I tightened my grip on the tie of the man I'd beaten into unconsciousness as I prepared for what was coming and curled my lip into a sneer. "I'll be waiting for you in hell."

Two shots sounded, and I flinched as I stupidly, involuntarily, braced myself to die.

But then a second passed, and then another, and I forced my eyes open to see William sitting slack in his wheelchair, with blood rapidly pooling onto his white button-down shirt.

I turned my head to the side and saw the most beautiful angel on her knees with a gun still aimed at William.

"Briar," I said numbly, and her head whipped around to face me.

Wide-eyed and terrified, her chest moving roughly from her too-fast breaths.

"Briar," I repeated, trying to get my mind to realize she was alive.

"Do I—do I do it again?" she asked shakily, and she started sobbing the second I pulled her into my arms. "Do I have to—?"

"It's okay," I crooned as I pressed a rough kiss to her forehead and then her lips. "Shh, Blackbird. It's okay."

She dropped her arms and let the gun slip from her fingers, and then she was gripping me with one of her arms as tightly as I was gripping her. Her other hand slipped to her stomach protectively, and the same thoughts and fears from earlier built inside me, but before I could ask, her entire body began shaking so hard. She was going to go into shock.

"You said—you said to do it again. To be sure. You said—"

I cupped her face in one of my hands, pressed my forehead to hers, and tried to speak as gently as possible when all I wanted to do was beg her to forgive me for not being fast enough, to beg her to assure me she was really here in my arms. "He's gone, Blackbird. He's gone; it's okay. You're okay," I whispered, then brushed my lips against hers. "You're okay."

"Everybody on the ground," a deep voice boomed from above me, and Briar recoiled from the sound, but I didn't release her and I didn't move.

I looked up at the man in the bulletproof vest, and demanded, "Take us to David Criley."

"I said ever—"

"Take us to David Criley," I ground out, and when it looked like he would argue, I said low enough that my voice wouldn't carry, "You're only here because I made this possible. She's going into shock. Tell Criley that Trent Cruz is demanding to leave. Now."

He stared at me with confusion and apprehension, but something registered when I said my name, and he hurried to speak into the mic clipped to him. After a few moments of silence, he jerked his head toward the front of the hall, and I stood with Briar in my arms to follow him—not once looking back at William, or the two men we'd left bleeding on the floor.

As soon as we were outside, my handler came jogging over to us, already talking about whatever was happening inside the hall, but I wasn't listening, and I didn't wait for him as I took off for an ambulance at the end of a long line of police and SWAT vehicles.

David caught up to us, his tone warning me that he wasn't happy. "What happened?"

"He was stabbed," Briar said immediately.

"I'm fine," I growled as I caught the EMT's attention and waited until they were surrounding us. "She needs to be checked out. She's been blacking out and close to fainting all night. Someone put a needle in her arm about five minutes ago, I don't know what it was filled with."

I stepped up into the back of the ambulance and reluctantly placed Briar onto the gurney.

"Lucas, please!" she said frantically and sat up, reaching for me when I stepped back.

I pressed my mouth roughly to hers, leaving it there when I said, "Let them make sure you're okay. I'm not going anywhere; I'll be right here."

Once she released me, I stepped out of the ambulance and watched her. Again, one of her hands fell protectively to her stomach, and I felt anxious and fucking terrified as I waited for something that I wasn't even positive was happening.

"You were stabbed?" David asked once the EMTs were looking her over.

"Right shoulder. I'll get it checked later."

I thought he was going to argue, but after a moment, he sighed and said, "Someone reported as soon as we entered. Were you near there? Do you—?"

"That was us," I mumbled. Without taking my eyes off Briar, I told him everything that had happened with William at the end.

"He didn't push it in," Briar said weakly from where she was now sitting up. "He put the needle in, but he wasn't able to push whatever was in it into me before you shot him."

My eyes shut, and the crushing weight I'd been feeling since I'd seen the needle sticking out of her arm vanished. "I saw you fall to the floor," I whispered, the ache in my voice revealing how gravely it had affected me.

"They were yelling at everyone to get on the floor," she explained. "I pulled out the needle and dropped to the floor."

A weighted breath rushed from me, and I opened my eyes to look at my blackbird. "I thought you were—"

"Briar!"

I stilled at the same time my blackbird did, and I watched as her face fell into horror and confusion when the deep voice shouted her name again, this time closer. "Oh my God," she whispered, and tears immediately fell down her cheeks. "Kyle?"

David and I were pushed out of the way as the man I had come to hate over the last six months rushed into the ambulance and took my entire world up into his arms, despite the protests from the EMTs, and kissed her like a man dying.

Thoughts I hadn't had in months reared inside me, dark and ugly.

Not the same, I thought on instinct.

But as the girl in front of me clung to her fiancé's arms instead of pushing him away, I wondered when I would finally comprehend that it was.

I'd always known I would lose her. Always known she would go back to him—choose him over me. And I had no one to blame but myself, because I'd been the one to bring them back together.

I stumbled back a couple steps and then another. My eyes dropped to her flat stomach as wonder and grief slammed into me.

David was saying something, but I wasn't hearing him. He put his hand on my uninjured shoulder, but I shoved it off as I turned and staggered away.

Chapter 48

SING

Briar

"Jesus Christ, Briar," Kyle said when he pulled away. Tears were streaming down his cheeks and his hands were cradling mine so his thumbs could brush my tears away. "Jesus Christ," he repeated. "I thought you were gone forever." He pressed a rough kiss to my mouth again, and I tried desperately to hold on to him so I wouldn't fall.

I felt weak. It felt like my body wouldn't respond the way I needed it to anymore after what I had done to William. I felt betrayed by my body's inability to do what I needed it to. I felt so confused . . .

Because Kyle was there, and I couldn't figure out how or why. But his mouth on my own let me know this was real and not a dream. And his mouth felt comforting, like an old blanket, but it felt wrong. It felt so wrong. And I didn't have the strength to push him away.

Seeing him after everything that had happened tonight was too much, and I felt so close to breaking.

"I've got you; you're gonna be okay. I've got you; you're gonna be okay. I love you . . . until we're old and gray, Briar Rose," he whispered, and I managed to jerk my head away before he could kiss me again.

"What are you doing here?" I asked, my voice sounding weak and breathless.

"I'm here to take you home."

"No," I said quickly, stopping his mouth just a breath from mine. "No, *how* are you here."

"The guy working with the FBI. Luke, or whatever his name is," Kyle said on a rush. "He contacted me to let me know where you were, and where you were going to be tonight so I could get you out of here."

Betrayal hit me swift and deep, forcing the air from my lungs, and I looked up to my devil—but he wasn't there.

He wasn't anywhere.

"No." Horror dripped from the word. "No, *no*! I have to go," I said as forcefully as I could.

The EMTs checking my vitals had left at some point after Kyle had jumped into the back of the ambulance, and one rounded the rear door when he heard me.

"We should really finish checking—"

"I have to go," I cried out, struggling to get from Kyle's grasp and off the gurney.

"Babe, what are you doing?" Kyle asked frantically as he helped me down. "You're safe; no one's going to touch you again. I'm going to get you—"

"Lucas," I yelled over Kyle's assurances, and avoided his eyes when he suddenly stilled.

"Babe . . ."

"Lu—*Trent*!" I yelled again as I turned in slow circles, looking for my devil, but my voice barely held any power behind it. My body went numb when I didn't see him, and overwhelming panic clawed at me.

"Briar, he was working undercover for the FBI," Kyle said gently and slid an arm around my waist to pull me closer. "But I can't imagine what it must have been like for you thinking he was one of the people in this trafficking ring. We'll find someone you can talk to."

I pushed feebly against his chest, unable to move against his hold.

"I don't need someone to talk to, I need——" I broke off when I saw him in the distance talking with a group of men, his head hanging low and his hand gripping the back of his neck. "Devil," I whispered, and somehow, impossibly, my devil's head snapped up, and he looked over at me.

I took a step in his direction at the same second he took one in mine, but Kyle stopped me. "I'm gonna get you help, Briar Rose, I swear to God." He looked as horrified as he sounded. He swallowed roughly a couple times before he managed to say, "It's . . . it's normal to feel something for a person that held you captive—especially that long. But even though he was undercover, that's all he was to you. Your *captor*."

"No, he wasn't, you don't understand."

"Briar, he——"

"I love him, Kyle," I shouted, but my voice was still just above a whisper.

His blue eyes widened with shock. "What the hell?" he asked softly, and his hold tightened.

Hard sobs wracked my chest, and I stopped trying to get away from him. Lifting a shaking hand up, I cradled his face and spoke through my tears. "I love you. I tried to get back to you in the beginning."

"What the fuck are you saying? What the fuck did he do to you?"

"I know who he is, Kyle. I know he's undercover. I've known for months. But even before that, I . . ." A sob caught in my throat. "I stopped trying to get away. He gave me opportunities to go, even bought me a ticket home, and I didn't take them. It wasn't because of any syndrome or anything else you might think—it was just him. I fell in love with him."

Kyle looked as if I'd just torn him open to let him bleed out, but the denial was there in his eyes. "No. No, Briar, *no*. That's Stockholm——"

"It's not. Not with him. I'm sorry. I'm *so* sorry." I pushed against his hold, and his arms loosened but didn't fall.

I turned toward my devil. He was waiting about halfway from where I'd last seen him, but he only took a step before Kyle tightened his arms around me and pulled me back.

Kyle's blue eyes looked like he was in so much pain, and his jaw clenched as he pled, "Briar, don't do this."

"I can sing with him," I said softly, and watched the impact of my words on the man I had once seen a future with.

None of what I had said had hurt him as much as that confession.

"I hate that I'm hurting you. I hate that you've hurt this whole time," I said through the tightening of my throat. "Please forgive me, Kyle. I never wanted you to find out this way."

"Babe, I—*Jesus Christ*." Fresh tears filled his eyes as he pled again, "Briar, don't do this. You're confused, you've gone through something . . . *fuck*, something so traumatic, and you're not thinking clearly."

After what we'd just gone through, the need to get to where my heart was waiting for me was overwhelming and made it nearly impossible to focus on what was right in front of me. But I owed Kyle so many apologies and explanations that would take time . . . hours and days and weeks.

And right then, I owed him that moment.

I curled my hands around his head and pressed my forehead to his. "Know that I love you . . ."

"Briar, don't—"

" . . . and I'll love you forever."

"We're supposed to *be* forever," he gritted out. "*Until we're old and gray.*"

"Please try to understand. Please try to forgive me. We had plans, but life changed them. I hate imagining the grief you lived with. I promise I would've put an end to it if I could've." Tears slipped down my cheeks when I whispered, "All I want is for you to be happy."

"*You* are what makes me happy."

I slowly released his face and searched his heartbroken eyes. "Please . . . let me go. I'm not that girl anymore."

"Briar." My name was nothing more than a forced breath.

Nearly a minute passed as he strained to digest what I was saying, before his arms fell limply to his sides, and he slowly backed away, his head shaking subtly as he did.

"I . . . I don't—" Another pained breath left him, and with one last agonizing look, he turned and staggered away.

I watched until he rounded the ambulance before I turned to find my devil . . . my heart . . . my *home*.

Lucas—*Trent*—watched me carefully as I walked toward him, and when I was nearly halfway he stalked toward me, quickly eating up the rest of the distance.

"You *idiot*," I seethed as he got closer.

"I know, Blackbird," he whispered just before he pulled me into his arms and pressed his mouth to mine.

His lips moved against mine roughly, his hands gripping me tightly, but his tongue slid against mine in a slow, torturous dance that could've made me forget about the night and everything that it had been filled with, if it weren't for the intense ache in my chest.

"You idiot," I repeated when his mouth moved to my jaw and then down my throat.

"I had to," he whispered when his lips met my collarbone. After one last lingering kiss there, he dropped his forehead in the same spot and pulled me impossibly closer.

"Had to?" I mumbled and wove my hands through his hair to bring his face in front of mine. "I chose you long ago. Why couldn't you see that?"

That devastating smile tugged at his lips, and his head shook once. "I know you did." The smile fell, and he let out a heavy breath. "But I didn't think I'd make it out alive, and I knew you planned to be with me every step of the way. He was the only way you'd leave—the only way to get you to safety once it all went wrong." He brushed his thumb over my lips, and a ghost of a smile played on his. "And even though your safe way out was waiting for you, your stubbornness almost got you killed anyway."

"It's where I belong," I said simply.

There was a long pause before he said gruffly, "You didn't stop him when he kissed you."

"I didn't have the strength to. I didn't have the strength to move until I realized you were gone." I searched his dark eyes, seeing the pain there, and asked, "Is that why you left?"

"I couldn't watch my worst fear play out in front of me."

"He knows where I stand now," I said softly. "He knows I can't be without you."

An ache for the man I had loved flared in my chest, but it was nothing compared to the thought of losing the one holding me.

"Trent?" I asked hesitantly. "Trent Cruz."

My devil regarded me silently for a few moments before dipping his head once in confirmation.

"That might take some time to get used to."

"Briar," he began warily, "have you ever thought what being with *me* means?" When I didn't respond, he continued, "I told you I was going into witness protection before I was pulled into this life. I was just told that the last of the trials ended a few months ago, every last member of my crew is in prison—and they're going to be there for a long time. That doesn't mean they won't have people who look for me. So even though this bust will be all over the news, I've been assured *I* won't be.

He searched my eyes and dipped his head close as he whispered, "I won't be leaving here as Trent Cruz, because I'd have to spend the rest of my life looking over my shoulder. I can't live like that, and I won't do that to you. But the second I stepped out of that building, I was no longer Lucas Holt. The house, the cars, the money . . . it's all gone except for what I made working at the company. The FBI have assured me of that, but I'll still be starting over again."

"When have I ever wanted the money you had?" I asked just as softly. "I don't need Lucas Holt, and I don't need a name from who you were a lifetime ago. As long as my devil is by my side, I have everything I'll ever need."

His lips brushed against mine softly, tenderly. The hand on my face dropped to my waist, and then the back of his knuckles trailed across my stomach in question.

My breath caught, and I looked up to find his knowing stare locked on me.

"Tell me," he began, his tone pleading, and his hand flattened against my stomach protectively, lovingly. "Tell me why you're light-headed and weak."

Fresh tears sprang to my eyes, and I choked out a soft cry. "You already know, Devil."

His eyes slid shut like he was in pain seconds before he fell roughly to his knees. He gripped my hips in his hands and pressed his forehead to my stomach, and stayed like that for long moments as I dragged my hand through his hair and cried silently.

And as I stood there with my devil kneeling before me, relief swirled through me when I realized we were both finally free.

"Almost lost you both," he murmured as he lifted his head to press his lips to my stomach. "I can't lose you."

"I know, but you won't," I said softly, soothingly. "We promised each other forever."

"Forever," he vowed.

Epilogue

INCREDIBLE

Briar

I followed the screams and giggles and turned the corner to see my husband running through the living room with our daughter on his shoulders. She had soft, golden curls that fell to her shoulders, a smile and laugh that made you melt over and over again, and the darkest green eyes you'd ever seen.

She was perfect, and she was such a light in our home.

A light among broken darkness.

My devil caught sight of me standing there and slowed down to walk calmly toward me while our daughter yelled for me and her baby brother in my arms.

"Incredible," he mumbled then leaned down to pass his lips over mine.

"What is?"

"The way you steal my breath."

Our daughter slapped his head. "I wanna kiss Mommy! I wanna kiss Mommy!"

My devil's face brightened, and he bent so I could receive a loud kiss from her. When he stood, he reached out with one hand so he could cradle our son's face. "And how is he?"

"Mad that he's awake. I'm about to put him down for a nap."

He huffed through his nose, his smile only growing as he watched his son with rapt attention. "Such a devil."

An amused sound slid up my throat. "Wonder where he got that from?"

He grinned mischievously at me as he leaned forward to kiss my neck. "I'll put the monster down then meet you in bed."

My eyes widened at his suggestive tone, and I bit back my smile as I stepped back. "Whatever for?"

His dark eyes flashed, and his next words sent a welcome shiver down my spine. "I was thinking for a little *more*."

"More chocolate?" our daughter asked excitedly and slapped his head. "Daddy, run around! And more chocolate!"

I laughed softly then turned to go put our six-month-old down for a nap.

In the three years since we'd left Houston, life had been as close to perfect as I thought it could get. There were hard times, as with any relationship, but my devil and our kids were my home—my everything.

At the beginning, we'd had to come up with a story for the media since Briar Rose Chapman had been splashed across the news so often, and we'd worried that people would recognize me once we started on our new life.

Kyle's mother reported that I had been abducted and held captive for six months, and that I would receive help from the best therapists. A while later, it was announced my engagement to Kyle was off, with reassurances that he still loved me and wished me well in my recovery.

After a while, the stories died down, and it was now rare that someone stopped me on the street or in a store to ask if they knew me.

Kyle and I had very little contact even when we created our stories. The last I'd heard he was engaged again, and I was happy for him—it was what he deserved. Someone to love him the way my husband fiercely loved me.

And my husband was . . . *my devil*, I thought with a heated shudder when he stepped up behind me after I had undressed, minutes later.

"She in bed?"

A sound of confirmation hummed in his throat, and his nose skimmed up my neck. "Tell me what you want."

"You already know, and you already teased me with it." I reached behind me to drag my fingers through his hair, scratching lightly down his neck.

"More?" he asked darkly and slowly fisted his hand in my long blonde hair.

"Always," I breathed as I waited eagerly for what would come. Because I wanted the pain with the pleasure until I couldn't separate them anymore, and I knew he wanted to give me both.

He was still my devil and I was still his blackbird, and I didn't want us to ever change. His dark was there, swirling around him, but it had changed the night we left Houston. It was as if something had broken inside him, and he'd never had to struggle to fight against it since.

He was free, as was I.

He was my darkness, and I was his light. And when we collided, it was still nothing short of incredible.

The spoken-for Princess of the Irish-American Mob, and the man who sets her world on fire with just one touch — but who would take her life if he knew who she was . . .

Look out for the next novel in the Redemption series

Firefly

Coming soon from Headline Eternal!